About the Young Four

The Young Foundation combines creat
social needs. We work on many differe
– including advocacy, research, and policy influence as well as creating new organisations and running practical projects. The Young Foundation benefits from a long history of social research, innovation and practical action by the late Michael Young, once described as "the world's most successful social entrepreneur" who created more than 60 ventures which address social needs.

www.youngfoundation.org

THE YOUNG FOUNDATION

SINKING AND SWIMMING
First published in Britain in 2009 by

The Young Foundation
18 Victoria Park Square
London
E2 9PF
UK

A CIP catalogue record for this book is available from the British Library
ISBN 978-1-905551-11-8

Printed by Solopress on 9lives Offset paper (FSC certified 100% recycled fibre) using vegetable inks.
Cover illustration by Claire Scully. Designed and typeset by Effusion.

Contents

About the programme

The research team working on this programme included Beth Watts, Dan Vale, Geoff Mulgan, Michael Dale, Rushanara Ali and Will Norman, with additional help from Alessandra Buonfino, Carmel O'Sullivan, Jane Franklin, Caspar le Fanu, Cressida Jervis-Read, Jacob Garber, James Copeland, Jonathan Graham, Katrina Forrester, Reema Mehta, Robert Patrick and Sarah Hewes.

The work was supported by the following organisations:

- Baring Foundation
- Barrow Cadbury Trust
- Bedford Charity (The Harpur Trust)
- Big Lottery Fund
- City Bridge Trust
- City Parochial Foundation
- Comic Relief
- Economic and Social Research Council
- John Lyon's Charity
- Joseph Rowntree Foundation
- LankellyChase Foundation
- Northern Rock Foundation
- Wates Foundation

The advisers to the programme included Lord Moser, Ian Gough, Danny Dorling, Sir Roger Jowell, Ruth Lister, Suzanne Fitzpatrick, Karen Dunnell, Chris Creegan, Peter Taylor-Gooby, Mike Savage, Nick Emler and the late Norman Glass. We are deeply grateful to both the funders and advisers for their enthusiasm, their expertise and their consistent commitment to the goals of the project. Any inaccuracies or omissions are, of course, our own.

In addition to this report, the programme has produced a series of detailed case studies (including reports on Bedford, Teesside, London and transitions), as well as background reports on a range of issues from theories of need to an interim report looking at the impact of recession and a related study of rural needs.

Preface

My link with this highly original project has been a fulfilling experience. As a social scientist I have obviously been interested in its central focus, namely the complex problems facing people in our society with all kinds of unmet needs, material or otherwise.

And the mix of research methods was appealing since so much of my professional life has been centred on social statistics and social surveys. It all takes me back to 1965 when I was lucky enough to be a founder member of the Social Science Research Council, one of many influential institutions we owe to the late Michael Young – the Young Foundation being another. The focus and approach of this study would have appealed to him.

Going back even further, to the Beveridge report in the 1940s, we are reminded of the five evils that epoch-making report identified; want, disease, ignorance, squalor and idleness. Of course those evils are now less prominent, but one can hardly claim that they have disappeared. Hence the importance of this study in throwing light on what remains to be achieved in confronting major social problems.

But it is vital to stress what this report does not do. It does not pretend to be a comprehensive and nation-wide survey on poverty. Indeed there is now need for such a major project, but that is a task for government and its resources. Meanwhile what we have here is, strangely enough, more ambitious. Its theoretical chapters show how complex the very concept of 'unmet needs' is in the real world. Material needs, for example, go well beyond shortage of money, covering a wide range of every-day problems. 'Psychological needs' are a different issue altogether, possibly but not always necessarily linked to material needs.

This research attempts to illuminate these intricate complexities and links, all in the interest of what 'unmet needs' mean for people, groups and areas with problems.

To achieve this, a sometimes bewildering mix of research techniques is used. Official statistics are brought into play where available and relevant; data from official and academic surveys appear throughout, notably the British Household Panel Survey (BHPS), a vital longitudinal survey. In addition there are the project's own case studies in London, South Wales, Teesside and Bedford, plus an intriguing picture of night workers and their problems.

By employing these different 'lenses' in looking at unmet needs, with varying depth, the report illuminates where policy intervention is needed, where data are too poor to be helpful and where more comprehensive research would now pay off. I commend the report as a valuable contribution to our understanding of the complex scenery of social needs in the UK.

Lord Claus Moser

Summary

This study provides an overview of where the most acute needs are in Britain today, and which needs may become more pressing in the future. It looks at why some people can cope with shocks and setbacks and others can't, and at the implications for policy, philanthropy and public action.

The study combines statistical data, research based on conversations with citizens as well as professionals, case studies and reflections on both past patterns of need and future possibilities. It has been supported by many of the UK's leading foundations,[i] together with the Economic and Social Research Council and a group of leading academics.[ii]

The current position

Recent years have brought some progress in how needs are met, including lower child and pensioner poverty, a narrowing of the gap between richer and poorer areas and between schools in richer and poorer areas. But health inequalities, inequalities of wealth and inequalities of income have widened. A large minority of teenagers (one in eight) remains detached from the education system and the labour market. Over two and a half million people remain on incapacity benefit and employment and support allowance. And the very poorest have seen their living standards stagnate or even decline. Over the last year the recession has raised unemployment, put downward pressure on incomes and will soon be followed by sharp cuts in public spending which are likely to affect the poorest most.

The landscape of support

People meet their needs through four main routes. They buy goods and services – like food or housing – through the market. They receive services – like healthcare – from government. They get support from charities, for example homeless shelters or drugs treatment. And they rely on family members and friends. These routes overlap and are of very different scales. The UK economy is around £1300bn in total. Government spending is around £620bn – an unusually high proportion of GDP, partly thanks to the recession. There are roughly as many hours of unpaid work as paid work each year in the UK, mainly within the family. By comparison total charity income is around £34bn and total foundation spending around £3.5-4bn.

Defining Needs

Many people may feel that they need a new car or a holiday. But our concern here is with socially recognised needs that can make a legitimate claim on others, whether through charitable giving or public support. These tend to be needs for things which help people avoid unnecessary harm and suffering. Our research shows that the public think of needs in this way and that they see psychological wellbeing and material prosperity as equally important. There is no simple hierarchy of needs: for some people, whether refugees or unemployed teenagers, a mobile phone may be a higher priority than having a square meal.

Statistics: measuring material and psychological needs

Needs can be measured in many different ways. Material deprivation remains significant, though much less than in the past. While obesity is a major problem, particularly for younger people, some older people still get sick and 350 die because of poor nutrition each year. Although the numbers have fallen, some still sleep rough on city streets, and have a life expectancy around 42. Some get by on very little money – like the asylum seekers surviving on £5 a day. Debt has always been a fear for poor families and communities, and recent years have seen a worsening incidence of unmanageable debt (which is not just an economic nightmare for many families but also a psychological one as well, closely correlated with mental ill health). Average household unsecured debt (i.e. excluding mortgages) is now over £9,000.

Although most people are content with their lives, a growing number, particularly women, are not. Between one in six and one in four people in the UK experience mental health problems at some point in their lives. The number of prescriptions for anti-depressant drugs increased from 9 million in 1991 to 34 million in 2007. There are also important psycho-social needs – some people have no one to talk to day-to-day or about important issues. New research shows that a million people have no-one to turn to and no-one who appreciates them. The groups most likely to have acute and persistent needs include the unemployed, lone parents and many living with disabilities, as well as half a million irregular migrants, 140,000 child runaways, a third of a million problematic drug users and 80,000 looked-after children.

Case studies

Detailed case studies look deeper into people's lives, experiences and conditions. The study of transitions examines how people cope, or don't cope, with transitions out of prison, out of families in crisis, or out of local authority care. Many of the most acute needs are associated with difficult transitions, and this is where many current policies and institutions fail. The study on Bedford focuses on teenagers, particularly those not in jobs, education and training, and shows the importance of help-seeking, resilience, attitude and social networks. The study on Teesside brings out the importance of family and informal supports that help people get by in a relatively poor working class community. The study in South Wales looked at workless households, and confirms that although these communities are resilient to shocks, such as the current recession, they may be lacking in 'adaptive resilience', the ability to connect to new opportunities. The study on Londons look at several groups. These include refugees (showing just how materially poor refugees are, but also the importance of religious and family networks for many); teenagers coming out of care (confirming the importance of their direct supports, whether these are family members or statutory services); and older people (showing just how isolated many feel, as friends and family have either died or moved away). Another study looks at which needs become apparent at night, whether in the lives of night workers, or through the eyes of emergency services that see some of the most marginalised people out on the streets or hitting crises when the majority are asleep in their beds.

Needs in the future

Highly likely future trends include: a long period of constrained public spending; an aging population requiring significantly more care and healthcare; a generation of teenagers facing even more difficult transitions thanks to the economic climate; and the effects of global phenomena such as climate change and rising fuel and food prices. Some less appreciated trends include worsening levels of stress and anxiety: anxiety and depression looks set to double during the course of a single generation. The family will continue to be an area of challenge – from children having children to a growing number of adults wanting to have children but being unable to do so, and from growing pressures on children and spouses to look after parents and partners to the unpredictable impacts of ubiquitous social networks.

Implications and directions for action

Most people in Britain live good lives and believe that they live in strong and supportive communities. Most are safer from crime and violence than they were a decade ago, and dramatically safer than their equivalents were a century ago. When they face setbacks most people bounce back. But Britain is a brittle society, with many fractures and many people left behind. From our analysis we recommend seven broad directions for change.

1 **Provide preparation, bridges and support for difficult transitions**
Many of the worst clusters of need are the result of difficult transitions. The ways in which we help people make these transitions – from being a teenager to being an adult, or from being in care or prison to independence – are inadequate and miss many of the things that matter most in making them work: good preparation, bridging support from reliable and sympathetic people, and resources such as housing or money as well as emotional help. Public agencies' responsibilities are divided by chronological age, and both public and voluntary organisations tend to divide by function

in ways that cut against what people need. At a time of acute pressure on money, this could be an area for long-term savings.

2 **Isolation – help to connect the disconnected**
Loneliness has become a stark feature of a more individualistic society. Millions like living on their own. But many are suffering because of the absence of people they can turn to for help and support. A growing body of evidence points to the psychological and physical harm that loneliness can bring. There are many good initiatives trying to address these needs – from befriending schemes to mentors – but they remain very much on the margins of policy and small in scale. Being without a roof over your head or a job to go to brings you entitlements, however meagre. Having no one to talk to does not.

3 **Provide access with 'no wrong door'**
People often access services that are not the right ones for meeting their underlying need. They may show up at A&E when their real problem is alcohol; they may turn up at a homeless shelter when their underlying problem is a mental illness. Access points need to be less devoted to functions and more to people. We need more institutions, advisers and access points which are holistic, rather than function specific. Many of the people and families that most need help are the least likely to take it up, sometimes because of chaotic lifestyles but also for reasons of stigma, distrust and disengagement. It is not enough to provide something useful: how it is provided also needs to build trust and confidence.

4 **Enhance resilience and psychological fitness**
Resilience matters and can be influenced. Everyone is bound to face shocks and setbacks at some point in life. But what makes the difference is how well we cope with these shocks, how well we bounce back. This is in part a matter of social support from family and friends, teachers or GPs, as well as skills and financial assets. But resilience – and psychological fitness in a broader sense – can also be learned, and enhanced.

5 **Rethink welfare provision through the lens of wellbeing**
The welfare state grew up to deal with physical and material needs (although it was often justified by its impact on people's dignity as well). It evolved to provide enough food to eat, cures for sickness, homes and jobs. In a society with relative material abundance the critical issues of welfare have become as much about psychology and relationships as about material things. The risks that matter most include mental ill-health and relationship breakdown as well as unemployment and poverty in old age. Indeed these psychological and psycho-social risks are more common across classes and regions than the economic ones, and perhaps a stronger basis for mutual support and solidarity. 'It could be you' certainly applies to mental illness, which affects a third of the population at some point in their life. It's time to

rethink welfare through this new lens, addressing the most important risks that individuals and families cannot deal with on their own.

6 **Focus on new and old necessities**
Over time many items move from being luxuries to become necessities. People living in rural areas are not alone in thinking of the car as a necessity. But the mobile phone is much the clearest example of this shift – invaluable and prioritised by everyone from refugees to unemployed teenagers.

7 **Invest in better social accounts**
The UK publishes regular economic accounts, but not comparable social accounts. And while government shares extensive data on production, consumption and finance, it doesn't map wellbeing, and data on psychological needs is patchy. We show how regular snapshots of social needs could be developed that could become as prominent in our national consciousness as economic accounts are today.

PART I

Introduction

'Sinking and swimming: understanding Britain's unmet needs' is the culmination of a series of studies undertaken by the Young Foundation between 2007 and 2009. Their aim was to map the state of need in the UK, using a wide range of research tools and combining national analysis with local case studies.

1 Background to the study

This is a study of who is sinking and who is swimming: of where the most acute needs are in Britain today, of why some people can cope with shocks and setbacks and others can't, and of the implications for policy and public action.

It combines statistical data, research based on hundreds of conversations with citizens as well as professionals, and reflections on both past patterns of need and future possibilities.

It sketches a complex picture – but also one in which there are some clear messages. It describes a society in which, even amidst a severe recession, most people are getting by, with a healthy standard of living and the means to meet most of their needs. But large numbers of people are at best struggling to cope with pressures ranging from job insecurity to debt, and some are sinking as their problems mount up. Often they face a vicious spiral as, for example, family tensions lead to heavier drinking or drug use, which in turn leads to greater tensions in the home, problems at work, worsening financial pressures and then a rupture which leaves people out on the streets with no one to turn to. Often it's the moments of transition that seem to be most fraught with problems, whether it's the transition out of care, or employment, or prison, or the nuclear family.

Britain has a great tradition of research that in the past powerfully shaped our society's sense of responsibility. Morally-inspired investigation of everyday needs first took off in the Victorian era in response to the suffering that accompanied industrialisation and the dramatic expansion of cities, parts of which became living hells of abject poverty, high crime and poor health. Florence Nightingale was not just a nurse but also a statistician of social facts. Charles Booth set out to study poverty in the 1890s with the intention of proving that concerns about poverty were exaggerated. He ended up showing the opposite, in an extraordinarily detailed account of the misery that was then to be found in London, the richest city on earth. Seebohm Rowntree studied poverty in York to equally influential effect, beginning a tradition of research that led to Peter Townsend's surveys and analyses from the 1950s onwards, Michael Young's poverty reports in the 1970s and Ann Power's studies of poor estates in the 1990s and 2000s. Around the world too there have been many impressive attempts to survey the needs of societies, such as the 'Voices of the Poor' studies, many of them mixing quantitative and qualitative analysis, the perspectives of experts and the perspectives of people living with acute needs.

These studies all start from some simple premises. One is that human need is not always visible. We may be able to see that someone is sleeping on the streets, or that someone is unhappy. But to understand need we have to dig deeper, to study the patterns, the trends and the clusters that may not be immediately apparent. These clusters show us that needs can amplify each other just as capabilities do.

Another premise is that the perspectives of people living with severe needs will always contain insights not apparent to those studying them. Beneath the statistics are real people and groups facing barriers and obstacles, devising their own solutions and also reflecting on the sources of their problems. Perhaps the most important premise of all studies of need is a moral one: that needs matter and that a good society is aware of itself, aware of who is thriving and who is not, and of who is in need of care and support.

This study has been supported by many of the UK's leading foundations, together with the Economic and Social Research Council, who wanted a new overview of the state of needs which could provide some steers on where action might be most needed as well as on where research might be most useful.

Recent years have seen intensive action to address poverty, including innumerable government initiatives. These have achieved some progress, including lower child and pensioner poverty, some narrowing of the gap between richer and poorer areas and between schools in richer and poorer areas. But according to many measures health inequalities, inequalities of wealth and inequalities of income have widened. A large minority of teenagers remain essentially detached from the education system and the labour market. And the very poorest have seen their living standards stagnate or even decline.

These uneven patterns of success and failure are now set to be shaped by a very different economic environment. A long period of economic growth, which led to an enormous rise in wealth at the top and significant advance in the middle, has, even if only temporarily, come to an end, leaving the market less able to meet people's needs. Even the more optimistic forecasts assume a period of high unemployment ahead of us. In parallel, sharp cuts in public spending are on their way, reducing the capacity of government to meet people's needs.

The arrival of a recession in the middle of this study reinforced our interest in understanding not just what people need, but also how able they are to meet their needs on their own or with others. Here we look not just at the structural causes of needs, but also at patterns of resilience, abilities to seek and find help, and the informal support structures in families and communities that are often invisible to governments.

The methods we have used are deliberately multiple, designed to look at needs through a variety of lenses, including quantitative and qualitative methods, analysis of needs in particular places, particular times, and through particular transitions. An overview of the methods we have used is provided in Appendix 1.

Part I sets out some of the background, including a brief overview of theories and definitions of need, along with our research on how members of the public themselves think about needs. This shows that most people now think of needs in terms of psychological wellbeing as well as material factors. It also shows that there is no simple hierarchy of needs: for some people, whether refugees or unemployed teenagers, a mobile phone may be as important or a higher priority than having a square meal.

In Part II, we turn to a broad survey of needs, based on statistics and research findings, drawing on the work of others and on our own analyses of longitudinal and other data such as the British Household Panel Study. One part of the analysis shows two distinct pictures of British society (see Figure 1 on the next page). The first presents the distribution of income and material wellbeing. This kite-shaped picture has stretched at the top as the rich have become much richer, and sagged at the bottom as a significant minority has seen their incomes stagnate even as the average has risen. In the middle the majority are getting by on fairly modest incomes, but those at the bottom, particularly those without jobs, have seen their living standards stagnate or fall. Overall men are richer than women; ethnic minorities tend to be in the lower income groups, but the picture is much more varied than it was a generation ago. Economic growth over many decades has left most people better off materially. But it has been associated with widening inequalities and widening disparities of pay, which are partly the result of technological change, partly the result of globalization, and partly the result of political choices on taxes and benefits.

A second picture shows the state of our mental wellbeing, with a picture that is almost a mirror of the first (Figure 1). Again the shape is like an elongated kite. In the middle most people are fairly contented with their lives, but there is a long and apparently lengthening spike of unhappiness, loneliness and stress. Women are more prominent in the lower reaches of the diagram.

These two pictures are connected. Greater inequality appears to be correlated with higher levels of stress, more anxious competition for resources and positions, and a weakening of the buffers of trust, family and friendship. Even during the economic boom, some of the indicators of mental wellbeing worsened (if you are curious to know where you sit in these diagrams, we have designed an easy to use tool which can be found in Appendix 3).

Figure 1 Distribution of equivalised household income (pounds per week) and subjective wellbeing (GHQ12), 2006-7

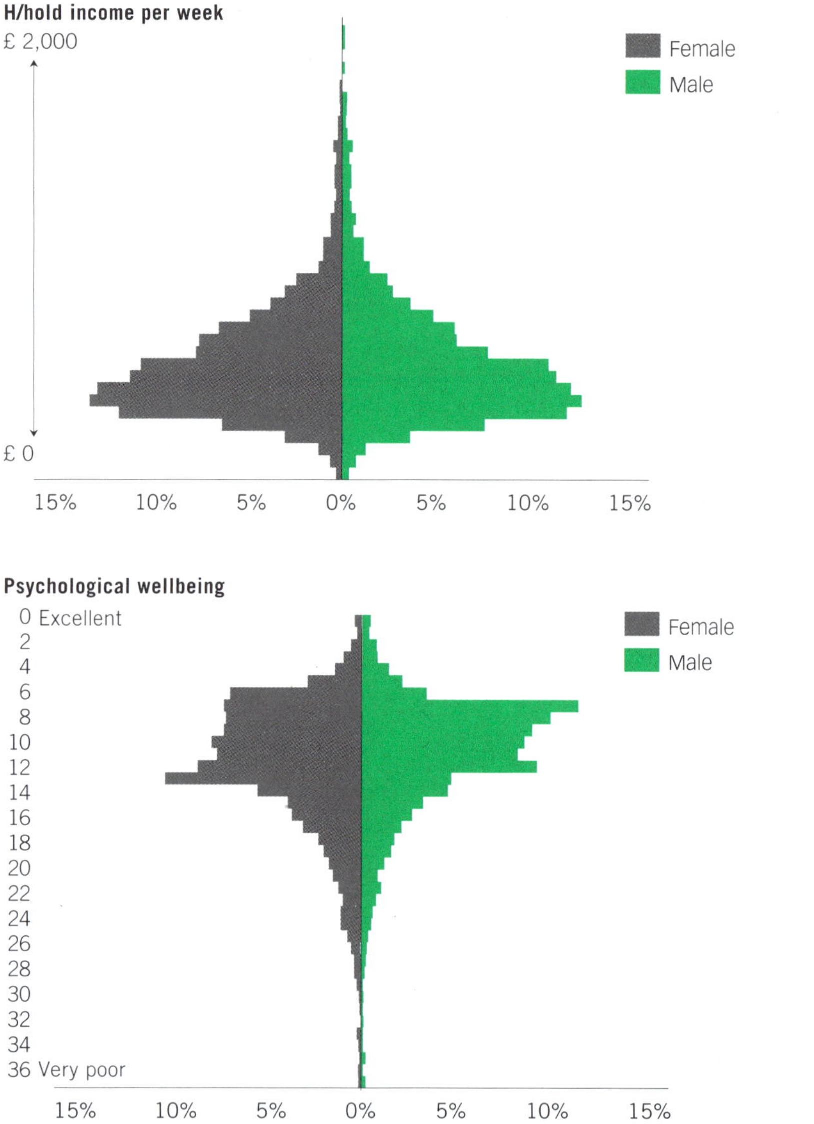

Source: BHPS analysis

Building on this starting point, the rest of Part II sets out in detail the patterns of need that can be found across the UK: the still striking numbers suffering from absolute material deprivation (like the elderly people sick or dying because of poor nutrition, or the people who still sleep rough on city streets, or asylum seekers surviving on £5 a day). It also looks at the patterns of income inequality and unemployment, as well as the worsening incidence of unmanageable debt (which is not only an economic nightmare for many families but also a psychological one, closely correlated with mental ill health). The number of people facing material deprivation – as measured by the numbers who can't afford such things as household insurance - has decreased significantly over the last decade. But a quarter still can't afford to feed a visitor once a month or a week's holiday away from home each year.

We then turn to the broader patterns of psychological need, ranging from acute psychosis to low level depression, as well as patterns of psycho-social support, like the people who have no one to talk to day by day or about important issues, or the half million pensioners who spend Christmas Day alone. These psychological and psycho-social needs were a primary concern of Victorian civil society, but they were then largely neglected by twentieth-century researchers and policy makers.

From this broad-brush analysis we then identify some of the groups with the most acute needs. These are the groups that show up however you look at needs. They include the unemployed, lone parents and many living with disabilities, as well as other vulnerable groups such as undocumented migrants, problematic drug users or looked-after children. We also look at who sits right at the bottom of society, identifying the bottom 1 or 2% (or put differently the bottom million) whether seen through the very different lenses of income, social status or wellbeing. For example, about a million have no one to turn to or no one who appreciates them (half of this group have a job or are married).

In Part III we dig down into a series of case studies that describe in more detail people's lives, experiences and conditions. The purpose of these case studies is to flesh out what's happening to some of the groups that are experiencing clusters of serious and persistent unmet needs. The case studies build on qualitative research, ranging from in-depth interviews and focus groups to ethnographic immersion in the daily lives of different groups.

The case studies cover a wide spectrum of contemporary life, including: older people in several places, highlighting in particular how many are isolated or afraid of crime; poor families in Teesside, showing the importance of informal mutual support; teenagers in Bedford, showing the importance of help-seeking behaviour or its absence; long-term unemployed families in south Wales, showing some of the ambiguities of resilience which can help people cope with setbacks but can also sometimes cut them off from opportunities. We also look at the experiences of elderly people, excluded young people and undocumented migrants in London, showing some of the complexities of need in a very mobile, dynamic and unequal city.

We also look in some detail at questions of transition – how people cope with the transitions out of prison, out of families in crisis, or out of local authority care. As we demonstrate, many of the most acute needs are associated with difficult transitions, and this is where many current policies and institutions visibly fail. We have also used another lens to look at need, examining which needs become apparent at night. We look at the conditions faced by night workers, and at the many people with problems who show up on the streets or come into contact with the emergency services at night.

From these studies we draw out some common themes. The case studies confirm the persistence of some kinds of 'classic poverty', including homelessness, alongside some very modern phenomena like obesity. And they confirm the still wide inequalities of opportunity that do so much to shape life chances (for example for the 12% of 16-19 year olds who are not in education, training or a job). But we also highlight other themes which have not been so high on the social policy agenda: these include the importance of resilience, 'grit' and persistence. Another important theme is help-seeking behaviour (whether it is middle-aged men unable or unwilling to access advice about health or teenagers needing help finding a job). Many find it hard to understand their own needs, let alone how to meet them.

All of the studies emphasise the continuing importance of social networks and the family, who are vital sources of help and whose absence leaves people particularly vulnerable. Having few social networks and little social support of this kind is arguably just as serious a problem as being poor in cash.

We then turn to what we can know, or guess, about future patterns of need. This is certainly not a science. The government recently tried to create a website to help people predict their income in retirement but had to close the project: future patterns of private pension provision were reasonably easy to forecast but there was simply no way to predict what sort of state pension people might receive in 30 years time. Nevertheless, there are some highly likely patterns and trends including constrained public spending, an aging population, a generation of teenagers facing even more difficult transitions, and the effects of global phenomena such as climate change and rising fuel and food prices.

Technology is likely to create new divisions and needs, as well as providing new ways to meet needs. A recent survey of young people (from Youthnet), for example, found that 75% couldn't live without the internet, and over 40% now use it to seek advice on health, sex and finance. We also point to some of the less appreciated trends that look likely to continue, such as worsening levels of anxiety and depression which, like obesity, are set to double in a generation.

Finally, we set out recommendations for action, focusing on how such issues as isolation, transitions and resilience could be addressed more effectively. Some of these directions of change might require additional resources. But many are about spending money more effectively, in ways that get to the root of problems rather than primarily dealing with symptoms.

Understanding individual needs and social contexts

The case studies and the conclusions analyse how people's ability to meet their needs is influenced by factors at three very different levels. The first is the level of the self, of individual skills and assets, as well as attitudes and dispositions. These can make a big difference to life chances as well as to how people cope with a shock or setback. There are stark inequalities of human and financial capital. Yet these are not the only assets that matter. There is now a large body of evidence showing the importance of dispositions and character to life chances and showing how they can be cultivated.[1]

The second is the level of day-to-day support, the networks of family and friends (and for some, GPs, social workers and personal advisers) that are so important to helping us get by. As we show, the family remains much the most important means for people to meet their needs (and conversely anyone without family or friends is bound to be much more vulnerable, and around seven million people suffer from a 'severe' lack of social support). Yet a surprising proportion of public policy and service provision effectively neglects the family and fails to maximise the potential it has to offer social support and meet needs.

The third is the level of systems and structures that range from the state of the economy in an area to patterns of power and powerlessness. Living in a town with few jobs, and few links to places with jobs, stacks the odds against an individual, however motivated they are to get on. Similarly, whether or not someone has rights, or can access the law to protect themselves (as in the case of undocumented migrants), greatly influences their chances of meeting their needs.

Figure 2: Three levels influencing whether needs can be met

Welfare and wellbeing

This framework provides a useful way of thinking about both the strengths and limitations of a welfare state that grew up in response to the last great financial and economic crisis, in the 1930s. At that time the overwhelming priorities were to meet people's material needs: housing, healthcare, income support for unemployment and old age were what mattered most. Policy makers could assume that many people who were materially poor lived in reasonably close-knit families and communities that could provide emotional support in hard times. The state's job was to meet material needs and to insure people against material risks; society's job was to meet most of the psychological and psycho-social ones. The solidarity that underpinned the welfare state was based on a shared understanding of risk: that for a majority of the population there was a serious risk of becoming unemployed, or sick and in need of hospital care, or getting old without adequate savings.

Sixty years later the picture is very different. Some people are still homeless, and classic poverty has not disappeared. We depend as much as ever on the state to protect us if we lose our job or become sick. But few people go seriously hungry, and few have literally nowhere to sleep. Decades of economic growth have created a society which by past standards is materially abundant, indeed that is as concerned with excess consumption, whether in the form of obesity, smoking, alcohol or gambling, as it is with under-consumption. Over the last decade the proportion of people unable to afford essentials, or facing fuel poverty, has come down sharply. And although nearly half of the adult population has little or no savings, a substantial proportion of the population now owns significant assets.

Yet during this same period society's ability to meet people's psychological and psycho-social needs appears to have declined. The buffers of religion and family that helped people cope with setbacks have been weakened significantly. There has been a rise of individualism. A more overtly meritocratic society has encouraged people to be more ambitious for themselves, but also made them more vulnerable to failures – and more likely to blame themselves (rather than fate or the class system) if things go wrong. Some of the shock absorbers – from faith to family – that helped us cope in the past have atrophied.

It's possible that a new basis of solidarity is slowly coming into view in which we are bound together by a new set of shared risks: the risk of loneliness and isolation; the risk of mental illness; the risk of being left behind. But these risks are not yet reflected in political settlements or policies, and are inherently harder to reach through the standard tools of public policy and provision.

Better data and research

Achieving this shift will require greater awareness of unnecessary suffering, as well as more effective action to reduce it. The two are of course linked. A good society is aware of itself and of who is in need of care and support. Yet the available data and research on psychological and psycho-social needs is much patchier and less reliable than data on material conditions. Some of our detailed research work has focused on designing and testing the questions that could be asked at regular intervals to take the nation's temperature, and assess our feelings of wellbeing, security, competence and autonomy as well as our physical health or income. Our hope is that this lead will be followed up both at the national level and through detailed local studies (details of how a national survey could be done are provided in Appendix 2, and we also provide guidance on how local studies could be done on the web). We believe that social accounts including subjective measures of wellbeing should be published alongside the more familiar economic accounts, and should aim to capture the many dimensions of need, as well as our capacities to meet them.

Brittle Britain

This study shows that the UK is a rich country, but with many poor people. It's a largely happy country, but one with many unhappy people. Some inequalities and divergences of experience are inevitable. But they are much wider in the UK than they need to be, and the result is a great deal of unnecessary harm and suffering. Too many parts of British society are brittle, vulnerable to shocks, stressed and in some cases close to the edge.

Past recessions often made people more aware of the needs of others and more willing to share their good fortune with others suffering bad luck. As we enter potentially more turbulent times, we hope that this report will help us better understand each other, help us better care for each other, and, in a small way, help us as a society to become more resilient in the face of adversity.

2 What are the UK's needs, why are they important and how are they met?

Why are we interested in needs? Having needs is fundamental to the human condition. Our needs, as well as our capacities to meet them and the opportunities we have to use these capacities, help to define who we are. They mark our passage through life. How we meet them affects how we organise our time and also marks many of our most important relationships, with parents, spouses, children, friends and colleagues. How societies institutionalise responses to unmet needs – whether through welfare, charity or markets – helps to define their character too. The needs of others matter, both because human nature makes us able to empathise and sympathise – to 'feel with' others – but also because most people want to live in societies that are marked by compassion.

But needs are never straightforward. As the late Peter Townsend, one of the great researchers on modern poverty, put it, "the concept of need is not easy to explore."[3] Needs can be absolute and relative, objective or subjective, universal or historically and culturally specific, and there are substantial grey areas between each of these poles.

2.1 Theories of need

Surveys of need face many pitfalls. Forty years ago it was observed of needs studies that:

> *This type of research attempted to identify the disparity between needs and resources where resources were defined with reference to the established pattern of professional services and community facilities. Not surprisingly, with unfailing regularity these studies concluded that there was a need for... whatever community service was the focus of the inquiry. Such studies were mired in a conceptual confusion from which they could not be rescued.*[4]

An alternative is to seek philosophical rigour in definitions, and then to deduce from definitions which needs count and in what ways. As we have explored in detail in accompanying papers, the theoretical literature on need is rich, imaginative and full of compelling arguments. But it has not led to any consensus about precisely what need is, let alone how it should be measured. While some studies still aim to define universal needs, most recognise that many needs are context specific: to take part in the life of a community we may need more than a bare minimum of nutrition and housing. Equally, while some studies think of needs solely as deficits – a lack of particular resources – many more have come to emphasise instead the links between capabilities, resources and assets, notably in the work of Amartya Sen and Martha Nussbaum.[5] Others have also pointed out that it is not enough to have capabilities without opportunities, for example in a dynamic economy. Otherwise you can end up overqualified but inactive. And while some studies draw on apparently objective data (for example, estimates of how much food people need in order to function) others draw on subjective data (for example about happiness or feelings of safety).

In the various stages of this project we have used a definition of needs that avoids some of the pitfalls. Drawing from the work of Ian Gough and Len Doyal we define the most important needs as those that help us avoid socially recognisable harm or suffering.[6] This definition connects back to the fundamental human drive to avoid suffering and to the moral imperative which any society has to reduce unnecessary suffering. It recognises that specific definitions of need are socially determined, rather than being timeless or universal. And it provides a broader perspective than poverty, which may be easier for people to grasp, since studies of poverty often struggle with public confusions about the relationships between absolute and relative poverty, and the fact that poor people now, as in the past, don't like to be labelled as poor.

This definition of needs also provides an opening both to questions of immediate need and suffering or harm (having food or shelter), and to longer term questions about how we gain the means to meet our needs (whether through opportunities, skills, mental habits or legal rights).

By emphasising *socially recognisable* harm or suffering we are distinguishing between needs and wants. Having unsatisfied wants (not being able to buy a Nintendo Wii or a BMW) may cause discomfort or upset, but this does not correspond to a socially endorsed recognition that the want should be satisfied. However, although needs and wants can be distinguished in this way, the boundary between them is contested and changes over time. Needs surrounding the Internet and digital technologies are a good example: is Internet access a need in the UK today? What about having a mobile phone? Clearly the answers to these questions change. A job seeker in a rural area may be able to make claims on others (or on the Job Centre) for a car or means of transport; an isolated elderly person may be able to make claims on others for a mobile phone or an emergency button; a homeless person may be able to make claims on others for help in learning a new skill or finding a home. But these claims are constantly being argued about and calibrated against competing claims, available resources and shifting social norms. The social recognition of needs is a dynamic process, and we see it as a strength of this definition that it does not pretend that definitions can be timeless.

Any study of needs is also a study of inequalities. As a rule, those with the most needs (the young and the old, the disabled and the sick) tend to have the least means to meet their needs. Societies have devised many ways for the well endowed to support the more needy, from the nuclear family to the charitable foundation and the welfare state. As inequalities widen these come under greater strain. In recent years there is evidence that market returns have become strikingly more unequal. Summary measures of inequality, such as the Gini coefficient, have crept up.[7] Tony Atkinson has shown that the welfare state now has to do more to achieve a given level of equality than in the past.[8] Less obviously, there is now mounting evidence, well-marshalled by Richard Wilkinson and others, showing the correlations and possible causal links between inequality and low life expectancy, high crime and distrust.[9]

Figure 3: The Gini coefficient* 1979 to 2007–08, Great Britain

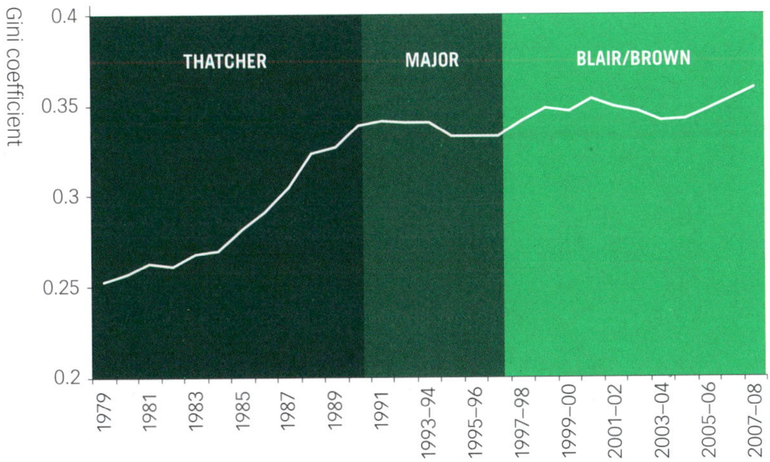

Source: Institute of Fiscal Studies

These statistical inequalities also sit alongside persistent structural inequalities, and what Charles Tilly called the "durable inequalities" that take shape along boundary lines, for example of gender or race, as privileged groups hoard resources and opportunities for themselves.[10] Such inequalities endure in part because people privilege their own needs, the needs of their families and others like them, over the needs of others. Kindness, charity and compassion are universal, but they tend to be weaker than these other forces of habit and hoarding.

* The Gini coefficient is a popular measure of income inequality that condenses the entire income distribution into a single number between 0 and 1: the higher the number, the greater the degree of income inequality.

2.2 How people understand needs themselves

While drawing on theoretical arguments, we also investigated what people themselves think needs are. We asked people from different backgrounds, of different ages and in different parts of the UK, to tell us what they need in life and what 'need' means to them. This is discussed in more detail in Appendix 2. One of the most important messages from these discussions is that although people have very complex perspectives on need, and on the relationships between wants and needs, the notion of needs was one that people readily identified with. Our discussions suggested that people automatically understand need as applying to both material and psychological issues. These are interlinked in how we live our daily lives and how we think about others. There was also passionate discussion about composite needs, such as the 'need for stability' and the 'need for peace of mind', as well as about poverty.

> “ **We feel very insecure because there is this feeling that if I can't manage myself I just better put up and shut up, I dread a bit as I get older, that if I can't do anything about it myself I'll just have to sort of hide away or something.**
>
> — Female, Focus Group in London of over 60 year olds

This study also showed that there are not necessarily common hierarchies of need of the kind once promoted by Abraham Maslow.[11] Maslow was right to distinguish different kinds of need (from subsistence needs to needs to do with wellbeing and self-actualisation). However, contrary to his conception of the hierarchy, we found that the way people classify needs depends on a range of other factors, not least the context or situation they find themselves in. For example, we interviewed one young man in Bedford who went without food for three days and elected instead to spend his last £10 topping up his mobile phone.

> “ **When I had money for food, I just used to use it to save up to take out a girl, it's not worth it at the end and it made me have bad health, really bad skin and just really, really skinny and it was horrible, it's like at the time you just think, I don't need food.**
>
> — Male, Focus Group in Cardiff of 18-24 year olds

So our responses to needs may also be shaped by contexts and moments. Our need for someone to talk to, a cigarette to smoke, a visit to a betting shop or a doctor will be very much determined by contexts and particular moments.* How we respond to needs in daily life may be influenced as much by our emotions as it is by rational consideration. And our view of what is or isn't fair is as shaped by deep rooted disposition as it is by rational argument.

> “ **If you feel that, you are either loved or looked after or somebody wants to be your companion or you're a part of an organisation or a group there is a reason to go on, so I think that is absolutely essential as well.**
>
> — Female, Focus Group in London of over 60 year olds

The study also showed that attitudes towards which needs are the most pressing and urgent can vary across the life course. At younger ages the more seemingly intractable needs, such as income and housing, loom large. Some of the more complex psycho-social needs, which are clearly present under the surface, may not be at the forefront of the young person's mind. Older people, having survived life's ups and downs, seemed to be more comfortable that many important needs have a habit of being met one way or another. They were concerned about averting more extreme or unpredictable needs. One way of thinking about this is that the further into life people get, the more concerned they are with 'smoothing out' the frequency and severity of acute needs and adversities that create acute need. Younger people, on the other hand, are more focused on the major challenges ahead of them.

* For example, addiction and compulsive behaviour counselling approaches warn that people are vulnerable to making poor decisions when they are physiologically in the grip of Hunger, Anger, Lust or Tiredness (HALT)

The study also reveals that people in middle age may be more conscious of the needs of those who depend on them, such as children, partners or elderly parents. People gave specific examples of prioritising the needs of their depedents ahead of their own.

For some people, the need to sustain a self-image (such as being a good mother) or to avert psychological discomfort (my daughter's friends all have an iPod and she doesn't) can become powerful even when what they actually deliver might be considered a preference, want or desire.

This research suggests a gap between how the public think and feel about needs and how formal policy and research treats them. Formal policy and research prioritises material needs over other psychological and psycho-social ones (being homeless sets in motion various statutory rights, whereas having no friends doesn't). It emphasises common hierarchies of need, with survival at the top. It is concerned with aggregates, whereas for the public the things that matter are more to do with whole people, situations and relationships. And policy is often concerned with what some consider to be fairly arbitrary numbers, such as the definition of poverty as below 60% of average incomes, a definition which is both unknown by the great majority of the public and not intuitively obvious either.

2.3 The interaction between material and psychological needs

An important aim of this study has been to look at both material and psychological needs and how they interact. Material needs include the essential things we need to subsist, for instance enough food to avoid malnutrition, and shelter and a source of warmth to protect us from harsh weather. Some of these needs are very specific to particular societies, for example in an economy based on bartering, access to regulated and affordable credit would not be a need. Psychological or psycho-social needs are generally more complex, including needs for autonomy, competence and relationships.[12] People have unmet psychological needs for many reasons: they may suffer from a mental illness or psychological disorder; they may have depression, or suffer from stress and anxiety. People also have psychological needs for personal security, so being in a violent or abusive relationship would also add to psychological needs. In addition to these psychological needs, people also need a host of other things in order to flourish: they need to have meaningful relationships with others, social contact and social support; they need to feel competent and capable in their environment; and they need to have choices and options about how they live and have some control over their environment. At a deeper level too they need recognition and dignity, meaning and purpose.

Material and psychological wellbeing are profoundly connected to each other.[13] Threats to physical wellbeing (violence, hunger, lack of shelter) have impacts on psychological health, and deficits in psychological needs (stress, isolation, low self-esteem and psychiatric morbidity) can affect our physical health, stifling people's motivation to eat a balanced diet or maintain their home, for example. There is also some evidence that threats to our sense of meaning and belonging lead to a more materialistic orientation – shopping really is therapeutic for some people, or at least an imperfect substitute for healthy relationships. There is also now growing evidence that mental dispositions such as optimism have a strong impact on recovery from physical illness, as well as on life expectancy. Furthermore, some material resources are required to meet psychological needs (the clothes we wear affect our self-esteem), and some intangible resources (motivation, competence) are required to meet our material needs.

2.4 The relationship between static needs and dynamic capabilities to meet them

Needs can be met in either static or dynamic ways. In the old parable, it is said to be better to teach a man to fish than to give him fish (and in its modern variant, it's even better if he can learn not to overfish). Where possible, it is better to provide people with access to jobs than with benefit payments, better to provide skills than food vouchers, better to provide relationships which may lead to opportunities in the future than pure dependence. In many situations people may simply need the equivalents of fish (or cash, or medical support). There is little point telling someone with advanced dementia that they should be more self-reliant. But in most situations a balance has to be struck between static ways of meeting needs and dynamic ones. These are all reasons why we have emphasised questions of resilience and help-seeking in the later case studies, along with the structures of opportunity in which people find themselves. Policies and programmes which focus on symptoms rather than causes are bound to disappoint.

2.5 How needs are met

This is primarily a study of needs, rather than of the many ways in which they are met. But the two are in practice interlinked, in particular because our main concern is with *unmet* needs. As a result, throughout the case studies and the research we have looked simultaneously at needs and the means people have to meet them.

As we have shown in one of the accompanying papers, there is a repeated pattern whereby people experience a need, learn that it is not peculiar to them, give it a name, and then either campaign for it to be met or develop new ways to meet it themselves.[14] A good example from several decades ago was domestic violence; a contemporary example is elder abuse.

The table on the next page summarises some of the categories of need and how they are met through the different systems of public provision, markets, civil society and the support of friends and family. Our main aim has been to look at the last row of this diagram ('Gaps'), at the groups and people whose needs are not being adequately met. The size of these different fields for meeting needs (and wants) is of course very varied. The market economy is about £1300bn in size: government's share in 2009 is set to be nearly half that, devoted both to transfers and services and its many responses to financial and economic crisis. The charitable sector accounts for around £35bn of turnover, though its social value may be much more. Foundations spend around £4bn, while corporate giving is barely a tenth of that, at least in purely financial terms. The informal or household field, however, is roughly comparable to the market economy according to studies in the USA and Germany, though it is difficult to put meaningful prices on day-to-day activities of this kind.

The importance of informal links and supports was confirmed by our research. In preparation for this project we commissioned a survey of public opinion to examine where people turn to meet their needs. Policy makers, not surprisingly, assume that state provision of pensions or hospitals, schools and social work dominates the picture. Businesses tend to assume that their provision of food, cars, finance and holidays dominates. Yet seen from the bottom up the picture is different. Most people turn to family and friends when seeking help to meet their needs.* For example, the vast majority (89%) of respondents said that they would turn to relatives, spouses and friends if they needed practical assistance (help around the home, with shopping and so on) as a result of being struck by illness.

Similarly, people would mostly turn to their family and friends when looking to meet their psychological needs. For instance, when very upset about a problem with their husband, wife or partner, one-third (32%) of respondents said that they would turn to their friends and another third would turn to other relatives, parents, or their children (31%). Few said they would access state services, with 5% seeking help from psychiatrists or counsellors and 3% doctors. Interestingly, one-fifth of respondents either indicated that that they would not turn to anybody in a comprehensive list (8%), were not sure who they would turn to (5%), or just would not turn to anybody at all (7%).

There are many fields where the market is predominant. For example, when faced with having to borrow money 47% would turn to a bank or building society, yet even here the second most common answer was 'parents' (14%). Overall, intimate relationships and friendships appear most important in helping to satisfy unmet needs, and their strength and weakness is decisive in shaping our wellbeing.

---

* We commissioned Ipsos MORI to carry out a survey of public opinion relating to social needs in 2006 (n= 2112). The sample was representative of groups according to gender, age (15 or over), work status, marital status and housing tenure.

Figure 4: Illustrations of how needs are met

	Material and physical needs	Care needs	Needs for capabilities	Psychological Needs
State	Benefits, NHS	State nurseries	State education	NHS
Market	Renting a flat	Hired childcare	Private education	Psychotherapy
Civil Society	Food parcels	Hospices	Community projects	Befriending services
Individuals, family and friends	Parental protection	Informal eldercare	Cultural capital	Familial love
Gaps	Rough sleepers	Single disabled elders	Illiterate school leavers	Untreated mentally ill

PART II

An overview of material and psychological needs: key facts and trends

In this chapter we provide an overview of the state of need in the UK, drawing on existing data as well as our own analyses. The aim is to supply some of the background to the more detailed case studies and analyses that we offer later on, through an overview of the complex landscape of needs – including both material and psychological data, data about different clusters and groups, and changing patterns over time.

We start with a snapshot of the whole population, before disaggregating the different dimensions of need. The figure below brings together psychological and material needs. Our primary concern is with the people represented by the lower left hand quadrant. These are the people who are both poor and less satisfied with their lives. Poverty and unhappiness often — but by no means always — come together.

We are also interested in the relatively prosperous but unhappy (and, as we show, by some measures a significant proportion of the people who are least content with life are not particularly poor), and we are interested in why some people appear to be materially badly off but are nevertheless living contented lives. As we show, some of the answers have to do with social wealth as well as material wealth – the strength of family links, friendships and others who can be relied on.

Figure 5: Material and psychological needs quadrant

We drew on UK data from the British Household Survey Panel to characterise these quadrants, using life satisfaction questions (excluding those that related directly to income) to generate a proxy indicator of psychological need and household income as an indicator of material need. Combining this information we were able to isolate and analyse groups akin to those in the diagram above. Below we profile each group showing their differences compared to the overall sample. More specifically, we summarise each group's relative likelihood of being represented among various classifications e.g. lone parent. This is indicated by values where '1' means equally likely as the overall sample and '2' means twice as likely.

Figure 6: Higher statistical likelihood of different groups appearing in our four quadrants 2007-08

Dissatisfied with life & on high income

Couple without dep. children	2.0
Hardly talks to neighbours	1.8
Poor or very poor health	1.7
Life lacks meaning	1.7
Life is not full of opportunities	1.7
Long-term sick and disabled	1.5
Separated from spouse	1.4
Area characterisation:	
'Aspiring households'	2.6
'Settled in the city'	2.0

Satisfied with life & on high income

Have a degree	1.8
Area characterisation:	
'Thriving suburbs'	1.8
'Aspiring households'	1.5

Dissatisfied with life & on low income

Unemployed	4.0
Dislike neighbourhood	3.0
Work is driving/travelling	2.4
Used social worker	2.4
Long-term sick/disabled	2.3
Separated from spouse	2.0
Life lacks meaning	2.0
Caring for sick/ disabled in household	1.9
Lone parent	1.8
Aged 16 to 20	1.7
Life is not full of opportunities	1.7
Full time family carer	1.6
Rarely involved sports	1.5
Area characterisation:	
'Public housing'	3.0

Satisfied with life & on low income

Unemployed	1.8
Full time family carer	1.6
Single elderly	1.5
No qualifications	1.5
Retired	1.4
Widowed	1.4
Area characterisation:	
'Village life'	1.4

Source: BHPS analysis

This table shows that while each of the four groups has a broad mix of people within it, on some measures there are stark contrasts that distinguish them from the general population and each other. The poor and unhappy are four times more likely to be unemployed than the overall sample. They are three times more likely to live in public housing areas and twice as likely to be long-term sick or separated from their spouse. Those who are on low incomes and satisfied with life (bottom right) were likely to be older – 1.4 times more likely to be 65 or over. Overall this group is more likely to be unemployed (twice as likely as the sample overall) but they were only half as likely as the bottom left group. Those who have high incomes and yet are dissatisfied with life (top left) are twice as likely to be couples who no longer have dependent children, are less likely to talk to their neighbours and more likely to be in poor health. Those who are satisfied with life and on high income (top right) are the least remarkable in terms of divergence with the overall sample but are almost twice as likely to have a degree. Both those rich and poor who are dissatisfied with life are more likely to think life lacks meaning and are less likely to think that life is full of opportunities.

We explore the relationship between material and psychological needs in more detail later on in the report. But first we disaggregate, looking at what lies behind this composite picture.

3 Material needs

We begin with the familiar territory of material need. Essential material needs relate to the necessities required for survival, such as food, shelter and warmth. If these needs go unmet or partially met then health suffers and life expectancy shortens. Prosperous societies like Britain are generally successful in meeting these essential needs. The various arms of the welfare state are meant to guarantee minimum standards as well as minimum incomes, yet there are important gaps, for example among undocumented migrants or isolated elderly people slipping into destitution.

3.1 The need to be adequately nourished

Food is a very basic human need. It figures here for two opposing reasons: because many people eat too much, and too much of the wrong kinds of food, and because a much smaller number have too little to eat.

According to the English Health Survey, over the ten years to 2007 the proportion of overweight or obese men rose three points to 65% and the proportion of overweight women rose four points to 56%. Figures for children suggest the problem is going to get worse, with both boys and girls recording an increase of 5 points up to 30% overweight or obese[15] (see 'Damaging consumption' in Chapter 14 for trends and potential implications in ten years time). The trends are occurring throughout society, albeit to a lesser extent among the affluent, for many reasons ranging from the much easier availability of food and drink to greater car use and children spending much more of their time in the home. The health implications are clear. Overweight people are more likely to develop problems such as heart disease, stroke, diabetes, certain types of cancer, gout (joint pain caused by excess uric acid) and gallbladder disease. Being overweight can also cause problems such as sleep apnoea (interrupted breathing during sleep) and osteoarthritis (wearing away of the joints).[16] The risk increases with the extent to which a person is overweight. Such illness can cause both unmet material and psychological needs. For example, gout and osteoarthritis may limit physical mobility, and at the more severe end cancer can impact on every aspect of life, dramatically compromising a person's ability to meet their own needs. Obesity has proven resistant to public policy, despite increasingly vigorous attempts to reduce sugar content in foods and bring down portion sizes, alongside public information campaigns and attempts to boost exercise.

The mirror of obesity is malnutrition, which predisposes people to disease, delays recovery, affects body function and wellbeing, and hampers medical treatment outcomes.* By global standards the UK does not have a problem of hunger. However, given the abundance of food in the UK it is surprising to discover that, according to the Malnutrition Advisory Board, five percent of the UK population are thought to be clinically underweight and two million people are malnourished.[17] While anyone can suffer from malnutrition, it is those with chronic disease, people living in deprived areas, and older people who are most at risk. One in seven older people have been assessed at medium to high risk, and this rate increases among older people in institutions. The extent of the problem is revealed when malnourished people come into contact with services. A revealing recent study found 42% of adults being admitted to hospitals were at risk of malnutrition.[18] Given these figures it is unsurprising that some consider malnutrition to be more costly to public funds than the more recognised issue of obesity and call for more screening of at-risk groups.[19]

Considering that the problem is largely reversible through providing adequate nutrition, it is perhaps unexpected that hundreds of people still die each year in the UK as a result of malnutrition or, more commonly, malnutrition in combination with another illness. During 2007-08, there were 353 deaths in England and Wales and 110 in Scotland from malnutrition. The trend in England and Wales has been relatively stable since 1998-99 with an average of 310 cases per year. Unsurprisingly, older people are over-represented, with those aged 55 or older accounted for 85% of deaths.

> **“ I paid my rent one week and I'd gone overdrawn in my bank account so they whisked a load of money away. I was left with £11.00 to go shopping for seven of us for a week. I just ended up with Baked Beans, bread and milk that I could water down ... I couldn't afford to go and buy the fruit and veg you know.**
>
> — Mother in rural Norfolk

Another indicator of unmet need which falls into this category is food poverty. Defined as the inability to obtain healthy affordable food, food poverty is twice as prevalent as malnutrition and is thought to affect four million people in the UK, although there is little information on whether the problem is getting worse or

* The literal meaning of malnutrition is 'bad' nutrition and therefore the term can encompass wasting (undernutrition) and/or obesity (overnutrition). Despite this, the term malnutrition is more commonly used to refer to undernutrition rather than overnutrition. It is in this sense that the term is used in this report.

better or whether certain areas of the country are worse affected than others.[20] The issue has only been thoroughly researched and recognised in recent years. Although not immediately life threatening, food poverty can be extremely detrimental to health, contributing to 30% of life years lost in early death, higher levels of disability, 50% of heart disease cases, 33% of deaths from cancer, increased falls and fractures in older people, low birth weight, and higher child morbidity and mortality.[21]

Those at risk of food poverty include people living on state benefits, who typically eat fewer portions of fruit and vegetables, fish and high-fibre breakfast cereals. Also workless households, who typically consume a higher number of calories, considerably more fat, salt and sugars.[22] Other statistically at-risk groups include households with dependent children, older people, people with disabilities, and black and minority ethnic communities. The concentration of food poverty can be explained by a culmination of economic factors (e.g. a perception of what represents good value), logistic factors (e.g. accessibility of shops) and cultural considerations (e.g. appreciation of what a healthy diet is). It has also come into sharper focus because of the simultaneous growth of out-of-town supermarkets and the closure of shops in poorer areas, leading to 'food deserts' where remaining small local shops provide poor quality choice and high prices.[23]

Figure 7: Section summary – Adequate nutrition

	Malnutrition	**Food poverty**
Extent of unmet need	2 million malnourished (UK)	4 million affected (UK)
Trends	No overall trend but malnutrition related deaths relatively stable	No data
Geographic variation	No comparable rates Deprived areas	No data Deprived areas
Groups more at risk	Older people Those with serious illness	Workless households Lower income households

3.2 The need for somewhere to live

Having somewhere to live is as essential a human need as food. Many people who do not have a home find shelter in different types of temporary accommodation, perhaps staying with relatives or in refuges. However, the most severe and visible type of homelessness involves sleeping on the street or, for instance, in abandoned buildings. The harm caused by sleeping rough like this is stark, reducing life expectancy by 30 years to an average age of 40-42.[24] Rough sleepers are reportedly 35 times more likely to commit suicide, and four times more likely to die from unnatural causes such as accidents, assaults, murder, drug or alcohol poisoning.[25]

There are thought to be around 800 people sleeping on the streets in the UK on any one night. The government collates night count figures, which are a snap-shot of people sleeping rough in key local areas during a specific night. There were 480 rough sleepers counted in England (Jun 2008),[26] between 128 and 165 in Wales (2008),[27] and the latest figures for Scotland (2003) counted 328 rough sleepers.[28] The problem is particularly pronounced in London. The capital has a constant flow of people sleeping rough, accounts for half of the English night count total, and has, according to St Mungo's homeless charity, some 3,000 people sleeping rough at some point during the year.[29]

Many different people are at risk of becoming rough sleepers. They are often victims of some sort of abandonment, dispute, abusive relationship or family breakdown. Also at risk are people leaving institutions without adequate social support: prisoners, cared for children and those leaving the armed services. Other more individual dispositions also put people at risk, including mental health problems, substance misuse, anti-social behaviour, lack of 'coping' or practical skills and learning disabilities.[30]

In England and Wales the number of people sleeping on the streets has decreased considerably. The night count data suggests a step-change reduction with a 73% fall between 1998 and 2003. Since 2003 levels have stabilised. The reduction followed a range of actions taken to meet a target set by the then Prime Minister Tony Blair in 1998 to reduce rough sleeping by at least two-thirds by 2002.[31]

BOB'S STORY

Bob is 44. His wife of 15 years died a year ago from cancer. He cared for her for the seven months before she died and found watching her health deteriorate really difficult. After she died, Bob "lost the plot completely". With hindsight he is surprised he didn't cope better, as he'd been in the army for 17 years and coped with friends dying, but this time was different and Bob found it impossible to cope.

After his wife's funeral Bob felt that he had to get away, to escape the house his wife had died in, to escape from people talking about her and to have some time to think. He left his home, family and friends and got on a train. Bob initially stayed in a bed and breakfast by the coast, to give himself time to think. He was drinking heavily and started to sleep rough as money began to run out.
Bob spent seven months like this, travelling around Britain, drinking and trying to decide what to do next. Bob tried to get in touch with a few organisations who he thought might be able to help. Every time he did they focused on his alcoholism, but Bob wanted to talk about his wife and get help to grieve.

Eventually, Bob got in contact with his old army regiment and they were able to help him. They organised for him to see a psychiatrist, who he still sees now, and which he's found extremely helpful. Being able to deal with his wife's death has helped Bob stop drinking. Bob found a hostel for rough sleepers which he stayed at for three months. He is now living in a shared house and hoping to start renting his own flat within the next year. This is really important to him as he feels that once he has got his own place he can start moving forward and can hopefully get back to work.

Figure 8: Street counts of rough sleepers for England 1998-2009

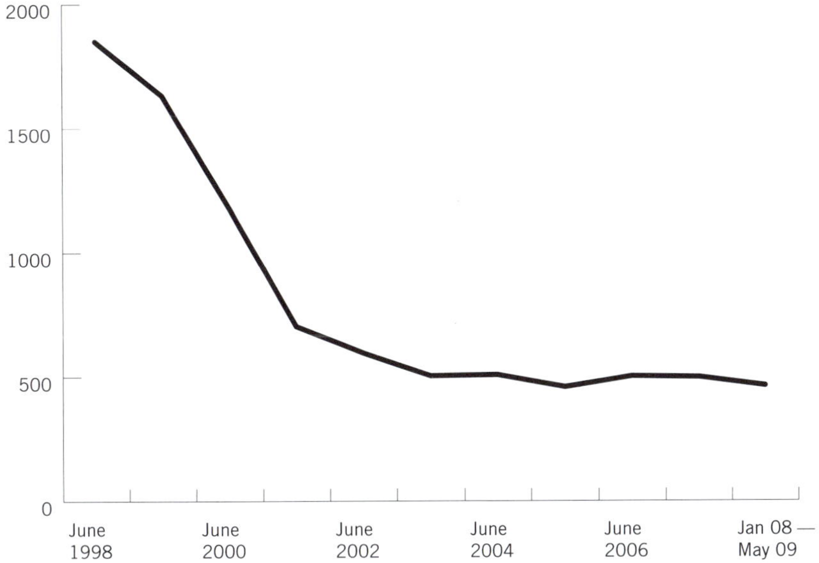

Source DCLG

While rough sleeping is a more visible sign of the need for shelter, homelessness is much more prevalent. A homeless individual, household or family has no accommodation which they are entitled to occupy, or it might be unreasonable for them to continue to occupy their present home. Such as keep individuals may find temporary accommodation staying with different friends. Bed and breakfast or hostel establishments are also used in an emergency to accommodate homeless households.

Due to differences in legislation, homelessness figures are presented independently for UK countries. In England, the number of households officially accepted as homeless in 2007 was 99,500, half the level of 2004 and well below levels a decade ago. In Wales the equivalent figure was 9,300, similar to a decade ago. This figure rose sharply between 2001 and 2004, falling equally thereafter. In Scotland there were 41,100 newly homeless in 2006-07. Here levels had increased and were a third higher than a decade ago but this is thought to be a consequence of new legislation introduced in 2001 and 2003 which led to the inclusion of homeless people without dependent children in the official figures.[32] Homelessness figures are also available for the English regions in percentages for 2008. These indicate that homelessness varies from a high of 0.6% of households in London and the West Midlands to a low of 0.2% in the South West.[33]

The data surrounding homelessness is largely administrative. As such the figures above relate to government criteria and do not cover all relevant groups. This was highlighted by a National Policy Institute 'hidden homeless' report in 2003, which estimated that there were 400,000 adults in Britain who met the legal definition of homelessness but were not accounted for in official statistics.[34] The table below summarises estimates, showing that the majority of homeless people are in overcrowded concealed households, that is, adults who are staying with friends or family because they have no other option and where the housing is overcrowded (and often insecure because of owner/renter dissatisfaction).

Figure 9: Estimated groups of homeless people not recorded in administrative statistics

Category of hidden homelessness	Estimated No.
Overcrowding in concealed households – aged 16-24	310,000
Overcrowding in concealed households – aged 25+	190,000
In a concealed household where the owner/renter is dissatisfied – aged 16-24	130,000
In a concealed household where the owner/renter is dissatisfied -¬ aged 25+	50,000
Hostels, night shelters or refuges	43,000
Bed and Breakfasts etc.	38,000
Involuntary Squatting	at most 10,000
People due for discharge from institutions	at least 1,500
Risk of eviction	1,000
Rough sleepers	700

Source: NPI

There are many causes of homelessness but 2008 official figures show that 37% of those recognised as homeless had lost their last settled home because parents, relatives or friends (mostly parents) were no longer able, or willing, to accommodate them.[35] A considerable proportion of homelessness, however, is due to people (mostly women) leaving abusive partners (13%) and another 6% is related to other violence or harassment. There are also 13% who struggled with arrears or lost rented housing and 7% who have left institutions' care or asylum support. Black Minority Ethnic (BME) groups were typically over-represented in England, accounting for over 25% of cases accepted by Government. If BME representation in the general population is used as a benchmark the proportion would be expected to be 9%.

Figure 10: Section summary – Shelter

	Rough sleepers	Homeless households
Extent of unmet need	Poor data. Estimated 800 on any given night (UK)	Households accepted as homeless: England 99,000 Wales 9,300 Scotland 41,000. 400,000 hidden homeless in Britain
Trends	Stable over recent years after large decrease before 2001 (England) No recent data (Scotland)	Lower than 10 years ago in England. Similar levels in Wales. Scotland levels elevated by more inclusive legislation.
Geographic variation	More prevalent in London	Higher in London and West Midlands
More at risk groups	Those with broken / dysfunctional/ abusive relationships. As with rough sleepers. Plus BME groups, younger people relying on relatives/ friends for accommodation.	Those leaving institutions. Those with mental health problems.

3.3 The need for warmth

Having access to shelter is clearly essential, but homes also require heating. Cold homes can at best result in an uncomfortable living environment and at worst increase the risk of illness and even death among the most vulnerable. In 2007-08 there were an estimated 25,300 excess winter deaths in England and Wales[36] and 2,180 in Scotland.[37] The proportions of excess winter deaths in the UK are paradoxically worse than those in colder European counties such as Norway and yet better than for warmer countries such as Portugal. This is because dwellings in colder countries are typically more thermally efficient. The trend in excess winter deaths has been improving in the long term: in England and Wales the number of cases has been progressively declining from the 100,000 recorded in 1950-51.

Figure 11: Number of excess winter deaths in England and Wales (1950-51 – 2007-08

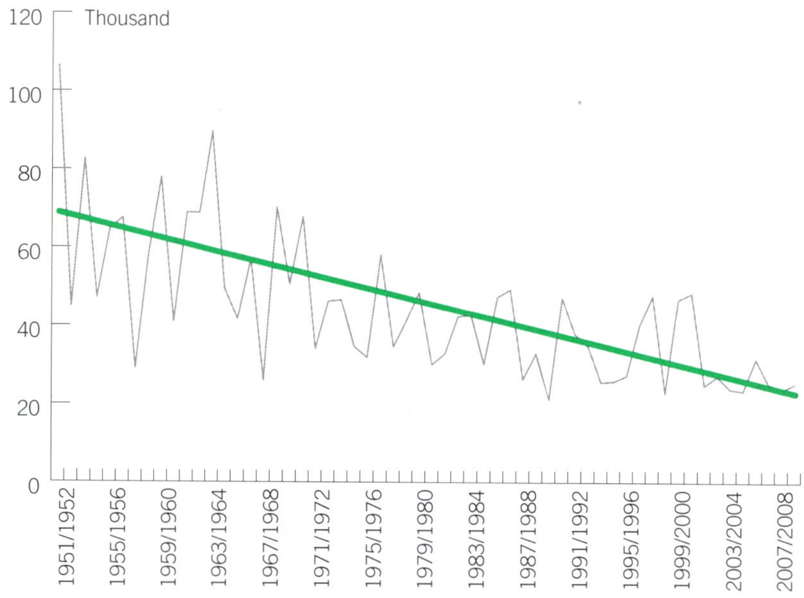

Source: Office for National Statistics

Winter death levels are contingent on diseases that cause sharp annual fluctuations. In the winters of 1998-99 and 1999-2000 flu epidemics increased the numbers who died, but in recent years, in England and Wales, winters have been mild and there have only been low levels of influenza (though 2009 brought serious concerns about a swine flu epidemic).[38] The elderly experience the greatest increase in deaths each winter. In 2007-08 there were 19,400 excess winter deaths among those aged 75 and over in England and Wales. In contrast there were 5,900 more deaths among those under the age of 75 (a much larger age group).[39] Older people are more at risk as they are less able to judge if they are dangerously cold so might not make efforts to warm up. They are also more likely to live in older, less thermally efficient homes and to be economical with heating to lower energy bills.[40]

Unmet need for warmth is also indicated by levels of fuel poverty. Fuel poverty is defined as a household that needs to spend more than 10% of its household income on all domestic fuel use; this includes appliances to heat the home to an adequate level of warmth. The problem was estimated to affect 3.5 million households across the UK in 2006, an increase of 1 million households since 2005 but down from approximately 6.5 million in 1996. There was some notable variation by country: Scotland and Northern Ireland recorded the highest proportion of households in fuel poverty (23%) compared to Wales (11%) and England (7%).[41] The higher proportion in Scotland is partially explained by differences in definition. In Scotland pensioners, the sick and disabled are deemed to require warmer homes than their counterparts in England. Other contributing factors include a higher proportion of pensioners and the long-term sick; Scotland's greater rurality; and a colder climate and higher wind speeds (especially in Northern-most regions) leading to a longer heating season.[42] Regional figures for England show the North East has the highest rate at 13% and the East the lowest at 5%.

Figure 12: Estimated number (millions) of households in fuel poverty by UK country 1996-2006

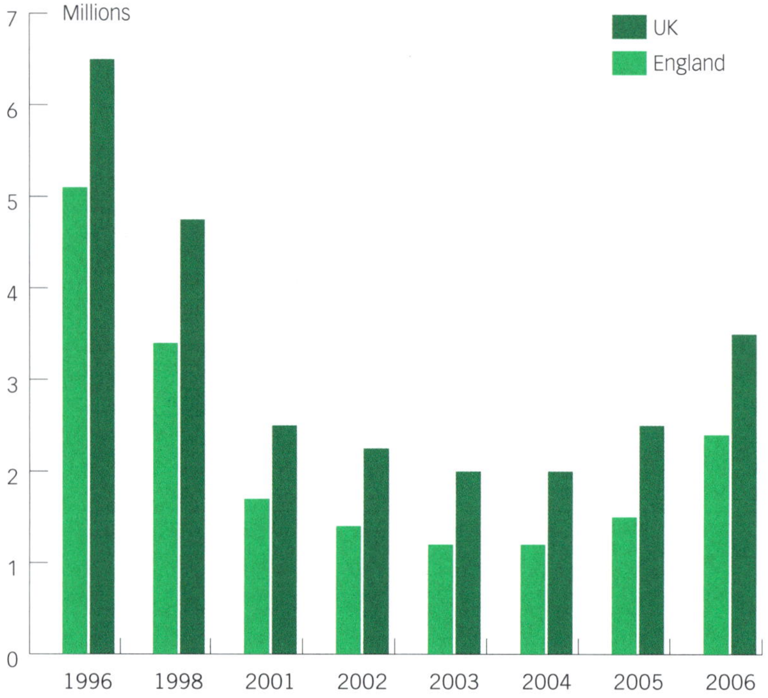

Source: DEFRA

The main causes of fuel poverty are low incomes and poor housing stock but it is also influenced by fuel prices and affordable energy.[43] There have been advances in the market to ensure that vulnerable customers are not disconnected,but increased prices still lead to colder homes as households with low incomes try to economise. [44]

Generally, fuel poverty is most likely to affect those in private rented accommodation (12% compared to 7-8% in other tenures); households renting social accommodation are often in smaller, more energy efficient dwellings. Additionally, single working-age people and pensioners are more at risk than couples or larger families. And rural areas are much more likely to be in fuel poverty compared to urban or suburban areas (44% compared to 28% in suburban and 26% in urban areas in 2005): rural residents may be more likely to live in larger and less energy-efficient properties.[45]

Figure 13: Section summary – Warmth

	Excess winter deaths	Fuel poverty
Extent of unmet need	25,300 (Eng & Wales) c.2000 Scotland	3.5 million households (2006)
Trends	Annual fluctuations depending on weather and disease but consistent long term reduction since 1970s	Down considerably on 1996 but increasing since 2004 (UK) Fluctuations depend on fuel costs
Geographic variation	Small regional variations in England	Scotland and Northern Ireland have higher proportions High in North East (Eng)
More at risk groups	Older people Thermally inefficient homes	Private rented Single working age/ pensioner Low income private tenants Rural areas

3.4 The need for a decent home

Living in a non-decent home means that the accommodation provides inadequate warmth, is in disrepair or has a lack of modern facilities. The English Household Condition Survey indicates that the proportion of non-decent homes has decreased from an alarming 45% in 1996 to 27% in 2006. In 2006 London recorded the highest proportion at 34%, followed by the South West (30%), and North West and Yorkshire & Humberside both at 29%. The lowest proportions were recorded in the North East (23%), East (24%) and South East (25%). There are no published figures for the rest of the UK.

People who rent privately are most at risk of living in a non-decent home. However, owner-occupied accommodation still accounts for the majority of the problem (two-thirds) by virtue of the fact that this is the most common type of tenure.[46] In England 30% of households in the poorest fifth were judged non-decent. The proportion might be expected to be higher for poorer households but such households are more likely to reside in public rented accommodation that typically have decent maintenance standards. A second indicator of inadequate housing is overcrowding. Overcrowding is associated with a higher rate of child accidents and the resulting lack of space, privacy and demand for resources can be a cause of psychological stress.

In the UK 5% of people and 2% of households live in overcrowded conditions. These figures have not changed substantially for a decade. Scotland recorded the highest rate at 12%* (Glasgow stands out, with 22% of households overcrowded) and Northern Ireland had high levels at 7%, while Wales was lower at 4%. London was by far the most overcrowded English region, at 17%, with most other regions between 5% and 6%. In terms of trends the figures have been stable in Britain between 1996-97 and 2006 at around 5%.

Overcrowding is four times as prevalent in social rented housing in homes owned by the occupiers (12% of people compared with 3%). One-third of those in overcrowded households (500,000 adults) neither own nor rent the property and are therefore living in someone else's home, usually their parents'. Surprisingly, almost half of these people were aged 25 or over.

JESS'S STORY

Jess is 17 years old and has a one-year-old daughter.

Jess's mother lives in the Caribbean. Until recently Jess and her daughter had been living with an aunt in a small two-bedroom maisonette in London. Jess's aunt has two children aged five and six, one of whom has learning difficulties, and is pregnant with her third child. The aunt's boyfriend also lives with them. The living conditions were very cramped, with Jess sharing the upper berth of a bunk bed with her daughter in one of the rooms. Jess was enrolled in a childcare course at a local further education college and receives about £100 a month in benefits. Her aunt has a number of part time jobs at a nursing home, a super market and informal childminding.

The combination of very overcrowded living conditions and very little money was the source of considerable tension between Jess and her aunt. Eventually their arguments grew to be too much and Jess moved out. She is now living in temporary accommodation with her daughter and is no longer attending college.

* Scotland has a slightly different legal definition of overcrowding, which may account for part of this variation.

Figure 14: Section summary – Decent home

	Non-decent housing	Overcrowded households
Extent of unmet need	27% of homes (Eng.)	5% of people 2% of households
Trends	Down from 45% to 27% (Eng.)	Unchanged for a decade
Geographic variation	London high as was South West, North West, Yorkshire & Humberside	Scotland high nationally London high
Groups more at risk	Poorer households (although significant proportion for all income bands) Private rented	Social rented Those who neither own/rent and their relations

3.5 The need for adequate transport

Adequate transport, meaning that people can travel affordably and without substantial inconvenience, allows people to access opportunities, be they economic (the journey to work), social (to see family) or practical (to supermarket or hospital).

People with access to a car are more likely to have their transport needs met. In Britain in 2006, 24% of the population did not have regular access to a car, while 44% had access to one car, and 32% to two or more. The proportion lacking a car was highest in Scotland at 29% followed by England at 24% and Wales at 22%. Rates varied across the English regions, from a high of 31% in the North East to 17% both in the East of England and South West.

Some types of people were less likely to have car access. For example, only 10% of working-age couples were without car access compared to 40% of working-age singles (both with and without dependent children). The problem was much worse for single pensioners, 65% of whom lacked access to a car. Interestingly, there is still a gender distinction among those who can access a car. In 2007, 25% of men either lacked a car or driving licence, but this proportion was much higher for women, at 40%.

Clearly, public transport is a necessity for those who cannot access or drive a car. In England 5% of people with a car found it difficult to access a supermarket but this proportion increased to 20% for those without access to a car. The equivalent proportions for visiting the doctor were 6% compared to 19% (three times as high); the hospital 22% compared to 41% (twice as high); the post office 8% compared to 17% (twice as high); and 4% compared with 12% for corner shops (three times as high).

Public transport is more important to those in rural areas, given that access to amenities is likely to be more difficult. People living in very rural districts are more likely to feel that their local transport needs are improving than are those in urban districts (37% compared to 21%).[47] In these cases access to a car may be vital to coping with everyday life; people living in remoter rural areas are arguably the most vulnerable to rising petrol prices, as well as facing higher prices for many commodities.

Figure 15: Section summary – Adequate transport

Extent of unmet need	24% no access to a car (Brit) 20% without car found it difficult to access supermarket (Eng.) 29% doctors 41% hospital 17% post office 12% corner shop
Trends	Proportions without car access is reducing, both male and female
Geographic variation	Scotland high nationally North East high Rural areas high
Groups more at risk	Single pensioners Single working age Females

3.6 The means to meet needs: income, jobs and serviceable debt

The phrase 'material needs' is used to describe both the essential needs covered above and the need for money. This is somewhat misleading, since money income can just as easily be used to pay for non-material things such as therapy, a visit to the cinema or bingo. But access to money is obviously central to how people meet their own needs, buying goods and services in the market. As we showed earlier, its importance is often exaggerated – a high proportion of our needs are met through friends and family, and not through purchases in markets or state provision. Money can't buy you love or friendships, or many of the things that matter most in life. But material wealth certainly helps in meeting material needs, and other things being equal, being well above the poverty line is likely to provide the basis to be happier in life

The need for adequate income

Researchers on wealth and poverty have long focused on what an adequate income is. Changing definitions – based on assessments of nutritional, housing and other needs – have been drawn on to set benefit levels. In parallel, researchers have studied changing patterns of relative income, both on grounds of fairness, and to reflect the fact that people are very conscious of relativities.

The conventional threshold for relative poverty in the UK is below 60% of the median (average) equivalised household income.* In 2007-08 this generally equated to, or was less than, £236 per week for a couple without children (the conventional benchmark).[48] Joseph Rowntree Foundation research argues that relative poverty has also been shown to relate to shortened life, poorer educational achievements and higher rates of child accidents in the home. Moreover:

> *Young adults who as children suffered financial hardship, were in trouble with the law or played truant have significantly greater than average chances of earning lower wages, being unemployed, spending time in prison (men) or becoming a lone parent (women). These associations exist independently of socio-economic background or experiences in early childhood. They are only partly accounted for by lower educational attainment.*[49]

More generally, there is the psychological impact of poverty in facing prejudice and stigma (as we show in the later case studies). It is common for those struggling to feel constant strain and deep-seated pessimism.

The majority of people in the UK are not affected by low income, yet in 2007-08 there were 11 million people, or 18% of the population, living under the poverty line. These statistics are derived before housing costs (BHC) are considered. When housing costs are factored into the calculation the figure increases to 13.5 million people, or 23% of the population.[50] The poverty rates among UK countries is different, with Wales recording the highest proportion at 24% (after housing costs – AHC) followed by England (22%), Northern Ireland (20%) and Scotland (19%).

In England, some regions are worse affected than others. People in the North East, North West, and West Midlands are most likely to live in low-income households before housing costs (all have 21% below the poverty line) whereas households in Inner London have higher rates after housing costs (30% compared to 21% overall). Those living in the South East are least likely to live

* More precisely, 60% of contemporary equivalised median household disposable income before the deduction of housing costs.

in low-income households before housing costs, with individuals in the East and South East of England least likely after housing costs.[51]

The national poverty statistics have changed considerably over the years. Starting in the mid-1980s poverty in the UK (using the 60% of average threshold) increased substantially from around 14% to 25%. Thereafter it levelled off until the late 1990s and then began a slow decline down to 20% by 2003-04. However, the most recent trend is an upward one, with 2007-08 levels at 23% – the equivalent figure in 1979 was 14%. The proportion on the very lowest incomes (40% or less of the average) has been increasing since 1985.

Figure 16: Percentage of UK individuals in relative poverty after housing costs, 1979 to 2007

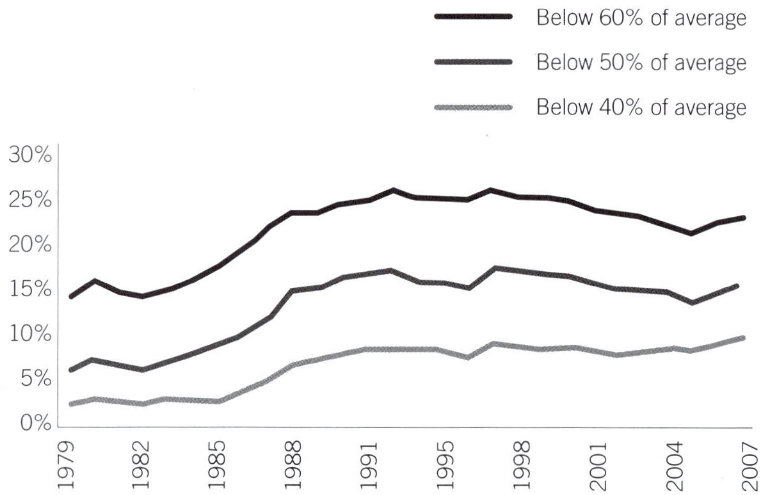

Source ONS

While there is a dedicated section on international comparisons later in the report, we note here that the proportion of people in poverty in the UK does not compare particularly well with other European countries. The UK had two percentage points above the average of 16% living under the poverty line BHC in 2007, with only four countries recording a higher rate.[52] The proportion of the population on low incomes in the UK is almost twice that of the Netherlands and one and a half times that of France.

Figure 17: Percentage of households on low income by European country 2007

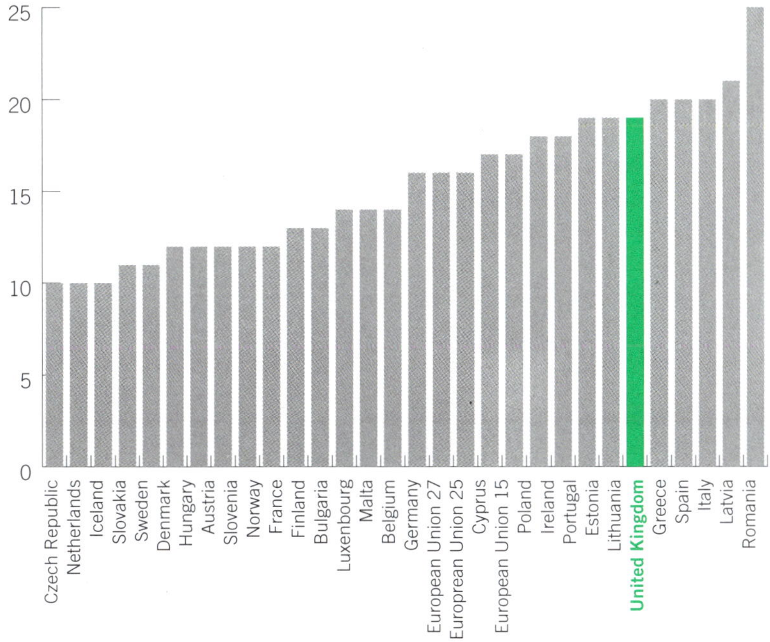

Source: Eurostat

Certain types of people and households are more likely to fall below the poverty line than others. Children are more than twice as likely to suffer from poverty as adults. Other groups more likely to be poor include those aged 85 or over, lone parents and households with a disabled person not receiving benefit. Not unexpectedly, workless households are at the greatest risk, with 70% below the poverty line AHC. Levels of poverty also vary substantially by ethnicity. Some Black and minority ethnic groups record up to 61% in poverty AHC. Department for Work and Pensions research has shown that the risk is greater for Bangladeshis, Pakistanis and Black Africans, and to a lesser extent Caribbean, Indian and Chinese people and that Muslims are more likely to be poor compared to other religious groups.[53]

While some people's experiences of relative poverty will be brief, some household types are at risk of sustained poverty, officially defined as being under 60% of the average income for at least three years out of four. Figures for 2001-05 suggest that 9% of all individuals were in persistent poverty during this time. This figure increased to 19% for single parents with children and 18% of single pensioners; pensioner couples also recorded higher levels at 13%. In contrast, couples without children appeared to be well protected, with only 5% in persistent poverty.

Poverty is often associated with debt. The average household unsecured debt (i.e. excluding mortgages) is £9,280. This is mostly comprised of personal loans (41%) and credit card bills (49%). Our analysis of the BHPS 2007-08 suggests that almost one quarter (24%) of UK adults (aged 16 and over) were making repayments on these types of loan. Those who had borrowed were asked if repayments were a burden on the household. A majority (58%) replied that the repayments were not particularly problematic. Just under one-third (30%) thought them to be 'somewhat of a burden'. However, a minority of 11% considered the repayments to be a 'heavy burden'. For the purpose of analysis we have considered these latter respondents to be over-indebted and compared various groups, using the 11% as a UK average benchmark.

Excess debt is a particular problem for 'lone parents with dependent children' (26%) and the 'single non elderly' (19%). Single elderly households felt the least strain typically with 80% saying debt was not problematic. Other studies have shown that over-indebtedness is related to age and that young people between the ages of 18 and 25 are most vulnerable as a result of increased exposure to and availability of credit.

When looking at housing tenure, the highest proportion finding repayments a heavy burden was for 'local authority rented' (23%, twice the UK average) and the lowest were those who owned outright (6%). An analysis examining the residential area of respondents (see footnote xiv for explanation about OAC area classification) indicated that those in 'blue collar communities' and 'city living areas' were slightly more likely to be over-indebted, with 15% feeling repayments were a heavy burden on the household compared to 11% overall.

With regard to trends, the proportions of the BHPS sample feeling that repayments are a heavy burden remained fairly stable during the 14 years to 2007-08 (between 10% and 11%). However there are other, perhaps more sensitive, measurements that suggest that personal debt has been increasing over recent years. Two of the main statutory insolvency instruments available to individuals in financial difficulties are bankruptcy and individual voluntary arrangements (IVAs). In England and Wales, the total number of individual insolvencies has increased from 30,590 in 2002 to 106,540 in 2008. The Office for National Statistics have described the trend as reflecting a similar increase in levels of consumer credit.[54] It is widely considered that the rapid increase in bankruptcies between 2003 and 2006 was attributable to economic factors rather than legislative ones, particularly the levels of high and increasingly unserviceable consumer debt.

Figure 18: Number (in thousands) of individual insolvencies (bankruptcies and IVAs), England and Wales 1991-2008

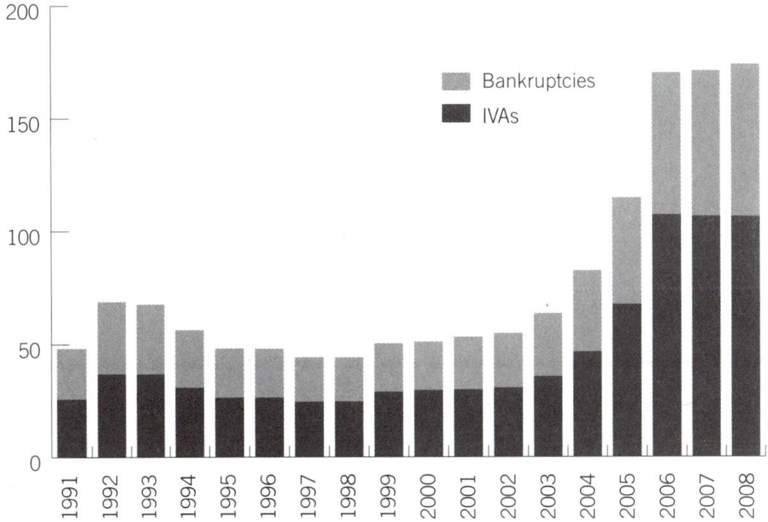

Source: ONS

There is little data on local geographic variations in debt. A recent survey comprising over 9,500 people in Britain who were worried about debt showed only slight regional variation with regard to unsecured debt.[55] Respondents in the North East demonstrated the lowest 'debt to pay' (debts as a proportion of take-home pay) disparity at 114% and respondents in the North West recorded the highest rate at 132% (a difference of 16%).

People are also at risk from over-indebtedness through secured lending. Mortgages often represent the largest single loan that any household will ever take. The average UK household debt, including mortgages, in 2009 was £58,370, which is six times greater than the average unsecured debt value of £9,280. Repayment problems on mortgages were small up until 2008 due largely to low unemployment and a rising property market. However the current recession, subsequent rising unemployment levels and a falling housing market have resulted in greater numbers of people struggling. The proportion of mortgage holders in arrears for three months or more has doubled from just over 1% in 2007 to 2% in 2008 and is forecast to double again in 2009. The figure below indicates the increasing rate of repossessions across the UK.

Figure 19: Number (thousands) of mortgage arrears and repossessions in the UK 2000-2009

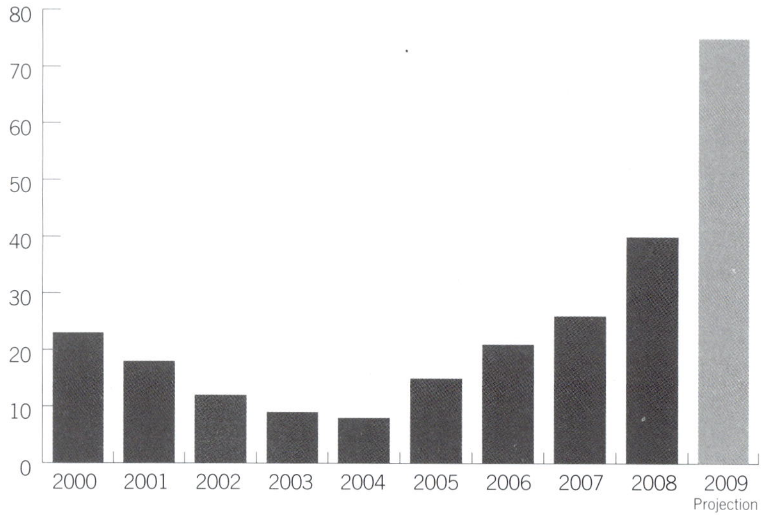

Source: Council of Mortgage Lenders

Those who invested in mortgage deals based on high multiples of income are among the most vulnerable, as are those made unemployed. In fact, at least 60% of those who become unemployed are in owner-occupied homes with mortgages, and that at least half of these people (and the households they live in) are vulnerable to mortgage arrears and ultimately repossession.

The need for employment

Unemployment not only impacts on income and the needs discussed in earlier sections but also has ramifications for psychological wellbeing (see the next chapter). Below we examine economic inactivity, unemployment, and also young people not in education, employment or training (NEET).

Labour market statistics for August 2009 show that 21% of the UK working age population are economically inactive, meaning they are not participating in the labour market.[56] The majority are long-term sick or disabled, some are fulltime family carers or students and a minority are discouraged workers. These groups are not only disadvantaged with regard to the level of income they can achieve, they are also at greater risk of going without the sense of purpose and competence a job provides (see psychological needs). Economic inactivity rates vary by country with the highest figures in Northern Ireland (30%), followed by Wales (24%), and England and Scotland (both 21%).

Figure 20: Relative need summary – Adequate disposable income

	Poverty	Financial strain
Extent of unmet need	13.5 million (23% UK after housing costs)	11% finding non mortgage loan repayments a 'heavy burden'
Trends	Relatively stable since 1998-99	Large increase in personal insolvencies and increasing levels of mortgage areas and repossession
Geographic variation	North East, North West, West Midlands, and Wales have high levels Inner London Urban districts	Poor data – little regional variation indicated Public housing areas
More at risk groups	Workless households Children Some BME groups Those aged 85+ Lone parents with children Disabled but not receiving benefit	Lone parent Single people Sub prime mortgagors Young (18-25) Unemployed

While the majority (around 80%) of the UK working age population are economically active, a rising proportion are unemployed. As of July 2009 the employment rate was 7.9%, meaning 2.47 million adults were without a job. The following figure illustrates how unemployment has spiked over the years in line with previous recessions of the 1980s and 1990s. The rate in recent years has been increasing since the low of 4.8% in 2004 but has increased rapidly from 2008 and continues in 2009, reflecting the current economic crisis (see Chapter 14 for more on this).

Some industries are more at risk than others with regard to the current recession and consequent redundancies. The highest rates of redundancy in the UK during quarter two 2009-10 were recorded for construction and manufacturing industries (27.9 and 20.1 per 1,000 employees respectively). These industries typically include higher levels of unskilled jobs, meaning that there may be a disproportionate social impact on those with lower incomes. Finance, intermediation and business services recorded the second highest rates (18.1 per 1000 employees), followed by distribution, hotels and restaurants (9.9), transport and communications (9.1), and lastly public administration, education and health (2.1). Although the rates are lowest in the public sector it is very probable that redundancies will increase here during the 2010-11 financial year, as the Government and opposition are both planning public spending cuts after heavy borrowing to address the recession.

Figure 21: Unemployment in the UK (%) overall and by gender 1971-2009

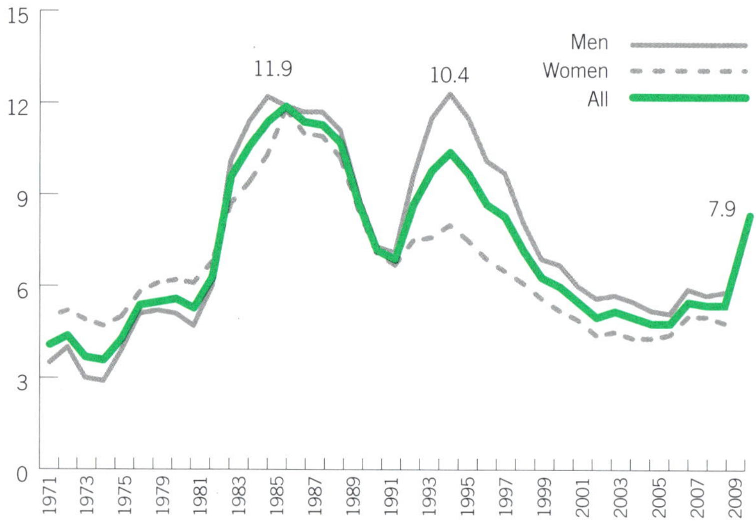

Source: ONS

National figures for April-June 2009 show that within the UK, England has the highest unemployment rate and count (7.9% or 2,086,000), followed by Wales at 7.6% (108,000 people), Scotland at 7.0% (188,000), and Northern Ireland at 6.7% (54,000).

Within England the regions with the highest rates were the West Midlands (10.6%) and the North East (9.8%), followed by London (8.9%) and Yorkshire and the Humber (8.8%); the lowest was the South East (5.9%). However, there will be great local variation, for example the unemployment rate was 14% in Lincoln (Lincolnshire, England) and 1.3% on the Shetland Isles.

Unemployment after education is particularly problematic as this means that young people do not engage with or gain experience from the labour market. The UK youth unemployment rate is generally higher than that of the overall working age population and varies considerably by UK country, with Wales the highest at 26% and Northern Ireland the lowest at 14%.

Figure 22: Number and percentage of 16-19 unemployed by UK country 2009

	Count	Percentage
Wales	22,900	26%
England	314,100	23%
Scotland	28,700	18%
Northern Ireland	4,800	14%
United Kingdom	370,600	22%

Source: Labour Force Survey

Many young unemployed people are also in neither education nor training (or NEET).* While this is of obvious detriment regarding life opportunities, research has also shown that if a young man is NEET for six months then by the age of 21 he is five times more likely to have a criminal record, three times more likely to have depression or mental illness, six times less likely to have any qualifications and four times more likely to be out of work.[57]

In the UK one in eight 16- to 19-year-olds is NEET, which equates to between 300,000-400,000 young people at any point in time. The rate is slightly higher than a decade ago rising from 11% in 1998 to 12% in 2008 (see Chapter 14 for trends that may affect levels of NEETs in the next ten years). The rate in Northern Ireland, Wales and Scotland was 12% in 2008. Among the English regions, Yorkshire and Humberside, West Midlands and the North East recorded 13%, with the South East and South West recording 10%. Internationally the UK does not compare well, ranking the fifth highest rate for male NEETs among 28 western countries.

The probability of becoming NEET is of course not equal for people from different backgrounds. Also, young females are more likely to be NEET than males (15% compared to 11% for 16-24). Department for Education and Skills (DfES) research in 2005 also suggested that those who were NEET at 16 tended to be from a less affluent background, have parents with low or no qualifications, or have had difficult experiences during Year 11, such as truancy and exclusion.[58] The research also suggested that parents played an extremely important role in determining whether their children become NEET. Parents who had positive attitudes about the value of education and were involved in their children's decisions about what to do after Year 11 were less likely to have children who were NEET.

* NEETs include those aged 16-24 who are not in employment; who are economically inactive but not a student; who are enrolled but not attending or not enrolled on a course; who are not recognised as doing an apprenticeship or having completed an apprenticeship; or who are not working or studying for qualification.

Research published in the Economic and Labour Market Review shows that 28% of NEETs aged 16 and 17 had no qualifications in 2008 (compared to 7% of the non-NEET group), and this rose to a quarter of those aged 18-24 (compared to 5% for non-NEETs).* The report describes how NEETs are four times more likely than average to live in a workless household and how a high proportion (41%) of NEETs aged 16-17 live with one parent only. The highest risk of becoming NEET was for those who had been in work previously with no training, whereas risk was lowest for those in education the previous year.

When asked whether they felt they would work again in the future, most NEETs aged 16-24 replied 'yes, definitely' (65%) although this was considerably lower than the non-NEET group (94%). Almost half of all those people who were NEET at age 16 were also NEET at 17, and over a third of those in this group at age 17 were still NEET aged 18.

In 2008, 49% of NEETs aged 16-24 were unemployed and 29% were economically inactive looking after family or home, whereas 8% were inactive owing to long-term illness or disability. The remaining 14% provided other miscellaneous reasons. There were stark sex distinctions, with 50% of young female NEETs looking after family compared to 3% of males.

Figure 23: Section summary – Employment

	Unemployment	NEETs
Extent of unmet need	2.47 million (7.9% UK)	300-400,000
Trends	Increasing (up from low of 4.8% in 2003)	Up 1% over the decade
Geographic variation	Higher in North East London North West	No substantial national or regional variation
More at risk groups	Construction, manufacture and finance employees	No or low qualifications Parents not involved in decision making Leaving employment without training Youth from workless household Youth from lone parent household

* This analysis uses academic age rather than actual age to help control for youths yet to complete their GCSE examinations.

3.7 The need for basic possessions and activities

While a good income is not a panacea for high levels of wellbeing, a certain level of wealth is required to meet some basic consumer needs, like being able to equip a home to a decent standard or go on holiday.

In terms of basic household appliances, the vast majority of UK household needs were met in 2007-08: 95% of households have a washing machine, 95% a freezer, 91% a landline phone, 91% a microwave oven and 98% a colour TV. These are needs where the market has been able to deliver affordable solutions for the vast majority and they also provide an example of yesterday's wants becoming today's needs. Even less basic possessions such as home computers are now common, although to a lesser extent, at 68%.

However, our analysis of BHPS revealed high levels of unmet need with regard to some other important basic possessions and activities. For example, almost one quarter of UK adults (aged 16 and over) are unable to afford a week's annual holiday away from home. A similar proportion (23%) could not afford to provide guests with a meal once a month. Thirteen per cent could not afford household insurance and another 13% could not afford to replace furniture. There were smaller proportions of unmet need at a more fundamental level, reflecting people's prioritisation of the essential: 6% could not afford to eat meat on alternate days; 5% could not afford new clothes; and 3% could not afford two pairs of shoes for each adult.

JODIE'S STORY

Jodie is 18 years old and five months pregnant. She lives with her 17-year-old boyfriend Lewis in London.

Jodie was severely bullied in her early teens and described school as a miserable experience. She rarely attended and eventually left school at 16 with no qualifications and few friends. At the same time she left home as a result of a violent relationship with her mother. Jodie spent months living in various forms of emergency accommodation and hostels. When she became pregnant she was offered the flat she now lives in.

The flat is sparsely furnished with a couple of old sofas they were given and a mattress on the floor. Jodie and Lewis both receive income support of £46.95 a month, which covers their rent and food:

"We're living off tins and takeaways at the moment. When we can get a cooker and a fridge, we'll be able to eat properly. We can live off what we have now, but it will be difficult when we have the baby."

The figures for almost all of these indicators have shrunk considerably from when the questions were first asked, some in 1996-07, some in 2003-04. The table below indicates that the proportion of respondents unable to afford basic possessions or activities had dropped by between 27% and 57% for all but two measures (redecorating and housing insurance). It is probable that this is due in part to increased access to different types of credit.

Figure 24: Percentage of UK sample who cannot afford basic possessions and activities

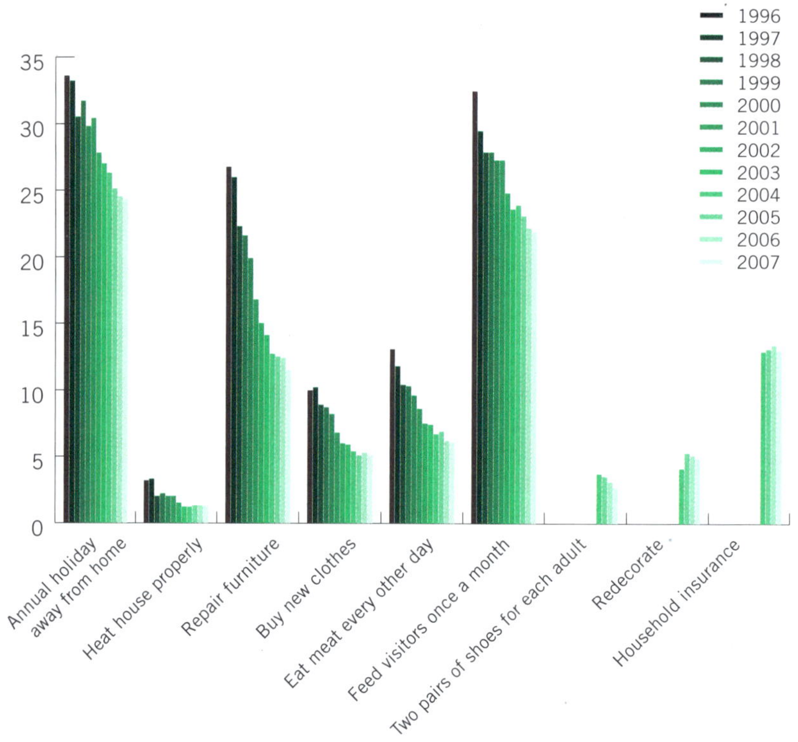

Source: BHPS analysis

There is evidence that the level of unmet need in this regard varies significantly across the UK countries, possibly reflecting regional priorities and preferences. For example, in 2007-08 the proportion of those who felt they could not afford an annual week's holiday away from home was highest in Northern Ireland at 33%, followed by 28% for Wales, 22% for England, and 21% for Scotland. Surprisingly, the proportion of those who could not afford household insurance in Northern Ireland (20%) was almost double the figure for England (11%, 13% for UK). There was further notable variation in the proportion that felt they could not afford to feed visitors once a month. This was 29% in Wales compared to 19% in Scotland (see figure below for other variations).

Figure 25: Percentages of households that cannot afford basic possessions and activities by UK country 2007-08

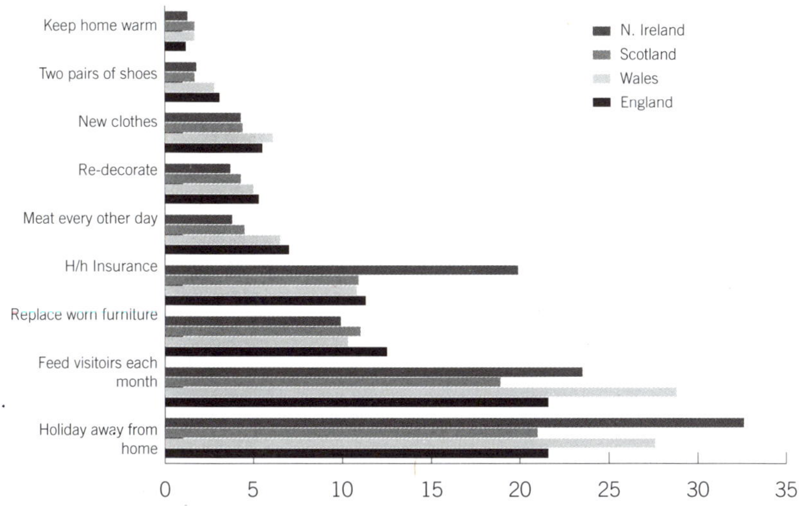

Source: BHPS analysis

To examine the level of unmet need among different types of neighbourhood, we analysed the BHPS data using census Output Area Classifications (OAC).* OAC uses local social and demographic statistics to group small geographic areas of the UK into one of 21 categories. For example, an area with a high level of properties being rented from the local authority or housing association would fall into the 'Public Housing' category. Figure 26 shows how the 21 different types of area have different proportions that cannot afford the basic possessions and activities listed above. Rather than present all the activities and possessions, we have provided a summary score where 1 indicates that a normal proportion could not afford basic possessions and activities and anything above or below one indicated high or low proportions. This analysis revealed that those living in public housing areas were clearly the most disadvantaged, with a deficit twice that of the overall sample and six times that of the least disadvantaged group, 'Prospering Younger Families' (see figure 26 for other variations).

* OAC data distils key results from the 2001 Census for the whole of the UK at a fine grain to indicate the character of local areas. It was created in collaboration between the Office for National Statistics (ONS) and the University of Leeds. It should be emphasised that the Output Area Classifications refer to general characteristics of areas. For more information about OAC see: http://www.statistics.gov.uk/about/methodology_by_theme/area_classification/oa/default.asp

> “I’m worrying now because I’ve got to get an iPod Touch for my daughter and she’ll go camping and then it’s all pushing together in my brain how I’m going to sort out this £165 thing for her sixteenth birthday and going camping... This has been pressurising me for about eight weeks and thinking about all these different ways ... this is all going round and round and round, and then I sat there the other night and I just thought oh shit to it, I’m just going to cancel my poll tax for a month. I just thought ... I’ve paid it every single month for the last God knows how long and I just thought oh they can just piss off this month, and then I’ll use that money. I’ll phone up and say I went online to my bank and I cancelled the wrong direct debit. I will pay it, but I need that breathing space.
>
> — Focus group participant, Cardiff

Figure 26: Basic possessions and activities inaffordability index by output area classification 2007-08

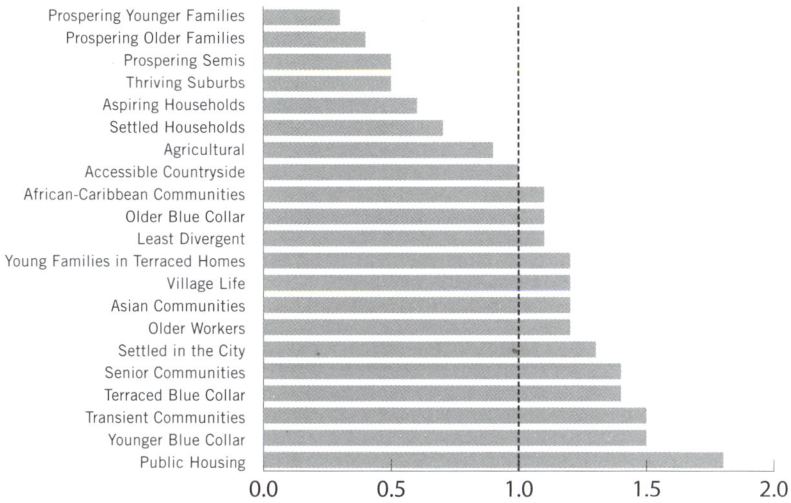

Source: BHPS analysis

Some stark disparities for the individual needs were hidden by the aggregated score. For example, only 9% of those living in 'Prospering Younger Families' areas could not afford a week's holiday away from home, yet the proportion was over 30% for 'Terraced Blue Collar', 'Younger Blue Collar' and 'Older Blue Collar' areas and 40% for those living in 'Public Housing' areas. At a more fundamental level, 12% of those living in 'Public Housing' areas could not afford to buy new clothes. This was six times higher than the figure for those residing in 'Thriving Suburbs' or 'Prospering Older Families' (2%).

We made use of the same composite score to look at variations for different types of household (e.g. 'couple with children' or 'single elderly' household). It showed that 'lone parents with dependent children' were more likely to be disadvantaged with around twice the proportion of these households unable to afford basic possession and activities compared to the average. This equated to a score four times that of the least disadvantaged group: 'couples with no children'. 'Single elderly' households were the second most disadvantaged at 1.8 times the average followed by households with '2 or more unrelated adults' at 1.7 times the average.

Figure 27: Basic possessions and activities composite score index by type of household 2007-08

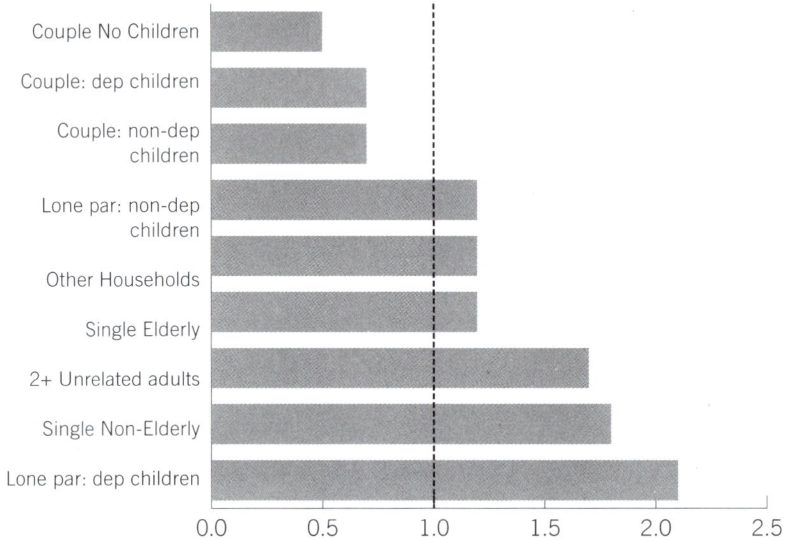

Source: BHPS analysis

Here again the aggregate analysis disguised some important contrasts concerning specific possessions and activities. For example, 'lone parents with dependent children' were least likely to be able to afford a holiday (44%), followed by 'single elderly' (38%) and 'single non elderly' (32%). The least disadvantaged households were 'couples without children' and 'couples with dependent children' (15% and 16% respectively). Only 3% of 'couples with no children' were going without new clothes whereas the equivalent proportion for 'lone parents with dependent children' was 9%.

When examining household income the level of unmet need corresponded intuitively. For each basic possession and activity there were much greater proportions of people who could not afford things in the lower income brackets (quintiles). In fact, those on the lowest income (in the fifth quintile) were twice as likely to be unable to afford the basic possessions and activities than the sample overall; those on the second lowest income (fourth quintile) were one and a half times as likely.

Figure 28: Percentages of households who cannot afford basic possessions and activities by (unadjusted) household income 2007-08

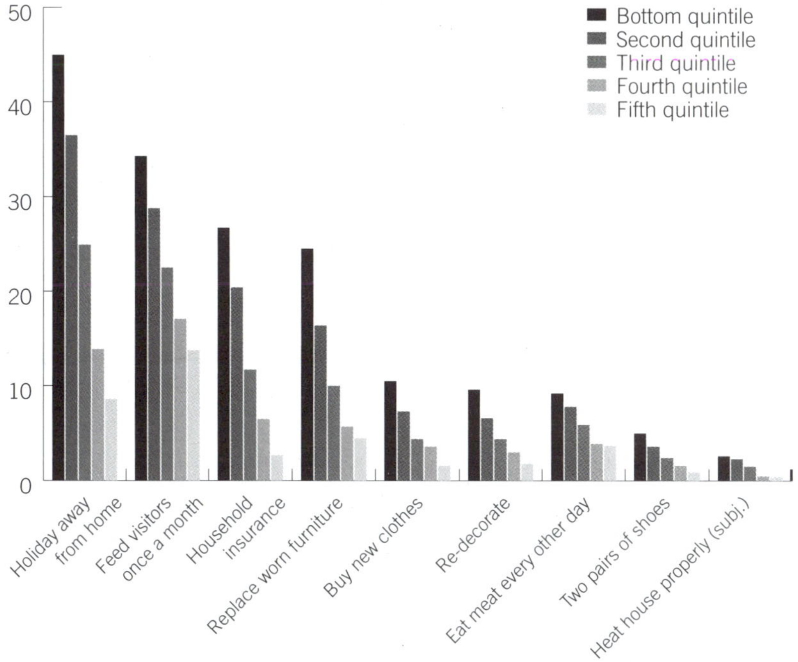

Source: BHPS analysis

While these inequalities are stark, it is worth considering them in context. Even among the poorest it was only the minority that were going without: new clothes (10% of the bottom quintile), eating meat on alternate days (also 10%) and being able to afford two pairs of shoes per adult (5%). Essentially, the majority of the UK's needs for these basic possessions and activities would appear to be met. There were, however, significant proportions unable to afford the less essential but still often taken for granted matters: being able to holiday, feed visitors, insure house contents, and replace furniture.

Figure 29: Relative need – Basic possessions and activities

Inability to afford basic possessions and activities	
Extent of unmet need	24% could not holiday away from home 23% could not feed visitors 13% insure household or replace furniture 6% eat meat on alternate days 5% afford new clothes 2.7% afford two pairs of shoes for each adult
Trends	Substantial reductions in the number of people who could not afford the listed basic possessions and activities between 1996-97 and 2007-07
Geographic variation	'Public housing' and 'blue collar' areas Northern Ireland high for inability to afford holidays and household insurance Wales high for inability to afford holidays and feed visitors
More at risk groups	Lower income Lone parents with dependent children Single non elderly

3.8 The need for basic skills and qualifications

Our basic needs are ones for sustenance and care. But we also need capabilities – skills, knowledge, wisdom – to help us navigate through life. These capabilities are the means through which we meet our other needs – finding a job, earning a living and coping with challenges. In Amartya Sen's words, capability is "a kind of freedom; the substantive freedom to achieve alternative functioning combinations (or, less formally put, the freedom to achieve various lifestyles.)"[59]

The lower a person's qualifications, the more likely they are to be unemployed and the more likely they are to be in low-paid work. Having no qualifications is also associated with feelings of low competence. For example, 19% of those without qualifications felt that they could not play a useful role in matters compared to 11% for those with a degree (see Chapter 4 on competence).

There are different qualification systems in the UK which mean figures for each country are not directly comparable, but broadly speaking around 9% of school leavers have low qualifications (fewer than five GCSEs at A*-C or equivalent) and close to 2% have no qualifications.

In England in 2007-08, 2% recorded no GCSEs and 7% recorded low GCSEs. In Scotland, 9% recorded a low level of SCQF passes and 3% recorded no qualifications. In Wales 13% had low qualifications (did not pass the 'level one threshold') but there were no figures available for no qualifications. And in Northern Ireland 10% recorded low qualifications and 4% recorded no GCSE passes. For each country there were slight reductions in low achievers compared to levels a decade earlier.

Socio-economic status has a bearing on low qualifications. Free school meals, a proxy measure of social-economic status, are strongly associated with low achievement and other indicators include: levels of unemployment; single parent households; poor performance at primary school; and parents with low educational qualifications. Further, economically disadvantaged students are more prone to attend poorly-performing secondary schools, and are less likely to benefit from teaching pitched at the right level, due to schools working to the 5A*-C GCSE target (or equivalent).

Some groups are more at risk of having low qualifications: most notably, low achieving boys outnumber girls three to two. There are also differences by ethnicity, as shown in the figure below. For example, Indian pupils are most successful in avoiding low levels of achievement, while African-Caribbean pupils, along with white working class boys, have much lower levels of educational attainment.

Figure 30: Percentage of 16-year-olds without five or more GCSEs (or vocational equivalent) for different ethnic groups, 2009

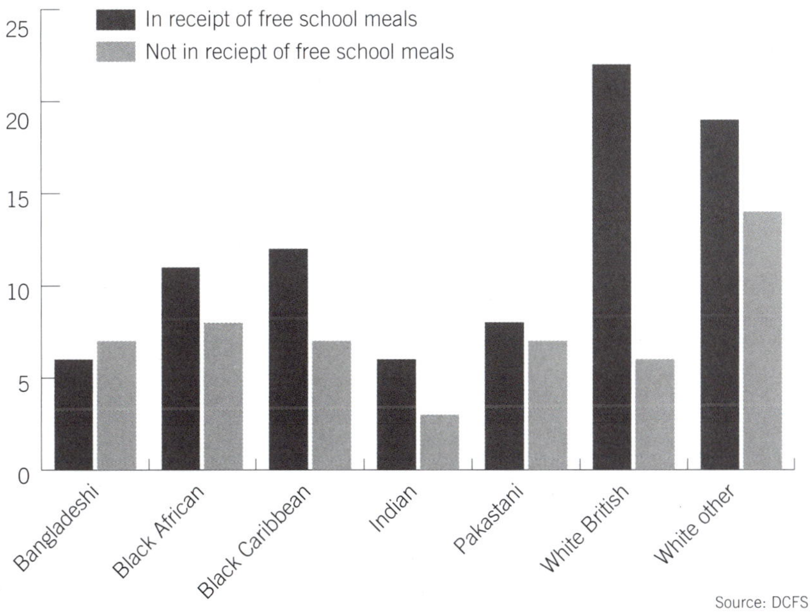

Source: DCFS

In addition to poorly qualified teenagers there were 5,014,900 working age people (13%) in the UK without qualifications in 2008. Here, too, the trend is down on 1997 although the rate of decline is greater overall (from 18% to 12% for those aged 20 to 65) than in the younger age group (from 9% to 8% for those aged 20 to 29). The figures for UK countries vary considerably with the lowest proportion in England (13% or 4 million) followed by 14% in Scotland (432,000), 16% in Wales (270,000), and, highest, 22% in Northern Ireland (237,000).

As well as lacking qualifications, significant numbers of adults leave school with poor basic literacy and numeracy skills. In addition to the obvious implications concerning employment, poor basic skills are indicative of other social disadvantages, for example not having a bank account or mortgage. Poor literacy generally limits the amount of information a person can benefit from and reduces learning and wellbeing provided through different types of literature. There are also psychological effects on self-esteem and feelings of competence. Further, there is the risk of intergenerational transmission, meaning that children of parents with low basic skills are likely to be at a disadvantage when it comes to their own learning.

The English Skills for Life Survey found that around 24 million adults had poor numeracy skills and 18 million adults had poor literacy skills in 2003.[60] In the English regions the lowest figures were recorded for the South East (40% low numeracy and 11% poor literacy) and highest for the North East (55% and 21% respectively). In terms of other UK countries, Wales recorded the highest proportions with 53% recording poor numeracy and 25% poor literacy. The data for other UK countries is less comparable but figures for Scotland in 2001 suggested that 23% may have 'low skills'.

Unsurprisingly, poor literacy and numeracy are closely related to educational history. In the English survey of adult basic skills, fewer than one in five (17%) of those with no qualifications at all reached 'Level 2' or above for literacy (1 being low), and the results were worse for numeracy. Housing tenure is also associated with performance, with only 25% of those renting from local authorities achieving 'Level 2' numeracy or above. In comparison, homeowners and private renters were approximately three times as likely to have achieved this grade. Lower levels of literacy and numeracy were also associated with socio-economic deprivation.

Despite these substantial numbers with poor literacy and numeracy, only a very small proportion of the sample (2%) believed that their weak skills had hindered their job prospects or led to mistakes at work, suggesting that they did not recognise a need to improve their basic skills.

Figure 31: Relative need summary – Qualifications and basic skills

	Low qualifications	Poor adult basic skills
Extent of unmet need	**Youth**: 2% no qualifications 10% low qualifications **Adults**: 13% no qualifications	18 million poor literacy 24 million poor numeracy (Brit.)
Trends	**Youth**: Low qual. down slightly on 1997-98 **Adults**: down by one-third overall but little change for 20-29 ages	Latest data 2003
Geographic variation	**Youth**: No substantial national variation **Adults**: N. Ireland high	North East and Wales high Renting public housing
Groups more at risk	**Youth**: Boys Free school meals/low inc. Lone parent Unemployed parent African-Caribbean Low primary performance	Poor educational history Socio-economic deprivation Routine/semi routine occ.

Recent research has provided many more insights into patterns of life chances, and some of the dynamic factors that explain how capabilities affect success and the ability to meet needs. James Heckman, a Nobel Prize-winning economist, has written that "life cycle skill formation is a dynamic process where early inputs greatly affect the productivity of later inputs in the life cycle of children. Skill begets skill; motivation begets motivation. Early failure begets later failure."[61] Our needs for capabilities are met, or not met, early and well before the beginning of formal education. It has been estimated that out of one million UK children with emotional and behavioural problems, 150,000 have been affected by perinatal stress in pregnancy. Then, in the early years, children's brains are strongly influenced by how much they are used, by the inputs they receive in terms of communication or engagement. A study by Hart and Risley of 42 families in the US found that by the age of four children from professional families had had 50 million words spoken to them, children from working-class families 30 million and children from families on benefits just 12 million.[62] More strikingly, the children from professional families had had 700,000 words of encouragement and 80,000 negative words whereas the child in the family on benefits had had 60,000 words of encouragement but twice as many words of discouragement. Studies of this kind confirm that the family remains much the most important educational institution.

Once children have started to spend significant amounts of time at school, family influences become somewhat less decisive. School performance remains highly unequal despite many efforts to bridge the gap. These imbalances – which correlate with geography as well as class – reflect the interaction of genes, environments, parents and schools. In terms of capabilities, numeracy, literacy and science have received much of the policy focus in recent years, and by some measures have improved significantly. But more schooling is unlikely to be an adequate answer. In one recent set of studies, for example, students' perceptions of their own effectiveness and confidence as learners drop significantly from key stage 2 to key stage 3. Thirteen year olds see themselves as less resilient, less resourceful, less curious and less good at team work than nine year olds.[63]

James Flynn, who has studied changing IQ rates globally, has shown that on average IQ rates are rising between 0.3 and 0.7 each year, in part as a result of the cognitive effects of living in more complex environments, in which concepts play a larger role.[64] His work points to the importance of environments in either enhancing intelligence or stunting it. Those environments include the immediate ones of the home and family, but also the influences of peers and the media as well as educational institutions. Flynn's insights are reinforced by analysis of upward mobility in the UK. Recent analysis of social mobility has shown that it declined between the 1958 and 1970 using cohorts of the National Child Development longitudinal study.[65] In the earlier cohort, there was little relationship between social and emotional competencies and parental income. In the second cohort, "parental income had much more impact on non-cognitive scores ... these scores ... impacted on earnings ... primarily through enabling children to achieve more in education." The authors concluded that "the UK has moved decisively away from [the goal of social mobility] through a strengthening of the social gradient associated with educational attainment. This in part stems from the growing importance of non-cognitive factors and the increased relationship between these variables and parental background." They continue to argue that policy "should focus on the personal efficacy (the sense that your own actions can make a difference), concentration and anxiety of children from low income backgrounds". Leon Feinstein of the Institute of Education has similarly shown children's dedication and capacity for concentration at the age of 10 has a much bigger impact on earnings 20 years later than their ability in maths. A sense of personal agency at the age of 10 is also more important to life chances than reading skills. Other research has emphasised the importance of self-discipline and persistence (as opposed to impulsiveness) which turn out to be the key causal variables that lie behind differential academic results and different patterns of success in later life. So we need formal knowledge and skills, but also other kinds of aptitude and mentality. As we show later in the case studies, these skills, dispositions and character traits are critical to understanding patterns of unmet need and differential abilities to seek out help.

4 Psychological needs

Throughout the twentieth century social and economic policy focused, by and large successfully, on meeting the very real material needs of the population, alongside much smaller scale provision for people suffering the most severe forms of mental illness.

Psychological needs are harder to identify and satisfy and are more likely to be unrecognised and to remain unmet. Psychological needs are ones which must be met for people to flourish in ways that go beyond physical health and embrace the social, emotional, mental and psychological aspects of life. Meeting these needs underpins both subjective wellbeing (self-esteem, relatedness etc.) and objective measures of wellbeing (educational attainment, social engagement, fulfilling work).

In this chapter we look at national quantitative indicators of unmet psychological needs. While there was very little information within national survey datasets and published statistics that suited our purposes perfectly, there was some proxy data to outline the extent of psychological need and identify which groups were likely to be more vulnerable. We recognise that some of the analytical tools may be weak in this section but this underlines that there is a problem of inadequate data and a need for further research. First, we look at the issue of mental illness, focusing on conditions where typically disturbances in thinking and perception are severe enough to distort perception of reality (i.e. forms of psychosis). We then move on to analyse the more common problem of poor psychological wellbeing, examining in detail five key psychological needs.

4.1 Mental illness

There is now a consensus that the prevalence of mental health problems is high in the UK. Surveys indicate that between one in six and one in four people in the UK experience mental health problems at some point in their lives and on many measures we compare badly with other countries.[66] The UK, for example, has one of the highest rates of self-harm in Europe.[67]

The treatment and diagnosis of mental ill health appears to have increased hugely since the early 1990s. For example, the number of prescription items for anti-depressant drugs has increased from 9 million in 1991 to 33.8 million in 2007.[68] Similarly, large increases have been recorded for Scotland (up from around 1 million in 1992-93 to over 3 million in 2002-03) and Northern Ireland (up from 0.3 million in 1991 to 1.5 million in 2007).[69] It should be noted, however, that this data relates to prescriptions and not to the number of people taking antidepressants and that the statistics do not distinguish the duration or strength of drug taken. As such, the upward trend will not equate to trends in rates of usage. In addition, an increased variety of drugs, recognition and treatment are also likely to have contributed to the rise.

Figure 32: Number (in millions) of antidepressant prescriptions in England, 1991-2007

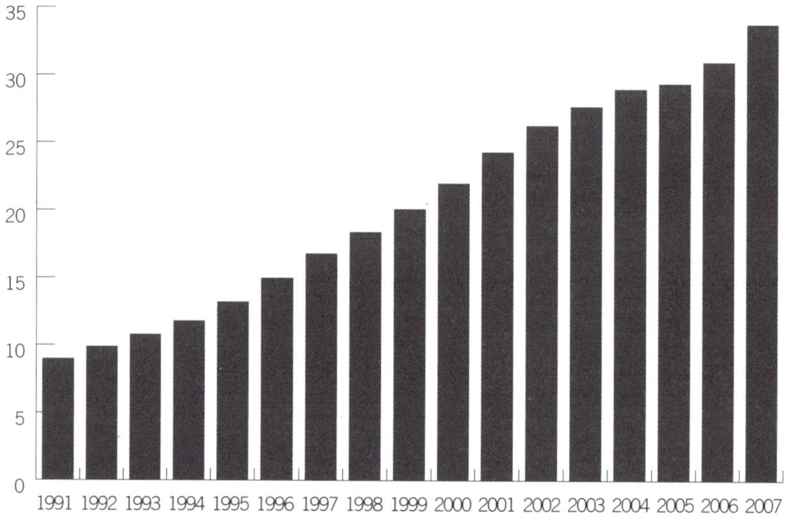

Source: ONS

Furthermore, there is a consensus that services designed directly or indirectly to meet mental health needs do not meet demand. For example, among people with depression, fewer than half have received any treatment, only 8% have seen a psychiatrist and only 3% a psychologist.[70]

There are many categories of mental illness comprising a wide range of behaviours, from more severe mood disorders (for example, persistent or fluctuating feelings of intense sadness or happiness) to acute personality disorders (which may involve extreme and inflexible personality traits) or psychotic disorders (which may involve hallucinations or hearing voices). The table facing shows a range of mental illnesses and their prevalence rates.

Figure 33: People estimated to be affected at some point in their lives by various mental illnesses

Mental illness	Estimates UK
Schizophrenia	0.3%
Bipolar (manic depressive)	1%
Obsessive-compulsive disorder	1-3%
Panic disorder	1%
Severe depression	15%

Source: NHS clinical knowledge summaries 2009

BECKY'S STORY

Becky is 35. She was diagnosed with bipolar disorder when she was 24 and since then has been in and out of hospital. Becky lives in a flat she has rented from the council for 13 years, but is currently trying to move because, for the past two years, she has been harassed by her neighbours.

Becky has been unemployed for the last three years. Previous, she had worked for 30 hours a week as a community mental health worker, but she found the job very stressful and got signed off sick. Becky eventually resigned as she felt the stress of the job had contributed to her getting ill again and she didn't feel able to return. Becky has left jobs in the past for similar reasons and is sad not to be in work. Reflecting on her experiences of moving in and out of work, Becky is upset she hasn't had more support in maintaining employment.

She wants work so she can feel that her money is her own, rather than being on Income Support, which she feels is someone else's money. At the moment, her financial situation is tight, especially during the winter when she has to heat the house while she is at home during the day.

Department of Health figures for England show there were 105,719 adult and elderly patients admitted to mental health care facilities in 2007-08, meaning they spent at least one day as a psychiatric inpatient. The equivalent figure for Scotland was 24,294, Wales 12,618 (2006-07), and Northern Ireland 6,896.

Women accounted for 56% of all cases in England in 2007-08. In terms of age, 4% of all cases were aged 17 or under, 23% were 18 to 35, 41% were 36 to

64 and 23% were 65 or over. The proportion of inpatients was higher for some Black and Minority Ethnic (BME) groups. For example, 19% of psychiatric service users in the Black or Black British group spent time as an inpatient compared to 10% of white service users. The proportions were also higher for mixed race people (14%) and those describing themselves as Asian or Asian British (12%). There were also ethnic disparities with regard to treatment under detention. Overall, 31% of all NHS psychiatric inpatients spent some time formally detained but this proportion was higher for all BME groups: the rate for those classified 'Black or Black British' was over 52%.[71] There is little consensus on whether the overrepresentation of BME groups is due to a greater prevalence of severe mental illness or whether people from some BME groups are less likely to seek early help from the NHS services.

Geographically, the rates of people using mental health services by English Primary Care Trust (PCT) showed large variations, ranging from 844 per 100,000 population (in Cornwall and the Isles of Scilly) to 4,294 (in Hammersmith and Fulham) during 2007-08; the English PCT average rate was 2,224. There was no obvious pattern across the country, although 15 London boroughs fell into the top 30 PCTS with the highest rates.

Identifying accurate trends for mental health issues using administrative statistics is very difficult given that they reflect treatment, not prevalence, and that awareness and recognition for various disorders can increase while the actual extent of the problem may be something quite different. Experimental statistics from the Department of Health indicate that in total 1.2 million individual adults had contact with special mental health facilities in England during 2007-08 (3% of those aged over 15), an increase of 4% on 2005-06. When using 2003-04 as a baseline, the overall increase was 10%; however, the extent to which improved recording contributed to this increase is unclear.

Figure 34: Number of people using adult/elderly NHS* secondary mental health services in England 2003-04 to 2007-08

	Admitted as patient	Only non-admitted	No care	Total
2003-04	113,772	814,252	150,992	1,079,016
2004-05	114,435	916,533	101,465	1,132,433
2005-06	111,088	930,374	108,010	1,149,472
2006-07	106,561	936,629	108,070	1,151,260
2007-08	105,719	982,704	102,119	1,190,542

Source: Department of Health

* Secondary services typically treat people with more severe mental health problems.

The Department of Health report accompanying these statistics shows that women accounted for the majority (70%) of the recent increase.[72] While such administrative data are improving with regard to those accessing services, general population surveys provide a more accurate means of measuring overall mental health. The Department of Health carries out such a survey; it estimated that the overall prevalence of psychotic disorder in 2007 was 0.4% (0.3% of men, 0.5% of women) and here the trends indicate that there has been no change since 2000.

In terms of groups more at risk, that survey shows that for both men and women the highest prevalence was observed in those aged 35 to 44 years (0.7% and 1.1% respectively). Prevalence was significantly higher among Black men (3.1%) than among men from other ethnic groups: the equivalent figure was 0.2% for white men and no cases (statistically) were observed among men in the South Asian or 'other' ethnic group. Interestingly, there was no significant variation by ethnicity among women.

The proportion of respondents with probable psychosis receiving some form of treatment (medication and/or counselling) was 85% in 2000 and 81% in 2007. In contrast with this high proportion of people with 'probable psychosis' who were receiving treatment, just two-thirds (65%) of people with 'psychotic disorder' in the past year were in receipt of treatment.[73]

While those at the more severe end of the mental health spectrum will have unmet psychological needs, those experiencing lesser mental health problems or poor psychological wellbeing will also have unmet needs, although they are likely to be less acute. We examine this much more common issue in the next section.

4.2 Poor psychological wellbeing

Mental illness is at the extreme end of the psychological health spectrum. While it severely affects the ability of people to meet their psychological needs, the number of people suffering from mental illness is relatively small. Poor psychological wellbeing, although less severe, affects many more people in the UK. The term 'psychological wellbeing' is a rubric that essentially relates to a notion of an ideal or happy state of mind as defined by cultural norms.[74] Most often it is measured subjectively by asking people to complete questionnaires relating to how they feel about themselves and their life.

People with poor psychological wellbeing are clearly more at risk of having unmet psychological needs. We have used the General Health Questionnaire (GHQ) to gauge poor psychological wellbeing among the BHPS UK sample and identify which groups are more at risk.* Initially, we concentrate on the overall measure of poor psychological wellbeing and then later we focus on some specific aspects relating to five key psychological needs.

The 12 GHQ questions are listed below. Participants are required to answer each one using a scale of 1 to 4 to indicate the extent to which they have been feeling a particular way. An overall score is calculated to indicate whether that person has poor psychological wellbeing. By definition this score is subjective and thus people in very different scenarios may record similar results and vice versa.

Figure 35: General Health Questionnaire questions

Have you recently...
... been able to concentrate on whatever you're doing?
... lost much sleep over worry?
... felt that you were playing a useful part in things?
... felt capable of making decisions about things?
... felt constantly under strain ?
... felt you couldn't overcome your difficulties ?
... been able to enjoy your normal day-to-day activities ?
... been able to face up to problems ?
... been feeling unhappy or depressed ?
... been losing confidence in yourself ?
... been thinking of yourself as a worthless person ?
... been feeling reasonably happy, all things considered ?

Source: BHPS

The overall 2007-08 GHQ results for the UK indicated that the majority (80%) were not at risk (scoring between 0 and 3 on a scale of 12). The proportion with a high GHQ12 score (between 4 and 12 – the conventional threshold) was 20%. This suggests that approximately 10 million people in the UK have poor psychological wellbeing and are at risk of unmet psychological need. The proportion varied slightly but significantly by UK country: Wales recorded 23%; England 20%; Northern Ireland 19%; and Scotland 18%.

* Developed by Sir David Goldberg "the GHQ is specifically concerned with the hinterland between psychological sickness and psychological health." The results of the questionnaire produce a score for each respondent; this data can then be used in quantitative analysis, comparing two groups within a sample, or the same sample on two different occasions, for example. Further, the scores could also be correlated with other clinical and social variables.

However, our analysis using Output Area Classifications (OAC) data showed greater variation by different types of neighbourhood across the UK. Some areas recorded as low as 15% with poor psychological health and some areas had a high of 28%. Those areas recording the greatest level of poor psychological wellbeing were 'Asian Communities', 'Transient Communities', and 'Public Housing'. Areas with the lowest proportions included 'Prospering Older Communities', 'Prospering Younger Communities' and 'Terraced Housing'.

At the individual level there was considerable gender variation, with 16% of males with poor psychological wellbeing compared to 23% for women (1.4 times as high). In terms of personality traits, poor psychological wellbeing increased, as expected, with propensity to worry easily: only 12% of those classified as less easily worried recorded poor psychological health compared to 37% for the most easily worried group. Similarly, those who were more likely to be relaxed and better at handling stress were less likely to have poor psychological wellbeing: 12% compared to 40% for those who were least relaxed and poorer at handling stress.

With regard to different household types, adults without children reported the lowest proportion with poor psychological wellbeing (17%) and lone parents with dependent children reported the highest (28%). Those who were married recorded the lowest proportion of poor psychological wellbeing (18%) and those who had never married recorded an average level (20%). Respondents who were separated from their partners in some way recorded higher levels of poor psychological wellbeing: those who were separated, widowed or divorced recorded the highest levels respectively at 29%, 26%, and 25%. This was congruent with findings from a separate study of the BHPS that found that relationships were protective of mental health and mental health was worse immediately after relationships breakdown. The research also found that the negative outcomes of separation were longer lasting for women.[75]

The following figure shows the varying extent to which poor psychological health is found within different groups among the BHPS data.

Figure 36: Percentage of UK BHPS sample with poor psychological wellbeing (high GHQ12) by selected variables, 2006-07

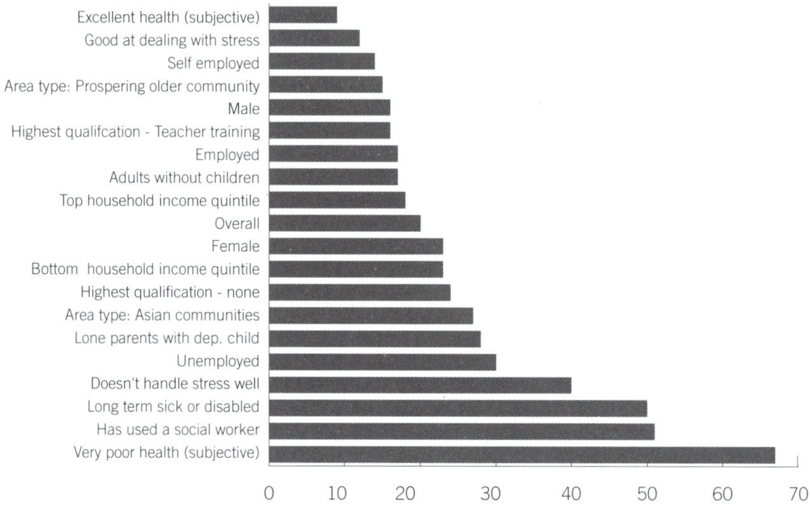

Source: BHPS analysis

There is a high level of association between psychological health and employment. Unemployed people recorded high levels, at 30%, whereas the lowest proportions were recorded for the self-employed (14%) and the employed (17%). Half (50%) of those economically inactive due to long term sickness or disability recorded high GHQ12 scores (2.5 times the average). High GHQ12, as expected, increased with poor physical health: the majority (67%) of those who felt that they were in very poor health recorded high GHQ12 (over three times the average); the equivalent proportion for those with poor health was still just over half (52%).

In terms of trends, analysis of the English health survey that uses a variation of GHQ suggested that the proportion of the working age population with poor psychological wellbeing decreased from 17% in 1997 to 13% in 2006, with women seeing a steeper rate of decrease. This may be a consequence of a more buoyant labour market and perhaps of the modest upturn in some indicators of social capital over the same period.

Figure 37: Percentage of English population at with high GHQ12 by gender 1994-2006

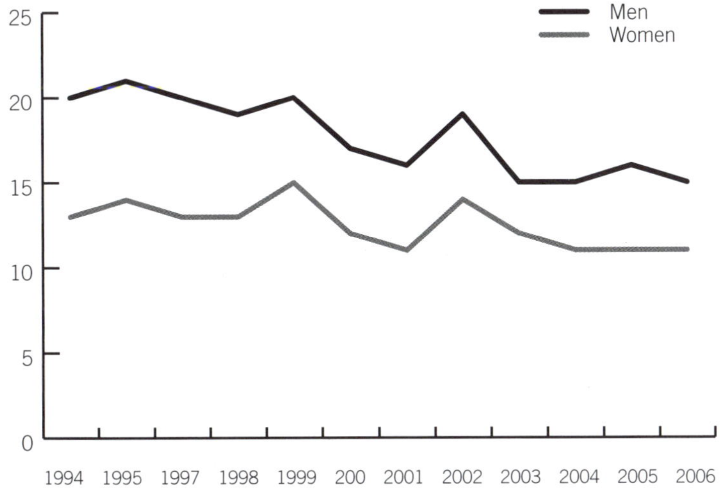

Source: English Health Survey

Figure 38: Psychological need summary

	Mental illness	Poor psychological wellbeing
Extent of unmet need	250,000 annual care facility admissions UK 0.4% with psychosis (Eng.)	20% of UK aged 16+
Trends	Contact with special mental health facilities up 3.6% on 2005-06 Psychosis prevalence stable between 2000 and 2007 (Eng.)	Overall downward trend between 1994 and 2006 (Eng.)
Geographic variation	12 London boroughs in 30 PCTs with highest rates	'Asian Community', 'Transient Community' and 'Public Housing' areas all higher
Groups more at risk	Women Black or Black British Mixed heritage Asian or Asian British	Very poor health Used social worker LT sick/disabled Unemployed Separated/divorced/widowed Lone parents Low income

4.3 The five key psychological needs

The General Health Questionnaire provides us with an indicator of overall psychological wellbeing. Within this, there are a number of specific psychological needs. The ten most commonly unmet psychological needs found in our forerunning research[76] are:

- Self-esteem
- Competence
- Autonomy
- Relatedness
- Security
- Physical thriving
- Pleasure and stimulation
- Meaning or self-actualisation
- Popularity and influence
- Comfort and reward

Our work echoes findings from the wider literature[77] that the first five (self-esteem, competence, autonomy, relatedness and security) tend to be the more important psychological needs in people's lives; they have also been developed as the cornerstone of several influential theories of need. We look at these in more detail below.

1 Self-esteem

Self-esteem is an important protective factor against unmet psychological need. Self-esteem refers to a person's appraisal of their own worth.[78] Literature suggests that it is important to have the right amount of self-esteem and the right kind. Having too much can lead to unrealistic perceptions of one's own situation and capacity. Research has shown that overly high self-esteem can lead young people to hold prejudiced attitudes towards ethnic minorities, reject social influence and engage in physically risky pursuits.[79]

To analyse self-esteem nationally we examined the 2007-08 BHPS UK sample who were asked if they had recently been thinking of themselves as a worthless person. The majority (65%) replied 'not at all' and a further 27% replied 'no more than usual'. However, 6% said they felt worthless 'rather more than usual' and 2% replied 'much more than usual'. These negative responses equated to 8% of the UK sample feeling more worthless than usual, indicating low self-esteem. In population terms this equates to approximately four million people aged 16 or over in the UK.

There were no substantial variations in the proportions of respondents feeling worthless for each of the UK countries, although there was some geographic variation. People living in public housing areas recorded the greatest proportion of people feeling worthless, at 12%, while prospering older families recorded the lowest at 4%. Women were more likely to feel worthless than men (10% compared to 6%) but there was no great variation by age alone. Marital status suggested that those who were married were least likely to feel worthless (6%) and those who were separated or divorced most likely, both at 12%. Lone parents with dependent children were high at 14%.

Economic activity had significant bearing, particularly on long-term sick and disabled people, 32% of whom felt worthless (4 times higher than average). Those unemployed also felt more worthless (14%), as did those undertaking full time family care (12%). Feelings of worthlessness were lowest for the self-employed (4%) and employed (6%). Health status demonstrated the greatest variation, ranging from 3% for people with excellent health to 41% for those with very poor health. Related to self-esteem is the need to feel competent, which we examine in the next section.

MACIE'S STORY

Macie is 16 years old and has a five-week-old daughter. They live with Macie's mother and three younger siblings in London.

Macie was put on the at-risk register at the age of 13 after she had unprotected sex with an older man. She left school at 15 after becoming pregnant with her current boyfriend. Macie's experience of education was an unhappy one. She was badly bullied since age 12, which resulted in poor attendance. She left school with no qualifications, few friends and very low self-esteem, "I couldn't do most of the stuff at school because I'm stupid. I didn't understand it and so didn't bother." Macie has little confidence and no aspirations to return to education or find employment.

2 Competence

The need for competence is met when a person feels capable of controlling their environment and able to foresee and predict the likely outcomes from specific events. Commonly this need is satisfied through education, knowledge and skills, experiences of success, cognitive skills and physical health.

The 2007-08 wave of the BHPS were asked whether or not they have recently felt they have 'been able to play a useful part in things?'* A minority (13%) replied 'more than usual', the majority (75%) replied 'same as usual'. However, 10% replied 'less so' and 2% replied 'much less so'. Combined, this indicated that 13% of the sample felt they lacked competence. There was no difference between UK countries.

The feeling of lack of competence increases steadily with age from 8% for teenagers to 19% for pensioners. As the figure below shows this gradual rise between the ages of 15 and 75 is followed by a steep increase such that by the age of 85, one-third (35%) of the sample lacked feelings of competence.

Figure 39: Percentage of respondents feeling a lack of competence by age 2007-08

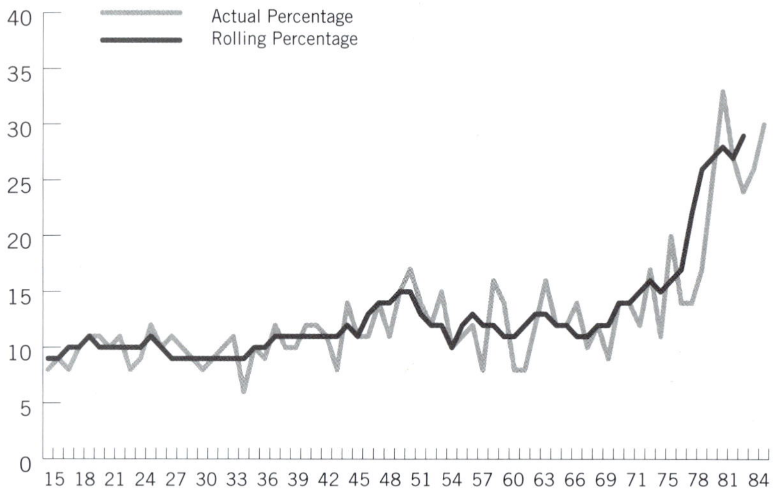

Source BHPS analysis

The proportion of those feeling they lacked competence was slightly lower for males compared to women (11% v 14%). Respondents who were married recorded similar levels to those who were single and never married (average at around 11%); however, separated respondents and widows in particular recorded higher levels (15% and 23%).

* With few other sources of data available, this question acts as a proxy for analysing levels of competence. This lack of alternative data underlines the need of further research into understanding unmet psychological need.

Economic activity recorded considerable variation, suggesting that a person's status plays a considerable part in determining their levels of competence. Unemployed people recorded a higher lack of competence at 20% and, interestingly, retired people recorded a similar high level at 18%. However, it was those who are long-term sick and disabled who indicated the highest level, with 38% feeling a lack of competence. In keeping with the earlier finding on age, the type of household most likely to be lacking feelings of competence was single elderly at 21% whiles couples with dependent children were least likely at 8%. There were some geographic differences with public housing areas recording the highest proportion at 17% and 'prospering younger families' the lowest at 8%.

Households with low incomes were slightly but significantly more likely to record high proportions feeling a lack of competence than those on high incomes: 15% compared to 11%.

> **“ I've worked all my life and I've been out of work twice. I just been out of work four months, which is the longest, and I'm thirty-eight. I've been out of work and I've just gone back into work now, they have given me nine weeks, but if I stayed out of work any longer I'd crack up.**
>
> — Male focus group participant, Cardiff

3 Autonomy

The need for autonomy is met when people feel in control of their own behaviour, making informed choices without external interference. This need is met when people have the option, information and resources to make informed choices, by avoiding traumas, shocks and crises, and being free of situations involving coercion and exploitation.

To look at autonomy nationally we analysed the 2006-07 BHPS sample who were asked whether 'there were times that they were not in control of their life'.* The majority (67%) replied 'not often' or 'never', but 28% replied that they were 'sometimes' out of control and 5% replied 'often'. Combined, these negative responses accounted for one-third of the sample (33%). This approximately represents 16 million people, 2.5 million of whom often felt out of control. Again

* Again, this is a proxy due to the lack of alternative sources of data.

there were no substantial differences to report among the UK countries but different types of location showed variations. Older workers' areas and blue-collar communities appeared to have high proportions lacking control (37%) but those settled in the city and people from Asian communities areas recorded the very highest proportion (38%). Young aspiring areas recorded the lowest proportion at 27% followed by African-Caribbean communities at 28%.

Women were slightly more likely to feel a lack of control than men (34% compared to 31%). With regard to age, 28% of young adults lacked control compared to 38% of pensioners. The relationship between growing old and lack of control was also indicated in comparing figures for different household types, although living alone also had a bearing. Single elderly people recorded the highest proportion (48%), followed by lone parents with dependent children and single non-elderly households (both at 39%), with couples with dependent children lowest (30%). When looking at marital status it was those who had undergone a form of separation that recorded the greatest levels of lack of control. Widows recorded the highest proportion (44%), followed by the divorced and separated (both at 39%). Those who had never married and those that were married recorded just below average proportions, both at 31%. Interestingly, those in civil partnerships appeared to have the smallest proportion who lacked control.

Economic status was highly associated with a lack of control, with 62% of the long-term sick and disabled lacking control. Retired people recorded the second highest rate (39%), followed by unemployed (38%) and full time family care (37%). Those with the lowest proportions were the self employed (26%) and employed (27%). But health appeared to be most predictive of variation, with only 20% of those in excellent health feeling out of control compared to 71% of those with very poor health (3.5 times as high).

4 Relatedness

Relatedness is the need for people to feel as if they matter to other people, that they feel cared for and are significant to others. This requires them to participate, feel involved and engaged with the social world around them, through a range of good quality relationships, including intimate ones (e.g. marriage, lovers, parents etc.), social ones (friends, clubs, neighbourhoods etc.) and wider family.

The 2007-08 BHPS sample were asked 'if there was anyone who really appreciated them?' and the majority (78%) replied 'yes, more than one person' while 19% said 'yes, one person' and 3% replied 'no, nobody'. For the latter there was no variation by country. When looking at area type people from Asian communities (i.e. areas with a high proportion of Indian, Bangladeshi or Pakistani residents) recorded the highest proportion replying 'nobody' (6%) followed by senior communities' (4%). Those areas classified as settled household, prospering semi-detached and agricultural recorded the lowest proportions (2%). There was no gender distinction, although children recorded the lowest proportion who felt unappreciated (2.4%) and mature adults the most under-appreciated (4%). Those who were divorced were high (6%) followed by never married (4%). Interestingly, separated people recorded the lowest proportion at 1%. Lone parents with dependent children also scored high (5%) as did single elderly and single non-elderly.*

A high proportion (11%) of the long-term sick and disabled thought that nobody appreciated them (almost four times the average), followed by the unemployed and full time family carers, both at 6%. The employed and retired were equally low at 2%. Those with excellent health had the smallest proportion feeling unappreciated, rising to 10% for those with very poor health.

In addition to the BHPS question on appreciation, we looked at whether people felt they had people to whom they could turn for support by analysing the 2005 English health survey. From answers to the seven questions (see table below) measuring perceptions of social support from their family (cohabiting and elsewhere) and friends, the majority (60%) of people did not feel they lacked support, one quarter of the sample reported 'some lack' and 14% reported a 'severe lack' of support. If extrapolated to the population of England this amounts to some seven million people feeling that they severely lack social support.

Figure 40: Perceived social support (%) 2005

People I know ...	Not true	Partly true
... do things to make me feel happy	4%	23%
... make me feel loved	1%	14%
... can be relied upon	1%	13%
... will see that I am taken care of	1%	13%
... accept me just as I am	1%	11%
... make me feel important	2%	17%
... give me support and encouragement	2%	16%

Source: English Heath Survey analysis

* Again these findings raise as many questions as they answer – reinforcing the need for much better survey research on psychological needs in the future

The individual questions showed that support was most lacking in being made to feel happy, important, and supported/encouraged (27%, 19% and 18%). It was more likely that respondents would know people who would be accepting, caring and could be relied upon.

In terms of the overall score, men were more likely to report a severe lack of social support (18% compared to 11%). There was little variation when looking at age alone, but the gender difference was apparent in every age band. Severe lack of social support peaked at those aged 35-44 for women (21%) and 45-54 for men (13%), although the proportions did not vary substantially by age group considering that older people are thought of as being more isolated.

Figure 41: Percentage of those severely lacking social support by age band and gender 2005

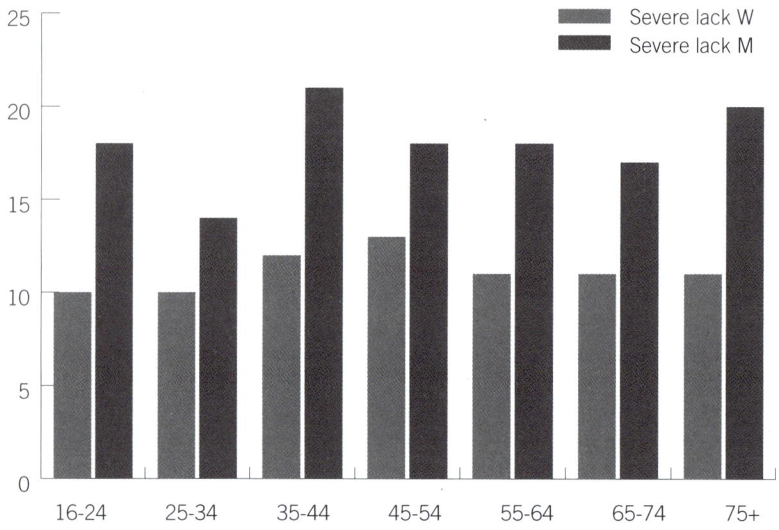

Source: English Health Survey analysis

The household type most likely to experience a severe lack of social support was single non-elderly with no children (21%); this increased to 47% when including 'some lack' of social support. A high proportion (20%) of those who lived in rented accommodation severely lacked social support. Ethnicity showed distinct variability, with 13% of white people recording a severe lack of social support compared to 27% for BME groups. One-third of the Black or Black British category reported a severe lack of social support. The sample size would not allow the BME category to be broken down further and it should be noted that there are likely to be culturally specific interpretations to the social support questions.

Social support varied by social class, with unskilled manual workers twice as likely to severely lack social support compared to professionals (22% compared to 10%). Income and support were also related. Those who fell into the lowest equivalised household income quintile recorded 23% severely lacking social support compared to 9% of those in the top quintile. These findings suggest that as well as having less financial capital, poorer people, on average, also have to cope with less social capital in the form of support. Further, a low level of social support was more likely in the most deprived areas, with 19% demonstrating a severe lack compared to 12% in the least deprived areas (see figure below).

Figure 42: Percentage of those lacking social support by deprivation or residential area 2005

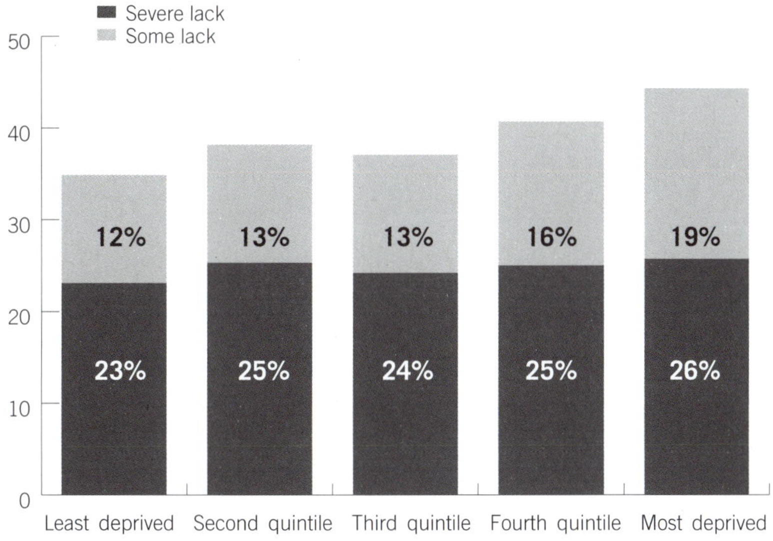

Source: English Health Survey analysis

Unsurprisingly, there were some strong associations between social support and wellbeing. Pessimism was higher among those with a lack of social support: 5.8% overall replied that they thought that their situation was 'hopeless'. The proportion was lower for those with no lack of social support (5%) and higher (7%) for 'some lack' and higher still (9%) for those with a 'severe lack' of social support. The pattern was similar for anxiety and depression. Overall 16% of the sample said they suffered from moderate depression and 2% said they were 'extremely anxious/depressed'. The proportions were lower where there was no lack of social support (13% and 1%), higher where there was 'some lack' (18% and 2%) and highest where there was a 'severe lack' of social support (29% and 4% – over one-third when combined).

Figure 43: Psychological need summary – Key psychological needs

	Lack of self-esteem	Lack of feeling competent	Lack of feeling in control	Feeling unrelated
Extent of unmet need	6% 'sometimes' 2% 'often'	10% feeling less competent than usual 2% 'much less so'	28% 'sometimes' 5% 'often'	19% with only one person 3% with nobody
Geographic variation	Public housing areas	Public housing areas	Settled in city Asian areas Older workers areas	Asian areas Senior areas
Groups more at risk	Very poor health LT sick/disabled Lone parent Divorce/separated	Very poor health LT sick/disabled Older people (esp. 75+) Widows Unemployed	Very poor health LT sick/disabled Single elderly Widowed	LT sick/disabled Very poor health Divorced Full time family care

5 The need for personal security

The need for personal security is the need to live without fear of victimisation, be it verbal abuse, threats, or serious physical harm. Below we examine the extent to which the fear of victimisation in general impacts on people's quality of life, and then focus on actual incidents of violent crime and abusive relationships, identifying who is most at risk.

The fear of crime is widespread but often people's perception of risk is mismatched with their actual risk of being a victim. The British Crime Survey, for example, shows that the general population estimated the likelihood of being a victim of violent crime at 17% compared to an actual risk of 3%, only one-sixth of the perceived rate. Worry about violence, burglary and vehicle crime has reduced over one-third since 1998-99, nevertheless, worry about victimisation has an impact on quality of life and the BCS showed how some groups are more affected than others.

When examining the adult sample (16+) overall, 35% of respondents stated that fear of crime had a high or moderate impact on their quality of life. However, this proportion increased to 47% for those residing in areas of high physical disorder and 46% for those living in multicultural areas. Correspondingly, Black and Minority Ethnic groups recorded higher levels than the white majority (46% compared to 34%). Asian and British Asian respondents recorded the greatest fear of crime, with just over half (51%) reporting a high or moderate impact.

SEAN'S STORY

Sean is 15 years old and lives with his mother and father in London.

Personal safety is a major concern to Sean. He talks about a constant feeling of fear and how he has to consider the risks, and potential risks, he might face on even the most local of journeys. A couple of years ago he attended a boxing club in a neighbouring borough and regularly used a local leisure centre. Because he was younger, his parents would take him back and forth. Now that he is older, and expected to make this journey himself, he doesn't feel that it is safe to travel to either of these clubs:

"I don't do it no more. There are the wrong people hanging around when I go there. I don't want to walk up there or get on them buses."

Sean thinks street violence is getting worse:

"I can't walk around without someone probing me. The other day, when I got this cut [pointing to a scar on his face], this boy just wanted a fight. I knew he'd bring his friends so I said just him. But then he pulled out a blade. I just ran. He would have stabbed me ... you can't walk around here any more. People look at you and you know they've got a knife. You can't get on the bus. For me to get to my girlfriend's house it's difficult because I'm not from round there. You have to have friends. It's safer to travel with them. When you are with a group of friends you feel less closed in."

There was a clear distinction between the impact on men (30%) and women (40%). Among household types, lone adults with children recorded the highest proportion (48%). Employment status also showed considerable variations, with employed people recording average levels (33%) and those unemployed and long-term sick or disabled much higher levels at 47% and 57% respectively. The impact in urban areas is higher than in rural areas (38% compared to 24%).[80]

Violent victimisation encompasses verbal abuse through to grievous bodily harm. The British Crime Survey (BCS) recorded 2,164,000 incidents of victimisation in 2007-08; the number of incidents reported has reduced by 48% since 1995. There were four offence categories: assault with no injury (which accounted for 42% of all violent incidents in 2007-08); assault with minor injury (22%); wounding (more severe, 22%); and robbery (14%) in 2007-08. Each of these categories recorded a large decrease since 1995, with the exception of robbery with a more modest 8% reduction.

Police recorded crime suggests that London is the region with the highest rate of violence against the person, at 23 per 1,000 population. The overall England and

Wales rate was 18 per 1,000 (Wales 17). The region with the lowest rate was the East of England at 13.

The BCS shows that men in particular are more at risk of violent crime (4% compared to 2% of women) and those aged 16 to 24 are most likely to be victims (13% men 6% women). Being single also increases risk (8% compared to 1% married). Economic status has some bearing, with students recording the highest rate (11% - probably because they are younger) followed by unemployed (9%), both of which compared unfavourably to those in employment (3%). Unsurprisingly, those who visited pubs and bars more than twice a week and those who were often out of the home also recorded higher rates.

For most people, therefore, the risk of being a victim of a violent crime is low. However, it is important to draw the distinction between those who experience a single or few incidents of violence and those who suffer from repeated violent behaviour. The most common form of repeat violent victimisation is domestic violence, where 45% of those involved are repeat victims.

Due to the sensitivity of the issue getting accurate figures for domestic violence is particularly problematic. The most credible statistics come from national victimisation surveys that ask about domestic abuse using anonymous self-completion forms. The British Crime survey does this. The BCS definition of domestic abuse includes non-physical abuse, threats, force and sexual assault carried out by a current or former partner or other family member.[81]

The 2007-08 survey results estimated that 5% of those aged 16 or over were victims of domestic abuse in the previous year.[82] The rate was higher for women but a comparable proportion of men were victims: 6% compared to 4.5%. These figures equated to some 1,688,000 people who had been a victim on at least one occasion (958,000 women and 727,000 men). The proportions increased when asking respondents about their experiences since the age of 16. Here 30% of women had been a victim of domestic abuse and 20% of men (25% overall). When focusing specifically on partner abuse the proportion of victims who experienced force was 18% for women and 10% for men.

In Northern Ireland, approximately 11% taking part in the 2007-08 crime survey (NICS) aged 16-59 reported having been a victim of domestic violence at some stage in their lives.[83] The Scottish victimisation survey showed that 10% of respondents said that at some point a partner had verbally threatened them or used physical force against them, falling to 3% for the reference period (Jun to Dec 2006).[84]

The risk of domestic abuse as recorded by the BCS changed when examining different socio-economic backgrounds. Female respondents who were classified as separated or from single adult households with children were most at risk, at 18%.

Figure 44: People (16+) most at risk (%) of any domestic abuse in the past year, 2007-08

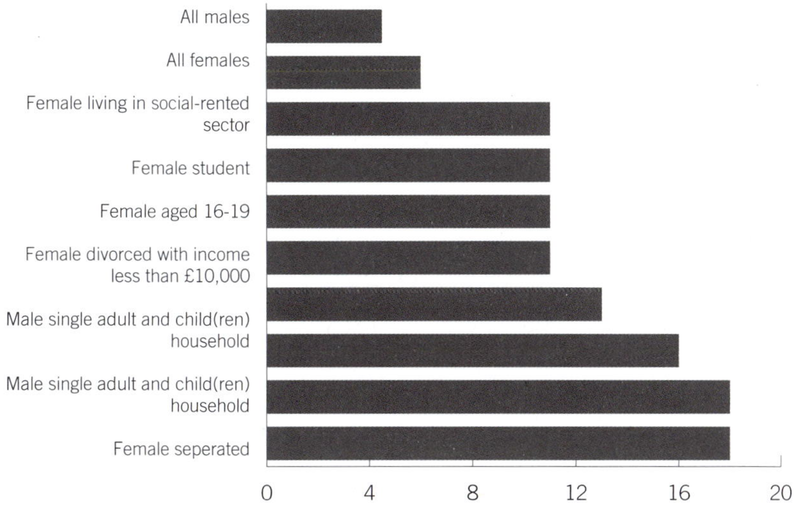

Source: British Crime Survey

BCS trend data was available from 2004-05 and is separated into partner and family abuse. There was no substantial change between 2004-05 to 2007-08 for either, ranging from 21.7 % to 22.8% for any partner abuse and 8.7% to 10.6% for any family abuse.

The regional figures available relate to face-to-face survey results (not the more accurate self-completion forms). Victimisation rates varied throughout the English regions and Wales, ranging from 14.5 per 1000 adults in Yorkshire and Humberside to 3.1 per 1000 in London (the overall England and Wales figures was 7.8 per 1000 and Wales was 6.9).

Figure 45: Psychological need summary – The need for personal security

	Fear of crime	Violent victimisation	Domestic abuse
Extent of unmet need	35% of adults in England and Wales	2,164,000 incidents Risk 3.2% (4.1% men, 2.3% women) 16+ Eng &Wales	5% 2007-08 6% women 4.5% men (E&W) Estimated 1,688,000 victims 16+
Trends	Worry about key crime types down one-third since 1998 (E&W)	Down 48% since 1995 (E&W)	No substantial change since 2004-05 for either partner abuse or family abuse (E&W)
Geographic variation	No regional breakdowns available Rural areas less affected	Violence against the person higher in London	Higher in Yorkshire and Humberside
Particularly at-risk groups	Areas of high physical disorder Multicultural areas Black and Minority Ethnic groups (partic. Asian & British Asian) Women Lone adults with children Unemployed and long-term sick or disabled	Men Those aged 16-24 Single Unemployed Student Visit pubs/bars 2+ times a week Often out of the home	Women Separated Lone parent household with child Those aged 16 -19 Income less than £10,000 Divorced Social rented

5 The relationship between material and psychological needs

Thus far our analysis has looked at individual needs largely in isolation of each other. However, as the personal profiles have shown, needs are not experienced in isolation. Threats to our physical wellbeing (hunger, lack of shelter) can have profound impacts on our wellbeing and psychological health, and deficits in psychological needs, manifested as stress, isolation or low self-esteem, can impact upon our physical health both directly and indirectly. Furthermore, some material resources are required to meet psychological needs, and some intangible resources (motivation, competence) are required to meet our material needs.

In later chapters, we explore how multiple needs – both material and psychological – are experienced by different groups of people through detailed case studies. However, before we look at how individuals experience and find help in meeting their needs, we look at the overall relationship between material and psychological needs at a national level.

We have carried out analysis of the BHPS data to understand the relationship between material and psychological need within the UK, initially using equivalised household income as an indicator for the former and the GHQ12 as an indicator of the latter. A principal limitation of this approach relates to the survey data. While BHPS data will represent the majority of the population and their experiences, it will not accurately reflect the most vulnerable groups who are not captured by surveys, for example rough sleepers, people with mental health problems or prisoners. Because of this the following analysis can say very little about the material and psychological needs of such important groups (a later section in this chapter explores the likely unmet needs of the most vulnerable groups in society). However, the survey does sufficiently capture people who are from low-income, average-income, and high-income households.

Department of Work and Pension figures on households below average income indicated that 18% of the UK population are from low-income households (see section 3.6), or 21% after accounting for housing costs, and thus can be considered to be at high risk of having unmet material needs. BHPS analysis using GHQ12 suggests that 20% of the UK are in poor psychological wellbeing and thus can be considered at risk of having unmet psychological needs.

When considering the relationship between material and psychological needs it is intuitive to suppose that people on low incomes would have higher levels of poor psychological wellbeing, given the well-documented social exclusion they face. Our analysis of BHPS supported this to a certain extent: the rate of poor psychological wellbeing increased from the average 20% to 23% when isolating those on low income. Those at risk of unmet material need were slightly but significantly more likely to be at risk of unmet psychological need compared to the overall population. When repeating the analysis but isolating the wealthy, the proportion decreased by a small but significant amount to 18%.

Figure 46: Psychological wellbeing by income banding 2006-07

	GHQ12 score			
	No risk	At risk	Most at risk	**Poor psychological wellbeing**
Low income	77%	13%	10%	**23%**
Below average	79%	13%	9%	**22%**
Above average	82%	11%	7%	**18%**
High income	82%	12%	6%	**18%**

Source: BHPS analysis

Essentially, this analysis indicated that those on low incomes were more likely than average to have unmet psychological needs and over 1.3 times more likely compared to those on high incomes, but that overall income did not have a very strong relationship with psychological health. This is congruent with relativistic arguments concerning income and wellbeing that argue that the impact of income is subject to changeable standards such as personal expectations (e.g. feelings that one should have a higher income), habituation (e.g. normalising the benefits of current income) and social comparisons (setting an income benchmark among your peers).[85]

When looking solely at those respondents with poor psychological wellbeing, and examining each of the individual questions within the GHQ, those on low incomes consistently record higher proportions of negative responses compared to those on high incomes. The only exception was for the question on feeling constantly under strain, where the proportions were equal.

Figure 47: Poor psychological wellbeing: negative responses to individual GHQ questions by high and low income groups

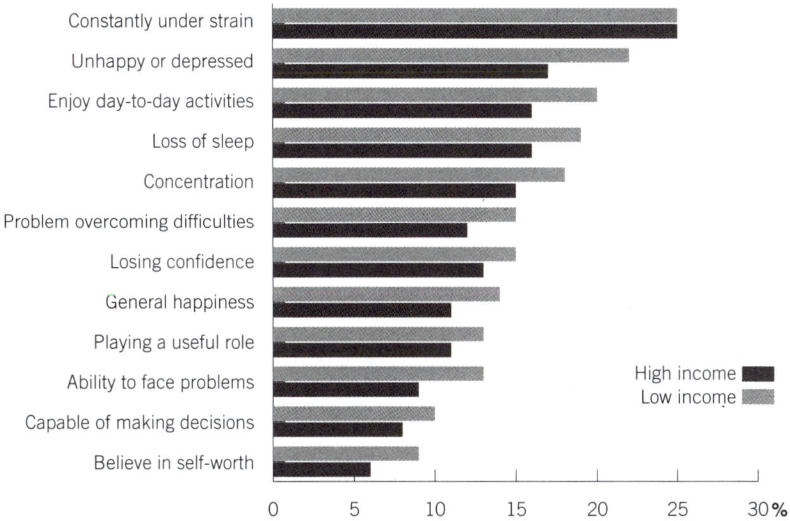

Source BHPS analysis 2006/07

We investigated further, moving on to relate psychological health with financial strain. Financial strain was measured within the BHPS through the question "How well would you say you yourself are managing financially these days?" Respondents were required to answer on a scale of 1 ('living comfortably') to 5 ('finding it very difficult'). There were groups within each income band who were finding it 'quite difficult' or 'very difficult' although the size of these groups increased as income decreased (see table below). The proportion feeling financial strain was 2.5 times higher for those on low income compared to those on high income (10% compared to 4%).

Figure 48: Financial strain by income banding 2006-07

	Living comfortably	Doing alright	Just about getting by	Finding it quite difficult	Finding it very difficult	**Finding it quite/very difficult**
Low income	24%	38%	28%	6%	4%	**10%**
Below average	26%	39%	25%	6%	3%	**9%**
Above average	33%	41%	21%	4%	2%	**5%**
High income	45%	35%	16%	3%	1%	**4%**

Source: BHPS analysis

Our analysis indicated that a minority of people who were finding it quite or very difficult in each income band were more likely to have poor psychological wellbeing. Only 14% of those living comfortably had high GHQ12 (compared to 20% overall). This progressively increased with financial strain: up to 58% of those finding it very difficult had high GHQ12 (see figure below).

Figure 49: Psychological wellbeing by financial strain 2007-08

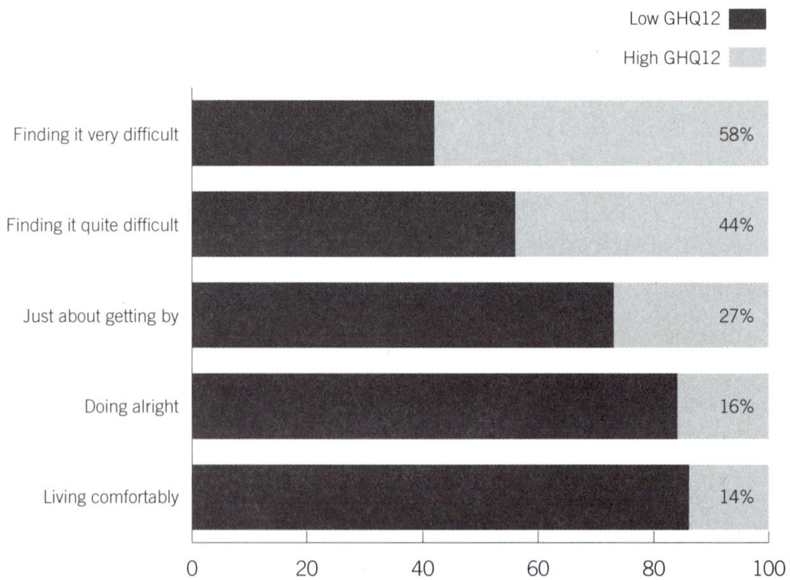

Source: BHPS analysis

We also wanted to understand if there a difference between the psychological wellbeing of those on low income with financial strain and those on high income with financial strain? The data suggested not, as it demonstrated similar proportions of high GHQ12 for both: 47% compared to 50% (the slightly higher proportion for those on high income was not statistically significant).

Figure 50: Those finding it quite or very difficult financially – income band by psychological wellbeing 2007-08

	No risk	At risk	Most at risk	**Poor psychological wellbeing**
Low income	54%	20%	27%	**47%**
Below average	52%	24%	25%	**48%**
Above average	53%	20%	27%	**47%**
High income	51%	22%	28%	**50%**

Source: BHPS analysis

This finding that poor psychological wellbeing is more prevalent among those experiencing financial strain tallies with a more complex study by the Financial Services Authority examining 'financial capability' and psychological wellbeing, also using BHPS. Here a financial capability index was derived drawing on a number of factors that indicated how well a respondent manages their finances regardless of income. The index included the above question on financial strain but also whether participants reported a worsening financial situation, whether or not they were saving, had housing payment problems, had had to borrow to meet payments, had to 'cut back' to meet payments or had been in housing arrears. The study found a strong association between financial capability and psychological wellbeing and between changes in financial capability and changes in psychological wellbeing. It demonstrated how greater financial incapability is associated with greater mental stress, lower reported life satisfaction, and a greater likelihood of reporting health problems associated with anxiety or depression.[86]

The above analysis suggests that unmet psychological need is more likely among households on low income and less likely among households on high income. Nevertheless this is an issue for substantial minorities in all income brackets. Considerably higher levels of poor psychological wellbeing were indicated among relatively small groups who felt they were struggling financially. People who were struggling financially were disproportionately found among those on lower incomes but were represented in all income brackets. Those on low income under financial strain had similar levels of poor psychological wellbeing as those with high income under financial strain.

5.1 The UK's material and psychological needs in an international context

This study is explicitly looking at need in the UK. But to make sense of the patterns here we need to be able to make some comparisons – both of the countries within the UK and of how we sit internationally. We have used selected statistics for the UK and other European countries to indicate levels of unmet material and psychological need.

A key indicator of material need that we use throughout this report is relative poverty. The relative poverty threshold is conventionally defined as 60% or below the average national income. Broadly, this indicator suggests that the UK has higher levels of unmet material need than Europe, recording a rate of 19%. The difference compared to some countries of similar standing is stark: the poverty rate in the UK was almost twice that of the Netherlands and one and a half times that of France. A related second indicator of material need is unemployment. Earlier figures showed that the rate of those unemployed aged 18 to 24 was no worse, with the UK and Europe both at 16% in 2007. However, considerable disparities appeared when examining proportions of workless households (i.e. households with no income from employment). These were more common in the UK (11% compared to 9%) and the proportion of children from workless households was almost twice as high (17% compared to 9%). Education figures compared more favourably, with 26% of UK adults recording low educational achievement compared to 31% in Europe for 2008.

Figure 51: Indicators of material and psychological need for the UK and Europe (relating to periods from 2007 to 2009

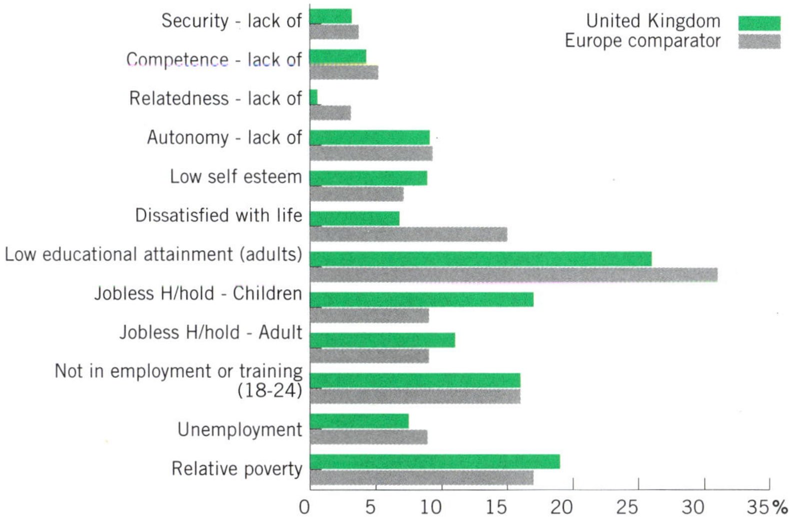

Source: EU 'Laeken Indicators' set & European Social Survey

In this study we have selected European Social Survey statistics that relate to aspects of psychological needs, although it must be noted that the questions asked are not an exact match to UK survey questions. When using life dissatisfaction as an overall proxy indicator of unmet psychological need, the UK appeared to have less of a problem than Europe as a whole, recording a lower rate of life dissatisfaction: 7% compared to 15%. However, when looking at more specific measures of unmet psychological need the difference largely fades. The proportion indicating low self-esteem (disagreeing, or strongly disagreeing, that 'In general I feel very positive about myself ') was similar in the UK and Europe as a whole (9% vs. 7%). Similarly, the proportion of the population appearing to lack autonomy (disagreeing or disagreeing strongly that 'I'm free to decide how to live my life') showed no great disparity, both each recording 9%. The proportions of people who felt a lack of competence were also similar (4% vs. 5%). The best indicator available to gauge security was respondents' levels of worry regarding being a victim of violent crime and again there was little difference. The UK proportion that worried 'all or most of the time' was similar to that of Europe (3.2% compared to 3.7%). However, the proportion feeling a lack of relatedness (unsure, disagreeing or disagreeing strongly that 'there are people in my life who care about me') was smaller in the UK (0.6%) compared to the European average (3.1%). Only a few countries such as Norway and Denmark recorded lower levels than the UK.

5.2 Indicators of unmet need: comparing countries within the UK

When looking at similar indicators that were available for the constituent countries of the UK the picture was broadly similar for each but there were some distinctions. Poverty rates varied between a low of 18% in Scotland to a high of 24% in Wales. Unemployment was similar across the countries at around 8% and the NEET rates were also similar at around 12%. The most obvious difference was the proportion of adults with poor qualifications in Northern Ireland at 22% compared to the UK figure of 13%. Also, Scotland appeared to record a higher overcrowded household rate at 12% compared to 5% for the UK. However, the most striking observation was the similarity in indicated levels of unmet psychological need (as measured by BHPS 2007-08). Wales recorded the highest level of poor psychological wellbeing at 22% but this was not largely different from the lowest rate recorded by Scotland at 19%. Likewise there was little variability when looking at measures for low self-esteem (8%), lack of competence (13%) and lack of relatedness (3%). The proportions lacking autonomy varied a little more but were all close to the UK rate of 35%.

Figure 52: indicators of unmet need comparing countries within the UK

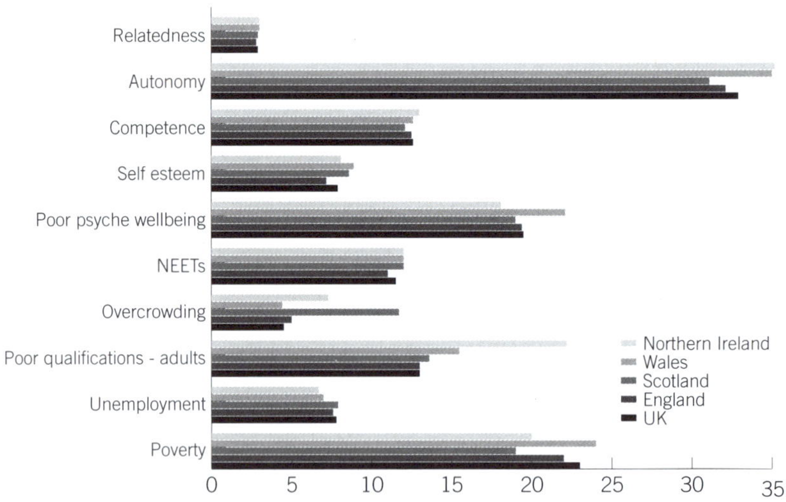

Essentially, the similarities appeared to outweigh the differences when looking at indicators of unmet need at the national level within the UK. Much greater variation and inequality is revealed when analysing different types of people and types of area, as demonstrated in the previous sections. In the next chapter we look in more detail at the types of people who are most vulnerable to having their needs unmet.

6 Groups most vulnerable to unmet needs

Thus far our analysis has concentrated on specific material and psychological needs and the extent to which they are being met as indicated by national surveys and administrative information. Some large groups, for example lone parents, repeatedly emerged from the data as being more at risk for a number of issues, suggesting they are likely to have multiple unmet needs and thus are particularly vulnerable. The multiple unmet needs that these groups are likely to face are described below. After this we move on to some specific groups who are at risk of more severe unmet needs and yet for whom the national data is poor, for example undocumented migrants or runaways. Here, in the absence of national data we have turned to smaller studies and provided a précis of the key material and psychological unmet needs that people within these vulnerable groups are likely to experience.

6.1 Most vulnerable groups as indicated by national survey data and official statistics

Seven key and potentially overlapping groups have been shown by the quantitative analysis to be more at risk with regard to multiple indicators of unmet needs:*

People living alone (make up 12% of households in Britain – this has doubled since 1971).[87] People living alone were not highlighted as at higher risk of having unmet essential needs, had only a few relative needs concerning risk of debt and poor transport, but were higher for nearly all the psychological need indicators that we used: poor general psychological wellbeing, lack of worth, lack of control, lack of relatedness and social support, more at risk of abusive relationships and violence generally, and with a quality of life more affected by fear of crime.

Lone parents (make up 16% of all families in the UK).[88] Lone parents with dependent children were more at risk of relative needs relating to poverty, financial strain and low qualifications. Psychologically they were more at risk of poor wellbeing, and at risk of lacking self-worth in particular. Their personal security was more at risk through abusive relationships, and their quality of life more affected by fear of crime.

Sick and disabled (5.4 million in receipt of relevant benefits in Britain) were more at risk of malnutrition amongst essential needs, poverty with regard to relative needs and were shown to be particularly at risk with regard to psychological needs, including being more likely to feel a lack of self-worth, a lack of control,

* While this quantitative approach benefits from drawing on national datasets that are largely representative, it inevitably cannot capture a lot of detail due to the aggregate and statistical methods of analysis. We more thoroughly explore multiple unmet needs, their interactions and complexities in the qualitative studies chapters later.

and to feel unrelated and incompetent. Their quality of life was more affected by fear of crime.

Low income (23% after housing cost in the UK)[89] households are more at risk of essential unmet needs regarding food and warmth. In terms of relative needs, they are more at risk of having poor skills/qualifications and non-decent housing, and were more at risk of poor psychological wellbeing and lower levels of social support.

Older people (10.5 million in the UK)[90] are more at risk of having their essential needs for food and warmth going unmet, are more likely to have unmet transport needs, and psychologically are at greater risk of feeling both less competent and lacking control over their lives.

Unemployed (7.9 million in the UK)[91] were more at risk of poverty, financial strain and low qualifications. They were more at risk of poor psychological wellbeing, lacking feelings of competence in particular, and more at risk of violent victimisation and their quality of life was more affected by fear of crime.

Minority ethnic groups (4.6 million in UK, 2001) were more at risk of homelessness. Some BME groups were more at risk of poverty, some more at risk of low qualifications, some had a greater risk of mental illness, and were more likely to have low social support (Black, Black British), and their quality of life was more likely to be affected by fear of crime.

6.2 Vulnerable groups for whom national data is poor

Some groups that are particularly vulnerable and likely to have severe or multiple unmet needs are insufficiently captured by national survey data and official statistics. We take ten of these groups below, provide estimates of their number and outline the nature of key unmet needs faced by each group. A full exposition of the variety of needs that these vulnerable groups face is beyond the scope of this section; instead we aim to identify the key overarching needs that are common within the group. Needless to say, each category encompasses a wide variety of individuals whose circumstances will differ.

Figure 53: Groups most likely to face severe, multiple and persistent needs – population or incidence estimates

Vulnerable group	Estimate	Some key needs
Undocumented migrants	533,000 UK 2007	Rights/protection from exploitation re income, accommodation etc.
Runaways	140,000 UK	Refuge and key relationships
Sex workers	80,000 UK	Exit pathways Refuge and safety Health and drug intervention
Problematic drug users	332,000 (opiates and cocaine) in Eng & Wales 2007; 51,582 (opiates only) Scot. 2003	Tailored effective treatment plans as well as holistic support to deal with the underlying causes of addiction
Isolated older people	11% of older people	Practical help accessing social support. Empowerment
Prisoners	74,000 sentenced, 15,000 remand UK 2008	Skills development and then accommodation and jobs support after release
People with dementia	700,000 UK	Early diagnoses, treatment support (including from spouses etc), and information
School exclusions	9,000 permanent exclusions each year (Brit)	Effective alternative education
Looked after children	81,100 UK 2007	Stability and reliable bonds with key individuals. Specific educational support
Travellers & Gypsies	200,000-300,000 UK	Adaptive services (esp. mental health and education) and legal settlement sites
Adults with neurodevelopmental disorder	8.2% with Attention Deficit Hyperactivity Disorder (Eng) 500,000 people with Autistic Spectrum Condition	Age-appropriate treatment programmes

Undocumented migrants

Undocumented migrants are without the official/legal right to remain in the UK and often live hidden from authorities. There are three classifications: illegal entrants, those outstaying their permitted period of stay and children born of undocumented migrant couples. They often enter the country illegally for the same reasons as legal migrants, for a safer environment, for work, to be with family etc. A recent study estimates there to be some 618,000 undocumented migrants in the UK in 2007.[92] The estimate for London was 442,000 or almost 72% of the UK total.

Undocumented migrants are in a uniquely vulnerable position with regard to meeting their needs, given that they are ineligible for support or are worried about asking for official assistance. For example it is common for individuals to be unable to secure local authority housing. Instead they have to turn to the cheapest and most deprived end of the private rental market with no recourse to ensure minimum standards.

Undocumented migrants' need for income is exacerbated by their ineligibility for government support when unemployed. This may lead some to attempt to obtain false documents from organised criminals that will enable them to work. Others work in the informal economy, often being exploited taking low paid or unpaid work. At its worst this might be forced labour reinforced by threats of violence or threats against family.[93] Those who have used trafficking networks to enter the country are more at risk.

The threat of being discovered by authorities also means that undocumented migrants are concerned about accessing services such as health (e.g. for work accidents or disease) and education (e.g. learning English). The threat is also detrimental to psycho-social needs, with many undocumented migrants finding it difficult to sustain relationships, owing perhaps to false personal information and a lack of money. The sustained psychological impact of the fear of being discovered generates stress and undocumented migrants often find it hard to plan for the future given their uncertainty, which diminishes their sense of control.[94]

Runaways

A report to a UK parliamentary panel counts some 140,000 incidents of children and young people in the UK who run away or go missing each year. The majority return safely after a short period but around 10,000 are hurt or harmed while away from home, some do not return, and approximately 50 children each year die or are killed while they are missing.[95] A significant number are running away from a harmful or abusive environment in the first place. These figures can only be approximate, due to a dearth of precise and detailed information. Data from some police force areas has been insufficient to enable insightful analysis. Two areas' records suggested that children who go missing are often looked after in Local Authority care, particularly residential care.[96]

The most recent comprehensive UK report[97] on the nature and extent of runaways was carried out 1999 by surveying those under 16 from a cross section of schools. Around two-thirds of children who ran away stayed in their local area, one in five ran to the nearest city while one in seven went further afield. The main reasons children gave for running away included violence, abuse, family instability, family conflict, neglect, rejection and drug problems, all of which relate mainly to psychological needs. Over a quarter of those who had run away had run away three times or more and over half of this group first ran away before the age of 11. From the age of 14 upwards, girls are twice as likely as boys to run away. The rates of running away are highest among white young people (10%), compared to 7.5% of children of African-Caribbean origin and 5.5% of those of Indian/Pakistani/Bangladeshi origin.

Many children said that running away gave them time to think and relief from the stressors causing them to leave. However, the longer a young person was away the greater the risks they faced. Young people sleeping rough were particularly at risk. Around a quarter of the young runaways slept rough, in back alleys, fields, parks and bus and train stations. Boys were more likely to sleep rough.

In addition to safe accommodation, runaways needed financial support while away. According to this study, some children were given food and money by relatives or friends, others took money with them. The remainder used more dangerous survival strategies, including stealing. A few turned to begging, rummaging in dustbins, and selling sex or drugs to survive. A third of the children who slept rough while away had resorted to one of these dangerous survival strategies. Children often sought help from services outside the hours of normal services.

Sex workers

Broad distinctions can be made between on-street and off-street sex workers, trafficked and non-trafficked workers, female and male workers, and so on – but even within these distinctions there is much heterogeneity. Because of this, and because of the hidden nature of their work, there are no robust statistics on the number of sex workers. The Home Office in 2004 estimated that there were as many as 80,000 people working in prostitution in the UK.[98] Of these, perhaps 5,000 are under 18 and as many as 70% have spent some time in care. Over half of current sex workers became involved before they were aged 18.[99] Close to one quarter (22%) of women in prostitution report being homeless or in temporary residence when they first started selling sex.[100]

Sex workers' nationalities vary with their location; there are perhaps 20,000 foreign sex workers in total across the UK, whilst the Metropolitan Police estimates that 70% of the women involved in off-street prostitution in London are non-British. A sizable number of these workers are assumed to be trafficked and thus working against their will, but no figures are available. Young women who have been trafficked into the UK and forced into prostitution will have multiple, chronic and persistent unmet psychological and material needs, although clearly their primary need is to be free of the people and circumstances preventing them from controlling their own lives.

Victimisation is a common factor among sex workers. Many come from violent households, with up to 85% of all sex workers reporting physical abuse in the family and three quarters of women in street prostitution reporting physical abuse by their partners.[101] Violence continues to be a threat whilst selling sex. The report *A Three-City Comparison of client violence against prostitute women* found that two-thirds had experienced 'client violence' of some form or other; 28% reported attempted rape. Only one-third of women in prostitution report client violence to the police because of worry regarding anonymity and credibility with the police.[102] Criminal records are also common. For example, 69% of women working in indoor prostitution and 93% of women in street prostitution use illegal drugs.[103] Drug use and criminal records provide obstacles to legitimate work. Sex workers will also find it harder to get a job as many have a history of poor school attendance and educational attainment.

Sex work (often in combination with drug use) also leads to significant health problems. Sixty-five per cent of sampled sex workers in London using crack were found to have an STI, compared with 44% of non-crack users.

Problematic drug users

Drugscope define problematic drug use as where the primary 'problem' is the effect drug taking has on the user's life, i.e. they experience social, financial, psychological, physical or legal problems as a result of their drug use. While this can encompass recreational drug use it normally relates to psychological and/or physiological drug dependency. The most commonly measured dependency is for cocaine (most often crack cocaine) and opiates (most often heroin).

There were an estimated 327,466 problematic drug users (here opiate and cocaine users) in England and Wales, of which 74,417 (23%) were in London and 51,110 (16%) in the North West in 2003-04.[104] In Scotland in 2003 there were an estimated 51,582 problem drug users in 2003 (here just opiates and benzodiazepines)[105] and 3,303 in Northern Ireland in 2006.[106] In a list of 18 European countries where problematic drug user (PDU) prevalence estimates were available, the UK recorded the highest rate at 10.2 per every 1000 16-24 year olds, which equated to between 39,700 and 42,100 PDUs in that age group.[107]

A Home Office study explains how individual risk of problematic drug use is propagated by a wide range of interconnecting factors, including a family containing problem drug users, family disruption, poor attachment or communication with parents, child abuse, poor performance at or exclusion from school, having a childhood conduct disorder, offending, and mental disorder (particularly adolescent depression and suicidal behaviour). The vulnerable groups identified are many, including the homeless, children looked after by local authorities or in foster care, prostitutes, truants, those excluded from school, young offenders, children from families with substance-abusing individuals and young people with conduct or depressive disorders.[108]

Problematic drug use distorts an individual's perception to the point where they can neglect even their essential needs, damaging health and risking death. Until the problematic drug user can fully appreciate the need to be free of dependency and be committed to stopping, then other relative needs such as employment or psychological needs such as constructive relationships will be undermined. Drug treatment services help clients to manage their dependency using structured treatment plans. This professional support is a key need for problematic drug users and the tailoring of their plan to specific individual circumstances is of primary importance.

Isolated older people

As people reach older age the number and quality of relationships with other people can deteriorate, leading to unmet needs for companionship and social support. Half of all people aged 75 and over live alone (since 2000 the figure has reached 50% for the first time).[109] Nearly half of all older people (about 4.6 million) consider the television as their main form of company.[110] Over 500,000 older people spent Christmas Day alone in 2006.[111] Just over 1 million older people (11%) in England always or often feel lonely.[112] Twelve per cent of older people (over 1.1 million) feel trapped in their own home. Further, 17% of older people have less than weekly contact with family, friends and neighbours.[113] Ipsos MORI research shows that the problem is more common among older people who are on low incomes or who have poor health. They are three times more likely to be isolated than older people in general and three times more likely to feel trapped in their own home. The most severely isolated and lonely are people over 75, particularly older women, those who are widowed and those living alone.[114]

The research suggested that older people need and want to be empowered to develop activities and to benefit from low level support services that help them to remain socially engaged and independent. Roughly one-third of older people wish to do one or more activities more often than they do, with family visits (12%) and meeting friends (10%) the most commonly identified.[115] Although isolation and loneliness are interrelated they can also be seen as distinct – isolated older people require practical help and lonely older people require social support.[116]

Both loneliness and isolation are perpetuated by the need for transport and communication. For example, over 75% of men and 50% of women over 55 who have given up driving have done so because of some form of disability. This leaves them dependent on friends, family or public transport, reducing the variety of available destinations and transport flexibility, and entailing a psychological cost of loss of independence.[117]

PATRICIA'S STORY

Patricia is in her late 70s and lives alone in a flat in a sheltered housing block. She often feels lonely and isolated despite several hundred people being housed around her. Patricia sometimes attends activity clubs during the week but she finds weekends especially hard as all her family live abroad. The accommodation complex gets eerily quiet at weekends:

"After 6 o'clock on a Friday it's like walking round a mortuary even though there are over 200 flats here."

She is not alone in feeling isolated, recently a neighbour she didn't know asked her for help:

"He just knocked on the door and said 'I'm sorry to trouble you but I was at my daughter's in Cardiff last weekend and I miss her. Could I come in for a chat?'"

The Internet has great potential to be an important source of social contact for older people with limited mobility. However, the potential is still largely unrealised, as a 2006 Ofcom study found that just 28% of people over the age of 65 have home Internet access, compared to a UK average of 57% for all households. This leaves them excluded, not only from the Internet's communication potential, but also limits their access to some government services. The demand appears to be healthy, as more than two-thirds of pensioners without the Internet said they would use it if appropriately supported.[118]

Prisoners

In the UK in 2008 there were 74,000 prisoners who are sentenced and a further 15,000 in remand. Prisoners are typically male (95%) and from a disadvantaged background. A recent survey of UK prisoners demonstrates that they are more likely to have health and social problems compared to the overall adult population. For example, half of the sample were unemployed before prison and 13% had never had a job. Fifteen percent were homeless or living in temporary accommodation. In addition to these material problems health was also a serious issue, with one quarter reporting a long-standing illness or disability. Mental health problems, however, were even more prevalent, with 10% identified as likely to have a psychotic disorder, 61% a personality disorder and one-third reporting symptoms of anxiety or depression.[119] Mental health problems were even more common for female prisoners. Most prisoners had used drugs before sentence: half had used cannabis and a third had used cocaine or heroin, the use of which were also more likely to be reported by women. Heavy drinking was reported by 36% of the sample and was more prevalent amongst men.

Data from nationally representative surveys of sentenced prisoners in England and Wales conducted in 2001, 2003 and 2004 identified the proportion of prisoners who had previously served in the armed forces at 4-6%.[120] A high proportion of these convicts had suffered some form of post-traumatic stress disorder after leaving the forces. Research by NAPO revealed that their convictions were often for drug- or alcohol-related violence.[121]

Despite strong aspirations amongst many prisoners leaving prison, very few – as few as one in ten according to one study[122] – succeed in finding a job on release. Many also face a lack of suitable accommodation. Both unemployment and instability are strongly correlated with re-offending or re-engaging in substance abuse. Moreover, reformed drug addicts find it hard to access continued support on leaving prison, making relapse more likely.[123]

Reflecting these issues, prisoners prioritised their skills-related needs rather than issues relating to their health or family. Close to half (48%) reported needing help finding a job, 42% improving qualifications, and 41% improving work-related skills. A large proportion (nearly one-third) wanted help with their housing situation. The proportion who wanted help addressing their offending behaviour was also around one-third.[124] See Chapter 7 on 'Transitions' for more detail on needs when leaving prison.

People with dementia

In 2008 there were an estimated 700,000 people in the UK who were suffering from dementia; it is estimated that this will rise to 1.4 million by 2038. Dementia has been described as a "global impairment of intelligence, memory and personality."[125] Local estimates in England vary from 5.2% to 9.6% of over 65s suffering. It can occur at any age but becomes more common with age, from 5-10% in the over 65s to 20% in the over 80s. Dementia actually refers to some of the symptoms which can present in a number of different afflictions including Alzheimer's and Parkinson's disease and a number of lesser-known conditions such as Huntingdon's chorea. While the most widely understood symptoms are memory loss and disorientation there are many other associated problems such as aggression, incontinence/constipation, malnutrition, wandering and falls, and communication difficulties. Unsurprisingly, depression is common among sufferers especially if the individual concerned is aware of the dementing process.[126]

Those with dementia and those supporting them benefit from early diagnoses and easy access to support and advice thereafter; this would include information on causes and future treatments. Currently too great an emphasis is placed on the provision of medical prescriptions at the expense of comprehensive post-diagnosis care. Other needs include being able to live in their own homes for as long as possible, ensuring minimum standards in residential care, and being involved in planning end-of-life care.[127] Dementia can also exacerbate many of the needs conventionally associated with aging, for example isolation and feeling a lack of competence and control.

Permanent school exclusions

There are approximately 9,000 children permanently excluded from schools in Britain. The figures have fallen since the late 90s from a high of 13,200 in 1995-96 to 8,500 in 2007-08. Boys account for four-fifths of permanent exclusions, with African-Caribbean pupils over-represented and Black Africans to a lesser extent (36 per 10,000 pupils and 16 per 10,000 respectively, compared to 13 for white students). Indian, Bangladeshi and Pakistani children are under-represented (3, 6 and 8 per 10,000 pupils). There is considerable geographic variation in exclusions, from a low of 2 per 10,000 in Scotland to a high of 13 in London.[128]

Qualitative interviews from a Home Office study have suggested that permanent exclusion leads to a chain of events that weaken the links between the young person and a conventional way of life – a transition "characterised by the loss of time structures; a re-casting of identity; a changed relationship with parents and siblings; the erosion of contact with pro-social peers and adults; closer association with similarly situated young people and heightened vulnerability to police surveillance".[129]

Young people excluded from school need effective alternative provision. In England some 135,000 young people, mostly secondary school age, spend some time in alternative education, such as pupil referral units (schools for those without a normal school place). Not all attendees have been excluded; some are principally involved due to special learning needs.[130] Many such children also need non-educational support – for example, it is increasingly accepted that the behavioural problems that can lead to exclusion can be linked to health issues like attention deficit hyperactivity disorder (ADHD), which must be treated and supported. The permanently excluded are also a group likely to overlap with other groups here – particularly looked after children – and are therefore even more likely to suffer from multiple and chronic unmet needs.

Looked after children

It is normally parenting problems (e.g. neglect) that lead to children being looked after by local authorities, either through a voluntary arrangement or through a court order. Children may be supervised while staying within their parental home, or looked after by kinship carers, foster parents, residential care homes or schools, or in custody. A parliamentary committee has stated that cared for children are frequently and often suddenly moved, miss too much schooling, and are left to care for themselves too early. The latter was evident in exam results in England (2008), with only 14% of looked after children achieving 5 GCSE grades A-C, considered the basic threshold of employability in jobs requiring formal skills. There are three primary factors that contribute to this under-achievement:

the detrimental experiences of children prior to being looked after; the disruption of sometimes multiple placements; and inadequacies of schools to target and support looked after children.[131]

Academic studies have also revealed that looked after children have higher rates of mental health problems, for example children looked after by Welsh local authorities had mental disorders, with 42% having clinically significant conduct disorders, 10% emotional disorders (e.g. depression anxiety) and 12% hyperactivity.[132] Further, looked after children recorded higher levels of psychopathology, educational difficulties and neurodevelopmental disorders, and 'looked after' status was independently associated with nearly all types of psychiatric disorder.[133] Leading on from this, it is unsurprising that there is a stark over-representation of looked after children in custody: up to 41% of children in custody in the UK have some history of being in care.

A key need of looked after children is sustained good quality relationships with key individuals including carers and social workers. Placement breakdowns threaten this.[134]

Travellers and gypsies

Gypsies and travellers are a long established minority group in Britain. It is estimated that there are somewhere in the region of 200,000-300,000 in the UK but precise figures are unavailable.[135]

Travelling lifestyles can mean it is challenging to deliver public services. Education is a prime example. A late 1990s report by Ofsted showed how primary school attendance for travelling children was improving but that secondary education was still of grave concern, with as many as 10,000 unregistered children at that time.[136] Travelling children are likely to suffer from stigma and social exclusion at school. Further, their parents are more likely to be under-educated and less likely to see the value of state education.[137]

Travellers and gypsies are more likely than the general population to be suffering from poor physical health and also have significantly higher levels of anxiety and depression.[138] There are many factors that contribute to this including poverty, insecurity about accommodation, loss of traditional means of employment and heavy burdens on women caring for large families.[139]

Travellers and gypsies often experience accommodation problems due to an insufficient number of authorised sites where they can settle. This has contributed to a considerable proportion settling on and developing unauthorised sites (one in five caravans in 2004) and this in turn creates tensions with mainstream communities.[140] Travellers and gypsies are also likely to experience the highest levels of racial abuse of all ethnic minorities in the UK.[141]

Adults with neurodevelopmental disorders

Neurodevelopmental problems stem from an impairment of the growth and development of the brain or central nervous system, often affecting brain functioning with regard to emotion, learning and memory. Disorders are wide ranging and include problems such as attention deficit hyperactivity disorder (ADHD) and autism spectrum condition (ASC). Many are detected during childhood and have services dedicated to their diagnosis and treatment. However, it has been recognised that the conditions can have an under-recognised impact in adulthood and older age. Kings College London attest that patients often become 'lost' during the transition to adulthood and that there are few services in place to meet the needs of adults with neurodevelopmental disorders.[142]

Attention deficit hyperactivity disorder (ADHD) is a condition resulting in inattention, hyperactivity and impulsiveness. Symptoms and behaviours include excessive problems with organisation, difficulties with activities requiring cognitive involvement, restlessness and impulsiveness that interfere with normal functioning.[143] While traditionally associated with young people, the problem can persist into adulthood.[144] In fact, in a recent adult psychiatric morbidity survey 8.2% of the adult population tested positive for ADHD characteristics. Prevalence was higher among lower income households and people who were economically inactive. The prevalence did not vary with gender but did decrease with age. One-fifth of those that screened positive were receiving some sort of treatment for a mental health or emotional problem. This meant that 80% were not getting any professional support.[145]

Autism spectrum condition (ASC) is a lifelong condition affecting how a person communicates with and relates to other people and how they perceive the world. It is thought to affect 500,000 people in the UK. The condition varies and affects people differently and so people are said to fall on the 'spectrum' of autism. However, people with ASC share a 'triad of impairments'. Firstly, they have difficulties using and understanding verbal and non-verbal language such as gestures, facial expressions and tone of voice; secondly, they have problems in recognising and understanding other people's feelings and managing their own; thirdly, they have problems in understanding and predicting other people's intentions and behaviour and imagining situations outside their own routine. People with the condition often have no obvious disability and some individuals will not want to have their condition recognised but still have a need for support. Parents and other relatives often provide the care and support needed, sometimes leading to extra stress within the home.[146]

6.3 Stuck at the bottom: the UK's most disadvantaged million

One of our aims in this study was to better understand the people who sit right at the bottom of society: those with severe, multiple and persistent needs. In the previous section we described the groups which show up repeatedly in both quantitative and qualitative research as suffering the most, as well as their rough numbers.

Another way to think of this group is as a percentage at the bottom of distributions. So if we lined up a randomly chosen hundred members of the population this would be the one or two people at the end of the line, with the lowest income and the poorest life chances. These would represent about a million people.*

We know that they are likely to include many with severe mental health problems, long-term unemployed and long-term drug users. But can we say more about who these people are, who moves in and out of the bottom group, and what they share in common? And can we be more precise in aggregating them into a single group?

Many apparently sound approaches to this problem turn out to be problematic. It's much easier to isolate, for example, the top 1% of income earners, or holders of wealth, than those at the bottom. The bottom 2.5% by income will include some (such as students) on low incomes but with good life chances. Defining through the lens of capacity may quickly lead to a focus on incapacities, such as dementia. Yet only a third to a half of dementia sufferers ever receives a formal diagnosis.[147] Or if we look in terms of access to assets, 75,000 young people experienced homelessness in the UK between 2006 and 2007 but this data was limited to young people who were in contact with services.[148] Data limitations also mean that the homeless, some of those in institutions, people without English language skills and those not inclined to collaborate with surveys are likely to be under-reported. Many of the poorest may have deliberately cut themselves off from state institutions and statisticians, and may be living perfectly contented lives.

Defining anyone as sitting at the bottom clearly depends on what lens or metric is used. By most definitions, a status right at the bottom will cover only people who have fallen through state safety nets. Even the minimal benefits of Job Seekers Allowance (providing £47.95 per week for 16-24 year olds and £60.50 per week for over-25s) will still leave individuals above the bottom 2 or 3%. So falling through the net will tend to mean either that there is an issue of legal status (such as being an undocumented migrant or asylum seeker), or bad luck, or a lack of skills in finding access to state supports. As our case studies show this is fairly common – seeking help is not normal for many groups in need. One recent study found that 24% of disadvantaged young people would never go to a specialist organisation for help and advice, whether because of lack of knowledge or lack

* The Cabinet Office Social Exclusion Task Force, for example, studied the bottom 2.5% in this way.

of trust.[149] Moreover, most services that are designed to meet the needs of the majority are not well suited to the needs of people living chaotic lives, or lacking the confidence to navigate complex systems of entitlements.

Despite the difficulties involved in defining a group at the bottom we have undertaken a series of analyses to suggest alternative ways of thinking about who sits right at the bottom of society. One approach was with a composite measure of disadvantage and suffering. For this we looked at people who were in relative poverty (60% or less of median equivalised household income), and who were dissatisfied with their lives (answering between 1 and 3 on a scale of 7, 7 being completely satisfied).

A higher proportion of this group (aged 16 or over) turn out to be economically inactive, and their unemployment rate was four times as high. They were three times more likely to be living in areas characterised by 'public housing' and were more likely to be living without a partner; they were over twice as likely to be a lone parent with dependent children. When asked if their life has meaning the group were over twice as likely to reply 'not often' or 'never'. Similarly, when asked if the future looks good this group is more pessimistic and they are less likely to 'look back on life with happiness'.

This group turns out to be fairly fluid, confirming many different research studies on movements in and out of the bottom groups. The idea of a permanent underclass – though popular in the media – has not been borne out by several decades of research. Instead we find a more complex picture, with a small group suffering poverty permanently; a much larger group bumping in and out of the bottom, occasionally finding work but not keeping it for long; and another group suffering periods of bad luck, unemployment or ill health but then bouncing back. According to the BHPS, for example, only 9% of individuals lived in households with below 60% of median income for at least three out of four consecutive years (2003 – 2006).[150] In general, different kinds of need are mutually reinforcing – so if someone is functionally illiterate they are also likely to be stuck with a low income or in insecure employment, which in turn will make them more likely to suffer inadequate housing. But people's ability to bounce back from adversity varies widely, and most people are fairly resilient (as we study in more detail in Chapter 13).

Most of the past definitions of the group right at the bottom have focused on material needs. But we have also used analytical tools to ask who would be at the bottom if we looked solely at mental wellbeing and capacity. Specifically we looked at BHPS survey data on people aged 16 or over who feel that a) no one would comfort them if they were very upset; b) no one really appreciated them, and c) no one would help from outside the household if they were depressed. This gives us a picture of the people who are least connected to human love, care and warmth, and who, in some eyes, would make as much claim to be at the bottom as people on very low incomes.

Figure 54: Percentage responses to questions on emotional support 2007-08

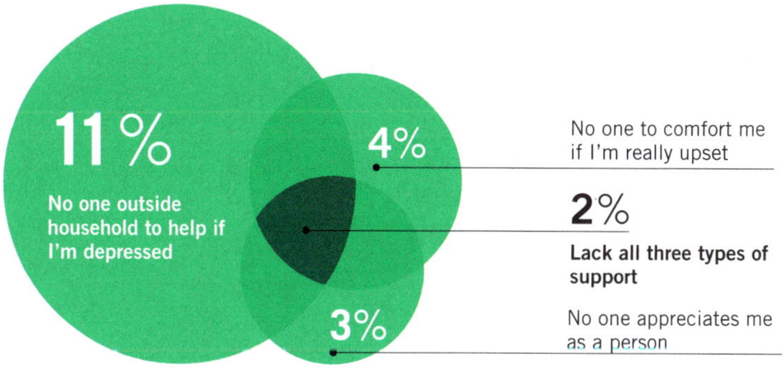

Source: BHPS analysis

This gave us a radically different account of a disconnected 2%. Some of the features of this group were perhaps predictable: a higher proportion without any qualifications, or doing unskilled work. Unemployment rates were higher yet a considerable proportion was working (46% compared to 56% overall), and income was not substantially lower. Their marital status was fairly typical (49% were married compared to 53% overall), nor were they predominantly living on their own (63% living in couples). They also talk a good deal to their neighbours (70% felt that this happened every day or once/twice per week compared to 77% overall) and frequently meet others either daily or once or twice a week (76% compared to 89%). The main difference with this group appeared to be that a higher proportion feel their health is poor or very poor, but this group still was in the minority (23% compared to 9% overall).

In other words there is a minority of people – perhaps around a million – who are deeply disconnected and unhappy with life, but who are living lives that on the surface look extremely normal.

Like all other measures of a group right at the bottom this group shows fairly high fluidity, with only around 20% still in the category after two years. These figures are suggestive rather than definitive, given that we are focusing on a small proportion, albeit of a very large survey. However, they demonstrate some of the complexities in thinking about what it means to be at the very bottom.

Perhaps this analysis also confirms the message from the previous chapter: there are many different ways in which people can slip into poverty, exclusion or misery. There are some common patterns which predominate in terms of the numbers – from the isolated elderly and disabled, to some migrants, or young people without skills or social networks. But it adds little to our understanding to bundle these different groups into a single category of the bottom 1% or the bottom million. Instead we learn more by disaggregating than by aggregating, and by looking at the dynamics of how lives change, rather than at snapshots. This is what we have therefore attempted in the case studies that follow – looking at the patterns of opportunity and suffering, rebuffs and renewals that lie behind the broader data.

PART III

Case studies

In this part of the report we move from the overview of the state of need in the UK to look at how people experience needs in their everyday lives. Quantitative data primarily focuses on specific needs, usually in isolation from each other. However, as many of the individual stories show, needs are not usually experienced in isolation. In the messy reality of life, people experience multiple needs – both psychological and material – at the same time.

Using interviews, focus groups and participant observation techniques we set out to dig deeper into the lives of many of the vulnerable groups who are experiencing clusters of unmet need, asking people about their situations, their needs and how they cope with those needs that remain unmet.

Through a series of six case studies we look at the needs of people living in Britain through different lenses. We look at needs in different geographic areas (London, Wales, Bedford and Teesside); we look at the needs of different groups (teenagers, migrants, elderly people, families on low incomes, and the long-term unemployed); we look at needs at night-time (exploring how needs at night vary to those in the day); and we look at needs through the lens of transition (investigating how people cope with transitions out of care, prison and violent relationships). The six case studies are:

1 Transitions

We were interested in exploring what processes or events could result in needs that were previously being met becoming unmet and problematic. Difficult or traumatic transitions – such as leaving prison, bereavement, unemployment or the end of a relationship – can act as such a trigger. We spoke to people In England and Scotland who had recently experienced a significant transition and found that a difficult transition can push people into homelessness, poverty or isolation and cause stress and anxiety. However, for some a transition can trigger a positive change, prompting some to access treatment for drug addiction, to rebuild damaged relationships or to rethink their goals and priorities. In this case study we explore what helps make a successful transition and what role service providers can play in supporting those who are most vulnerable.

2 Needs in London

London is one of the wealthiest cities in the world, yet it is also home to some of the most stark inequalities and pockets of poverty in the UK. Its size, diversity and economic standing make it a unique area of the country with unique needs. This case study looks at the specific needs of those living in London and what makes them different. We look at the overall picture of needs across the capital and delve into the lives and experiences of some of the Londoners who fall below the official radar.

3 Worklessness in Wales

The overview of need in the UK showed that those without work are among the most vulnerable groups. We were keen to look at the impact long-term worklessness has on a community as well as the individuals affected. We focused on Merthyr Tydfil in South Wales, in an area which has experienced high levels of economic inactivity since the decline of the coal mining and steel industries.

4 Needs at night

All the available data shows how needs vary according to variables such as geographic area, age, ethnic background, socio-economic status etc. In the course of this study we were keen to look at need through a more uncommon lens, that of time. How do needs vary at night compared to during the day? In an exploratory case study we looked at those who regularly work night shifts – finding out about their needs and the members of the public they encounter. By following the night workers throughout their shifts we uncovered a largely invisible workforce with distinct needs of their own, as well as insights into how the needs of the general population differ at night.

5 Low income families in Teesside

This study looks at the lives of families living on low incomes in Teesside in a time of economic recession. It paints a picture of people getting by in challenging circumstances. Despite the difficulties associated with financial pressures, high levels of debt, poor employment prospects and low levels of education, there are few signs that material poverty necessarily means a low quality of life. This study shows the importance of informal mutual support to surviving on low incomes and the continued importance, and strength, of families. Those households who can draw on extended families and wider networks of friends are more likely to be resilient to shocks that might push others further into difficulty.

6 Teenagers in Bedford

While in Teesside we focused on how vulnerable families drew on their own resources to help meet their needs, in Bedford we looked at how young people who were not in unemployment, education or training talked about needs and how they sought assistance in meeting their needs. Again, we demonstrate the importance of social networks for vulnerable people seeking support.

The chapters here provide summaries of the more detailed case studies which are being published separately, as well as being available to download.

7 Exploring the impact of life transitions in England and Scotland

7.1 Introduction

Everybody experiences transitions during their life: out of school, into and out of employment, into retirement and older age. People have to cope with bereavement, the onset of illness and transitions through parenthood; others have to negotiate more unusual transitions, out of prison or mental health care.

This study asks 'what makes a successful transition and helps avoid transitions creating unmet need?'. It looks for answers in the stories of 34 people, living in England and Scotland, who have recently experienced transitions, ranging from leaving prison, to bereavement, to redundancy.

The stories gathered are rich and diverse, and reveal how transitions affect every aspect of people's lives: their emotions and mental health, their finances and their relationships with others. Threading through these very different stories are some important messages about the things that help people experience transitions as transformations, rather than setbacks or periods of adversity.

To deal with transitions, people need to have stability in a few key areas of their life: they need a stable home, an adequate income and supportive relationships with friends and family. Having a positive attitude to transitions and seeing them as an opportunity for learning and self-discovery can also help motivate people to seek help and stay focused when things are difficult. Opportunities to prepare, where possible, and engage with supportive services can minimise the disruptions associated with transitions.

This study shows that while some people benefit from these things and make transitions with relative ease and success, others do not. In particular, vulnerable groups, including those leaving prison or abusive relationships and those with mental health issues, are often forced to negotiate transitions without adequate financial resources, in the context of an unsettled family life and with nowhere to call home. Moreover, for some of these vulnerable groups, opportunities for service providers to help them prepare for the changes ahead are often lost. In these circumstances, transitions can push people into positions of unmet need from which it is hard to escape.

7.2 The experience of transition

The people we spoke to told us very different stories of transition. For some, even traumatic transitions were a springboard, prompting them to find better ways of meeting their needs or providing opportunities for learning and self-discovery.

For others, transitions involved lurching unsupported into new circumstances. Often this lurch destabilised and undermined the resources and relationships that helped others through transition, leaving people constantly fighting to meet their needs adequately.

ERIKA'S STORY

Erika is 42 and lives with her 5 children, aged 12 to 20. She's been in more than one abusive relationship, with the most recent ending four years ago.

Erika has struggled since then. She spent some time in a refuge and found it difficult to find somewhere permanent to live. She moved into a rented house, but had constant problems with the landlord. They went to court frequently and Erika struggled to get advice and advocacy. This wore her down and she explained:

"I had to fight and fight every step of the way. I don't know, in the end if someone says no, you accept it. I didn't have any fight left in me."

Although for the last few years Erika has been single and life has become easier, she's still dealing with everything she has been through. She thinks she has learnt a lot, but that there are a lot of emotional issues she hasn't dealt with yet. She suffers from night terrors because of the abuse she suffered. Erika is also struggling to settle into her new home:

"It's the fourth place I've tried to turn into a home and every time it's been taken away. So there are fears from the past, and I'm struggling to put roots down because I'm afraid it'll be taken away again."

Erika is not close to her family and so hasn't been able to rely on them for support. She's found having her children around helpful and has also relied on friends and people who've been through similar experiences, who don't judge her and can empathise.

Transitions were processes that people managed, controlled and made choices about and that thrust them into situations and circumstances over which they had no control. Making a transition successfully seemed to involve steering a course through change and engaging with choices and options, but also coping with circumstances you would not choose and cannot alter. Pete, who is 42, lost his wife to cancer and was made redundant, learnt that "if you are worried about something, do something about it ... If you can't do anything about it ... there is no point in worrying about it." Erika's experiences were different: she struggled to achieve a balance in situations which seemed out of her control.

7.3 What makes a successful transition?

Having a foundation of stability in a few key areas of a person's life can help anchor them through transition and buffer them from the worst impacts of change. Where a transition could be foreseen, preparation could help maintain stability and avoid chaotic changes that magnify the challenges of managing change. Delving further, people's situation across the following areas of their life was fundamentally important to their experience of transition:

Relationships and support
Emotional and practical support from friends and family provide a crucial resource for people negotiating transition.

House and home
Having a decent, affordable home provides a stable base from which to manage transitions, offering escape and respite from other challenges and difficulties.

Income and work
Living on a low income makes negotiating transitions harder. Being unemployed often makes transitions harder for this reason, and also because jobs are a crucial source of routine, motivation, identity and self-worth.

Attitudes to transition
Some people saw their transitions, despite being challenging, as experiences to learn and draw strength from. Having this positive attitude was harder for those lacking social support, with chaotic lives and multiple needs.

In addition to people's situations in these four areas, **flexible and understanding guidance and support from service providers** could provide assistance during a transition and was especially valuable to more vulnerable transition-makers lacking financial resources and social support.

7.4 Preparing for transitions

Preparing for transitions can help minimise their destabilising consequences, but those we spoke to had very different opportunities to prepare for the changes ahead. Young disabled people, for example, who we spoke to about their experiences of leaving education, benefited from tightly managed and formalised plans. These 'transition plans' guide and assist the person through change, ensuring that their basic needs are met and aiming to help them develop and achieve their ambitions.

This level of planning was unparalleled among other participants. Sometimes preparation was not possible as transitions were sudden or unexpected, such as bereavement or leaving an abusive relationship. For others, the transitions were foreseeable but few preparations were made.

The clearest example of where opportunities to prepare for a difficult transition were not taken was for those leaving prison. The day of leaving prison often involved a stressful struggle to meet a basic need for shelter. Several people we spoke to not met by anyone at the prison gate, immediately returning to rough sleeping, drug use and, all too often, offending. The weeks after release were often an extended struggle to secure an income, stable accommodation and ways of managing and overcoming addiction. Those who could rely on support from their family, in particular for accommodation, seemed to fare better. Those without such support seemed to be at heightened risk of reoffending and/or a return to drug and alcohol abuse.

Where possible, improving opportunities for transition-makers to plan and prepare for change would help minimise the risk of transitions leading to unsustainable or damaging outcomes. These opportunities are too often lost. It is important to recognise, however, that preparation and planning do not necessarily ensure good outcomes: in spite of careful planning and the minimisation of serious need, the care leavers and young disabled people we spoke to often lacked opportunities to find fulfilling activities and/or employment and failed to realise their aspirations in the longer term.

CHRIS'S STORY

Chris is 25 and has been in and out of prison four times in the last few years. They have all been short sentences, from a week to four months long. He went to prison the first time because it was the only way he could see of getting help. After falling out with his family, Chris had been sleeping rough, begging and stealing to fund his drug habit:

"I were on self destruct … I smashed a window, waited for the police to come, got arrested … I actually waited 'cos I wanted that much help."

Going to prison was daunting for Chris. He was not able to take advantage of the courses and workshops because he was serving short sentences. He was often ill due to drug withdrawal.

Chris has left prison four times now. He has not been able to rely on his family because of what he has done in the past and has not wanted to contact friends because that would mean he would definitely start drinking and taking drugs again. Leaving prison felt like "walking out of that gate back into the big bad world again". He had been told he would get help finding accommodation but this never materialised. The first few times he just went "back to square one" to the nearest off licence and drug dealer.

The last time Chris left prison was different because he knew what it would be like and where he might be able to go for help. Before he was released he had organised to return to a drug treatment centre that he'd been to in the past:

"This time, I knew I wasn't just walking out of them gates into the hell, as I call it. I knew I was going to be safe, I'm not gonna be on the streets, I'm not gonna be in the cold."

Chris has now begun a drug treatment plan and he is determined to stay off drugs and alcohol. Eventually he wants to get back in touch with his Mum, have his own flat, and find a job.

7.5 Relationships and support

People's friends and family were often pivotal in providing them with both practical and emotional support during transition, from food when people could not afford to buy it themselves, to somewhere to stay rent free or someone to cry with and rely on when other options had not worked. Family and friends, and in particular children, were also an important source of motivation for people, spurring them to get through hard times.

Jack (who has been out of prison for a year now) explained how tightly he has to budget his income and how important family help can be at the end of a week:

> *I'm struggling with money at the moment. Yeah, a big part of it goes on gas and electric, sometimes I'll struggle for food and stuff like that. If me Mum lends me something I can get food with that or if she can't afford to lend me anything then I'll just go to me Mam's and have a meal at her house.*

When people spoke about family support they were referring to a broad range of relationships, extending beyond traditional ideas of a 'nuclear family' to include extended family, surrogate and foster family and even close friends.

Social support did not only come from friends and family. People also relied on strangers who they met at the beginning of the transitions (through support groups, for example) who offered them non-judgemental support or empathy that other friends struggled to offer as people moved through transitions.

Social support, however, cannot be seen as a panacea for helping people through transitions. Importantly, some people simply did not have these networks to draw on, or had only small networks, sometimes of one older parent, that were not durable in the long term. A lack of social support was often a problem for very vulnerable people, including those who had spent time in prison or had mental health problems.

People sometimes actively distanced themselves from family or friends to escape reminders of traumatic experiences or to avoid returning to previous patterns of behaviour such as drinking or drug use. Alternatively, relationships had been undermined by past patterns of behaviour, like drug abuse, offending or staying with an abusive partner against the advice of others.

As well as relying on others during transitions, people were often in a position of being relied upon or needed by others. To fully understand the impact of transitions on people's needs, the lens of the individual is therefore insufficient. People often prioritised the needs of others over their own and faced trade offs. This was particularly the case for parents and those with caring responsibilities

JULIE'S STORY

Julie is 45. She owns her own house (with a mortgage) and lives with her two children who are 14 and 16. Eighteen months ago her husband of 16 years, Luis, died suddenly in a road accident.

Luis' death has been hard for Julie to adjust to. They had lots of plans about what they would do when the children left home and now Julie feels that everything has changed.

It has also been hard financially since Luis died. At the moment, Julie receives Widowed Parent's Allowance, but that will stop in two years. To make sure she can take care of her kids and keep paying the mortgage, Julie is retraining and taking a university degree. She is also working 20 hours a week at a local pre-school and taking care of both her children, the youngest of which has Asperger's Syndrome and needs a lot of support.

Julie has not relied much on her family and friends. Her own parents are both dead and she described her siblings as quite needy, so she doesn't want to rely on them. Luis' family live nearby, but they have not been supportive either.

Julie thinks she tends to look inwards when things are difficult anyway – she doesn not think it is sensible to rely too much on other people, because you might "get your fingers burnt". Julie has not wanted to see her friends much since Luis died. She explained:

"I've cut out most of my old friends – sounds awful really – because they don't understand what I'm going through. They can't have the empathy that I need."

At the moment, Julie is focusing on looking after her children and giving them a good start in life. After that, she can start to think about what she wants to do with her life. Having the kids to look after gives her "a reason to get up in the morning." Without them, she does not know how she would have coped.

7.6 House and home

Having a decent and stable housing situation was an important factor enabling people to negotiate transitions successfully. The people we spoke to were in very different housing situations and these played an important role in their experiences of transition. Transitions themselves often destabilised people's accommodation, especially for those spending time in prison, leaving abusive relationships or whose transition involved a dramatic reduction in income.

People's housing situation was an important resource during transitions on two different levels: it provided transition-makers with basic shelter, a necessary condition for being able to manage a transition well. Furthermore, a person's home was invariably the site from which they accessed other basic resources that are practical requirements during transitions, such as a phone line.

Those who owned their homes or had tenancies with housing associations tended to have the most stable accommodation, although worries about paying the mortgage sometimes made owning a home stressful. Those in serious housing need clearly had the hardest time negotiating transitions and many of those we spoke to had spent time sleeping rough, staying in refuges or homeless shelters or temporarily with friends and family. Others had experiences of living in small cramped accommodation, in areas they did not like, away from their friends or family or where they were being harassed by other local residents. These type of experiences overshadowed their lives and compromised the extent to which people could negotiate transitions successfully.

7.7 Income and work

As we have seen, employment provides people with a means to earn an income and buy the things they need. Crucially, it also provides routine and a sense of identity and purpose. Transitions, however, often destabilised people's attachment to the labour market, which is reflected in the fact that only a minority of those we spoke to were in employment at the time of interview. Maintaining employment and managing mental health problems and/or grief were particularly challenging for some.

Those we spoke to who maintained employment through transition tended to be in professional or managerial jobs. Transitions disrupted the employment of those in routine, intermediate or manual occupations far more, suggesting that broader social inequalities may be reflected in people's experience of transition.

Many of those who took part in this study were out of work before, during and after their transitions. This was often connected to longer histories of vulnerability, involving disability, mental health problems, drug abuse or low educational attainment. Some of these transition-makers were desperately seeking work, but facing barriers due to long-term unemployment, a lack of confidence and a lack of options relating to educational attainment or conditions in the labour market. This group were clearly missing out on the foundations that employment provided in other people's lives.

Another group were not in work due their serious needs in other areas. Finding employment was not a priority for Chris, for example, as he struggled to move on from a pattern of offending, being in prison and accessing drug treatment. Chris needs a foundation of an adequate income, stable accommodation and a positive environment before he can manage to start working.

ROB'S STORY

Rob is 36. He is married, but doesn't have any children. He and his wife would like to have a baby, but since being made redundant several months ago, Rob is relieved not to have the responsibility of taking care of children.

Rob is an active person and has found it frustrating not having work to do. He wants to get back to work as soon as possible so he can make himself useful, rather than being a "deadweight, waste of space" which is how he feels at the moment.

The process of applying for jobs has been hard for Rob. Receiving letters saying that he hasn't got jobs is getting depressing. Rob is dyslexic and finds it hard to fill in lots of application forms. He has also found going to the Job Centre a difficult experience, because he hasn't received as much help as he would have liked and does not feel that the advisers there really care about his situation. He doesn't see the point of having to go if you just sign on and then leave.

Rob has also found it difficult because most jobs are looking for people with qualifications. Although he has 15 years of experience, Rob has no qualifications. He has got to go back to college to get his Maths and English GCSEs but is putting it off because he finds the idea of going back to the classroom a bit frightening.

Rob has a supportive family. His Mum, Dad and Nan have tried to keep him motivated to apply for more jobs and also helped them out by giving them food parcels and cooking them meals. He has relied most on his ex-colleagues, who were also made redundant when the store they worked in shut down. He has found their support helpful.

7.8 Attitudes to transition

All of those we spoke to had been through challenging transitions. Many expressed a sense of pride in how they dealt with their experiences and felt positive about what they had learned or how they had changed. They expressed a strong sense of ownership over their experiences of transition, explaining how they had grown stronger and had now had a different outlook on the world.

EVA'S STORY

Eva is 33. She lives alone and works as a manager in a graphic design company. Eight months ago, her boyfriend (with whom she was having a long distance relationship) was murdered. Eva was badly affected by his death and took a month off work to try and come to terms with it. Her employers were very understanding about her being away and coming back when she was ready.

Eva went to bereavement counselling which she found extremely helpful. She also thinks that the she's coped well because of her attitude and outlook:

"I'm just naturally positive. I think it's because I've been through a lot in my life. I think the more you've been through the more you know that you're going to be ok."

Eva thinks that her background, spirituality and her relationship with her mother have helped her cope too. Both her parents are Chinese but live in Spain. Eva believes she inherited her spirituality from her parents which has helped her:

"I have some eastern philosophies that are very positive. Sometimes people when they suffer bereavement, they can't see the light ahead, whereas with me, I think I was able to realise how, and eastern philosophy teaches you, that you are part of a very big thing and you are a very small part of it, and everything is as you wish it to be and if you want to get better you will get better."

There were also contrasting experiences, with people finding it much more challenging to interpret things positively or to see how they had learnt or grown because of them. This was sometimes because the experience of transition had profoundly challenged their sense of who they were. This was the case for several of those who were made redundant. For others, framing their experiences in a positive way was impossible, as their needs were so immediate and their lives so chaotic. Furthermore, for this group, the past did not offer examples of predictable or manageable experiences, which sometimes led to despondency and a focus on short-term needs and priorities: life was about 'getting through' not 'moving on'.

It was clear from the people we spoke to that having stability (a decent home and stable job etc.) and people to talk to made it easier for people to narrate and frame their experiences in a positive way, suggesting that this factor relates to other measures of advantage, once again underlining the significance of anchors through change and social support in negotiating transitions.

7.9 The role of services

This case study does not offer an evaluation of services available to transition makers, but it does shed some light on the kinds of service that helped people most. Those who took part clearly found services most useful when the culture of provision recognised the importance of the human interaction involved in delivering services, practical support and advice. Services that made people feel that someone cared, that professionals had a stake in their success and offered guidance and flexible support were spoken of most highly and often inspired people to want to 'give something back' and help others in the future when they'd dealt with their own situation.

These services were contrasted with others that made people feel controlled, judged or castigated and that were more concerned that people met statutory requirements and behavioural conditions, and that often did not acknowledge or fit with the stresses (often emotional and psychological) that people were facing at particular stages of their transition. These kinds of services risked alienating service users who felt that this support could be rigid and stigmatising. Unemployed people and those who had left prison most often felt like this, and were constantly worried about their benefits being sanctioned or going back to jail if they missed or were late for an appointment.

Another barrier to engaging with or making the most out of services was how people's needs were defined and prioritised. For some, this process was open and collaborative. Others, however, seemed to have the perspectives and priorities of service providers forced upon them.

Conclusions

Transitions are a crucial lens for organisations across the statutory and third sector seeking to understand, prevent and address unmet needs. Because they involve shifts in how a person's needs are met, they are a time of vulnerability and exposure to risk, as the stories in this chapter have shown.

The message of this case study is that there are a few basic foundations that can make people's experiences of transitions much easier. Having a stable home, an adequate income, supportive relationships and a positive and optimistic attitude can provide the stability and resources people need to deal with big changes in their life. Furthermore, when transitions can be foreseen, preparation can help ease the process of change and minimise destabilising effects. Support and advice from a whole host of organisations can also buffer people from the worst impacts of transition, especially when their approach is non-judgemental, flexible and responsive to that person's needs.

Not everyone benefits from these foundations, however, and in these circumstances transitions can be chaotic, stressful and become extended periods of struggle and adversity. This was particularly the case for those we spoke to who had left prison, left abusive relationships and had mental health problems. These experiences were often connected to having small or brittle networks of social support, limited opportunities to work and a low income.

The stories also suggest that younger people, especially those from disadvantaged backgrounds, might struggle to deal with transitions more than others: they are more likely to be homeless, staying with friends or family or living in private rented housing. They are likely to be just starting out in the world of work and may not have been through experiences in the past that have shown them the tricks of dealing with challenging situations well. In other words, the foundations required to make a successful transition may not have developed enough for some young people. Helping ensure that young people make these first and seminal transitions successfully may provide them with the resources to cope with other challenges in later life.

8 Mapping Needs in London

8.1 Introduction

London is one of the wealthiest cities in the world, which has seen rapid economic growth in recent years. Yet it is characterised by stark inequalities, containing some of the richest and poorest parts of the country, often very close together. The capital is a vast, complex city whose needs are as varied as its people. But there are some striking common patterns, distinct from other cities in the UK and distinct from the UK as a whole.

More than any other city in the UK, and perhaps even in Europe, London has become a city for the mobile – the average Londoner moves house every four years. It provides economic opportunities on a large scale, for everyone from city financiers to the people who clean their offices. Even the undocumented migrants working in insecure jobs, and constantly worried about being caught by the authorities, mostly want to stay and can earn more cash here than at home. And although the recession is markedly reducing London's attractiveness, it is unlikely to be hit as hard as other parts of the country. Its economy is more broadly based than is often assumed, and potentially more resilient.

The people who are losing out most are now the immobile and the stuck. Our analysis shows that 16% of Londoners – about a million people – are living in material poverty and are unhappy with their lives. These are predominantly the elderly, sick and disabled, and lone parents. They are the people who are living in the middle of a great world city but are afraid to go out, or lack the resources to make anything of the city. They feel stuck, bypassed by the world, ignored and forgotten. Many are not good at asking for help and their social networks are small. Many were born and brought up in London, but have seen their traditional sources of support disappear.

By contrast, many of the recent arrivals in London are also poor and insecure, but are plugged in to dynamic social networks (albeit often small) and dynamic cultures. The extraordinary flourishing of churches, temples and mosques, community groups and centres across the poorer parts of London has been accompanied by a growth of the arts, music and dance. These are all examples of communities meeting their own needs. London as a city is welcoming economically but not so welcoming socially. Yet many have created their own social support structures that enable them to cope and get by.

The implications for London are profound. The people most missing out are often invisible – poor at articulating their needs or accessing the networks that link into funding. They are in many ways the groups who are always most at risk in big cities – the elderly and the sick – but they are suffering even more as the very dynamism of London corrodes the communities around them.

We explore traditional and emerging needs in London and compare the unmet social needs of people living in London with the rest of the country. Some of the key questions we explore are: what makes London different? What are the specific needs facing those living in London? What and how can we learn about those at the very bottom and off register? What measurement tools can be used to understand those at the very bottom?

8.2 London's population: diversity and churn

As we have seen, certain groups of people in modern Britain are more vulnerable to their needs remaining unmet. Thus the characteristics of an area's population are key to understanding its needs.

London is a city characterised by its hyper-diversity. It is the most ethnically diverse city in the UK: in some boroughs, such as Newham, the proportion of the population from minority ethnic groups exceeds 50%. More than 300 languages are spoken by London's schoolchildren.[151] There are 34 communities of foreign nationals in London with more than 10,000 members, and a further 20 communities with more than 5,000 members.[152] According to the DfES, in 2004 English was a second language for 50.3% of London's school pupils.[153] Immigration has already changed and is likely to continue to change the city culturally, economically and spatially in significant ways.

Figure 55: Ethnic population projections in London

	2006		2011		
	Count	%	Estimate	%	Change
White	5,115,200	67.9%	5,105,400	65.3%	-2.5%
Black Caribbean	362,200	4.8%	375,600	4.8%	0.0%
Black African	453,400	6.0%	512,100	6.6%	0.5%
Black Other	189,400	2.5%	208,600	2.7%	0.2%
Indian	498,500	6.6%	547,700	7.0%	0.4%
Pakistani	167,800	2.2%	189,700	2.4%	0.2%
Bangladeshi	176,400	2.3%	204,200	2.6%	0.3%
Chinese	101,000	1.3%	117,000	1.5%	0.2%
Other Asian	228,300	3.0%	255,900	3.3%	0.2%
Other	246,100	3.3%	300,200	3.8%	0.6%
Total Population	7,538,400	100.0%	7,816,400	100.0%	0.0%

Source: Greater London Authority 2005 Round Interim Ethnic Projections - Sc8.07

London's population is growing and also changing in composition. The capital's population will continue to be younger than elsewhere in the UK. Those who move to London tend to be young adults, such as students or those in their first jobs, while those moving out of London tend to be older, including many families with young children.[154]

London experiences three main types of mobility: international mobility, including families migrating to London from other countries for varying periods of time; migration between London and the rest of the UK; and (cross-border) migration between London boroughs. These forms of mobility have a significant impact on the structure of London's population.[155]

So the city's population is younger, more diverse and more transient than elsewhere in the UK. However, rapid movement threatens the validity of statistics, particularly where census data serves as the foundation. For example, the London Boroughs of Brent and Ealing have carried out research that suggests that there is census undercount in their boroughs of 2,000 and 3,300 respectively. East London and City Health Authority estimates that the area's population is 30-40,000 more than official figures. Across London this would suggest the under-estimation of the population may exceed 1%, or upwards of 100,000 people.[156]

The difficulties in data collection in London are not limited to the population census. As with some needs on a national level, data is not collected or is patchy for a number of vulnerable groups (including sex traffic victims, runaways, those working in the informal economy, etc.). Nevertheless, we have collected estimated figures for some of the more vulnerable groups in London's population in the table below:

Figure 56: Vulnerable groups in London

Vulnerable group	No of individuals (Estimate / Service data)	Year	Source
Undocumented refugee and asylum seekers	442,000	2008	LSE/GLA Economics
Adult Numeracy entry level 1 or below (16-65)	302,785	2003	DCSF
Adult Literacy entry level 1 or below (16-65) KS1 5-7years	222,800	2003	DCSF
DDA disabled	171,400	2005-08	Labour Force Survey
Referrals of children to social services (U18)	89,770	2007-08	DCSF
Problematic drug users	74,000	2004-05	GLA
Dementia	63,919	2007	Alzheimer's Research
Ex offenders under probation service	42,700	2007-08	Ministry Of Justice
Youth crimes dealt with by YOTs	28,623	2002-03	Youth Justice Board
People accessing secondary mental health services	214,925	2007-08	MHMDS: Mental Health Minimum Dataset NHS

People squatting involuntarily	8,000	2004	National Policy Institute
Prisoners 21+	6,284	2009	Ministry of Justice
Rough sleepers	3,000	2007-08	St.Mungo's
Looked after unaccompanied RAS children	2,000	2006	DCSF
Permanent exclusions	1,170	2006-07	DCSF
Prisoners under 21	950	2009	Ministry of Justice
Imminent risk of eviction	700	2004	National Policy Institute

Undocumented refugees and asylum seekers were the greatest estimated sub-population, with 442,000 thought to be in London. Adults with poor literacy comprise the second most common vulnerable group we could gather statistics on (302,000); a similar figure for numeracy was recorded (222,800). The number of people accessing mental health services in London is also high (214,925). Some of these groups will inevitably overlap to a greater or lesser extent, increasing vulnerability.

8.3 Indicators of unmet need: What needs are more prevalent in London?

Due to the nature and make up of London's population, certain vulnerable groups are more prevalent in the capital than elsewhere in the country, and statistics indicate that some unmet needs are more pronounced in London. The diagram shows the figures for London (green dots) as a multiplier of the national comparator (dashed circle – here anything above 1 shows a higher rate for London).

When drawing comparisons between London and national figures, the most prominent disparity was recorded for overcrowded households, followed by adults lacking basic literacy and people from low-income households (especially children). Violent crime and unemployment were also all above the national comparator. The level of poor psychological wellbeing in London was similar to the rest of the UK but the rate of people accessing mental health services was higher. There are slightly fewer children with low GCSEs than nationally. It should be noted that other metropolitan areas are also likely to have higher rates compared to national figures when examining the indicators above, but the widely available aggregated regional figures often mask this.

Figure 57 Comparing London rates* to the national average (comparative area in brackets)

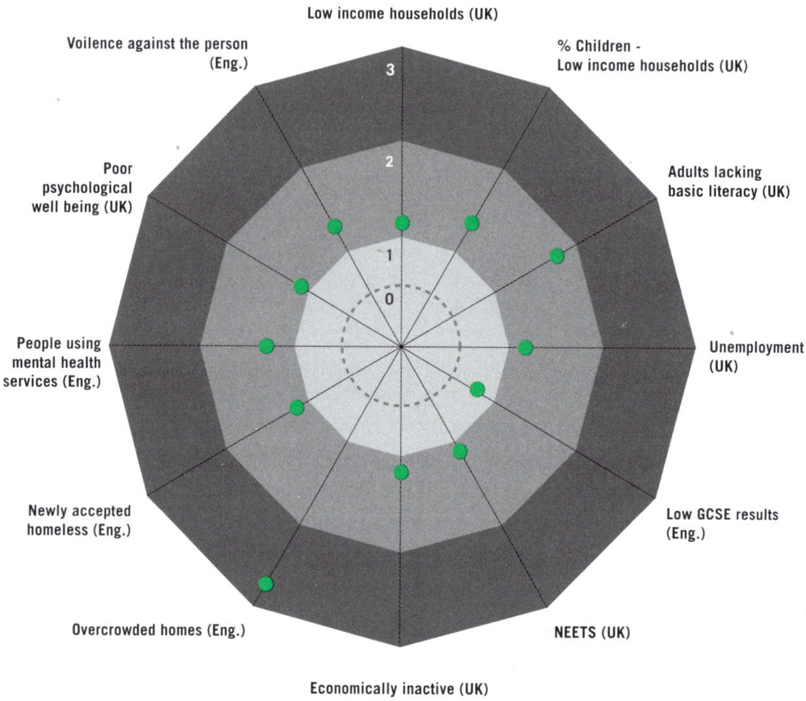

8.4 Poverty & inequality – the need for a sufficient income and status

In 2005, London ranked sixth in the league table of the world's richest cities.[157] London has a far more polarised distribution of income than other regions of Great Britain, with the nation's top earners working alongside large numbers of workers earning extremely low wages. London's population diverges from the overall pattern in the UK; high earners and those on low incomes are over-represented and middle earners are statistically underrepresented in London.

At the poorer end of the spectrum, GLA statistics show that during 2007, over two million Londoners were in income poverty, equating to 27% of the population. The equivalent UK figure was lower at 22%.[158] Migrants make up a disproportionate number of London's low paid workers and as many as 46% of all of London's

* Rates and percentages were collected for the London region and divided by the equivalent figures for the available national data (sometimes only figures for England were available). The collected statistics relate to years between 2003 and 2008.

'elementary' jobs (labourers, postal workers, catering staff and cleaners) are filled by migrants. People from Sub-Saharan Africa, Latin America, Eastern Europe and South Asia often find it especially hard to secure well-paid work, even if arriving in the UK with good skills and qualifications. Many have experienced de-skilling and downward social mobility on entering the British labour market. A significant proportion of working age migrants who currently live and work in London but were born in Ghana (50.3%), Ecuador (59.5%), Serbia and Montenegro (45.6%) and Bangladesh (45.2%) are found in the lowest paid occupational groupings. This includes jobs in personal services, sales and customer services, processing and plant operatives, and elementary occupations.

One of the areas where inequalities are most acute is child poverty. Although rates have fallen across the country since 1997, the level of child poverty remains high in London.* London has a higher number of children in income poverty compared to the rest of the country. During 2004-07, two out of five children (41%) in London lived below the poverty line after accounting for housing costs. Inner London has very high rates of child poverty – nearly half of all children live in poverty (48%).[159] The four areas with the largest proportion of children from families on benefits are Tower Hamlets (49%), Islington (46%), Newham and Hackney (both 41%).

Furthermore, London has the highest percentage of all regions of children living in workless households, at 27%. Rates are exceptionally high in Inner London, where around one third (32%) of all children live in workless households. While the rate is lower in Outer London (21%), nevertheless it is still well above the rate in the rest of the UK (15%). Children from certain ethnic groups face a very high risk of living in workless households;[160] the 2001 Census found that 40% of Bangladeshi children in London lived in workless households, and Black children also faced very high levels of household worklessness, above 30%. The rates were lowest for Indian (11%) and White British children (20%). Children in Inner London face the highest risk of being materially deprived, with nearly one-third of children experiencing material deprivation, double the national rate.[161] However, in line with national trends, London rates did show some improvement over the period 1996 to 2001, falling from 27% to 25%, although there has been no significant improvement since. The high rates of child poverty in London are mainly due to adult unemployment and economic inactivity.[162]

* This remains the case whether one adopts the 'official' poverty line of 60% of median income or uses the 50% or 70% measures. Trend data over the last twelve years show that national improvements in child poverty rates have not been evident in London, where rates remain high.

8.5 Housing and overcrowding – the need for a decent home

London has the highest number of rough sleepers in the country – official counts suggest a total of 248 rough sleepers on London streets on any one night, that is, roughly half of the national total.[163] Over the course of a year outreach teams contact almost 3,000 people sleeping rough in the capital – approximately half of whom are newcomers to the capital's streets. People end up on the street for a range of reasons such as poverty, debt, unemployment, family breakdown or health issues. As we have seen for some already vulnerable groups, transitions such as leaving care, prison or hospital, can be trigger points that lead to rough sleeping. Among rough sleepers 45% have alcohol, drugs or mental health problems, and 40% have been in prison, 12% in care and 7% in the armed forces.[164] Migration is also a significant factor affecting homelessness in London, where up to 20% of rough sleepers are A10 nationals (from the 8 EU accession countries plus Malta and Cyprus).[165 166]

In addition to having a disproportionate number of people who do not meet their essential need for shelter, London is also disproportionately bad at providing decent homes. The development of the London economy has put pressures on the London housing market. Over 37% of London's local authority homes do not yet meet the Decent Homes Standard; the proportion of unfit homes is particularly high in some inner London boroughs. The impacts of poor quality housing are often exacerbated by fuel poverty, the inability of a household to keep their home warm at acceptable cost; approximately 360,000 London households were affected by fuel poverty in 2007.[167]

In 2004 - 2007 there were estimated to be just over 200,000 overcrowded households in London, almost half of them in social housing. However, in recent years the most striking change has been a sharp rise in overcrowding in the private rented sector (from 7% of households in 2000-03 to 11% in 2004-07). Black and minority ethnic households are disproportionately likely to be overcrowded, even when family size is taken into account.[168] The numbers both in essential need of shelter and in relative need of decent housing are likely to get worse in the context of the current economic climate.

Overcrowding, living in temporary accommodation and sharing amenities for cooking, food storage and washing are all associated with stress and depression. Homeless children are three or four times more likely to have mental health problems than other children. They are also at greater risk of having behavioural problems, such as aggression, hyperactivity and impulsive behaviour, that can harm their progress at school. The high cost of housing, combined with the shortage of affordable housing, also presents challenges in attracting and retaining teachers and public service workers in London and is an increasing source of concern.[169]

8.6 Unemployment, worklessness and inactivity

Despite being one of the primary drivers of the UK economy, London has higher unemployment than the UK average. Greater London has more unemployment than Scotland and Northern Ireland together, and the unemployment rate in Inner London is twice the national average. London also has much higher levels of very long-term unemployment than the rest of the UK, concentrated in the 18-24 and over-50 age groups.[170]

As with so many of our indicators, need is unequally distributed through the population. The Labour Force Survey (LFS) shows that people whose first language is not English have relatively low employment rates at 52%, compared with 74% for those whose first language is English. In 2006, the employment rate for Black and Minority Ethnic (BME) Londoners averaged 58%, far lower than the rate for White Londoners (75%). Within the BME population, there is considerable variation in employment rates by ethnic group. During 2004-06, the employment rate ranged from 39% for Bangladeshi Londoners to 69% for Indian Londoners. Within the Black population, the employment rate for Black African Londoners (54%) was significantly lower than the employment rate for Black Caribbean Londoners (65%).[171]

London has the highest female unemployment rate in the country: 7.3% compared to 6.6% in the North East and 5.1% in the country as a whole. Of the mothers that are not in work in London, 25% have never worked – this is the highest percentage in Britain, and reflects cultural preferences in some BME groups, to some extent. Fifteen per cent of mothers have never worked in the country as a whole.[172]

8.7 Low skills and poor educational attainment

London has distinctive labour market demand and supply characteristics, including levels of skills and educational attainment. There are 1.25 million people aged 16-74 in London without qualifications, which is equivalent to 24% of the population.[173] London is also distinctive in terms of the occupational and industrial structure of its employment, with a large service economy, the greatest concentration of jobs in higher level occupations and a greater proportion of employment in managerial, professional and associate professional occupations than in any other region. The picture is one of increasing polarisation in skills demand and supply.[174]

An 'east–west divide' is apparent on many skills indicators, with east London displaying a greater prevalence of poor skills than west London. Whereas jobs demanding higher level skills are open only to people with such skills, jobs requiring low skill levels are open not only to people with low skills but also to people with higher level skills if they are willing to 'bump down' in the labour market to fill them. This means that in terms of absolute numbers of jobs those with poor skills have a smaller pool of jobs available.[175]

The number of young people not in education, employment or training (NEETs) in London has risen to 12,090, or 5.8% of 16- to 18-year-olds in March 2009.[176] The London Borough of Barking and Dagenham has the highest concentration of NEETs in the country – one in four young people. London's record on educational attainment for poorer children is promising, with London outpacing the rest of the country,[177] but there are still big challenges. NEET status stands in the way of individuals and society achieving optimum productivity, social inclusion and good health. It may also perpetuate a worklessness culture that can be passed on to future generations and result in NEET status being reinforced in families and communities across generations, affecting young people's aspirations and life chances.

The improvements at primary school erode when children move into secondary school and for those children who are failing the prospects are bleak. It is now widely recognised that the UK has a problem with the transition from primary to secondary school. Many young people, especially those in transition periods, experience a lack of self-identity and the soft skills associated with having self-confidence. Low self-esteem can lead to low expectations and aspirations. In London, 18% of all families with children have no academic qualifications, compared to 15% in Great Britain. 32% of those in London living below the poverty line have no qualifications.[178] Conversely, however, 33% of all families in London include someone who has a first degree or higher qualification, the highest for any region in the country – for Britain as a whole it is 21%.

There is a clear and predictable difference in the attainment of pupils from the poorest and the wealthiest areas, and there are also differences in the attainment of pupils in the groups in between. Pupils living in 'intermediate' income areas, which would not necessarily be classified as either poor or wealthy, are less likely than young people from more affluent areas to achieve nationally expected levels of attainment at key stage 2 and in public examinations.[179]

Educational underachievement is not confined to children living in poverty. While poverty as measured by eligibility for free school meals (FSM), is associated with low attainment in all ethnic groups, the impact is not the same across those groups. Nine out of ten Chinese pupils and four out of five Indian pupils entitled to FSM nonetheless achieved one or more higher-grade pass at GCSE or equivalent in 2006. By contrast, approximately half of White British pupils entitled to FSM did not achieve any GCSE passes higher than a grade 'D' in that year.[180]

8.8 Health needs

London is a city with profound health inequalities; the most deprived communities have life expectancies eight years lower than those in more affluent areas. This is starkly reflected in the illustration below, which shows that life expectancy declines by one year for each underground station you pass through as you head east from Westminster to Canning Town in East London. There is a clear relationship between income inequality and health inequality. People who earn lower incomes have shorter average life expectancy and higher levels of mental and physical illness or impairment than those who earn higher incomes.

Travelling east from Westminster, each stop represents nearly one year of life expectancy lost →

Electoral wards just a few miles apart geographically have life expectancy spans varying by years. For instance, there are eight stops beteen Westminster and Canning Town on the Jubilee Line – so as one travels east, each stop on average, marks nearly a year of shortened lifespan.

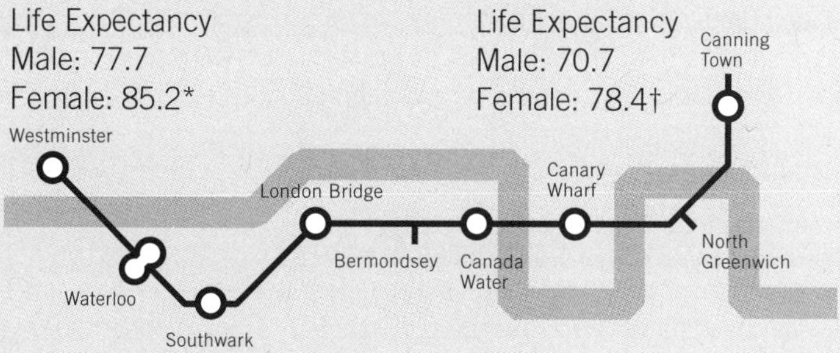

London Underground Jubilee Line

*Life Expectancy Westminster Male: 77.7 - (CI 45.5 - 79.9), Female: 85.2 - (CI 82.2 - 88.2).
† Life Expectancy Canning Town Male: 70.7 - (CI 69.0 - 72.5), Female: 78.4 - (CI 76.7 - 80.2)

Source: London Health Commission (2007)[181]

Between 1991-93 and 2005-07 London saw the highest increase in life expectancy at birth of all UK regions. Male life expectancy rose by 4.6 years to 77.9 years in 2005-07 and for females it increased by 3.1 years to 82.4 years. However, the difference between the borough with the highest life expectancy and that with the lowest life expectancy in London continues to increase and stood at 8.8 years for males and 8.0 years for females.[182]

At 5.1 infant deaths per 1,000 live births, London is close to the overall England rate. However, there are wide inequalities in infant mortality between London boroughs.[183] Boroughs with high levels of deprivation such as Southwark, Newham and Haringey have infant mortality rates of almost double those in the richer boroughs of Wandsworth, Richmond and Kensington and Chelsea.[184]

As with the rest of the UK, cardiovascular diseases and cancers are responsible for the most deaths in London. However, in addition to these 'big killers', London's population faces its own set of specific health challenges. The prevalence of infectious diseases such as TB and HIV is especially high in London. London accounts for approximately 40% of TB cases in the UK and 57% of England's known cases of HIV. New diagnoses of HIV in England remain highest in London: in 2005, 42% of all new HIV diagnoses were from the London area, including 319 among 16 to 24-year-olds.[185]

Other health challenges include obesity. In 2003, London had the highest percentage of obese children aged 2 to 15 years of all the English regions and significantly lower levels of physical activity among children and young people than the England average. Poor diet causes ill health and shortens life expectancy. Variations in access to healthy food link directly to health inequalities across the capital. In some parts of London, people struggle to access affordable nutritious food. There are concerns that the issue of food access may be more pronounced: thirteen wards across three London boroughs have been identified as 'food deserts' - areas where there is no provision of healthy food. In Newham more than two-thirds of residents live more than 500 metres from the nearest shop selling fresh fruit and vegetables.[187]

Compared to elsewhere in the country, London residents are less likely to use a GP and more likely to use accident and emergency services.[188] In London, unequal experiences of ill health are compounded by inequalities in access to services. Levels of funding and service provision vary across London boroughs and Primary Care Trusts. An inverse relationship exists between local health needs and resource distribution, with the proportion of GPs per 1000 population (weighted for age and need) significantly lower in the more deprived areas of north and east London.[189]

Many communities report that when they try to access public services they experience a range of physical, practical, or attitudinal barriers. Some services are of poor quality and do not meet the specific needs of London's diverse communities. This is a particular issue in relation to the provision of more personal services, such as health and social care, where sensitivity to cultural issues and individual needs are critical if services are to be acceptable and effective. The lack of timely access to language support is a significant barrier for people who do not have English as a first or preferred language, including British Sign Language (BSL) users. Difficulties in arranging for appropriate support such as interpreters or advocates can lead to lengthy delays in care, with consequent negative effects on outcomes. Lesbian, gay, bisexual and transgender people and deaf and disabled people have reported negative experiences of health and social services. Thus many of the Londoners who are most vulnerable, and most in need of health or social care services, may be least likely to know how to access services and what their rights to them are.[190]

8.9 London's psychological needs

The data from the 2007-08 British Household Panel Survey London sample suggests that levels of overall poor psychological wellbeing (as measured by the GHQ) are the same in London as the rest of the UK. Levels were also similar when running the analysis by age and gender. The figures were also largely the same when examining proxy measures of some specific psychological needs: self-esteem, autonomy and relatedness. While there were some statistically significant distinctions in comparing London with the rest of the UK sample they were small (see diagram below).

Figure 58: Questions relating to specific psychological needs

	Proxy measure	Answer	London	UK (excluding London)
Self-esteem 'I am worthy'	Have you recently been thinking of yourself as a worthless person?	"Rather more / much more".	7.9%	7.9%
Autonomy 'I am in control'	We would like to know how often, if at all, you think this applies to you… Not in control of life?	"Often".	3.7%	5.0%
Relatedness 'I matter to others'	Is there anyone who you can really count on to comfort you when you are very upset?	"No, no-one".	4.6%	3.6%

Source: BHPS analysis 2007-08

While the levels of unmet psychological need of London's general population would appear to be similar to the rest of the UK, there is evidence that the capital has a greater number of people suffering from poor mental health, as we discuss in the following section.

8.10 Mental health

In terms of more severe mental illness, over 26,500 London residents were admitted to hospital for psychiatric treatment in 2003-04. This was significantly higher than the national average. London also has a considerably higher percentage of inpatients with psychotic disorders, at 23% of inpatients compared to a national average of 14%.[191]

London has higher rates of more common mental health problems and severe mental illness than the national average, according to needs indicators. The capital has high levels of homelessness and single person households, both of which are associated with higher levels of mental illness. Also, London has a large refugee population and self-reported mental health problems are around five times higher among refugees than in the general population.[192]

People with mental illness from minority ethnic communities in London face a number of particular challenges and barriers in accessing appropriate services. Some individuals are more likely than the average population to be treated in inpatient and forensic psychiatric services, and Black people are less likely to be offered 'talking therapies' than the white population. Individuals from minority ethnic groups can find mental health services difficult to access because of language problems or cultural issues. Less than half of mental health services provide information about themselves in other languages. One-third say they have difficulty getting translation services. Mental health services have far fewer connections with minority religious organisations than with Christian organisations. All have connections to Christian churches, while only 80% have connections to Islamic organisations and 55% have connections to Hindu organisations.[193]

Availability of psychological therapies is patchy both in primary and secondary care. Most providers believe that significant numbers of people who would benefit from these therapies do not gain access to them. The quality of facilities for women varies hugely in London, from very high quality women's crisis centres to wards that lack separate accommodation for women. Moves to address this are hampered by the need in some places to rebuild premises at significant capital cost. Unusually high nurse vacancy rates in London are, in some cases, resulting in 50% or more of staff budgets being spent on agency staffing. This particularly reflects shortages of inpatient psychiatric nurses, but London also had significantly higher vacancy rates for community psychiatric nurses than the rest of the country.[194]

8.11 Violent crime

London suffers from more violent crime than the national average. Metropolitan Police Service data shows there is clear overrepresentation of African-Caribbean and African-born male victims in cases of murder and serious violence. In 2007-08, Black African-Caribbean youths constituted 50% of London's GBH and murder victims, whereas white European youths constituted 29%. Further, young Black victims of GBH and murder increased by 23% between 2005 and 2008. This ethnic disproportion is most evident among teenage homicide victims. Of the 26 teenage murder victims in London in 2007, 22 were identified as being African-Caribbean. During 2008, 21 of 27 victims were of African-Caribbean background.[195]

The under-18 secure population for England and Wales was 3,019 in 2006-07. Nine per cent were in custody in London (259 young people), and 25% were from London (approximately 750 young people). The ethnic origin of the young people in custody in London comprised 39% Black, 29% white, 11% dual heritage, 6% Asian and 1% other minority ethnic groups (15% not recorded). Only 7% of the young people in custody in London were female.[196]

8.12 Drug use

Estimates suggest that there were 327,466 problematic drug users (PDUs) in England in 2004-05, of which 74,417 were resident in London. This was the highest number of PDUs in any region and is approximately 1% of London's population of 7.5 million people. Inner London boroughs (Islington, Hackney, Southwark, Camden, Lambeth, Tower Hamlets, Westminster, Kensington and Chelsea and Hammersmith and Fulham) account for nine out of the top eleven places with the highest rates of problematic drug use in England. In contrast, the outer London boroughs of Bexley and Richmond upon Thames have the sixth and the nineteenth lowest prevalence rates in England. The estimated prevalence of crack cocaine use is far higher in London than in any other region, at just under 10 crack cocaine users per 1,000 population. London also had the highest level of opiate use of any region, with around 11 opiate users per 1,000 population. In contrast, the prevalence of injecting drug use was lower in London at approximately three per 1,000 population, compared with a national average of just over four.[197]

Many previous studies have found that men are more likely to use drugs problematically than women. Recent Home Office research indicates that this gender difference is even more pronounced in London. The estimated rate of problematic drug use was approximately four times higher among men than among women in the capital city, compared with a ratio of three to one nationally. It appears that London has a lower rate of problematic drug use among the 25-34 year age group but higher rates among the 16-24 and 35-64 age groups. It is particularly noteworthy that the rate of problematic drug use among London's 35-64 year olds was more than twice as high as the national figure for the same age group.[198]

Qualitative interview findings

We now turn to the findings of qualitative interviews carried out for this case study. We explored the experiences of several socially excluded groups which our research indicated would be particularly vulnerable to unmet needs. We also conducted interviews with front line workers to explore their understanding and perspective of the unmet needs of those they were working with. Our interviews focused on the experiences of undocumented migrants (refugees, asylum seekers and failed asylum seekers), socially excluded young people (including those excluded from school and care leavers) and elderly people (including those with high support needs) around London.

Relative poverty, dissatisfaction with life, higher levels of depression, more fear of crime and anti-social behaviour and greater disposition to loneliness were all common among older respondents. London also has one of the highest concentration of undocumented migrants in the UK, and there were widespread multiple needs among those we spoke to. Legal barriers to employment and the lack of legal status was the single biggest problem for undocumented migrants, including asylum seekers, seeking to meet their material needs (appropriate shelter, food, clothing). Depression and mental health problems were common among those interviewed.

8.13 The experiences of undocumented migrants

The estimated numbers of refugees and asylum seekers who claimed UK asylum during 1991-2005 (cumulative) and who were living in London in 2005, including dependants, totalled up to half a million people, or 6-7% of the city's total resident population. This figure includes people with refugee status, or other positive decisions on their claim; those with asylum claims still pending in 2005; and rejected asylum seekers who have remained in London.

Our interviews with undocumented migrants uncovered a number of themes around the needs facing these individuals. We reached interviewees through organisations working closely with them to provide social, financial and emotional support. There is, not unexpectedly, great diversity among those who fall into the category of undocumented migrants, including their countries of origin and the factors that drove them to arrive in the UK. Some were trafficked, others left to flee persecution and war, and others arrived to work. Some arrived seeking asylum (and had been waiting for some years for decisions to be made on their claims), and others were refused but remained as failed asylum seekers.

The highly diverse nature of undocumented migrants and the circumstances they face helps to explain why understanding and meeting their needs is so complex. Many of the undocumented migrants to whom we spoke are managing to send money home to their children to go towards their education, showing a strong desire for a better life for their children. Almost all of the research participants wanted to stay in the country and wanted their status to be regularised.

Legal status

The single biggest issue facing this group was their lack of legal status, as it held them back from working, accessing the appropriate health and social care support and building stable lives for themselves and their children. There was a general feeling among those we interviewed that they were stuck in limbo, leaving them feeling vulnerable to abuse, helpless and lacking control of their lives and with little to look forward to in the future. One female interviewee, of Nigerian origin, discussed how her experiences were bound up with being vulnerable to exploitation and violence by traffickers:

> *I am not a lazy person. All I want is just peace. If I got my papers – that would give me peace. I don't want my children to pass through what I have passed through. I want them to go on and study. If we go back to Nigeria [the traffickers] will kill us. They are getting on well here ... These people they can do anything. I just want safety for my children.*

The same interviewee spoke of her experience of coming to the UK under the belief that she would be studying while also working as a nanny. She was given a false passport and forced to work as a prostitute by traffickers.

> *As soon as I got there they said I couldn't go to school. I had to go to the street ... and I was beaten and I was forced to go to the street and work ... I used to be so scared. I lost so much weight. I was hiding behind the window. I have been alone going through this for almost three years with my two children.*

Another striking theme from the interviewees was their frustration at their inability to work, earn a living and contribute. This was common among those who had been educated in their countries of origin and had been in jobs with considerable responsibility, but now found themselves completely disempowered because they were unable to work in the UK:

> *I really want to get status and then I want to work, to contribute, to benefit the society and the economy. I am not used to doing nothing and to be given hand outs. I used to be hard working and I want to be like that again. I want to work and to give back to the community. You might work but if you don't have status you don't feel free. You think the police will appear at any time.*

Many of the interviewees who were in receipt of vouchers spoke of their frustration at being able to purchase goods in only a small number of outlets. This affected their ability to purchase cheaper goods from markets or culturally appropriate clothing or the food of their country of origin. This heightened their awareness of their powerlessness to affect everyday matters such as what they could eat or wear.

Lack of access to services

Lack of access to health and other services was a major issue for this group, leading to both pressures and risks to the lives of the individuals as well as the service providers.

> *The exclusion of vulnerable groups from health care brings along major risks like individual suffering and exploitation, a risk for public health in general, demand for emergency services which are far more expensive, the creation of backstreet services ... Not being regular migrants means that they don't have a lot of rights to services or benefits ...The other big issue is health. We have had people who have come to us and said in the later stage of their pregnancies 'help, I am pregnant - I haven't gone to get any of my scans' and this is almost at the point of giving birth because that is when they feel it is safest to go. People fear they can't access health care or will be found out. They don't know whether they should register their children in this country or not.*
>
> — Interview with health service provider working with undocumented workers

Older refugees may be particularly affected by isolation, and suffer mental health problems, including depression. Barriers to the access of health services can be harder for older refugees, and include language barriers, particularly for older refugee women, lack of confidence in going out, and uncertainty about entitlements. This problem was identified in one of our interviews:

> *The government should make centres for older people and make sure that whoever speaks their language make them understand and make projects for older people who have got any experience, to make them not lose that experience ... They want to do voluntary work, they want to do other things for the community and give something back but the facilities are not there and this is the government's problem.*

Where do they turn to for support?

There was widespread dependence on informal support from friends, family and networks through churches and community centres. These were crucial in providing practical support (such as finding accommodation), and also financial and emotional support. Faith and religion was important to several interviewees and they highlighted the fact that church groups helped broaden their social networks. Those who arrive with a partner or family members or those who have an established social network do better than those who have few or no family or friends in the UK. As well as these informal social and family networks, the undocumented migrants we interviewed depended heavily on charitable and third sector organisations working in this field for signposting to appropriate help such as vouchers, clothes and other material support, as well as advice on accessing healthcare, counselling and other services.

NINA'S STORY

Nina came to London six years ago. She managed to get a student visa but she did not study for very long. She had trouble understanding the lessons and she got bored. Initially she came to London on her own, without her husband and her daughter but they joined her three and a half years later. She misses her home country but feels very glad that her family are here with her:

"Now that I have my daughter here I am much happier. When she wasn't here I had to work every hour of the day not to think about her. I feel much more at peace now. My daughter is happy here. At first she didn't want to come over but now she is happy – she has good teachers and lots of friends. Now she doesn't want to go back."

Despite her illegal status she has managed to find work but her jobs are tedious and she works very long hours:

"It is easier to make money and make ends meet here but I work much longer hours here, six days a week and usually 12 hours a day. To start with I used to clean offices in the morning and houses in the afternoon; then I would work in a restaurant every evening until 11. Now I work as a cleaner in an underground station and I still work at the restaurant on weekends."

Nina says she feels lucky that she has never had a bad experience but she would like to work less so that she could spend more time with her daughter:

"I would like to work fewer hours. I don't see my daughter enough. I leave at 6am and I come home at 11pm; I leave her sleeping and I come home when she is asleep."

Even though life as an undocumented migrant is often uncertain and insecure she would like to remain in London. She says that her faith and her family give her courage:

"I am always optimistic; I do not like negativity or negative people. I am happy here; I thank God that I am here. Nothing bad has ever happened to me in this country. I have met good people."

Fear

Another major theme that emerged from these interviews was fear – fear of being discovered without the appropriate legal documentation for being in the UK. Those with children were fearful for their children and the effects of their circumstances on their lives. One of the service providers we interviewed described how common it was for people to be forced to work long anti-social hours on very low wages, with wages often being withheld:

> *You hear cases of people not being paid at all, for a month to months and pay is withheld. Others are being told money is being deducted for tax purposes even though they have no papers. But where on earth is this 'tax' going'? There are also stories of withholding papers. There have also been some cases of physical abuse.*

Another undocumented migrant explained:

> *I do feel anxious and fearful about my illegal status. I worry that they will catch me or deport me, my husband or my daughter ... You have to keep the fact that you don't have documentation very quiet – people take advantage, feel more powerful than you – you can't stand up for yourself. My previous landlord didn't give us our deposit back for no reason at all – but he know we couldn't complain to anyone about it...*

Fear was prevalent both among male and female interviewees. However, in the case of female interviewees who were working illegally, they were particularly fearful of violence and abuse, with some pointing to their own experiences of violence or the threat of physical violence. One interviewee, Lara, spoke of her traumatic experience of being raped when she went to find accommodation.

LARA'S STORY:

Lara arrived in London in 2000 having left her home town in South America to get away from her abusive partner.

She has three children who she left in Ecuador; she did not have the money to bring them to the UK with her and they are now living with their grandparents. Overall, Lara's time in the UK has been very difficult and on many occasions she has been exploited due to her status as an undocumented migrant:

"I tried to get status as an asylum seeker ... I wanted to bring my children over here with me. I was told about a lawyer in Liverpool who could help me. I handed over my passport, all my documentation and quite a lot of money ... he turned out not to be a lawyer, just another crook. He left me with nothing."

She decided the best thing to do was to try and get on and work, which was difficult without papers, but eventually she found work as a cleaner:

"I work mainly for my children and my father. I send money home. One of my daughters is studying at university and she needs financial support. She wants to be a business woman. I have to support them; I am both a mother and a father for them … It is hard to make ends meet, but I get by. I am alone; no one else will help me."

A few months ago Lara went to view a room for rent in a block of flats and was sexually assaulted:

"There was a man showing me around and we were alone in the building … he forced himself on me … I didn't know what to do … I didn't call the police, I couldn't call them, I was too scared so I didn't do anything … I don't have legal status here so there was nothing for me to do … A few months went by and I was feeling so awful … I didn't know what was going on, so I went to hospital – it turned out that I was pregnant. No, no it cannot be, I said ... I tried to be strong … how? Why? It can't be."

She managed to gain contact with a charitable organisation who work with women refugees and asylum seekers which has since been giving her support and helping her to cope including by giving her access to a psychiatrist.

"I found out about this organisation in April 2008, after all of this had happened. They have helped me to survive. I have lost my confidence after everything that has happened to me … it was hard for me to come here ... I felt very … insecure … dirty … I couldn't look at people in the face – even the young women here ... They finally convinced me to see a psychologist here. She was great … but they wanted me to carry on coming regularly – I didn't want to, I didn't want to keep talking, crying, dwelling on the past. I wanted to get on with things and be strong."

Lara often feels lonely: "I have no family here – I am alone". But despite all that has happened Lara wants to remain in London:

"My dream is to be here legally – there would be more work for me, I could support my family properly and afford to go back home. I want to pay tax, I want to work hard, that's all immigrants want to do here … I am alive, at least I am alive. Ugly things have happened, but what can you do … I have three kids that still depend on me … I have to send money back to my father who is very ill … these are the things that I need to think about, that keep me going.

Trafficking and prostitution

Research conducted by the Poppy Project investigated on-street prostitution in 10 boroughs. The majority of the women are African Caribbean, British (both Black and white) or Irish. Substance misuse is a significant issue for women selling sex on the street. One hundred and eighty-two chat lines were identified, as well as sixty-six lap dancing clubs across 17 boroughs of London. Anecdotal evidence from women trafficked into the United Kingdom suggests links between prostitution and lap dancing.

The so-called 'iceberg phenomenon' is used in connection with descriptions of trafficking for sexual exploitation and the identification of trafficked people. According to this model, the tip of the iceberg, which represents the cases we know about, constitutes around 10% of the actual number of people trafficked. It can be assumed that the same is true for other forms of trafficking, although the percentage could possibly be even lower, given that enforcement and prosecution, as well as other attempts to identify victims, have so far mainly focused on trafficking for sexual exploitation.

Our research indicates that the children of undocumented migrants will often be isolated, marginalised and live in fear. The main sectors in which undocumented migrants work are construction, restaurant cleaning, care work and domestic work. The sectors associated with female undocumented workers are sex work, domestic work and cleaning. Undocumented migrant workers often do not speak English and are isolated from wider society. Generally, those we met were unaware of their rights under the law. The vulnerability of these migrants means they can be forced to work in conditions that are coercive.

> *Prostitution is an area that we as an organisation would like to find out a lot more about and work with women who find themselves forced into it. It is notoriously difficult to get to such women, especially women who have been trafficked. There is certainly a problem there amongst Latin American women. I have spoken with other organisations who work in this area and they have also found it difficult to contact Latin Americans in particular. We have had phone calls, especially from Brazilian women, who have been trafficked for sex work or they have married into relationships which have become abusive once they arrive. I have also come across Columbians and Bolivians who have been trafficked into domestic work.*
>
> — Interview with service provider

8.14 The experience of elderly people living in London

A significant number of London's older people are among the most vulnerable, suffering from social exclusion, poor quality housing and a lack of access to essential social support and facilities. Older people are more likely than other groups to be living in poverty and suffering the effects of low quality and inappropriate housing. There is a shortage of sheltered and specialised accommodation for older people and many have to wait for lengthy periods of time for an occupational therapy assessment for necessary home adaptations.

Most of the older people we interviewed did not portray London as a generally age-friendly city; they see it as big, impersonal and anonymous. The fragmentation or disappearance of traditional sources of support and social networks were common experiences.

Fear

The fear and isolation experienced by older people was one of the key findings of the research. Fear of the external environment and the contrast with the relative safety of their childhood were common themes expressed by those we talked to.

TOM'S STORY

Tom lives in sheltered accommodation in West London, built especially for older people. He is happy with the quality of accommodation but he, and many others who share the sheltered housing, live in fear of crime. There are no security staff, just cameras, and no staff at all after 6 o'clock. He says safety and security are big issues:

"There are many infirm people living on their own in one bedroom flats leaving their door open for their carer because they can't get up to open the door and that is how people go in. … They [thieves] pick on people on their own without families coming in – they pick on the vulnerable. People with family have lived here without having things stolen."

He feels London has changed compared to what it used to be and he thinks that his neighbourhood has changed on every level. Tom doesn't find his neighbours friendly and he puts it down to the increase in cars and traffic: "It's changed completely, absolutely completely. We used to play out in the street, y'know, but kids miss that now."

He feels that he is now in a minority of real Londoners: "It's not London anymore. There's not many of us left"

While fear of crime is widespread within the elderly community, it is not just a perception. Many of those we spoke to described their experiences of being victims of crime:

> *One sat down next to me on the bus. I'd got my bag like this [clutched across lap]. She got her hand underneath my bag and how she ever did it I'll never know ... I don't think you'd ever win they are so clever.*
>
> *They work two as a team ... A guy standing on my shoes, I can't move. I said excuse me I'm trying to get off the bus and, of course, by the time it was sorted out another guy behind me had my wallet, credit cards and everything.*

The public realm can also be a hostile place for many older Londoners. Poor public transport facilities and the lack of accessible public toilet provision were commonly mentioned as limiting mobility and acting as barriers to independence. The reduction of independence can lessen opportunities for leisure, physical activity, engagement with the community – thereby limiting the chance to maintain vital social networks.

Older people's safety and security is a very real concern, both at home and in public open spaces. This can lead to a loss of confidence and a reluctance to leave the home. As one interviewee put it bluntly, "older people don't want to go out at night." This can lead to a general deterioration in their health and wellbeing.

The physical environment in which people live has a strong bearing on their health. Poor quality housing, the way neighbourhoods are designed and the availability of open space affects their health and wellbeing both directly and indirectly.

Loneliness

Changes in older people's social networks and the local environment were often felt to be beyond people's control. This included relationships with families, friends and neighbours and changes in the community. One of the consequences of an increasingly transient population is that traditional sources of support – family, community and social networks – have been eroded. The absence of friends and neighbours was a cause of loneliness. One person said that without family, weekends were the worst part of the week:

> *Weekends are difficult for people if you don't have family to see...We all get a bit upset Friday night knowing Saturday and Sunday will be grim. [Have you any friends in this block?] None at all. I miss my old neighbours, yeah, definitely.*

Lack of intergenerational contact can often manifest itself among older generations as a fear of young people and of crime. Fear of young people gathering in public spaces is one of the key factors leading people to perceive there is much more crime than there actually is:

> *I wouldn't go out at night, definitely not, not unless I was with someone that I knew.*

In some cases poor housing contributed to loneliness, as one woman complained that the hospital would not discharge her husband back to their home because of poor housing conditions, so she was left alone while her lifetime companion remained in care:

> *I didn't have central heating in my flat so they wouldn't let my husband come back and I had to put him in a home.*

MARGARET'S STORY

Margaret is 80 years old and has lived in London all her life. She is disabled in one leg and the opposing arm. Margaret lives on her own. She used to have the support of a carer, but was unable to continue paying for their help. A local voluntary organisation sends someone around to help her wash, do chores and provide some transport. Since having a recent hip replacement Margaret has found it difficult to get around and it takes a lot of energy to make basic physical movements. When asked how she was finding things since her operation, she remarked:

"Not fine at all. I'm worse off now than I was before. I was in pain before with my hip but now I cannot get about whereas I could before. Now I have to keep sitting down to rest 'cos I get out of breath and it takes me a long time to do anything."

The most significant impact of the operation has been that she is no longer able to care for her husband at home and he has had to move into residential care. Despite Margaret's mobility problems, she is able to take a taxi to visit her husband once during the week and at weekends:

"I do look forward to seeing him but I find it a big effort. As much as I like it I get worn out ... feel very tired by the time I get up there."

Both of Margaret's children live in London. Her daughter lives nearby but she rarely sees her. She is, however, in good contact with her son, but he lives on the opposite side of the city. He tries his best to visit, but it's not always easy for him. When he does come, he helps with shopping and visits his dad in the care home. She doesn't have many friends living nearby and feels isolated:

"The ones across, that have moved in over there, they are these ... erh, Somalis are they? Whatever they are called. I don't see nothing of them, they are in and out ... I miss my old neighbours, yeah definitely ... Now people are not very friendly. All my old neighbours have died off. They have all gone and so now everyone that comes in are all foreign, it's not like your own comp ... it's not like what used to be there. Before you would stop and have a little chat but you don't get that now."

Support for older people

Declining health, particularly mobility, has a considerable effect on older people's lives and they draw on family, friends and formal services to cope. Health and social care often does not meet the needs of London's elderly population because of poor location and accessibility problems. While older people are entitled to free public transport, more specialist transport services, such as Dial-a-Ride, are a priority for older people in the capital. One interviewee commented, when asked if she saw her GP regularly:

> *No I don't much... You have problems getting through to them in the first place. You're standing such a long time waiting to be connected.*

The quality of London's environment, the accessibility of the public realm, and the provision of basic facilities such as accessible places to meet, public toilets and street furniture are often inadequate in meeting the needs of older Londoners. Many also feel that an increase in cars and traffic have made the streets less people-friendly.

Moving to a more suitable property had made a positive difference to a few people. However, the process can take time, and practical and emotional obstacles can put people off moving.

How people navigate the ageing process depends upon the resources that they have available when they enter later life and often relates to their past experiences.

8.15 The experience of excluded young people living in London

We interviewed young people from a range of backgrounds including those who had been in care since childhood and young people who had been excluded from schools. We asked them about their experiences of schooling and family life. Disaffection with education was predictably widespread. Most of those interviewed had regular absences from school, got into trouble with teachers, or played truant:

> *Before I got here, like the first day, I woke up, I thought, you know, I'm gonna get ready for beef. ['Beef?'] 'Fights'. 'Cause it's that a school yeah, everyone's got kicked out, innit. Bare fights. ['Bare?'] 'Lots'. And then everyone's like bare bless, innit, 'cause I'm the only person on my own, innit.*

Our findings from the transitions case study have already highlighted the difficulties experienced by some young people going through transition periods and the findings of the London case study resonate with this. The young people we spoke to experience a lack of self-identity and associated soft skills. Lack of confidence is a big obstacle for young people. Low self-esteem can lead to low expectations and aspirations.

Transitions from primary to secondary school, school to work and out of care are stages where serious problems emerge. Absence from school, while the numbers are relatively small, becomes a problem with potentially serious long-term consequences for individuals.

Lack of joined-up services:

There was much criticism of social workers' interactions with young people, combined with the observation that the system in London is thoroughly overstretched.

> *They see so many social workers, the system's completely overloaded... Some of them, I don't know why they're in the job, if they don't like it so much, others, they just have too much to do.*

SAMANTHA'S STORY

Samantha has been staying in a hostel for a couple of months. She doesn't like the way that young people are moved around between hostels and bed and breakfasts:

"It causes problems ... It's like a waiting game ... we don't know whether we are coming or going, and at college, we're just supposed to 'get on with it'."

She describes the hostel as being somewhere young people are 'parked': "It's a dumping ground". Moving on can be very difficult. She has seen people move out when they reach 18 who find it very difficult to manage money and fall into petty crime.

She thinks it is easier for boys to get work, especially part- time construction and labouring. For girls things are different: "All Connexions want to do is to send you to college to do courses". She says that young women find it harder to get work. It is mostly part time work, especially in retail, that is available and she thinks older women are seen as more trustworthy and mature. When it comes to getting a job, she comments, "it seems to be about who you know".

She says that for a lot of girls it is even questionable whether getting a job will make them better off. Many of her friends think that they won't get a flat without having a baby, suggesting that it is almost a logical decision or progression to get pregnant. "Seems like their only choice – they don't want to go to college, they can't get a job".

Support

When it comes to asking for help and support a lot of the young people we interviewed mentioned the limited number of people they want to turn to, due to past experiences. One worker in the hostel for care leavers in the hostel remarked that "these [young people] been let down too many times", so that "they put up a wall":

> *A lot of them aren't used to having care ... they have had problems in care in the past, and this past history colours the way they feel about being 'cared for', and sours relationships in new care settings. 'They're so fed up of being shifted about'. The hostel takes people from several different boroughs and this can cause tensions when some boroughs give their young people more money, through different systems.*

Some of the young people we talked to commented that when they encountered difficulties and problems they only had themselves to rely on. Others said they relied on their support workers and saw them as family members:

Say you could ring one of your friends and say, can you help me, and they could say, I'm busy, you gotta do your own thing. Deal with it yourself, innit.

JANE'S STORY

Jane has worked in a hostel for young people for 13 years. Many of the teenagers that she encounters have been in care since babyhood. She says there is definitely a stigma attached to being in care and that for most of the young people that she works with, long-term friendships and relationships are almost impossible to maintain. She says the hostel represents something of a 'last resort' for the young people who live there. Many of them end up in the hostel if they have been 'cancelled', i.e. asked to leave where they were staying before.

Jane's day can be very varied and she often finds herself playing many roles: "Everyday is different, no day is the same". When we visited the hostel, Jane was helping Martina, a resident of the hostel, negotiate looking after her money, persuading her to put £10 of her 'giro' into a named envelope so that she'd be able to pay back the money she owed someone. It would also mean that she had enough cash to get a bus to see her baby son who is in care.

Jane tells us that Martina spends all her money on weed and this is the reason she is in debt. Martina frequently runs out of money both to eat and to get the bus, so she frequently walks several kilometres to see her son.

The hostel and youth centre (a pupil referral unit) we visited were dilapidated, dirty and in a state of disrepair. Conditions were cramped and uncomfortable. Young people were visibly aggravated by these conditions and it further reinforced their feelings of being forgotten about and ignored. When asked what could be improved one respondent commented:

[laughter] I know they put money in like youth centres and that. No one really goes – people go, but I don't. It depends what activities they got yeah. People still leave it with the little kids one, people, like over the age of 16 they don't bother.

When asked how people react when they discover that they can come to the centre, one young person replied, "they call it bad breed school." There was considerable stigma associated with being excluded and the young people we talked to were acutely aware of that. What was clear from the interviews, especially with the teenagers at the pupil referral unit, was that most were very bright and lively and had strong characters. Their support workers pointed to the fact that it was these characteristics that the mainstream education system often had difficulty coping with, due to pressures on the need to meet targets which left little room to tolerate disruptive behaviour.

Conclusions

London is and will remain a world city of increasing plurality. It is characterised by huge inequalities, which are likely to continue to grow. While London has significant wealth, there is a sizeable population who are at the very bottom and who lack the material and social means to get by and make the most of living in what is a vibrant, dynamic and thriving city. What was clear from our qualitative interviews with undocumented migrants, vulnerable elderly people and excluded young people is that their lack of opportunities and resources (and in the case of undocumented migrants, lack of legal status) left them feeling stuck and bypassed. The experience of fear, of change, of crime, of loneliness and isolation was particularly strong among the elderly interviewees. Among undocumented migrants, fear arose from their lack of legal status, which contributed to them not being able to raise matters with the authorities when employers or landlords were taking advantage of them. There was also a fear of violence, including sexual violence. Many of the undocumented migrants we interviewed reported feelings of anxiety and depression. Among the young people we spoke to, the services that were offered to them and the relationships they had with those service providers appeared crucial to whether and how they got on.

9 Exploring the impact of worklessness in South Wales

9.1 Introduction

This case study looked at the unmet needs of the economically inactive in Merthyr Tydfil in South Wales, an area of the country that has experienced high levels of unemployment since the decline of heavy industry in the region.

According to the latest data (February to April 2009), 24% of the working age population of Wales is economically inactive. Since the mid 1990s, the number of people who are economically inactive in Wales has reduced, but at a slower rate than unemployment. Economic inactivity is now a greater problem for every age group from 35 years onwards, especially for older people, and women are more likely to be economically inactive than men in all ages.[199]

More generally, worklessness is one of the great needs in modern society where so much depends on the recognition and status, as well as the income, associated with work. Worklessness is particularly damaging in communities that grew up with a strong work tradition, with the values and rhythms, historically shaped by heavy manufacturing or extraction industries. More than a generation after the arrival of mass unemployment in these areas, the long economic boom has had relatively little impact on opportunities. The one positive aspect of this is that these communities are likely to be more resilient in a downturn – as they have little left to lose. Community remains strong – but the very bonds of community can be disabling as well as enabling, holding people back from taking opportunities, or risking a new life somewhere else.

9.2 Understanding economic inactivity

Economic inactivity (like poverty, teenage pregnancy or long term illness) tends to be concentrated in areas that experience multiple needs. Our research highlights 'need clusters' – where unmet needs are clustered with other, different, needs. It is critical to understand the complex interaction between multiple needs and deeply entrenched material and psychological issues that impact on people in these areas. Even if no causality can be assumed, economic inactivity is deeply connected with other needs – material and psychological. This case study shows how economic inactivity is a difficult cycle to break as it involves complex and interconnected needs. Concentrating on only one set of needs will not solve economic inactivity.

- Wales has more people in receipt of out-of-work benefits than in most of Great Britain
- Sickness or disability is the main reason why working age people claim out-of-work benefits in Wales
- Mental or behavioural disorder is the medical condition most likely to be exhibited by working-age people who are claimants of out-of-work disability benefits, namely Employment and Support Allowance or Severe Disablement Allowance (SDA). These comprise two-fifths of all claimants.

Our research highlights that psychological needs, such as lack of confidence, poverty of aspirations and lack of autonomy, are significant among people experiencing high levels of economic inactivity. However, all too often the focus of research and policy seems to be on more material needs such as social care and benefit claiming, with less attention being given to the emotional and psychological needs underpinning the experiences and lives of people themselves.

Recent research by the Royal Institute of British Geographers on mapping happiness and wellbeing across the UK showed that some of Britain's happiest people live in Brecknock, Montgomery and Radnor in Powys, both in Wales. However, at the same time two former coal-mining communities in Wales were found to be among the least happy in the UK: the Cynon Valley and Rhondda Valleys. These latter are also areas characterised by high levels of economic inactivity. The research found that along with not being in employment, the intrinsic nature of 'place' influences happiness and wellbeing, including the local environment, lack of green spaces, the stereotypes and stigma around a place, and local crime rates. These conclusions resonate with our analysis of unmet needs in Merthyr Tydfil.

Most poverty-related needs in Merthyr Tydfil have remained broadly constant over the past decade. According to the statistics, lack of basic skills and prevalent long term illness remain big issues and are significant barriers to entering the labour market:

- 23% of the total population and 18% of the working age population in Wales report a limiting long-term illness according to the 2001 census, which is higher than the figures for England (18% and 13% respectively), and an increase on the figures from the 1991 census.
- There is some evidence of a link between a lack of basic skills and poor labour market outcomes. Within Wales the areas of highest needs are found in the Valleys, although the problem is not confined to this area. Aside from the obvious social costs, including an individual's ability to manage ill health and absorb health information, poor basic skills are generally identified as a major contributor to economic inactivity.

While the lack of basic skills and the long-term health problems of these communities cannot be discounted, the key finding from our research is that psychological needs are generally significant in communities experiencing high levels of economic inactivity. This means that any approach to tackling the complex nature of these needs requires a holistic approach, particularly in the context of an economic downturn.

The areas where these needs seem to be more deeply entrenched may be concentrated in and around the South Wales Valleys, but economic inactivity is more widespread affecting both urban and rural areas. Rural areas face considerable challenges: transport links, issues to do with mobility and access to jobs and services. There has been some debate on the unit of measurement of deprivation, highlighting that existing data may hide small pockets of deprivation in rural areas. Often, 'pockets of disadvantage' exist in rural areas, surrounded by relative affluence, and these 'pockets of disadvantage' also go unnoticed in areas of low population density.

Some groups suffer more than others from multiple and complex needs, for example those suffering from mental illness and single parents, no matter where they live, but those who come from communities that have historically been affected by economic inactivity are particularly vulnerable.

9.3 Primary Qualitative Research

Our interview sample was relatively small. It included selected service providers in Cardiff (who had both national and local experience of needs) and targeted interviews undertaken in Merthyr Tydfil. Our conclusions are based on a correlation with the findings of the wider study.

Merthyr Tydfil has one of the highest rates of economic inactivity in Wales and is currently also suffering the effects of the economic downturn. The research focused on the Gurnos estate, once one of the largest housing projects in the world when it was built in the 1960s. At this time heavy industry was thriving, jobs were plentiful and people moved to the area from all around the UK to work.

But since then, Merthyr has suffered like other parts of the country that used to depend on heavy industries. And like many other post-industrial towns, the decline of this sector fundamentally changed the composition of its labour market, firstly with a move to light manufacturing, which needed fewer skilled workers and subsequently fewer jobs as the service sector became more dominant.

Our interviewees spoke of being 'written off', 'forgotten about' and 'isolated'. Decades of economic growth and prosperity seemed to have bypassed the town. The local precinct on the estate is run down and dilapidated; the school on the estate reported very low levels of educational attainment and for many years there had been only one GP working single-handedly, for 6 hours a week. This has meant that residents have had to travel into the centre of town to visit a GP, despite the high incidence of health problems on the estate.

The current economic downturn is also touching Merthyr Tydfil and what is left of light manufacturing has been badly affected during the current recession. The Hoover factory closed in the spring of 2009, with a loss of over 300 jobs. The factory opened in the 1940s and has provided generations of Merthyr families with jobs, at one point employing over 5,000 people. Its closure was a shock for the town and represented the end of an important chapter for its residents.

9.4 Stigma and prejudice

Merthyr Tydfil regularly appears on lists of the worst places to live in Britain. High levels of economic inactivity and the related reliance on benefits has meant that the town, and the Gurnos estate in particular, has become synonymous with deprivation and disadvantage. Merthyr has been labelled 'sick note capital' of Britain and 'benefit scrounger hotspot' by sections of the media, and interviewees felt that this label has influenced aspirations and expectations, especially amongst the young generation:

> *I suppose it's like a self-fulfilling prophecy if you're told you are rubbish. You're going to believe that. So [young people's] aspirations are very, very low and it's trying to break that that is so difficult.*
>
> — Community Worker

The estate has also been associated with high levels of crime and anti-social behaviour. Interviewees told us that while there were still problems the situation had improved a lot in the past few years, and that this reputation does not reflect the behaviour of the majority of young people:

> *When the young people were asked what it is like living on the Gurnos, one young person said, I love living on the Gurnos – I love the people. What I hate is how the Gurnos is labelled. And when people say where are you from? and we say we're from the Gurnos people automatically think that we're not good.*
>
> — Youth Worker

9.5 Too much and too little belonging

Trade unions and political parties no longer occupy the central position they once did in the South Wales Valleys, as membership rates and low turnout levels in elections demonstrate. However, the solidarity that used to exist in the form of trade union membership and political participation has not completely disappeared. Instead it exists in different, less formalised ways, as members of the community develop coping strategies to help them to overcome difficult circumstances.

The community in Merthyr has suffered severe job losses and shocks in the past decades which appear to have had the effect of bringing people closer together in the face of adversity. This resonates with the findings in Teesside, where people meet their needs using social support and other non-financial strategies. The local networks we identified appear to be very strong, with high levels of informal support – for example, childcare responsibilities are shared locally between friends, families and neighbours on the estate. The importance of strong local networks and the support they provide, especially in the face of shocking events, was described by one resident whose house was badly damaged by fire:

> *We had a bad house fire in 2003. The whole house went up. I was out and [my boyfriend] was babysitting. There was an electrical fault ... but we were lucky, I've got my mother living nearby, she helped out ... my friends who live nearby too.*
>
> — Resident

Local networks and strong feelings of belonging within the community can become sources of support in times of need. However, our research and interviews showed how this could also have negative consequences insofar as the reliance of very close social networks could often result in a lack of autonomy and control. Close support from relatives, friends and neighbours in similar situations, can lead to lack of self-confidence, initiative and the motivation to engage actively in job seeking. If needs for childcare, help in case of serious financial trouble, and everyday support and companionship are efficiently fulfilled through local networks and mutual support, need to improve the quality of life, to retrain or to find a job is not as pressing as it could be. We found an example of initiative being curbed by the others in the case of a young mother, who was successfully retraining in order to change her life but found it very hard not to give up because of the pressures of her unemployed partner.

Some of our respondents felt unwilling or unable to take or apply for jobs more than a few miles away from the estate they lived on. They felt anxious in the face of unfamiliar circumstances. Access to public transport further compounded this problem with a view that this could inhibit people's ability to take up jobs and access public services, even in other areas of the town. Distance appeared to constitute a significant physical and mental barrier:

> *I don't have experience of living anywhere else. If I go anywhere, I miss home ... here you know everyone, you know where everything is ... It'd be different living somewhere else.*
>
> — Resident

One interviewee expanded this view into her social life, telling us that most of her socialising took place on the estate "I don't know about the town really, all my friends are here around me."

9.6 Lack of Confidence

The changing nature of the work now available could potentially reinforce low self-esteem and lack of confidence – pay can be low (all too often, a low pay job would be no more financially viable than existing benefits payment) and employment is sometimes temporary in nature. The individuals we spoke to did not believe that even applying for a job was something that they were capable of doing:

> *I mean I have come across people who never had a CV and wouldn't even know what to put on it. It's the attitude of 'I can't have a CV because what I've done is not worth mentioning'. But if you actually sit with them and get them to tell me about the jobs they've had, what they did actually do there. When I build up a CV for them and you show them, they go: Oh my goodness.*
>
> — Job Broker, Merthyr Tydfil

JENNY'S STORY

Jenny, aged 27, has lived on the Gurnos estate all her life and she can never see herself leaving. She had her first daughter aged 16 and she has never had a job. As a teenager she got into some trouble and she has a criminal record. Now she is fearful at the thought of going to an interview because of her record.

However, after much encouragement from local community workers, she recently went for an interview at the local hospital to work as a care assistant and she had to apply for a CRB check. Jenny is dreading hearing the result and now she doesn't want to return to the hospital. She told us:

"It's just the fear. I've had the CRB check before, and it's the way it's worded, the way it is written down; it says 'theft'. Like when I was young we all went into Boots and pinched plasters, and things like that … it just sounds worse than it was."

She has already been on a work experience placement and she really enjoyed it.

"It was brilliant. I just like that feeling, you know, of getting up in the morning, putting on the uniform, and going, and even like I wasn't being paid, I just liked that that feeling."

Jenny would really like to get a job. She says if she could do anything, it would be working with reoffending youths, but because of her criminal record she feels that she will always be judged and doubted.

9.7 Poverty of Aspiration

In both urban and rural Wales, lack of aspirations is a problem, particularly after long periods of redundancy or in areas that have suffered from generations of inactivity:

> *I asked 'what do you want to do when you leave school?' It was all like: 'work in Tesco' or 'Asda'. Well, I said, don't you want to be a pilot? And they said: well, we're from the Gurnos. So it's trying to break that.*
>
> — Youth Worker

The influence of people around them appeared significant in shaping people's willingness to retrain or find employment. The kinds of dreams and aspirations people had were all too often faced with a low ceiling of expectation of what someone from Merthyr or the Gurnos estate in particular could ever imagine or hope to achieve. This was often due to the fact that many young people are growing up without seeing any older member of their family in work. The absence of positive role models has a detrimental impact on aspirations and expectations, making it very hard for those trying to encourage people back into work to inspire them and convince them that employment could improve their lives:

> *Maybe their fathers never worked and it's very difficult to use an argument like you could be better off or you're missing out on – when some of them are not really missing out. Because the jobs they would go and find, they wouldn't be any better off.*
>
> — Community Worker

> *Do all the things mummy didn't do, go on holiday with your friends. I always say things like that with them. But, [one of my daughters] wants to be a shop-owner, and the other wants to be a police officer. So I always say, go to college, go to uni, have a laugh. Things that I didn't do, I'd like them to go, but I don't know.*
>
> — Young Mother

MARK'S STORY:

Mark is the manager of the community centre on the Gurnos Estate and he has been working there for the last 5 years. He enjoys working with people, especially young people. A lot of them have been excluded from school activities; some have been excluded from school altogether. His work involves re-engaging them and making them feel worthwhile. But he says that this is a gradual process and a lot of patience is required. Gaining the respect of young people in a scarred community takes time and work.

Some seemingly straightforward tasks have proved difficult for the young people he works with. For example, he described trying to organise a trip with a group of 16 year olds. They were nervous about picking up the phone to inquire about hiring a minibus; they didn't know what do to:

"They can't use a phone, they are afraid to use a phone for something like this. They've just never done it before."

He also described his frustration when asking parents to contribute one pound for swimming trips. Many parents refused but he saw some children spending even more money on sweets and crisps down the road, instead of going swimming. He says:

"It's a difficult culture to try and change. We are trying focusing on the younger elements. You are trying to break a habit."

But despite these difficulties, there are reasons to be optimistic. Mark told us of how the women on the estate have been involved in various projects based at the community centre with some success. These initiatives have tried to build their confidence, help them gain new skills and, crucially, open their eyes to the skills they have already acquired through life experience:

"We have had success with projects aimed at getting women back into work, or at least getting them thinking about getting back into work. A skill that they have, obviously, is running a home. And I think what they didn't appreciate what they were capable of. They didn't count themselves as having any skills. And yet when you break it down into separate terms, you might go: look, you brought up a family, you have managed a budget, you know you feed six children and keep a home running or whatever. So when you put all these labels on, then they realise that there is a lot they can do. It's just re-labelling it."

9.8 Negotiating Gender Roles

Women continue to have higher inactivity rates than men, but the gap between them has more than halved since 1984.[200] There has been an upward trend in the inactivity rate for men and a downward trend for women over the 24-year period in both Wales and the UK (even though women are still more likely to be economically inactive than men). Our research showed that barriers to economic activity are deeply affected by a change in traditional gender roles in a changing labour market and that this is having an impact on household relations, on who is more likely to retrain and on the role that institutions can have in encouraging and carefully managing this shift.

The shift in the composition of the job market has led to a decline in the availability of jobs in the somewhat male-dominated manufacturing and industrial sectors, with an increase in jobs in the service sector. Such jobs are 'people-centred' and require different skill-sets for which substantial re-training may be required.

However, we found that the women we spoke to were more eager than the men to take on jobs in the health and retail sectors and the service sector:

> *My boyfriend, he's not working, he was working before Christmas, labouring ... He's out of work now, but he's said if I was going work, he would have to go back ... He said something the other night, a little comment, like, um, 'Oh I'd better pull my socks up, and start visiting the job centre everyday'. So he felt like he should be doing that too just because I was going out and trying to get a job. I was like 'why didn't you think of that a couple of weeks ago, when you lost your other job, why now, just because I'm doing things?'*
> — Young woman

According to community workers and service providers we spoke to,, it was often the case that men over 30 or 35 on the estate considered themselves too old to be retrained, or to go back to education and find a new job in a different sector. If they had worked as qualified tradesmen or trained mechanics, the thought of having to re-skill completely to gain employment in the service sector was often too daunting a prospect. One respondent told us of the difficulties faced by this group:

> *The male age group is the hardest to reach. I would say 30 to 50. We have very little success in this one particular area. The jobs are all about customer service, really. It's dealing with people. Maybe you've spent your life in a mine, in heavy industry and never talked to anybody.... There is certainly a big percentage of that group that are going to find it very difficult to find suitable work. And they are unlikely to return to the labour market. Because they may see the jobs that are out there are beneath them. They are not given a chance to use what they were trained to do ... It's customer service really. It's people dealing with other people. Maybe you have spent your life in a mine, in heavy industry and never talked to anybody ... And it is quite probable that, not just here, but in many areas you still got the black economy. And they are working plus claiming benefits.*
>
> — Community Worker

Conclusions

When asked about the economic crisis, our interviews told us that they 'had seen it all before' and that 'it was nothing new for the town'. There was a sense that the community was powerless to change the situation but that 'it would be ok, it always is'. This view provided a sort of insulation, and combined with the very strong reliance on spatially bounded communities, strong resilience against shocks and difficulties.

Tackling economic inactivity is likely to be even more difficult during the downturn and, with spending cuts, more than ever the problem will require innovative and grassroots solutions. However, the economically inactive are an interesting example of a group that is not likely to be too affected by the downturn. Their income has been maintained throughout, and prices of food items have in some cases decreased through price wars in Britain's high streets. But a return to employment will be made more difficult with fewer opportunities for those who have been out of the labour market for some time; those who are already on the margins risk being further marginalised.

In this context, and as the economic downturn continues, there is an increased challenge for service providers to balance the demands on their services between active job seekers and the economically inactive. This may highlight a need for more personalised, local grassroots solutions which are designed to tackle both the material and the psychological barriers that people face. Importantly, the assets and capabilities that exist in communities afflicted by very high rates of economic inactivity must be recognised and nurtured in ways such as not just to provide people with everyday support and resilience but also to encourage people to be inspired and change their own lives.

10 In the shadows: needs through a night-time lens

10.1 Introduction

In looking at needs in the UK we were keen to look at issues through a new lens, one which has been relatively under-researched and of which most people are generally unaware. We wanted this to be an exploratory study, investigating an area on which there was little data but where there might be significant need. We decided to look at needs at night. Are certain needs more apparent during the night than during the day? We chose to do this by looking from the perspective of those people who are regularly active at night.

Using participant observation as the main methodology, we followed a range of different night workers as they worked their shifts, going where they went, seeing what they saw and asking questions as we went along. This approach allowed us not only to look at those needs that are more acute at night, but also at the needs of the night workers themselves.

10.2 The lonely city

"Night-time [in London] is the lonely time," said one of the paramedics as we started one night shift. "Drinks, drugs and self-harm – you get more of those on nights." The ambulance crews explained that they are called to far more incidents of self-harm and attempted suicide at night, as we were to find out:

> *Around midnight we get a call for someone who has cut their wrists. We put on the sirens and accelerate east along the A12. A police car arrives at the small housing estate at the same time as us and our blue lights illuminate the blocks. We climb the stairs and reach the flat, which has a new unpainted front door. "I've been here before," one of the policemen says. "My mate kicked in the old door." There is no need for anyone to break the door down this time, as it is swinging open. We go into a dimly lit, sparsely furnished one bedroom flat. The floor is strewn with clothes, shoes and litter. A young girl in her early twenties is sitting on a sofa, smoking a cigarette, sobbing. The ambulance crew try to comfort her and put a dressing on the wound on her wrist which they don't think is serious. "I thought I was getting over depression," she cries, "but I'm obviously not." The police are anxious for the ambulance crew to take her into hospital, as they are unsure what do to. "I don't want to go to hospital," the girl insists. "I've been in loads of times. They don't do anything. They don't give me anything. They can't help." She has self-harmed on a number of*

occasions and her wrists are covered in scars. The ambulance crew persuade her to come in and see a doctor, but they know the girl is right. "She's not serious enough to be admitted, so she'll sit around in A&E, a nurse will look at her, she'll go home and we'll be back out here in the early hours again. It's a cycle."

During the same evening we were called to two similar incidents. The ambulance crew explained that this is a common type of night call. They are frequently called out to lonely or isolated young people with psychological needs that are not deemed serious enough to warrant a clinical intervention or admission to hospital. In one case we saw the patient wander out of A&E even before we had processed the paperwork. The ambulance crews were resigned to the fact that it was probable that they would return to the flats to treat the same patients. "We're patching people up but nobody is dealing with the underlying problems."

10.3 Vulnerability and violence

One of the police officers commented that people seemed to be more vulnerable at night, or least those who were most vulnerable surfaced at night. Like the ambulance men and women, the police are another one of the frontline services that have to deal with consequences of unmet need at night:

The police van turns a corner and we see a couple arguing in the shadows of the back street. As the blue lights go on the man looks up, momentarily stares at the van and then turns and sprints off in the opposite direction. Two of the policemen jump out of the van and run after him. Jane, the remaining constable, gets out and talks to the young woman. The woman is dressed scruffily and is unstable on her feet. She is speaking incoherently and we have trouble understanding what she is saying. Jane searches her and finds a crack pipe and a several condoms in her pocket. Jane finds a bus pass in another pocket and types the woman's name into the van computer. She is 24, has no registered address and has learning difficulties. The computer profile indicates that the woman has been in trouble with the police for both drugs offences and prostitution. The other two policemen walk back trying to catch their breath, having been unsuccessful in catching the man who ran off. "There's nothing we can do about her," Jane explains as the woman stumbles down the street. "She's done nothing wrong. We can't arrest her. We're not social services. There's nothing we can do. We'll probably see her on this patch again tomorrow night. Sad isn't it?"

Jane expressed similar views to the ambulance drivers, observing that not only that particular unmet needs seem to be more prevalent at night, but also that those services that operate at night are only able to treat the symptoms, not solve any problems – leaving many of individual service providers cynical and frustrated.

Most violent crime is committed at night, particularly around concentrations of nightclubs and pubs.[201] In London 120 extra police officers are drafted in at weekends to patrol the entertainment hotspots in Westminster and Soho. Our interviews with nightclub security staff suggested that these extra officers were needed, as they witnessed and had to break up fights on a nightly basis. Nearly all the incidents we were called to with the police at night involved drugs, alcohol, violence or a combination of all three.

10.4 Britain's night workers

In looking at needs at night from the perspectives of those working at night, it became increasingly clear that the night workers themselves had a significant number of needs that were unmet or only partially met. This study allowed us to dig deeper into this and reflect on the needs in a workplace, rather than the other areas of life that have been the primary focus elsewhere in our report.

Night work is not a new phenomenon; evidence of working night shifts goes back at least as far as Roman times and the level rose during the Industrial Revolution. However, it was the transformation to heavily mechanised industrial processes during the twentieth century that saw dramatic increases in round-the-clock working. Modern industry is dependent on expensive equipment that becomes more cost-effective if it is operating, and therefore manned, 24 hours a day. Changing lifestyles in the late twentieth century have led to the rapid growth of the 24 hour service economy as workers demand more flexible working hours and consumers want shops, services and leisure activities to be open later into the evening, if not throughout the night. Not only do all these shops, banks, call-centres, transport systems etc. need to be staffed beyond the traditional nine-to-five working day, but the maintenance, cleaning, restocking etc. require staff to work after these services have closed to the public. The result is that levels of night working are increasing and are likely to continue to do so if, as Leon Kreitzman argues, we are moving towards a 24 hour society.[202]

The nocturnal workforce is split into two distinct groups: those who work at night at regular intervals as part of a rotating shift system and a smaller group who permanently work at night. The Labour Force Survey shows that over 1.3 million people in the UK regularly work at night. Of these, over 300,000 people are permanent night workers. However, it is likely that this is a considerable under-estimate as many of those who we met during this research were reluctant to provide personal information because they were working informally or as part of an unregistered second job such as driving mini-cabs, cleaning or security staff.

The night workforce is predominately male, as shown in the figure below. In part, this gender imbalance is due to the nature of the jobs that work at night, such as the construction workers, engineers, security etc., which are traditionally male dominated industries. However, as the night-time service economy continues to grow, it is likely that in the future more women will be working at night.

Figure 59: Different night shift patterns by gender

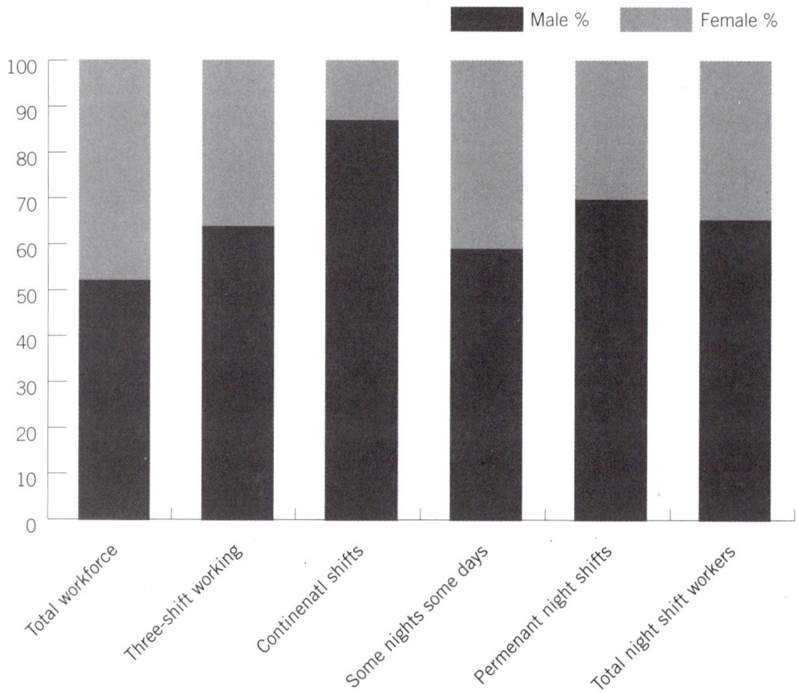

Source: Labour Force Survey

The majority of the night workforce is white (86%), but this is a significantly lower proportion than in the overall workforce (92% white). Conversely, there are proportionately more people from Black and Minority Ethnic (BME) backgrounds working at night, compared to the overall UK workforce. During the time we spent observing the night workers, it became clear that there was a difference between the types of jobs held by the white night shift workers and those from black and minority ethnic backgrounds. Those from BME backgrounds appeared far more likely to be doing the jobs that paid less, were less secure or more menial, such as cleaning and security jobs, refuse collecting, and mini-cab driving. The more professional jobs with rotating shift patterns, such as the police, ambulance service, and London Underground Station staff were predominantly white. In some jobs the roles were completely split along ethnic lines, for example there were teams of construction workers on the underground who were almost entirely Afrikaans, while the station cleaners were groups of West Africans or Bulgarians. The rickshaw drivers in Soho were mainly Columbians with smaller Turkish and Polish contingents.

Much of the night-time economy is invisible to most of us. However, when one spends time walking the streets, hanging out in coffee shops, looking beyond the closed office doors or being shown around a city's hidden infrastructures, the diversity of the types of work that are happening every night quickly becomes clear. There are the cleaners, the hospital staff, the emergency services, the security guards, the night bus drivers, postal workers, mini-cab drivers, prison staff, factory workers, call centre operators, transport engineers, carers, haulers, market workers, and the people who monitor the sewage systems, power stations and computer server hubs, to list but a few.

Figure 60: Proportion of night workers by industry type

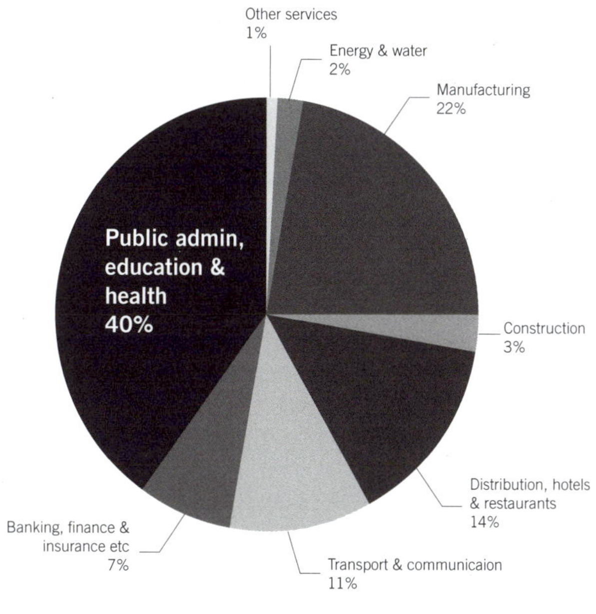

Source: Labour Force Survey

The figure above shows the breakdown of the UK's night workers by industrial sector according to the Labour Force Survey. Although just over 20% of the night shift workers are part of the manufacturing sector, the service sector is much more active at night, with the public sector (most notably health) the biggest employer.

10.5 Why do people work nights?

Typically those we spoke to worked at night out of financial necessity. As Marko, a Bulgarian who walks through the London Underground tunnels every night collecting litter, explained, "I do it because I need the money, only for the money ... When I started this I didn't think I'd still be doing it in three years time. I need the money. What else can I do?"

Marko's story was a common one; many people work nights out of necessity. They don't enjoy it or want to work when the rest of us are sleeping, but they have to – either due to financial necessity or lack of other options, like Marko, or because night shifts are simply part of the job, as with the emergency services. Many night workers are incentivised by higher wages, for example the shop fitters who we interviewed were paid 50% extra after 10 p.m., and the Westminster Traffic wardens are paid £9.75 per hour compared with their daytime counterparts who receive between seven or eight pounds an hour.

For some, there were a number of advantages to working at night and they preferred it to working during the day. For example, the contractors repairing or testing equipment on the Underground could only work from 1 a.m. to 5 a.m. because of the trains, yet they are paid for a full shift. Others found that working at night allowed them to do other jobs (such as many of the cleaners) or to study during the day. Workers said that working at night let them use the day to do their chores or get other things done. As Kevin, a construction supervisor who has been working nights on a permanent basis for 12 years, said:

> *There are pros and cons to nights. Working nights means I can get stuff done during the day. I finish up, go home and sleep until about 12. After that I can get the car fixed or do the shopping. In any other job I'd have to tell the governor and you can't just skip out to go to the dentist or whatever.*

There was a widespread appreciation of 'the quiet of the night'. For some this meant that they were able to get on with this with "no governors about", as one shop fitter put it, or allowed people to do the jobs they felt they were trained to do without interruptions or distractions, as a police sergeant explained:

> *It's a different style of policing at night. It's actually stopping crime. We have a proactive approach, stopping people and vehicles rather than just chasing all over London reacting to people's calls. During the day the traffic's terrible and you just can't get anywhere. You end up dealing with tourists and people all over the place. You'll see, it's a very different city at night.*

THE STUDENT NIGHT WORKER

Rafiq is a 22-year-old Pakistani who has lived in the UK for four years. He works night shifts in a small grocery shop and off-licence in the London Borough of Westminster. Rafiq works from 10 p.m. to 6am five days a week. He is studying to be a chartered accountant and is engrossed in a textbook when I walk into the shop. Rafiq explains that he attends college three days a week and is able to study when the shop quietens down from 3 a.m. to 6 a.m.

"It's usually busy at weekends and quiet during the week. The nights are much calmer than days. The problem is sleep. I'm sure I get sick more often. I feel dizzy and my face swells up, you know? … I've been doing this for two years. Another six months and I'll stop. It's good because I can study and get paid at the same time. I actually get paid 30% more at night. But my social life is finished, man, totally gone. I don't see anyone. I don't have a girlfriend because of nights and I can't see how I'd meet anyone new. It's impossible."

Rafiq advises me to avoid drinking coffee and red bull.

"They make you feel bad. One cup of tea during the night, that's what I do. Exercise is important too. I try to swim at the weekend if I can, but often I just want to sleep."

10.6 Accidents

Some of the most catastrophic industrial accidents in history have occurred due to human error during night shifts. These include the Chernobyl and Three Mile Island nuclear accidents, the Exxon Valdez oil spill and the Bhopal toxic chemical leak. While these accidents are extreme in their scale, they reflect that night workers are at greater risk of sustaining an occupational injury or causing an accident than those working day shifts. [203, 204] A number of studies show that some industrial injuries are three times higher on the night shift compared to the evening shift.[205] Those working night shifts have impaired physical performance, poorer reaction times and mental arithmetic,[206] and overall lower cognitive performance.[207]

> *I hate nights. Absolutely hate them. Some people actually prefer them. I hate it. I've always been an early morning person. Even if I go out with friends, I'd always be the first one home. I find it completely unnatural. It's got to be significant that the SAS and all that strike at 4 or 5 in the morning because they know that they'll get the least resistance. People are not alert at that time.*
>
> — Healthcare worker, London

During our fieldwork such dips in performance and energy levels were particularly noticeable between 4 a.m. and 5.30 a.m. in workers across all job types: conversations and jokes dried up, bedside manners became more abrupt, drivers slowed down. People physically changed: red eyes staring into the middle distance, faces covered in a sheen of cold sweat, shivers as people put on an extra jacket. It was easy to see how accidents could happen.

It is not just the accidents in the workplace that are of concern – many of the night shift workers reported accidents on their journeys home after working through the night, as one of the paramedics warned:

> *By the end of the shift, you've got to be careful ... I live out in Essex. I get in the car and drive back with the windows open. After a busy night you feel drunk, all fuzzy, you know? There are nights when I've had no recollection of getting home. There was this one bloke who worked here who was burning it at both ends. He had a new baby and was punching overtime, nights all the time. He had an accident with a lorry on the way home; ended up dead.*

Alarmingly, such stories were common. Nearly all the night shift workers that we spoke to had similar stories of road accidents or near misses that had affected them or one of their colleagues.

10.7 Health

It is not only accidents at work or on the way home that affect night workers. Shift and night work has been linked to a wide range of health problems including breast cancer,[208] prostate cancer,[209] non-Hodgkin's lymphoma,[210] cardio-vascular disease,[211] gastrointestinal disorders[212] and pregnancy problems.[213]

Typically the night workers we spent time with had unhealthy lifestyles, eating large amounts of junk food, smoking excessively, and many were overweight and admitted taking little exercise. Nearly everyone thought they drank too much caffeine and there was an obvious alcohol drinking culture associated with many of the jobs. It was not uncommon for night workers to use alcohol to help them sleep after the shifts, one had even been recommended by his doctor to have the "odd nip of brandy" to help "send him off."

> “ I rarely eat at home when I'm on nights. I get by on cigarettes, tea and toast. I can't be arsed to eat.
>
> It's carbs and grease on night shifts. Kebab shops are the only things that are open.
>
> We do eat shit though...pizzas, fish and chips, kebabs. We probably end up drinking more too. Helps you sleep in the days. Of course it affects your health. It buggers up your sleep pattern completely.
>
> I drink Red Bull and coffee all the time, day and night ... I take food from Tesco's, sandwiches or something from China Town. It's expensive. I never can eat healthy food, it's impossible with this job.
>
> — Quotes from various night workers

Many of the medical conditions affecting night workers have long been attributed to their unhealthy lifestyle choices. However, recent research in the United States indicates that the risks associated with disrupted sleep patterns remain, irrespective of lifestyle. In a laboratory experiment, subjects whose sleep patterns were disturbed produced less leptin, a hormone that signals the body to stop eating, and experienced increases in blood glucose and insulin. Levels of cortisol, a hormone released during periods of stress and linked to a number of medical conditions, also increased dramatically.[214]

There was an awareness of the health implications of working regular night shifts and workers expressed concern for their health and how their work might affect their life expectancy. There is no data available on how the life expectancy of night shift workers compares with the general population, but we were repeatedly told by those we interviewed that they were amazed how many of their former colleagues had been diagnosed with terminal conditions (often cancer) early into their retirement.

Those over 50 years old complained that they were finding it harder to cope with night shifts than they had done when they were younger. They explained that sleep patterns were becoming increasing erratic or they were finding it harder to sleep in the day. For example, Pete, a 62 year old ambulance man, said:

> *I never had a problem with nights in the past. Until about five years ago. I used to be able to sleep for about five hours in the daytime, but that went down to four and now I'm lucky if I get three. You can manage one or two nights, but by the end of the fourth you really begin to feel it.*

Ali, a 53-year-old traffic warden who works nights in the London Borough of Westminster echoed this:

> *I feel it walking the whole time. It takes it out of you and it gets harder with age. But what can I do? I can't change my job. There are no other jobs available.*

10.8 Social lives and relationships

There was a distinct camaraderie between fellow night workers which was evident across all the sectors – even the police and prostitutes exchanged friendly conversation about how their nights were going and how many hours they had left before they would head home. Although the camaraderie between all of those working at night was clear, the strongest social ties were between co-workers. It was common for the shift workers to socialise together after work, as one of the nightclub promoters explained, "It's the best part of the job. I love it at night. There're great after-work parties for staff." As with many who work during the day, this time was an important mechanism for winding down after the shift and coping with the stress of the job. As one of the ambulance staff reflected, "There's a good social life in the service. We've been surfing and there's a drinking culture. Everyone has a dark sense of humour. I suppose it's the way we cope."

Mike is head of security at a large London nightclub:

> *I've been in this game for 10 years. I like it as I can live during the day. I can get to the shops, the bank and everything. I can get by on five hours sleep ... I'd say 80% of door staff have no social life. We get home see the kids and then crash for a few hours. That's our world. It's different to everyone else's.*

The close social ties at work and the solidarity between fellow night workers was seen as the good side of working nights. However, far more people were quick to identify how night work damaged social lives. One of the rickshaw drivers gloomily explained:

> *I don't make friends. Other people do activities at weekends, I cannot. My only friends are other rickshaw drivers. On Saturdays we buy beers and drink them in the garage when we finish, we drink from 5 a.m. until maybe 11 a.m.*

The lack of social lives affected many of the younger night workers' opportunities to form relationships. Franco, one of the rickshaw drivers, explained, "The problem with working nights is that you're always alone. You can't go out with the girls. None of my friends have girlfriends." These sentiments were repeated time after time among the younger male interviewees.

Night work also put stress on some of the relationships of the older night workers. Ali, the 52-year-old traffic warden, told us, "My wife gets lonely. I don't see her much. I go to work when she comes home. She goes to work when I am asleep." Mike, one of the underground workers, said much the same thing, "We're like ships that pass in the morning. I come in and she goes out. It's not healthy."

10.9 Family life

Whether night work had a positive or negative influence on family life was a common topic of conversation on many of the night shifts we participated in. For some, the fact that their working hours opposed their partners' made it easier to share childcare. For example, Keith, a police constable with two children, said that when he's working night shifts he can get home in time to do the school run before he goes to bed. Terry, an engineer on the underground, thought the same:

> *One of the pros of the night is that I see more of my family than in normal life. My partner is a teacher and so we have much more flexibility in childcare. I usually get home, have something to eat and take the kids to school. I then come back and crash.*

This was not the case for everyone, as night work can make organising childcare far harder. Bill works for London Underground and has two children aged six and ten:

> *The childcare costs a fucking fortune on nights: eleven grand last year. My missus works early and so we need a nanny in the morning because I can't get back by 7 a.m. Some people say nights makes childcare easier, but it doesn't.*

For lone parents the situation is even harder; research by the Day Care Trust highlights the major gaps that exist in childcare provision for shift workers, which can exclude single parents from employment that involves evening or night-time work.[215]

While the debate over whether night working assists with the logistical aspects of family life will no doubt continue, there was much more of a consensus that working at night was to the detriment of the quality of the time and the energy people had when they were spending time with their families and children. As Pete, the paramedic in his 60s, said:

> *I felt like I was missing so much of the kids growing up due to the job. You're never there during the day, even if you're doing nights you're trying to get over the last one, or prepare for the next. With shift work time goes so quickly and you're always out of sync with everyone else.*

10.10 Management and support

Complaints that the needs of those working at night are not sufficiently understood or taken into account by their managers or their colleagues working in the daytime were widespread. One of the shop fitters moaned:

> *The office don't think about it. They call us at 9 a.m. when we're trying to get some kip, or book us into some hotel in the middle of town, so noisy you can't sleep.*

While such oversights are undoubtedly annoying, there were other ways in which the night workers were clearly lacking the support structures and facilities required to ensure they were working safely. Much of the unhealthy eating was happening because of the unavailability of other alternatives, for example nearly all the police canteens in London are closed at night. The ambulance crew we followed worked from 6.30 p.m. to 6 a.m. without any substantial break – the three cups of tea we had over this period were only obtained by essentially 'chatting up' the nursing staff in the hospitals where we dropped off our patients.

As a recent Home Office report rightly noted, from the workers' perspectives, "there is no such thing as a good shift system",[216] i.e. there will never be a single approach to night shift work that will suit everyone. Nevertheless, changing shift patterns are among the most stressful aspects of night work. As one of the ambulance drivers commented:

> *I do 12-hour shifts and don't have a life outside work. I just can't do stuff in the day. I'm all dazed. It's not safe, I don't feel safe to drive or treat a patient at 4 a.m. On an eight-hour shift I could cope. These 12-hour shifts,*

I can't do them. They [the new 12 hour shift pattern] were introduced here in January. Management love it. We only have one change over. For us eight hours [shifts] were much better.

A change in shift patterns caused similar consternation with the police team we followed. Their eight-week rotation, which included a Monday-to-Friday night shift, had changed to a four-week pattern where they do a Friday and Saturday night, from 10 p.m. to 6 a.m.

The chief inspector says that we can do the two nights, have a couple of hours sleep on the Sunday and have the rest of the day with our families. Most people end up sleeping during their rest day. It's down to resources ... it's only really busy on Friday and Saturday nights. They didn't want to pay for us to work the whole week of nights, when it's quiet. I preferred the old shifts. Your body can't get used to just doing two nights.

Shift patterns affect the biological clock, sleep and social lives, and shift work can lead or contribute to a range of medical conditions and illnesses. The way the shifts are organised has to accommodate the type of job, but understanding the needs and views of those working shifts must be an important part of the design of shift systems. This research has shown that in many cases this is not occurring.

Conclusions

The majority of our service infrastructure is designed for use in the daytime. However, particular problems (isolation, vulnerability, violence) appear more common or regularly surface at night. Those services that do operate at night are ill equipped to adequately meet these needs, resulting in a number of different people falling between the gaps or being marginalised.

When it came to the needs of those working at night, it is clear that night shift work is an important part of the modern economy which is likely to continue to grow in the foreseeable future – especially within the service sector. However, little attention has been paid to those working at night in terms of who they are and whether their needs differ from the daytime workforce. We have found that those who work at night have significant unmet needs that go unnoticed and unreported.

A growing volume of medical research is highlighting the serious health implications of working night shifts and, as this case study has shown, many of the medical dangers are being amplified by the unhealthy lifestyle choices being made by – or forced upon – the night workers. There is a clear need for raising awareness of the risks of night working, among workers and those responsible for managing their shift patterns and working environments. The trade unions and Health and Safety Executive should be playing a more significant role in this education, pressuring for new legislation and enforcing existing regulations.

With the majority of night workers in the UK employed in the public sector, the government needs to take notice of the risks these people are being exposed to. In 2009, after studying research by the International Agency for Research on Cancer, the Danish government began paying compensation payments to women in professions such as nursing who developed breast cancer after working regular night shifts. As one commentator put it, night working has the potential to be the "next asbestos",[217] raising the possibilities of widespread legal action and large compensation payouts.

11 Exploring family resilience in Teesside

11.1 Introduction

This study explores how men and women in low-income households in Teesside meet their needs in economic adversity, using social support and other non-financial strategies. We look at the role of non-financial assets within the household economy, and in particular at social support, the difference between women and men's access to and control of these means of meeting needs, and how dynamics within the household contribute to success or failure.

Our research is based on detailed interviews with participants, in their own homes, working with them to understand their needs and listening to their stories and strategies they use to get by.

The Teesside conurbation has an extremely large concentration of deprivation, in the context of a proud industrial heritage based around steel, heavy engineering, shipbuilding and, more recently, chemicals. These industries struggled in the recessions of the 1970s and 1980s with mass redundancies, especially by the larger employers such as British Steel and ICI. Manufacturing decreased dramatically and social problems increased in line with the high levels of unemployment. Conversely, business start-up rates were one of the lowest in the country. The EU classified Teesside as a region that was in industrial decline and meeting the deprivation levels of Objective 2 of the ESF. Some progress has been made in recent years both to diversify the economy and to build on existing industries. Tees Valley remains the largest heavy industrial complex in the United Kingdom (petrochemicals). By and large it is typical of other UK areas recovering from the loss of traditional manufacturing industries and shares ACORN and Mosaic classification types with areas on the Clyde, Liverpool, South Yorkshire and the West Midlands.

Individuals in economically disadvantaged places and periods of time tend to face very limited choices, but despite this, they demonstrate determination, resourcefulness and innovation in developing life strategies to cope with daily challenges. These strategies may be based on the support of family and friends, or on reducing certain behaviours and consumption patterns. Some strategies may be long term, including accruing assets such as saving for a car, but most often they are short-term measures to get through to the next pay packet or benefits payment.

Within close communities of interest, limited assets will be shared readily even within relatively poor communities in order to prevent the most serious effects of poverty. This, however, might not be done in such a way that allows households to build assets and address their long-term poverty sustainably. Couples tend to cope better than single people, both in terms of physical and financial assets, and certainly in terms of measures of psychological wellbeing, including optimism and self-esteem. The more assets households have, the more likely they are to be resilient to shocks that might push others further into poverty.

Households in this study generally appeared to have developed relatively robust coping strategies, which seemed to centre around a communal set of behaviours which were either openly negotiated or embedded and habitual.

MEL AND STEVE'S STORY

Mel and Steve have been together for 23 years and have three children. During that time Steve has been made redundant three times. Mel has had various jobs, some of them part time. They have spent long periods where their only income has been from state benefits.

"We've been through some pretty tough times, especially when Steve was laid off for a couple of years ... I had a bit of depression after the second baby and we had a few fights, but we got through that. I've never thought for a minute that we wouldn't be together ... and anyway I'd rather be poor with Steve and my girls than rich without them ... no contest. After all we've gone through I reckon we could deal with whatever life throws at us."

11.2 Positive outlook

The households that reported the least unmet need demonstrated a significant amount of confidence and optimism, and seemed to be the most likely to use humour when describing their situations.

> *He's been made redundant six times since we got married, you'd think he smells or something, God bless him. He might be useless but I do love him...*

These families also appeared to regard themselves as being less 'needy':

> *You talk about needs, well I don't reckon we are any different to most folk, even those in rich areas down south ... We need a roof over our heads, food on the table and to feel that our children are safe.*

Even in the situations where people admitted that they had 'gone without' something that they might have needed or wanted (food, a holiday, new shoes), those with a positive outlook seemed overall to report fewer and less pressing needs and suffering than others. For example Gary and Michelle, who have four children and who are both economically inactive, reported regularly skipping meals and taking their children to eat at relatives', whilst not eating full meals themselves:

> *You've just got to do what you've got to do ... I remember it was the same in my day ... me Mam never seemed to eat anything, she just lived off fags, but she made sure we all ate like kings.*

There were also families who had gone through not only the economic shock of redundancy or over-indebtedness, but also health and mental health problems. A common feature of those who reported most positively on these seemingly intractable problems was the cheerful and upbeat way in which they were reported and the absence of negative descriptors, other than those which deployed a kind of gallows humour.

> *Yeah, Matt's been shuffling along like Quasimodo since the operation, the kids have a good old laugh at him ... course he can't pick up Gemma any more and swing her around, but that's probably just as well, she almost puked all over him one time...*

The challenge of mental health problems seemed to be something that was a little more difficult for people to be optimistic about. Generally, when the condition was ascribable to either an understandable adaptive response to difficult situations (such as 'the baby blues' or 'being depressed after he lost his job') or where the condition was a clearly defined medical condition requiring a single drug (such as lithium carbonate for one woman with bipolar disorder) the general damping effect on general optimism seemed less severe.

> *She's fine as long as she remembers to take the pills, and I'll soon know if she hasn't. It's just one of those things ... can't be helped.*

11.3 Routines and rituals

The families that took part in our research generally observed reasonably set patterns of communal behaviour. This was particularly the case where there were pre-teen children in the house. However the households that most often did things together, whether it was eating together, playing games, doing household chores or undertaking visits, were also the ones which complained the least about having unmet needs.

The language used to describe daily activities was one of informed intimacy rather than otherness, "he likes his soaps, does Dennis ... I like to sit with him even though it's not really my thing". Family time was mentioned by a majority of people as being particularly important to them.
Spending time together is vital for a family and promotes continuity and a stable

family life. Time spent together can range from having family meals, doing chores together, running errands to having fun. Sharing family time together has been shown to reduce the chances that children will get involved in substance abuse, smoking and early sexual activity that can put their mental and physical health at risk, particularly in adolescence. Unfortunately, family time appears to be dwindling due to increased demands on parents, responsibilities and time strain (a phenomenon that includes the lack of spontaneity to respond to children's needs, fatigue, and an inability to disconnect feelings from work). Effective ways to reduce time strain and increase family time include: family housekeeping activities, using commuting time to have meaningful communication, discussing future plans, or participating in fun learning activities.

11.4 Stable family roles and communication

Typically the adults interviewed, whilst displaying gender roles which might be described as being at the more traditional end of the spectrum, seemed secure in what was expected of them and in what they could expect of others. The most successful households were by no means without stress, but they seemed to have a longer-term perspective on the trials and tribulations of daily life:

> *She's never really done the money stuff, which is ok, I suppose. I mean there isn't much and anyway the kids is her patch so I can't complain. I mean if we really need to sort something she'll listen ... whether she understands I don't know ... she can't count for toffee.*

A notable aspect of the interviews was how open the married and cohabiting adults were with each other, during and around the interviews. There seemed to be a kind of clarity and openness of emotional expression, and an exceptionally collaborative approach to problem solving:

> *So thank God Jill knows this woman in Eston who could help look after the kids two days a week ... I was really tearing my hair out ... I didn't feel I could turn down the cash but you can't leave Sammy and Jordan on their own.*

11.5 Strong support networks

There was also plentiful evidence in our interviews of both extensive long-term and also more recent individual, familial, and community networks, which enabled people to share resources and responsibilities. This ranged from neighbour-provided child-care and car-pooling for work or study, to the shopping for elderly relatives and, nearly universally, telephone calls and visits to give emotional and social support.

> *So I was telling Briony ... I speak to her most days on the phone ... even though she's only down the road ... drives Keith mad ... but I tell him it's on 'Friends and Family' ... anyway she's so good, I mean when we split up last year she really helped me hold the fort till he got his act together and stopped the boozing.*

11.6 Goal focus and crisis prevention

Adults commonly talked openly about targets for their household, usually in the form of income generation, improved housing status or the hoped-for developments and successes of their children or elderly parents. These goals seemed to be shared household objectives and each adult had some role in taking concrete steps towards that end.

> *What we'd really like is to get out of this flat and rent a house so me Mam can live with us and Jack can be nearer his friends in Grangemouth. When Paul gets more work we reckon we can afford it, fingers crossed.*

FRANK AND DENISE'S STORY

Frank and Denise are both divorced and have been living together for 8 years. They live with Denise's two teenage children from her first marriage. The children's father lives on the same estate with his girlfriend and takes the children every other weekend and in the holidays. Frank is in receipt of Incapacity Benefit for a long-term back condition. Denise augments their benefit income by helping out at a hairdressers.

"I get irritated when I feel that I have to do everything and we've had it out a few times, you know, just because he can't work doesn't mean he can't help out around the place. I think it's really down to his last missus, who mollycoddled him. I mean he couldn't cook or anything when we got together. Now he's good as gold sorting the food out when I'm working or getting other things done, what's needed to be done." (Denise)

"It was difficult at first what with her kids – I never had me own and they were a bit shy like, well suspicious you might say. But their Dad wanted to see them regular like and that has really helped. We can plan what we do all four of us or just me and Denise cos we have this routine. We all really look forward to the kids coming back but also Denise and me get some time to ourselves, so everyone's happy." (Frank)

11.7 Using financial assets to meet needs

Family wellbeing is closely associated with how well finances are handled. In times of financial hardship, resilient families provide reciprocal and high levels of warmth, affection and emotional support for each other, and a sense of promise for a brighter future. Financial pressures can lead to family tension and stress and can affect emotional wellbeing and interpersonal relationships at all levels in the family (e.g. individuals' emotional lives, marital interactions between adults, and the caretaking environment of the children).

The combination of psychological, social and economic burdens can put families at higher risk of multiple problems and crises beyond their control (for example unemployment, substandard housing, crime, violence, substance abuse and a lack of health care).

> *I wouldn't trust him to do it – he'd probably end up buying beer. One time he came back with dog food and we've only ever had cats ... and they wouldn't exchange it.*

Money worries were common, with widespread reliance on state benefits and the regular use of short- and long-term loans. One example was Trish, a single mother who went back to work but earned little more than the minimum wage and had ended up hugely indebted.

> *You wouldn't believe it but they let me take out four credit cards ... it was about 12 grand in total ... I didn't spend it on nothing special ... just clothes for the kids, trips, a telly and other stuff I couldn't afford on my wage. They promised me a managerial position but nothing's happened yet and that was near off three years ago.*

People seemed to be extremely adept at finding bargains and making their finances stretch between payday or benefit payment day: "I went an extra mile just to get the two-for one offer at Iceland. Usually skip breakfast..."

But there were still families who struggled with lumpy expenditure patterns and one-off unforeseen disasters, who experienced poverty in all aspects of their lives. There also seemed to be a widespread tendency to forsake quality of purchase for quantity. Multi-purchase offers and the stock found in discount 'pound shops' seemed to dictate the contents of many shopping baskets.

> *We don't really buy fresh, like in the old days. It's too far to go and too pricey. I love mushrooms though; you can get two cans for a pound.*

Prioritisation in budgeting followed an interesting pattern, with food only jointly most important, along with ICT (TV, DVDs and top-ups for mobiles) and, in the households with smokers, cigarettes. In fact, there were cases where nicotine was described in priority terms as trumping protein. "I reckon after I've bought tabs for the week there's about fifteen quid left for meat, bacon and cheese. We have to go to the supermarket for those."

The demands of non-priority creditors (that is, loans taken which are not secured on property or for which the default penalty is imprisonment) took up more emotional energy and attention than other financial commitments: "I only had a tenner left after paying the Provy and getting the food in. And we had bills that week too."

JIM AND COLLEEN'S STORY

Jim and Colleen have been together for 34 years. They have three children, all of adult age. One son has recently moved back to live with them. Colleen was diagnosed with manic depression (bipolar disorder) in 1991 which has largely been managed in the community with medication, although she has been sectioned four times and Jim eventually took early retirement from his job working for a large petro-chemical firm to spend more time with her.

"It was hell when we didn't know what was wrong with Colleen and she was behaving really odd. She went out one night completely naked and started ranting about Jesus. The kids were really shocked. The police took her away and the doc told us she had manic depression. She were in a locked ward for two month and I was left with the three kids to worry about and me job. I was really lucky Colleen's sister, who's not married, moved in for a while and helped us get back on our feet … I dunno what we'd have done without Shirley."

11.8 Using human capital to meet need

Families tended to make use of the skills, knowledge and time of all individual members whatever their age. This was particularly apparent in those households that appeared to have been most successful in avoiding severe, entrenched need. For example, one family sent their two teenage daughters to spend the day with their grandparents most weeks, not for childcare but to make sure that the frail and disabled elders had company and support for basic household tasks. The granddaughters, although only 15 and 12, were more trusted than the Polish domiciliary care worker who came in for two hours three days per week.

Severe mental health problems seemed to present the greatest threat to individual and family wellbeing, regardless of the economic status of the household:

> *I used to be a workaholic, holding three jobs down, but it did my head in. Even though we needed the money, I just couldn't cope and the doc signed me off sick ... the stress.*

It was common for households to have one or more adults experiencing significant long term disabling health conditions, and this also had the effect of eroding both financial wellbeing and confidence. Again, the most successful households tended to be the ones where the sick or disabled members had clear and positive roles and were not merely viewed as victims who were a drain on the family resources.

> *I put me Mum first, after all she'd looked after me and my Gran when I was young and I wasn't going to let her rot ... By the time she went (died) I'd been away from work since I was in me 30s ... who's going to take me on?*

Many people perceived themselves as not having the necessary skills, qualifications or experience to attract potential employers in the job market, despite evidence to the contrary in their accounts of other parts of their lives where they clearly had transferable skills and experience.

> *My son asked me to help him with a CV ... I mean what do I know? I couldn't put anything on mine ... except babies ... and he couldn't on his ... except school, and that were no good ... anyway where have I got the time? I'm so busy with the house, the girls and running the toddlers club, especially now Doris has retired and I have to do the bookkeeping as well.*

11.9 Using social capital to meet needs

Families and individuals with a very strong system of family and friendship support were both better at identifying their own needs and better at identifying the needs of others. They were more comfortable talking about needs, less sceptical, damning and untrusting of public services and quicker to seek help in resolving problems.

> *Bill and Kath across the road were having real problems controlling their young lad. He was dealing and stole a load of money from his Mam. But they wouldn't call the police, just didn't trust them not to lock the boy up ... anyway they're a very proud family, well we all are round here ... Well, see, we'd had the same problems with our Paul and he got some help, down in London, and now he works as a drugs counsellor ... came back and helped out ... it's the least we could do – they were so good when Dawn lost her first baby.*

Many common and everyday activities seemed to be routinely pooled in an exchange of human resources and time that had clearly been operating for a long time. For example, sharing the feeding and care of younger children was something that was in most families the norm. It was often regularised too.

> *I don't cook Fridays or Sundays cos we go over the road, and we have the boys round here on Tuesdays after school, help them out like.*

The use of community groups, religious organisations and community projects was also higher in these families and seemed to provide not only practical and emotional support but also a healthy pressure valve to relieve the internal tensions brought about by worklessness, depression and domestic problems.

> *Just helping out there on a Saturday morning takes me out of myself and I always feel a bit more relaxed afterwards, even when I know I've got to go back to the grind.*

Conclusions

In our interviews, insecurity, a lack of financial stability, a lack of confidence or trust in services, and a widespread feeling of social neglect were commonplace themes. However, this study also found that many families who do not have much in the way of financial resources are extremely adept and innovative at finding solutions to social needs which involve the exchange of human and social capital and the sharing of problems and burdens.

All types of assets are important in meeting needs, but are not on their own as important as the interaction and interdependencies between them. Assets also seemed to be spread widely; from file sharing in music downloads to play equipment, bikes and even cars, there seemed to be an open culture of 'freecycling' which had evolved through necessity and ingenuity rather than negotiation and formalisation.

Adverse events that threaten or jeopardise one set of satisfiers (such as the effect of redundancy on financial satisfiers or marital breakdown on human satisfiers) often have a domino effect on other satisfiers, and on individuals' and families' abilities to acquire those satisfiers. These vicious circles seemed to be more likely to affect those with smaller family and social networks. Virtuous circles were also evident, and again seemed to be more likely to occur where there was strong familial support.

12 The needs of marginalised young people in Bedford

12.1 Introduction

In this case study we shift the focus from looking directly at needs and how people experience them to looking at how people seek assistance in meeting their needs. Our study was conducted in Bedford amongst young people, many of whom would be categorised as not in education, employment or training (NEET). We chose young people aged between 16 and 25 as they are known to be a vulnerable cohort, particularly those at risk of being NEET, being substance dependent, having mental health problems, or being homeless, learning disabled or single parents. All the research and data show high levels of unmet needs amongst these young people.

But why Bedford? What do the experiences of young people in Bedford tell us about the nature of unmet needs in the United Kingdom? Bedford, in some ways, could fairly claim to be 'everytown'. If you were to place Bedford on a line ranking all British local authorities in order of deprivation, disadvantage, and diversity, it would sit right in the middle. It has all the socio-economic and cohesion problems of the city, all of the connectivity and isolation problems of the countryside, and pockets of social problems and pressure points just like all the other places Britons call home, but none in great excess nor any too insignificant to be safely ignored by policy-makers and community leaders.

12.2 Young people in Bedford

While Bedford comes in the middle nationally on many variables, it does somewhat worse in rankings relating to children and young people (e.g. low birth weights, proportion of pupils failing to reach level 4 at Key Stage 2, proportion of 16-year-olds failing to get 5+ GCSEs).[218] Furthermore, several areas of Bedford have significant levels of deprivation, with several wards among the 10% most disadvantaged in England. The most intense pockets of deprivation in Bedford lie in the inner urban wards of Cauldwell, Castle, Kingsbrook and Harpur. All these four wards rank in the top 10% most deprived wards in England and within the top 2% most deprived wards in the East of England. All four wards have a high ethnic minority population, chiefly Pakistani and Bangladeshi.

These deprived areas of urban Bedford have many young people not in education, employment or training (NEET). They also have far greater basic skills deficits than the region as a whole. Data at county level shows that more than half the population are lacking basic ICT skills (52.6%), more than 45% lack basic numeracy skills and around one in ten lack basic literacy skills. Just over half of pupils (51%) in these wards leave school each year without five or more good GCSEs – this group are most at risk of becoming NEET. In Bedfordshire as a whole, 6.5% of 16-18 year olds were NEET in 2007, compared to an East of England figure of 5.8%.[219] Pupil attainment in Befordshire is below the regional and national average, with fewer pupils leaving school with five or more GCSEs at C grade or above than the East of England as a whole.

The most deprived areas in Bedford, including the wards of Goldington and Kingsbrook, show both extremely low levels of pupil attainment and high levels of child poverty, with 35-40% of children under 5 living in low income households.[220] Furthermore, Cauldwell ward ranks in the top 1% most deprived areas across England for 'Children and young people's education', with Kingsbrook and Goldington not far behind.

SHARMAINE'S STORY

Sharmaine is 20 and has been in trouble with the law on a number of occasions due to a drug dependency. She got into drugs when her boyfriend, who was a dealer, introduced her to them. Although the relationship is over she still uses "from time to time", and, with no qualifications, has not been able to find and sustain work. She was assigned a Connexions caseworker when she was 16, but does not feel that she "got anything out of it". When asked whether she had sought help for her drug use or any other social problems, such as her housing situation, she gave the following answer:

"They don't care about people like me, they just view us as scum, lowlifes, who don't do nothing. They look down at you like (the teachers did) at school. Anyway the guy I was with told me I wasn't to tell nobody about the drugs or he'd do me damage. Now I don't even qualify (for Connexions) so nobody cares anyway. They're all like, just get a job. Well who's gonna give me a job? ... I don't really get on with my family ... yeah my friends just tell me not to worry about jobs and shit, and don't trust anybody, not even them."

Previous local work and consultation by the Bedford Charity (The Harpur Trust) has identified the high incidence of mental health problems amongst the young people and some significant barriers to seeking help from statutory and other services. Our work also uncovered a perception among service providers that children making the transition to adulthood are a particularly hard group to access; staff from a counselling service in Bedford explained:

I think they're the most difficult to catch hold of. They're not proactive in looking for themselves more often than not ... it's very hard to connect with those children if they don't want to ... if the child or young person doesn't want to attend, doesn't want to engage, then that's ok as far as we're concerned, you can't force them.

This perspective highlights the fact that from the perspective of service providers, young people often fail to engage in help-seeking behaviour by looking for assistance in alleviating and tackling their needs.

Sixteen to eighteen year olds not in education, employment or training (NEET) have become a central agenda for both national and local government in recent years. Here we have broadened the age range because our work identified a gap in research and intervention for 18-25 year olds making the transition to adulthood. This group no longer qualifies for youth services and are formally adults, although they are in a vulnerable and transitional period of their lives, as the evidence presented above illustrates.

12.3 Understanding NEETs

Nationally, the proportion of young people not in education, employment or training (NEET) has remained stable at around 9-11% since 1994.[221] On average, throughout the year there are approximately 450 young people who live in Bedford, have reached their statutory school-leaving age and who are NEET.

It is common for these young people to have complex lives and they are also more likely than their peers to have learning difficulties or disabilities, be supervised by the Youth Offending Service or be ex-offenders, teenage parents and/or have mental health problems. It is also more likely that young people who are NEET will have grown up and live in a household where there is no-one who is working.

The evidence is clear that young people NEET, whilst not forming a homogeneous group, do tend to be difficult to engage with on an individual level. Many will not have attended school consistently, especially in the latter years of statutory education, and many will not be currently engaged with other services. These factors, coupled with the likelihood that the lives of young people NEET will be complex and chaotic, mean that they may lack confidence and the resilience necessary to independently access and maintain a place on a programme.

What does it mean anyway, NEET? It's just a label ... another way for them to put us into a box. I'm a real person, man. Not a NEET or an excluded youth or a juvenile whotsit ... It's really stupid.

Young people in the NEET group claim that their experience of school was unsatisfactory and feel that it contributed to their position. Low levels of attainment were attributed to changes in staff, bullying, issues relating to transition to secondary school and school exclusion. In addition, failure at school and poor relationships with teachers resulted in negative perceptions of further education and training situations that were similar to school.

Interestingly, yet unsurprisingly, the characteristics of those most likely to be NEETs closely correspond to those groups who are most vulnerable to unmet needs. In comparison to white students, Pakistani and Bangladeshi young people aged 19 are more likely to be NEET, whereas Indians were least likely to be NEET. Young people with a disability or health problem are three times more likely to be NEET. Young people with special educational needs or mental illness are twice as likely to be NEET as those without.

Also highly predictive of ending up NEET is having a history of school exclusion or truanting. Persistent school truants are seven times more likely to be NEET at age 16, which probably correlates with low attainment. It has been estimated that two-thirds of teenage mothers, equating to around 20,000 young women, are NEET. Other characteristics of the NEET group include being looked-after young people, young carers, young people involved in crime and young people whose parents have poor educational qualifications.

Ben is 21 and out of work. He lives with his parents and has mild learning difficulties.He told us:

> *I don't need much ... you know... Me Mum gets me what I need. I'd like to have me own place near (to his mother) but that ain't gonna happen. I need money really. And a job...*

12.4 Young people's perceptions of their needs

As with many others, the young people that we talked to in Bedford did not naturally couch things in the language of need, rather they were likely to talk in words such as "I want", "I should", "it would be good/nice" or "I've got a right to". Therefore, in order to explore their underlying needs, we discussed with the young people their view of what they were aiming for in their lives in the short to medium term. One young man responded that all he wanted was to "get a job ... so I can get some decent clothes and a car". On further exploration, the clothes appeared to be instrumental to his need for self-esteem and identity and the car a key factor in his need for independence and meaningful relationships (particularly for a girlfriend).

The second most common initial expression of needs by the young people was for the resolution or elimination of a particular problem. Their most common problem was their inability to find a job, but the next most common were broadly characterised as relational conflicts, whether with a partner, family member or another member of the community.

The need for a job

There was a clear consensus among those who were not in employment that they wanted jobs. They generally recognised that they need qualifications to get a job but saw this as a barrier to getting "any job". When asked what their plan was to get a job, the participants generally responded that they weren't sure, or talked about qualifications. On being asked what sort of qualifications would be most useful, people rarely mentioned the type and level of course that they felt would be needed and it was uncommon for anyone to spontaneously volunteer a specific vocational training subject (those that did were young women mentioning childcare). Responses to questions about what sort of work people wanted commonly involved "retail" or "in a shop", reflecting a widespread perception amongst participants that there were limited employment opportunities in the Bedford area, especially in the current economic climate.

BEN'S STORY

Ben is 21 and out of work. He lives with his parents and has mild learning difficulties. He told us:

"I don't need much … you know … Me Mum gets me what I need. I'd like to have me own place near (to his mother) but that ain't gonna happen. I need money really. And a job..."

MAC'S STORY

Mac is 17 and lives with his grandmother.

"Gran's getting on and she needs lots of stuff doing … she's only on a pension and that … I try to help her out … if I had the money I'd take her on holiday or something ... she needs a break"

The need for money

Most of those we spoke to were not in work and all of them mentioned money as being a huge issue for them. It was common that the younger participants still lived with family members, although this was as often with grandparents, siblings or other extended family members as with their parents. This reflected the high reported incidence of family breakdown.

Those who lived with family members had extremely varied financial relationships with their families. Almost all participants expressed their need for money to buy clothes and for mobile phones.

Those who lived in sheltered accommodation such as the local Foyer and YMCA reported finding it extremely hard to make ends meet. Two could not make calls or texts to the researchers at one time or another due to insufficient funds to top up their phones.

The need for meaningful things to do

The young people we interviewed identified the lack of activities and things to do as being a major blight on their lives and a cause of the anti-social behaviour and street violence that so many of them described in some of the more deprived parts of Bedford. "The kids have got nowhere to go and nothing to do so of course they hang out there," said one young man aged 18. "But then the police moved us along even when we weren't doing nothing wrong".

While participants could list local youth centres, leisure centres and other venues, the perception was usually that "you have to go to Milton Keynes or Luton to do good stuff". Alternatively, the younger end of the cohort said that the youth venues were "no good to us", either because they were "boring", "naff", "full of 12 year olds" or "there's always trouble there".

The main needs identified by the young people we interviewed are represented in the table below.

Practical needs	Psycho-social needs
Skills and training	Things to do – activities and leisure
Help finding more suitable accommodation	Someone to talk to about a problem
Advice on housing and legal issues	To be near to family and friends
Help with literacy and numeracy	Control over domestic situations
Help with applying for things and budgeting	A place to stay of their own – independence
Life skills training	To feel safe, secure and stable
Financial inclusion	Support to cope after the impact of abuse, violence and crime
Help with childcare and relative care	A sense of belonging
Education	People to be with for company

12.5 Young people's perceptions of services and solutions

It was common for the participants in the study to have encountered one or more professionals working for either Connexions or another of the many statutory and voluntary services working with young people in the Bedford area. Most contact was established through the provision of 'entry to employment' (E2E) training, although many young people told us that they were extremely bored by E2E training provision, and also that the content did not match their long-term aspirations. This provides some evidence to suggest that lack of aspiration was not, of itself, a problem; instead, routes to achieve those aspirations should be identified in order for young people to succeed. Some of those we spoke to had even taken steps to avoid certain E2E training providers because they said it might make their problems worse. There was a perception amongst both young people and practitioners that certain providers took on young people who had been involved in drugs or other criminal activities or, worse, who had been bullies them at school. This for some young people acted as a disincentive: "I knew Kevin was on that course and he's trouble, like, so there's no way I'm going what with what he did to me before".

12.6 The views of those providing services for young people

Connexions was commonly understood among the practitioners we interviewed to be an agency overly concerned with tackling NEET numbers, at the expense of engaging with the real needs experienced by young people. Their responsibility for tracking and monitoring NEET young people was widely perceived as an inefficient use of time, given that resources are generally overstretched.

The Personal Advisors (PAs) we spoke to estimated that their caseload was at least twice as high as that which would allow them to give an optimal service to their clients, and the amount of time spent chasing phantom appointments, waiting for people and following 'dead-end' leads was seen as overly high and rarely compensated for by the ability to replace that lost time with other face-to-face work.

The Connexions PAs were seen by other practitioners and young people alike as helpful in getting some young people to meet their own needs, but their impact is limited due to being over-stretched.

The following is a list of common barriers identified by young people:

- A perceived lack of suitable opportunities or a lack of qualifications/experience; Lack of funds preventing them from engaging;
- An inability to travel to college/workplace;
- Being unaware of what options are open to them and available, and/or being undecided about the sort of job or course they want to do;
- Childcare issues;
- Having a criminal record;
- Lack of decent jobs or courses available in their area;
- Emotional Barriers – lack of confidence, fear of the unknown, lack of motivation;
- Personal issues and personal circumstances arising from family or housing problems, to health issues and a lack of transport.

12.7 Impact of major life events and social problems

Young people's responses to major life events are diverse and not easily predictable. Some of the most positive and confident participants in the study, for example, were those with the greatest number of severely adverse life events, such as those who had been bereaved or subjected to violence and displacement.

Young people were asked whether they felt that any particular events had made it more likely that they would suffer from problems or unmet needs in the future. These events were identified as ones that appeared to the young people to 'mess up' their life and make dealing with troublesome issues "a complete nightmare", as one young girl put it. Examples of such events and situations included the intervention of police or social services following incidents of abuse and violence, bereavement or the breakdown of relationships, particularly ones where there was a child involved.

We also asked people to speculate as to what it is about individual young people that means they will be more or less severely affected by such events and situations. More replied that it was something to do with the individual's personal "strength" or "bottle" than focused on external factors such as whether or not there was a high level of social support. One young woman, aged 17, saw it as a simple choice – "either I can just lie down and go yeah I'm screwed or I can get on ... I mean it's not like someone died is it? There's no choice really". In her opinion some people's personalities were quite simply stronger than others. In her eyes they were the people who "didn't need help" or wouldn't want "a fuss made".

The same young woman took a slightly different view of the amount of time and emotional energy that it took her to "get over" an adverse event which she felt had been avoidable and had not been "nobody's fault". Her experience of serious disputes with her manager at a bakery, her only ever job, had "put her off" trying for another job. "It's not worth the hassle when there are bitches like that", she said. She saw the workplace as an arena where she had no control and was not able to display any resilience, not least because someone else "had all the power and it went to her head".

12.8 Attitudes towards the future

When asked questions about the future, the first and most striking feature about the young people's responses is that virtually none of them saw their future in Bedford. Even those with families in Bedford expressed the same feelings.

These negative views were largely attributed to a lack of vitality in Bedford, "nothing changes here"; very favourable views of other places, "why would you stay in Bedford when you could go (to) London?" and, most frequently, pessimism about the economic opportunities locally "if I want a decent job I'll have to move".

The researchers asked the participants to imagine that in ten years time they were living the kind of life that they aspired to - usually a settled job, home and relationship or family. We then asked them whether they thought that this pathway was likely to have been achieved without any assistance from third parties, with a certain amount of assistance, or very largely due to the assistance of a third party.

The young people predominantly answered that they would probably have been significantly assisted by somebody, whether it was a friend, family member or outsider, at some crucial stage along the pathway. It is possible to speculate that this shows that the idea of efficacious and even transformative help is not alien to the young people, whether or not they have actually experienced it. When pressed respondents tended not to have in their mind exactly who would have played such a role but it was a feature of most of the interviews that the young people could at least imagine a situation where their lives turned around.

Finlay is 20 and has been in and out of the criminal justice system. He also has two children by two different mothers. He was born and brought up in Bedford. He told us:

> *[they] don't think I can get me act together but I know I can. It's just there's no point even trying to get (a job) ... anyway I'm gonna go and live with me brother in London, it's different (there).*

FINLAY'S STORY

Finlay is 20 and has been in and out of the criminal justice system. He also has two children by two different mothers. He was born and brought up in Bedford. He told us:

[they] don't think I can get me act together but I know I can. It's just there's no point even trying to get (a job) ... anyway I'm gonna go and live with me brother in London, it's different (there).

Conclusions

This study reinforces what previous studies have found: that young people tend not to seek help from professional sources, especially for stigmatised areas such as mental and sexual health or substance dependencies, preferring to seek informal help before they turn to formal resources. Young people tend to turn first to friends for support with emotional and sensitive personal problems, before seeking the counsel of parents. The young women we interviewed were significantly more likely to seek help than young men, particularly for help with mental health problems. The young men tended to be more likely to rely on themselves and also not to recognise that there was an important problem that needed to be solved.

Different types of problems lent themselves to different ports of call for help – relationship advice was sought from friends, health advice from parents, and educational advice from teachers and so on.

We also found that the most common predictors of effective help-seeking were low levels of family conflict, the belief that treatment or intervention will be efficacious, previous experience with services, and having had fewer school problems.

Assistance from others was often seen as a mixed blessing, and as a consequence some young people in need decide not to seek help from available resources at all – effectively working against their own self-interest.

PART IV

Responding to need now and in the future

In this final part of the report we begin to draw our conclusions and look to the future.

First, we summarise some of the overall patterns from the case studies, both in relation to patterns of unmet need and how people meet them.

Then we map how needs might evolve, focusing on public spending, unemployment, demographics and ageing as well as science and technology, diversity, anxiety and other emotional states, isolation, damaging consumption and climate change.

Finally we turn to directions for future action.

13 The dynamics of need

In this chapter we draw together the evidence presented so far, and begin to consider what it implies for some of the thorniest questions about need. What causes unmet need? How do people cope with having unmet needs? How do they get their needs met? What protects people from vulnerability?

13.1 Explaining the incidence of unmet need

The case studies have shown how people do or don't succeed in meeting their needs. They demonstrate how particular individual or community circumstances determine people's ability to meet their needs, and that both risks and capabilities operate at several levels:

- Self: those relating to the individual, including their assets and skills as well as attitudes, habits and dispositions.
- Support: those relating to people's immediate networks of support, including family members, friends and GPs.
- Structures and systems: those relating to more structural and macro factors such as the availability of work in their town or region, whether they have rights and entitlements, or the impact of environmental factors such as climate change.

They are then shaped by the interaction of:

- Assets, capabilities and opportunities – such as money or skills, living near a good local school or a buoyant labour market.
- Risk factors – such as having a criminal record or a history of mental illness, or living in an estate with very high worklessness.
- Protective factors – such as strong family supports or entitlements to care.

To illustrate this, it is helpful to return to the story of Julie, who we met in Chapter 7. Julie lost her husband in a road accident and has been struggling to support her two teenage children. She had few immediate networks of support to fall back on; her parents were both dead and she did not feel her siblings or friends were able to offer the support she needed. Yet her children provided her with a sense of purpose, and by focusing on their needs Julie was able to draw on her self-determination and resilience. She was able to gain additional skills by retraining at university and found a job at a local pre-school. Julie was helped by the financial asset of owning a house (although mortgage repayments added to her stress) and additional state support through the Widowed Parent's Allowance. Julie's story shows how the interplay of different types of support, resources, opportunities and protective factors can help individuals overcome crises and allow them to continue to meet their needs.

Julie was able to deal with the loss of her husband through drawing on her own capabilities, assets and other protective factors. However, as we have seen, not everyone has access to such resources. There are also significant risk factors that can hamper people from meeting their needs. The case studies show that risks are often concentrated (or have especially adverse impacts) at particular stages in the life course or among particular groups. Being a child of drug-addicted parents stacks the odds against you in many ways, as does being a child in care. We know that the number of frail and disabled older people is growing and that the number of people at ages typically involved in caring for them is shrinking in relative size. And we know that the further contraction of demand in the labour market for unskilled young men means that unless today's 16 and 17 year olds can gain skills and aptitudes they risk a lifetime of insecure employment and income.

13.2 Who is meeting needs

By historical standards we are a very dependent society. Very few of us can provide our own food, energy, healthcare or housing. We rely day in and day out on the work of others to feed us, clothe us, protect us, transport us and finance us. Most of us depend on support from all sectors – from private companies operating in commercial markets such as supermarkets, from government agencies like the NHS, from charities and from our family and friends.

Where the market is the main provider, access to cash is all-important. Being an asylum seeker with a spending entitlement of under £40 a week makes lack of cash an overriding concern. Many others on low incomes trade quality for quantity in 'pound shops', and the poor pay more for many items, from food to credit and utilities – the so called "Poverty Premium".[222] And market provision feels very different if you live in a remote rural community, with patchy provision and high prices.

Where the state is a primary provider, there is sometimes universal provision (usually bringing with it issues of uneven quality, as in primary schools) and sometimes rationing, as with varying entitlements to care. There are the shifting patterns of fees – from council house rents to public transport. And there are shifting patterns of conditionality, particularly for those without jobs. Governments are generally competent at dealing with major shocks or risks that are fairly homogenous. This is the case when many people are made simultaneously redundant or need a particular kind of health care or treatment (for example for swine flu). But government programmes tend to be poor at dealing with people in the round, at care and continuity, let alone love. And they are increasingly struggling to cope with the huge expansion of diversity, with all of its implications for everything from sensitive diagnosis of health conditions to the funding of community centres.

Civil society and community organisations have again become more visible as providers, though where in the nineteenth century they often paved the way for state provision, now they often provide under contract to the state. Their services have been professionalised immensely in the last two decades and now tend to be more accessible, holistic and barrier-free than in the past. As in the past, they are better at seeing people and places in the round. But provision remains uneven, and often what is funded is not the fundamental need. Some charities were set up to deal with particular conditions rather than their causes. Moreover, institutions and resources in civil society can reflect the needs of the past rather than the present, perhaps an inevitable result of the way foundations and endowments are established.

As we have already shown, the family and household remain the primary place where our needs for sustenance, health, support and learning are met. But household size, family configuration and strength vary enormously across the UK. The number of single households has risen markedly over the last generation or two, and in some areas, such as those explored in the London case study, we are seeing a return to multiple occupancy overcrowded urban properties. Young people are having to remain living with family for longer, and many in middle age are struggling to support their parents as they navigate the messy decisions that come with declining health. At all ages many want to escape their families, which can be cauldrons of hate and resentment as well as havens. And much seems to depend on micro-cultures and norms: for example we saw greater intra- and inter-household co-operation in the Teesside housing estates than in the ones in Bedford.

13.3 Adverse events and life course transitions

Major shock events often have a big impact on our needs. The psychological as well as material impact of job loss was an important theme in three of our case studies. Adverse events are by and large unavoidable over the life course, but some of them have a far greater impact than others. The onset of severe disability or of primary responsibility for caring for a severely disabled person brings a huge number of new needs. Bereavement, divorce, incarceration and victimisation are all common enough examples of adverse life events, many of which we explored in our transitions case study. They are all usually unexpected and some of the power of their effect on need derives from their suddenness. All have been shown in research to not only create new needs but also to erode people's capacity to seek help and cope with challenges. Various scales measuring the power of psycho-social stressors regularly put these events at the top of social risk factors for mental health and wellbeing deficits.

Life course transitions appear to work in a similar way, although often played out over longer periods of time and in more predictable ways. Each transition, such as the path from youth to adulthood, from employment to retirement, from health to infirmity or from institutionalisation to independence can have profound effects on the needs people have and their ways of having them met. We saw those in our transition study who on release from prison suddenly had to take responsibility for their time and finances, and those in our Bedford study who were finding the adjustment from school to employment extremely challengin. But the importance of transitions has been underplayed in public policy until recently.

Both adverse events and life course transitions affect people very differently. Some people are not only able to recover from the trauma of shock events relatively quickly, they are even able to turn them into growing and learning opportunities that leave them stronger and happier in the future.

Similarly, some people make life course transitions enthusiastically and without great distress, while others find the experience traumatic and sapping. Our case studies demonstrate that some of these differences can be explained by socio-economic buffers and anchors (such as having a secure financial and housing base) and some by psycho-social buffers and anchors (such as having effective social support systems or a strong faith). Some people use coping strategies to handle psychological stress and anxiety, but in ways that help them to absorb shocks rather than overcome them: narrowing their expectations, their ambitions and their activities. They can end up hardened and tougher, but less able to realise opportunities in the future.

This sort of 'survival resilience' contrasts with a more proactive and adaptive kind of resilience that involves finding new sources of internal and external support (for example seeking help, as some young people did in Bedford) or planning for the future (as some of the households in Teesside did). The critical factors that make such proactive resilience possible include: robust levels of self-esteem and optimism, humour, being comfortable admitting that things are difficult and seeking help from others. They also often include previous experience of trauma having been overcome and the existence of strong personal frameworks of meaning, identity and belonging. All of these contribute to an increased likelihood that adverse events and challenging transitions will not deplete wellbeing or leave severe needs unmet.

We have adopted one of the definitions of resilience used in the literature on ecological systems to summarise the point. Resilience is at heart 'the capacity of an individual, organisation or system to absorb disturbances and reorganise itself while undergoing change in ways that retain or enhance its capacities to think and act'.[223]

13.4 The mechanisms for meeting needs

Drawing on the case studies, we have developed a model for making sense of how people come to meet their needs. It sets out the stages people go through to recognise and then act on their needs. For every stage there are potential barriers and enablers. Many of the participants in our fieldwork bore testimony to the barriers facing them, even when a need had been identified. For example, Sharmaine in Bedford had already identified that she required help and support to free herself from the grip of drugs and find employment. But many barriers lie in the way of her having those needs met. Some of these are personal to her, such as stigma and mistrust of services, and some are external, relating to the shape and availability of services and other structural conditions, such as eligibility.

The key stages in the process of meeting need are laid out in the following table, along with an account of what might be experienced subjectively at each point and the most common barriers we have observed in this study. It is striking that many of the barriers do seem to lie at an individual psychological and attitudinal level, particularly at the earlier stages. In the later stages, structural and external factors play a more important role.

The first stage is identifying a need. Most of the participants in this study seemed to identify readily with the concept of need, relating it to current or imminent suffering or hardship. Some were actively involved in identifying needs for others less able to do so, such as their children or elderly parents, especially where there were cognitive challenges, for example through dementia or learning disabilities. The perception of suffering varied hugely across individuals, with some ascribing high levels of suffering to social problems relating to threats to their dignity, status and self-esteem, while others were much more focused on hardships relating to economic and health outcomes. These differences do not relate directly to the level of economic disadvantage or even to objective health status. There are major psychological drivers that are important to explore if we are to understand how needs and hardship are perceived and distributed. For example, mental health problems play a major role both in creating new needs and in inhibiting people's ability to deal effectively with existing needs. This came out in all of our case studies – perhaps not surprisingly, since severe mental illness (psychosis) and mental disorders (neurosis) are experienced by around 17% of people at some time.

The distribution and magnifying effect of mental illness is connected with poverty, however poverty might be defined. People who are poor are at far higher risk of having either psychosis or neurosis than those who are not poor. Having lower educational attainment, being unemployed or being economically inactive are also very consistent predictors of psychosis and neurosis.

Perhaps more surprisingly, recent research has consistently shown that having a physical illness and two or more recent adverse life events are high risk markers for having a mental illness (six times more likely than those without physical illness and three times more than those with fewer than two recent adverse life events).[224]

The second stage in the process is 'internal activation': the realisation that a need which you feel or perceive is actually able to be met, is important and therefore should be met, and that you are intending to ensure this happens. There are many potential barriers to this happening. Simple lack of awareness of the existence of a satisfier that might meet that need (such as was expressed by some of the young people in Bedford) or feeling that you don't deserve to be helped can deter help-seeking and stall the process at this point. We have seen that the resolution of acute psychological needs can be particularly difficult to activate, since the satisfiers can appear very complex or stigmatised and shame, guilt and hopelessness are more commonly felt.

The barriers to internal activation range from stigma, pride, stress and cultural inhibitions to having terrible previous experiences of services and distrust – and it is often hard to disentangle which one is most important. But it is safe to say that most of the participants in our research experienced barriers of this kind (a point that is recognised in much of the literature on low take-up rates and reluctance to seek help).

The third stage in the process of meeting needs is the effective expression of demand. In the market that means having the money to buy something and the knowledge of where to buy it. But for many of the needs we were studying there was neither money to buy things nor anything available on the market. Many of the people we spoke to were not particularly confident about asking for help or approaching formal services, especially where the responsibility lay with the individual to self-refer and make the case for entitlement themselves. Many of the young people under 20 that we spoke to were entitled, for example, to support from Connexions, but found it hard to make demands, or relied on trusted intermediaries such as a family member, community sector advocate or key worker.

The fourth stage is the availability of a satisfier to meet the need. In many cases there may simply be no available service or opportunity to meet that need, for example there may be no respite services available for the carers of a multiply disabled child, or domiciliary care for someone with arthritis may have been rationed out under the Fair Access to Care Services programme for social service resource prioritisation in England.

Many of the barriers at this stage are political and economic. Here we reach fundamental political questions about which needs should make the greatest claim on public resources. Even before the current economic crisis, government was tending to move away from providing some lower level supports, concentrating resources instead on the most acute needs (for example of old people) or needs associated with statutory duties (such as child protection).

Figure 61: The key stages in the process of meeting need

	Process	Subjective experience	Potential barriers
Identification ↓	Need felt or identified	I'm suffering or if I don't get this sorted I will suffer	Lack of knowledge, absence of perceived suffering, cognitive or mental health impairment, denial
Internal activation ↓	Need acknowledged as satisfiable and a priority for action	This need can be met. I have a right to have it met and it is important that it be met. I want it met.	Lack of awareness and motivation, pride, stigma, mistrust, bad previous experience, competing priorities, hyper-stress,a culture, perverse incentives, fatalism, learned helplessness
Demand expression ↓	Need expressed effectively as demand for existing satisfier	Here is my need X, please provide me with satisfier Y to which I am entitled by virtue of Z	Lack of confidence, assertiveness, power, opportunity, support, legitimacy, knowledge, language determination or organisation; wrong approach, strategy, timing or data
Availability ↓	Satisfier available, affordable, accessible, offered and accepted	They are offering me Y in an acceptable way at an acceptable time, place and price and with acceptable reciprocal demands	Non-existence of satisfier, rationing, expense, ineligibility, inaccessibility, exclusion, conditionality
External Activation ↓	Satisfier provided in full, in time and effectively	I am getting Y as promised	Service provided partially, badly or at the wrong time, service different from that promised
Satisfaction	Need satisfied	Y seems to work, my need is being met	Need more complex than thought, dependent upon resolution of other needs, only temporarily met, or met in a way that causes more need

Government has also tended to move towards services that can demonstrate some cost-benefit gains (such as Family Nurse Partnerships) rather than ones based on entitlement. Meanwhile the market meets some needs effectively (from clothing to cars to sex), but struggles to meet the needs of those who are in the bottom 20% of society, and is inherently ill-designed to meet human needs for care, compassion, or love.

The fifth and sixth stages are the external activation of a service or good to meet need and the satisfaction of the need. Many everyday needs are met in straightforward ways, such as the need for food or warmth. Indeed these are met far more straightforwardly than in past eras. But some needs are inter-related and there seems to be a cumulative or magnifying effect. Families that we observed in Teesside who had to deal with the challenges of disability often had to deal with over-indebtedness and family tensions as well. Badly or temporarily met needs can cause more unmet needs in the future, particularly when the response is to deploy a coping strategy that avoids the underlying cause (pretending that there is no problem) or tries to compensate for it (turning to drink or another compulsive habit).

One very striking feature arises from this picture. The choices facing people appear to be more complex than in the past. But many lack the confidence, skills, knowledge or friends to help them navigate their way from stage 1 to stage 6. This is particularly the case for people living chaotic lives.

The wealthy now spend a growing proportion of their income on advisers of all kinds, to help them with financial choices, career choices, psychological troubles or how to decorate their homes. Some of these advisers guide their clients through the stages outlined above – identifying and understanding their wants and needs and then finding ways to meet them. The relatively poor, by contrast, facing much more difficult choices on the whole, have access to far fewer, and far more stretched, services to help them think about choices and their life course. Some of these are provided by the state through services like Connexions, personal advisers at Job Centres or probation officers. Some are provided by the voluntary sector, for example through Citizens Advice Bureaux. But they can rarely devote enough time to each of their clients, and are usually juggling their scarce time. The result is a substantial group who simply feel at sea much of the time, out of control of their lives.

13.5 Resilience

Resilience has become a much more common object of study because of the recurring empirical observation (also found in our case studies) that there are enormous variations in people's responses to all types of environmental hazard and threat. Indeed, one of the earliest attempts to empirically measure resilience was prompted by observation of the resilience, fortitude and bravery shown by Ernest Shackleton and his crew in the Antarctic one hundred years ago.[225]

The notion of resilience focuses our attention not so much on the risks and threats that people face but rather on the strategies they use to cope with them, and rise above them. Much has been learned about both physiological and psychological resilience. Research shows that physiological resilience is increased by having been born to a healthy mother after a normal gestation and brought up in a clean, safe, warm and dry home where income is adequate to needs.[226] It is also influenced by mental factors, including optimism, and social factors, including strong social networks.

While traumas can be debilitating, many people quickly bounce back. There is evidence of 'steeling' effects, in which successfully surviving situations of stress or adversity can produce improved functioning and increased resistance to future stress and adversity.[227] Older children who experience having to cope with family poverty sometimes appear to gain additional psychological strengths, just as the body's ability to resist disease comes in part from being exposed to risks in controlled circumstances.

Mel and Steve, participants in our Teesside study, had experienced multiple economic setbacks, as well as health problems and family difficulties, and yet they displayed an extremely resilient attitude towards the slings and arrows of misfortune and even described themselves as resilient.

This sort of resilience is common. A large proportion of children recover from short-lived childhood adversities with little detectable impact in adult life. But resilience decreases with the severity and multiplicity of adverse events.[228] In other words, where adversities are continuous and severe and protective factors are absent, resilience in children, and then adults, is likely to be rarer. This is particularly the case for people with severe mental health problems. One study of adults in their 30s who suffered serious mental health problems in their adolescence measured their resilience and found that there was a high association between the impact of early mental health problems and poor adult mental development and functioning.[229] Resilience is also critical to our ability to cope with transitions. One study found that people who describe themselves as resilient before their loved one died were less likely to have enduring grief symptoms at 4 and 18 months after the loved one's death.[230] They did experience symptoms consistent with grieving, but unlike non-resilient people, managed to continue functioning in their lives.

Yet resilience varies across families, and for the same individual across different parts of their life. No one knows precisely how these dynamics work, or precisely how resilience is shaped by experiences, or whether the various factors that inform adult resilience interact or are cumulative. However, it is clear that a central role in the process of developing resilience (or grit), or lack of resilience (or brittleness), is taken by adverse or challenging life events or transitions.[231] A good example is widowhood and divorce, which can both be seen in the figure below to cause a serious dip in psychological wellbeing. Wellbeing takes some time to recover its pre-existing level, but it is striking that it usually does recover, even after serious traumas.

Figure 62: Marital transitions and annual psychological wellbeing scores over time (GHQ12 mean score)

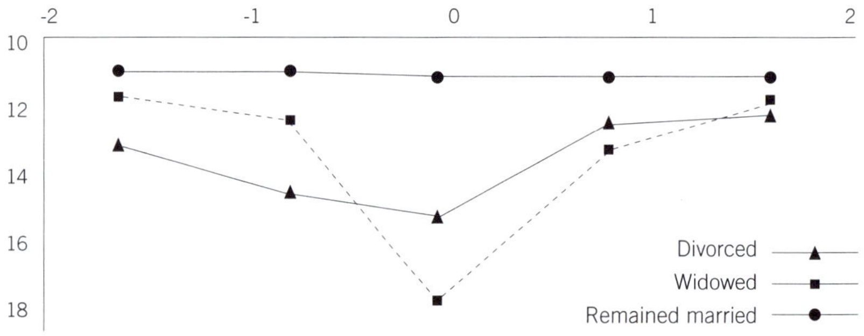

Source: BHPS

Adverse events, social problems and crises are common occurrences during the life course.[232] Our case study on transitions found that when people experience a crisis, one of the first things they do is attempt to regain a sense of equilibrium by processing the event internally. They can then respond either with a survival resilience – in which they shrink back and harden their defences – or with a more adaptive resilience that helps them grow out of adversity. Although most people do bounce back, how they bounce back can vary greatly. The following diagram aims to provide a way to think about these dynamics.

Figure 63: Conceptual framework for resilience

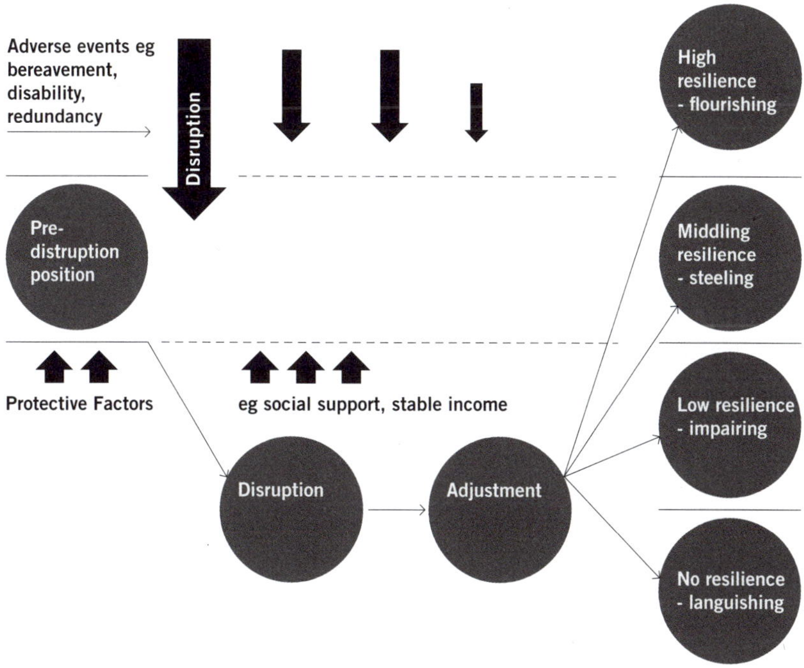

Healthy resilience requires a 'good-enough' level of both self-regulation and self-esteem. Recent research has found that "high ego-resilient people are characterised by their ability to exert appropriate and dynamic self-regulation, whereas low ego-resilient people (i.e., ego-brittle) tend to rigidly under or over self-regulate." Too much self-regulation in this context means trying too hard to exert control, or being too neurotic.

For children, the most common sources of anxiety are chronic and transitional events. Chronic problems will usually have more lasting effects than acute adversities. This has enormous implications for social policy and services, which often tackle severe and acute presenting needs (such as a crisis) at the expense of severe and chronic needs (such as the absence of good quality parenting). A study of Dutch adolescents with parents with bipolar disorder found that negative life events significantly increase their liability to experience mood disorders, with the negative effects of the life events decaying steadily by 25% per year after they occurred.[234]

Our understanding of resilience is that it is more than merely the ability to 'bounce back' after experiencing trauma or stress, but also about having sharper antennae to avoid future threats, and being better able to experience stressful situations with more equanimity or more 'neutrally', from missing a bus to breaking a leg to losing a job. Another recurrent theme, well expressed by the more resilient families in the Teesside housing estates, is the ability and motivation to re-frame adversities so that the beneficial as well as the damaging effects are recognised.

13.6 Factors enabling resilience

Resilience seems to be fostered by protective factors and inhibited by risk factors.[235] But context is crucial, and one mix of factors may prove beneficial in one situation and detrimental in another, whilst people may be resilient to some things and not others, and at some times and not others.[236]

Resilience can be developed in a retrospective fashion, as people make sense of their lives and previous adversities in constructive ways. And for many people 'turning point' events, such as marriage, promote recovery. Getting together with Denise was certainly the turning point for Frank in Teesside. He talked freely about the transformation that had taken place in the eight years since they had got together, in stark comparison to the previous 40 years of a life in which he says he "couldn't cope" with things and "made the wrong decisions ... always."

The ability to recover and bounce back after adversity is not always pro-social. Some of the individuals who have demonstrated the most resilience to adversity can do so by being 'hardened' and overly self-centred.[237] An excessive pre-occupation with eliminating risks can be damaging: too much fear is disabling, as is being too neurotic. And some actions that appear likely to support resilience can backfire: e.g. giving teenagers too much responsibility too early, or providing a targeted intervention to children of drug users that, through labelling them, reinforces their sense of otherness.[238] Finally, while self-esteem is a crucial factor in the promotion of resilience, it is more likely to grow and be sustained through developing valued skills in real life situations, rather than just through praise and positive affirmation.[239]

As we have seen, protective and risk factors operate at three levels, from those of the self through those of the family and support networks to those of the wider community. The table below summarises these.

Figure 64: Protective factors promoting resilience

Self: individual level – from transitions and Bedford study	Support: family level – from Teesside study	Structure: community level – from London and South Wales study
Emotional regulation Effective coping skills	Stability of intimate relationship	Community involvement and cohesion
Internal locus of control Self-efficacy Belief systems Increased education, skills and training Previous physical and mental health Past social and cultural experiences Exposure to and recovery from trauma Temperament and personality Problem solving skills Social skills Sense of purpose and meaning Gender	Family structure Supportive vertical relationships Family cohesion Social support Stability of housing environment Stability of income Humour and communication Well defined but malleable roles Equity of effort and responsibility	Safe neighbourhoods Access to quality schools and child care Access to quality healthcare Sensitivity and availability of quality social services Infrastructure Labour market

Resilience can be enhanced at each of these levels – from teaching children how to cope with emotional shocks, through family support, to more effective public institutions. Yet there is a clear need for better understanding of what makes communities resilient. We've suggested some of the key factors in the table above, but there are big gaps in the available knowledge, and it's important to distinguish between different kinds of resilience. Many of the communities that suffered the shocks of deindustrialisation in the 1970s and 1980s have developed strong survival resilience: the ability to absorb shocks and cope with setbacks. They also developed coping strategies – including strong mutual support in some cases. But they are arguably less well-placed for adaptive resilience. Our definition of resilience is the ability to respond to challenges in ways that leave greater capacity behind. This sort of adaptive resilience is rather different from survival resilience. If the latter is about having thicker skin, the former is about seeking out new opportunities, and learning fast how to cope with setbacks. One thesis which is implied by our research, and warrants further testing, is whether more diverse communities may be better at this kind of adaptive resilience.

13.7 Help-seeking behaviour

One of the key determinants of unmet need is the extent to which people seek help. In our Bedford interviews it was clear that although many of the young people were in desperate need of help, they had no idea where to find it. Misha, who had been abused by her stepfather, said that she "didn't dare ask for help, in case he found out and came to me again". Laurence had been diagnosed with ADHD and problematised at school and lived in constant fear of the authorities "making me feel like a little boy again".

Help-seeking behaviour is the process of actively seeking out and using social relationships, whether they be formal or informal, to help with personal problems. Unlike many other social transactions, the objective in help-seeking is intensely personal, and therefore the barriers will also tend to be personal and often psychological.

Our fieldwork has demonstrated the complexity of the help-seeking process. It is not simply a process of identifying need, deciding to seek help and carrying out that decision. At each of these decision points, factors can get in the way: need may not be identified; if identified, need may not be translated into intention; and intention does not always lead to action. These observations have led us to a pathway model of the dynamics of seeking help, represented in the diagram on the next page.

Figure 65: Conceptual framework of the process of help-seeking

Internal determinants	Help-seeking intention	Tipping point	Determining help pathway	Choice of help source	Help-seeking first approach
Self-awareness, self-image and self-esteem Unsuccessful self-help attempts Help-seeking attitude Distress and inability to cope Perceived helpfulness of previous help-seeking experience Cultural, attitudinal and social influences, social comparison	Problem identification Recognition of the need for outside assistance Readiness for self-disclosure Awareness of existence of satisfiers Willingness to relinquish some degree of control to a helper	Decision point – individual wants and decides to seek help for need	Geographic and emotional proximity of help Perceived effectiveness of help Perceived cost of help – money, reciprocal demands and penalties Perceived accessibility of help Perceived stigma in using help Perceived reliability and rustworthiness of help	Dependent on sources of help available	Approaches formal mainstream service provider Approaches informal service provider such as family or friend Approaches community sector service provider No approach made

The process begins with awareness of symptoms and recognition that a significant problem exists that may require intervention. Many factors in this contemplation phase can influence the intention to act. However, as we have seen from the individuals who did finally seek help in our qualitative studies, such as Lucy who ended up in hospital with a drug overdose, there is often a tipping point that triggers the actual decision to seek help. Not least of these preconditions is that the help-seeker must be willing and able to disclose some of their inner state to that source. The barriers to this can be immense, as we have seen in the transitions case study.

Of course, help can be sought from a wide variety of sources varying in their level of formality – some from informal social relationships such as friends and family and some from formal professional sources. Increasingly, help can be sought from sources that do not involve direct contact with other people, such as the Internet, and this may have the effect of removing some of the internal barriers in the pathway to seeking help.

However, some groups are far less likely to approach formal services than others. For example, our evidence from Bedford confirms that young people tend not to seek help from professionals, and tend to seek informal help before they turn to formal sources. In addition, our findings mirror those elsewhere which indicate that in contrast to women, a man is more likely to rely on himself than to seek help from other people, and is also more likely to deny the presence of a problem in the first place.

Surveys and service data have constantly revealed particularly low rates of help-seeking for mental distress amongst young adults. As few as 17% of young adults with mental distress[240] and fewer than a third of those with a clinically defined disorder may seek healthcare.[241] These estimates for young adults are much lower than comparable figures for all adults. In fact, large-scale surveys of all adults reveal an association between help-seeking and age, whereby help-seeking is least likely to occur in those aged 16–24 years.[242]

The experiences of the NEET young people in Bedford confirm that the quality of the first interaction young people have with a particular type of service is hugely important in predicting whether they will turn to formal services in the future. One bad experience can tarnish all professional services in the eyes of many people. Equally, if someone has experienced the transformative effect of help given by a third party, they seem to be much more switched on or attuned to the possibility that they might find assistance in resolving a future problem.

To shed light on the help-seeking behaviour of those with psychological needs we analysed the extent to which people with anxiety and depression problems sought professional help. Only a minority of the UK sample (8%) stated that they suffer from anxiety or depression. Although the majority of people suffering from anxiety/depression were women (72%), men were proportionately more likely to have accessed a psychologist (17% compared to 14%).

The proportion of the subsample that had used a psychologist decreased with age: 33% younger people; 24% young adults; 18% middle aged; 16% mature adults; 14% seniors; and only 5% of pensioners. Those renting from local authorities were slightly less likely to have accessed a psychologist (10%) compared to those who were owners with a mortgage (14%).

So it appears that the disinclination to seek professional help with psychological needs is widespread across the life course and does not improve with age. Clearly there are cultural and historical factors that go towards explaining these differences, with the role of stigma and pride featuring highly at the older end of the spectrum.

14 Emerging and future unmet need

14.1 Introduction

Thus far we have looked at the current state of unmet need. In this chapter we look at some of the challenges of the future. It is of course impossible to be certain about any aspect of the future, and there is no shortage of examples of people getting things wrong in the recent past, for example the swing from ignorance about the impact of AIDS on British society to greatly exaggerated fears that came from underestimating how well medical science and changing behaviours would contain it. But by drawing on a range of methods – from forecasting and foresight to scenarios and thought experiments – we can map out something of the likely landscape over the next few years.[243]

Our starting point was to consider a range of trends and then assess how important they might be for the development or satisfaction of unmet needs over the next ten years until 2020. The trends we centred on were:

- Public spending
- Unemployment
- Demographics and ageing in particular
- Science and technology
- Diversity
- Anxiety and other emotional states
- Isolation
- Damaging consumption
- Climate change

Any futures exercise risks being overly influenced by the latest short-term issue, be that economic, technological or demographic. The obvious candidate here was the recession and its impact on government finances. But, whatever the prospects for economic recovery, we felt confident that the impact of recession on public finances will remain a major factor during this time period, and perhaps a decisive one for many people facing severe needs.

14.2 Pressures on public spending

The sheer scale of the crisis facing the public finances is widely understood. The combination of falling tax revenues and rising demand for spending has already driven public borrowing up to historically high levels. Substantial cuts are likely in many public services, potentially as high as 10-20% over the next three to four years. Public capital spending has already juddered to a halt, ending a decade of (by historical standards) generous investment in the buildings of poor areas, from estates to schools and GPs surgeries. It remains to be seen which services will be hit hard; health and education may be partly protected, but other local government services look likely to be squeezed. It also remains to be seen how much the cuts will be the traditional ones, like bearing down on existing models of service provision within functional silos, or whether more creative models will be adopted that save money by dealing with the causes of high cost demand (for example, dealing with the causes of readmissions to hospitals, or recidivism in crime).

Areas of the country that are particularly dependent on public sector jobs are likely to be hardest hit. Between 1998-2007 70% of jobs created in UK cities were in the public sector, and then, between early 2008 and early 2009, while the private sector lost around 450,000 jobs public sector job numbers continued to rise (by 55,000). Forecasters now expect cuts of several hundred thousand jobs in the public sector, and that cities which are most dependent (such as Newcastle, with 32% of jobs in the public sector, and Barnsley, with 35%) will suffer most.

Looking at the bigger picture, however, it is not clear yet how either a short or a sustained recession, and public spending cuts, will affect overall income (and wealth) inequality. Previous recessions often reduced inequalities even though they also led to increases in poverty.

Figure 66: Income distribution for the total UK population 2006-07

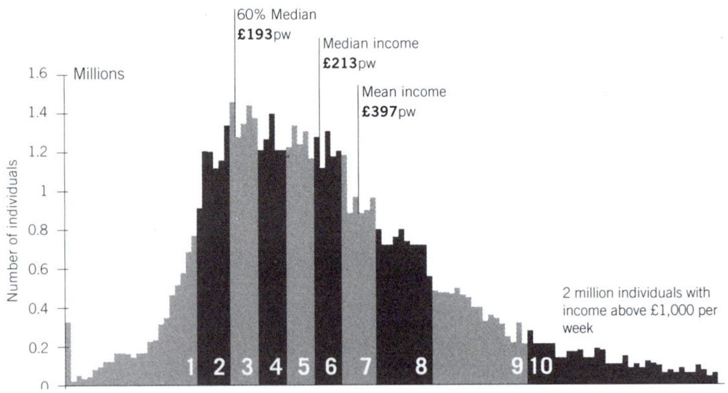

Source: Households below average income

The degree of inequality has not changed much in the last ten years. After reaching a peak in the mid-nineties child poverty has declined while measures of the income distribution (like the Gini coefficient) have changed relatively little, with some improvements in the middle of the income range, and accelerating inequality at the very top and the very bottom. Broader economic pressures to widen pay differentials have combined with a more redistributive government policy, roughly balancing each other out. Some of the pressures at the top may abate, particularly in the financial sector. Yet redistribution is also unlikely to continue at current levels. Areas that are relatively investment intensive – such as transport and housing, which make up 40% of all public sector investment – are set to be relative losers in a very tight spending settlement (with private investment also stalled). This suggests no improvement, and a possible deterioration, with regard to unmet housing needs. Similarly, deterioration in the provision of public transport could contribute to problems of social isolation.

14.3 Another lost generation?

Unemployment could remain high for several years. The younger generation are likely to be disproportionately affected by this. Unemployment in the teenage years is associated with significantly lower earnings later in life – 12% to 15% by the early forties, even leaving aside educational effects. This will be an additional drain on public funds.[244]

Figure 67: Number (in thousands) of UK unemployed

Source: Labour Force Survey, Oxford Economics

As we have seen, employment matters not only for the income it provides but also for self-esteem and wellbeing. The long-term impact of the 1980s recession was so great that people talked about a 'lost generation' who never made a successful transition into the labour market and have suffered irregular employment prospects ever since. There are clear dangers of a similar pattern repeating itself. With unemployment growing so much, there will inevitably be an increase in workless households and in young people becoming NEETs. The number of NEETs is likely to rise significantly, as they have in previous recessions (see chart). There were already three quarters of a million 16-24 year old NEETs at the end of 2008, up by 76,000 from the previous year. Given that these numbers did not decline during the boom, the prospects for 16-18 year olds entering the labour market at a time of high unemployment look particularly bleak.

Figure 68: NEET rates among 16-18 year olds

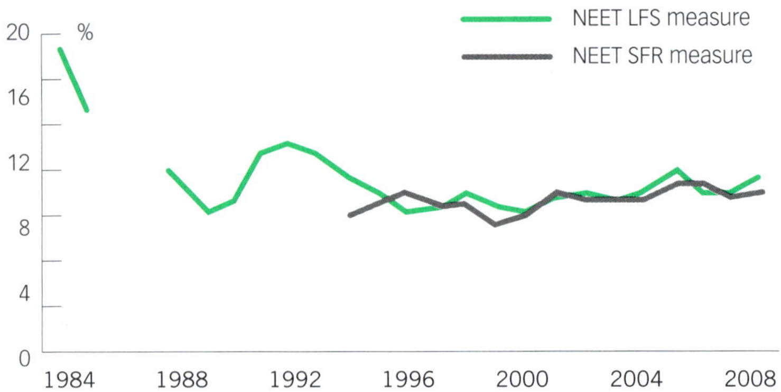

Source: Statistical First Release (SFR) 'Participation in Education, Training and Employment by 16-18 Year Olds in England' and analysis of Labour Force Survey[245]

Our work in Bedford identified lack of skills, opportunities, and qualifications as being common barriers for young people entering the labour market. But it also showed the importance of emotional factors such as confidence, persistence and motivation: in a difficult climate there will be an even greater imperative for these young people to be resilient, able to cope with shocks and rebuffs.

14.4 Demography and an ageing population

The UK population is expected to rise substantially, to nearly 72 million by 2033. Two-thirds of the increase will come from migration and from the children of migrants (which we look at below). But part of the growth is because people are living longer as a result of the vast improvements in infant mortality, the eradication of many infectious diseases and broader improvements in healthcare. Across the world, life expectancy is rising and potentially accelerating with important implications for employment and pension policies. The number of those aged over 65 will rise by 2.5 million between now and 2020, while the numbers of very old (80+) will increase significantly over this period from 2.8 million to 3.7

million (a rise of 30%).

Ageing will have many effects on needs – and on society's ability to meet them. A basic question is whether healthy life expectancy will increase. The table below suggests it will but not to the same extent as life expectancy itself. The result appears to be that the proportion of life spent in 'good' or 'fairly good' health is decreasing.

Figure 69: Health indicators

	Women		Men	
Year	1981	2001	1981	2001
Life expectancy	76.8	80.4	70.9	75.7
General HLE	66.7	68.8	64.4	67.0
Per cent of life in 'good' or 'fairly good' health	86.9%	85.6%	90.0%	88.5%

Source: ONS

Expert opinion is divided over whether it is inevitable that morbidity will grow more than mortality. It is possible that the combination of new knowledge, new treatments and new cultures of ageing could together contribute to a much more positive picture. But the most likely outcome is a substantial growth in need amongst the elderly, particularly given the limited prospects of more effective treatments for dementia. There will be both acute needs and lower level needs for care, befriending and day-to-day services. It remains unclear how these will be paid for, and what mix there will be of formal service provision and informal provision within families and communities.

Conversely, however, there will be many more opportunities for people to realise their ambitions, and potentially new sources of support for others, through changes to life cycles. If current trends in longevity, fertility and later childbirth continue, a woman born today would spend over 35 years (50% of her adult life) in the post-family phase (see chart below).

Figure 70: The changing life-course (in this case women). Average time spent in different stages for women.

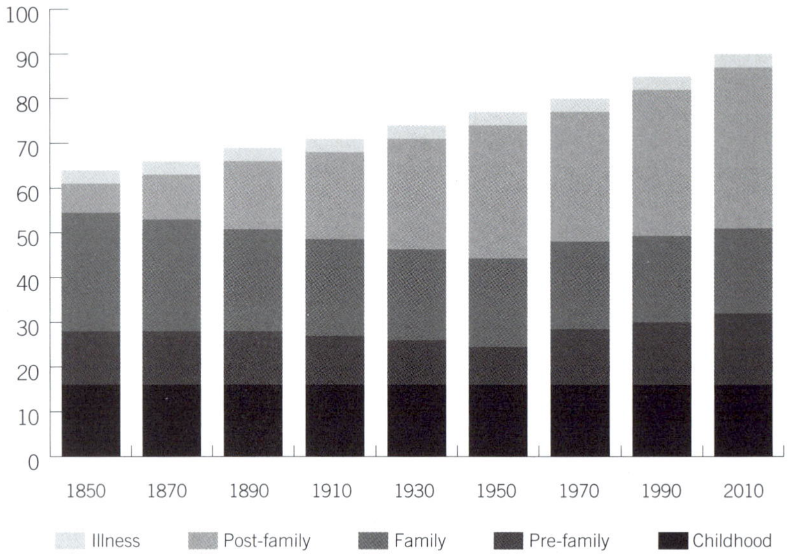

Source: Symmetrical Family, ONS, Trajectory

The changing shape of the family is bound to be a decisive issue both in creating needs and in determining how they are met. The numbers of children having children has remained fairly stable, despite many efforts to reduce it (the UK and USA stand out as particularly bad examples), with many causes ranging from low aspirations to poor sex education to misconceived incentives. A period of high youth unemployment is likely to worsen the situation, making it relatively more attractive for teenage girls to have a child as a shortcut to status and meaning (and, in a few cases, a flat). A growing number of adults want to have children but are unable to do so, partly because of the lengthening period needed to establish careers. There are growing pressures on children and spouses to look after parents for the reasons set out above, and because it is unlikely that governments, or markets, will provide reliable sources of care (because of the scale of the tax bill on the one hand, and the failings of insurance markets on the other).

A longstanding concern about ageing has been how to reshape work to allow for a slower and smoother transition from jobs to retirement. After falling in the 1980s and early 1990s, employment has been growing again for those aged over 50 (up five percentage points from the low in the mid 90s for men) – and for those past retirement age (particularly so in the last eight years). Many older people want to keep a job, even if only part-time, to retain not just income but also companionship and self-worth. And given the problems of pensions (particularly for the low paid) the need to work longer in life is likely to grow stronger over the coming decade. The potential impact on the finances of older, poorer people – and maybe even those who have had their pension pots decimated by the financial crisis – could be severe.

It is unlikely that service provision for the elderly will be able to be sustained in its current form as the population ages. Informal support networks, such as peers, friends, family and neighbours, will have to play a greater role in meeting the needs of older people in communities, with a growing role for assistive technologies of all kinds. This will be particularly important in rural areas, where there will be more pressure on services because the population is older and is spread over a wider geographic area. Social networking technologies are also likely to be increasingly used to orchestrate informal support networks.[xxii]

Physical infrastructures will also continue adapting to changing needs. For example, housing designed for easy adaptation for different life stages allows people to live independently in their own homes for longer, contributing to better health, improved wellbeing and obvious cost savings for health services. Such design features include pre-plumbing downstairs rooms so that they can be easily converted into bathrooms when people become less mobile, and designing staircases to be sufficiently wide to allow rails or stair-lifts to be fitted.

14.5 Diversity: conflict and rivalry?

The last decade brought a dramatic increase in inward migration as the buoyant UK economy attracted labour from around the world and particularly from Eastern Europe. But there have also been some less well-known and more surprising changes, such as the growth of the South American community in London or the Chinese community in Northern Ireland. While the number of immigrants from Europe has declined, it will continue to influence the population structure. Immigrants (from Europe and Asia) are younger and more likely to have children, with implications for births,[246] age distribution, education and health. The fertility rate for foreign-born women is significantly higher than for UK-born women (at all ages). In fact two-thirds of the increase in births since 2001 can be attributed to foreign-born women.[247] The table below shows the large change over a relatively short period (2001 to 2007) in the proportion of all foreign births accounted by women from Poland – not in the top ten in 2001 and second highest of all countries in 2007 – and the continuing importance of births to women born in the Indian sub-continent, with Pakistan, India and Bangladesh accounting for the other three of the top four countries of origin.

Figure 71: The ten most common countries of foreign-born mothers only, UK 2001 and 2007

2001			2007		
Country of birth	Live births	Percentage of all live births	**Country of birth of mother**	Live births	Percentage of all live births
Pakistan	15,111	2.3	**Pakistan**	18,311	2.4
Bangladesh	8,218	1.2	**Poland**	13,333	1.7
India	6,735	1	**India**	12,478	1.6
Germany	4,673	0.7	**Bangladesh**	8,850	1.1
Ireland	4,589	0.7	**Nigeria**	6,702	0.9
Somalia	3,202	0.5	Somalia	5,952	0.8
United States	3,070	0.5	Germany	5,564	0.7
Nigeria	2,643	0.4	South Africa	4,708	0.6
South Africa	2,322	0.3	Ireland	4,258	0.6
France	2,065	0.3	Ghana	3,784	0.5

Source: Birth registrations

This is potentially important for future needs because some of these groups have much higher rates of child poverty.

Figure 72: Children's poverty rates (%): rolling average (BHC) Great Britain

	2001/02-2003/04	2002/03-2004/05	2003/04-2005/06	2004/05-2006/07
White British	20	20	19	20
Indian	28	28	30	27
Pakistani	59	56	53	54
Bangladeshi	72	66	65	58
Black Caribbean	31	27	30	26
Black African	38	30	37	35

Source HBAI DWP

Increased migration combined with an economic slowdown may also influence attitudes to welfare. Data from Ipsos MORI suggests a rise in anti-immigrant feelings (see table) and also declining support for respecting the wishes of minority groups. Other data shows that British citizens increasingly expect immigrants and other minorities to adopt a British way of life and are less supportive of preserving diverse cultures. This could be a source of tension in areas experiencing greater competition for jobs and housing and greater pressure on public services. Anecdotal evidence indicates a decline in conflict resolution skills in urban communities compared to a generation ago, with unions, community workers, churches etc. playing a less central role in people's lives. Added together these suggest a high risk of unrest in many cities.

Figure 73: "There are too many immigrants in Britain" (%)

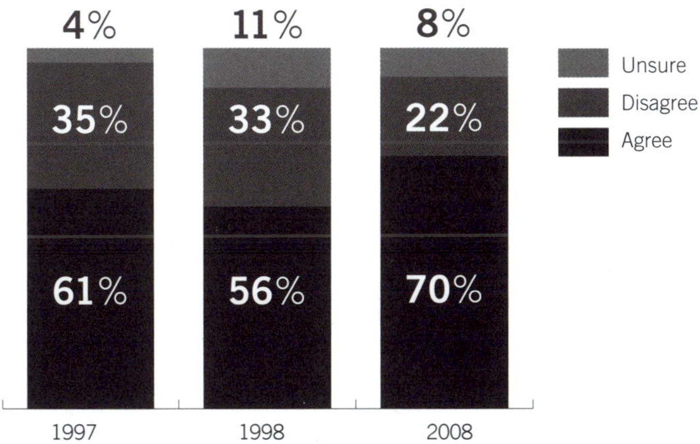

Source: Real Trends. Ipsos MORI

The potential impact of immigration clearly depends on its future rates, sources and on whether some groups might return home. Some numbers are rising inexorably, such as refugee numbers. Others may be levelling off – for example the number of Polish migrants arriving in the UK seems to have peaked. Rising sea levels and flooding caused by climate change (see below) are likely to create large global population movements. Some of the most vulnerable areas, such as Bangladesh, have strong ties to the UK. Significant flooding disasters in these regions will result in large numbers of people wanting to join relatives who now live here.

14.6 Isolation and social support

Throughout our study, we have consistently found people living alone (whether elderly, young people or single parents) to be among the most vulnerable groups in society. While the majority of people living alone are contented, a significant minority are not. Social and demographic change has tended to increase the number of single person households, encouraging the dispersal of the family and leading to a decline in community support. All of this is deemed to be increasing isolation and reducing social support.

The number of single person households in England has grown from 5.7 million in 1997 to about 7.5 million now and is expected to increase by another 1.8 million, to a total of about 9.3 million by 2020. Yet much of this increase is in fact in younger singles, out of choice, or divorced people, who typically remain single for not very many years. Those most at risk of isolation are older, widowed men and women whose numbers are growing because of increased longevity and longer periods alive for surviving spouses.

While it is true that the family is more dispersed than in the past, the impact is often over-estimated – most people still live quite close to where they were born and the vast majority stay in touch with their extended family. For example, analysis of the British Social Attitudes survey looked at changes between the 1980s and 1990s in the proximity of family members. Reflecting the increasing importance of the car, proximity was measured by the time taken to reach a particular relative by whatever means. Among married and cohabiting people with one or both parents alive, over half lived within 30 minutes of them.[248]

As an example, Willmott's own analysis of the 1992 repeat[249] of his and Michael Young's Family and Kinship in East London 1950s survey showed that although propinquity has declined contact had remained remarkably similar, albeit increasingly via the telephone (see table).

Figure 74: Contact (meeting or telephone) with mother (married subjects with mother not in same house or flat) – white families, Bethnal Green

	1955	1992
Daily contact	34%	53%
Weekly contact	69%	73%

Although the telephone was a key substitute for face-to-face contact in the early nineties, we now have the added medium of the Internet, with continuing growth in use by the over-60s (see below).

14.7 Anxiety, psychology and emotional needs

Awareness of health is increasing, in part thanks to improved diagnosis, more easily accessible information and a greater expectation of good health. The paradoxical result is that although people are better generally, as shown by improved infant mortality figures and increased longevity amongst other things, they do not feel better. Self-reported illness on the British Household Panel Survey has increased for all conditions except sight (where there have been real medical advances) as the chart shows.

Figure 75: Rise in self-reported health problems represents greater health concern among public

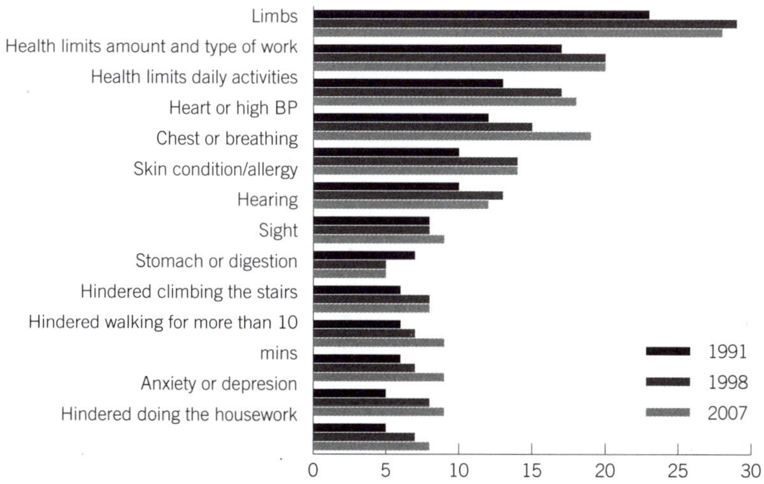

Source: BHPS analysis

Those reporting anxiety, depression and related problems have increased the most in proportionate terms over the last decade and a half. If we extrapolate current trends we can expect 12% of the population to be suffering in this way by 2025.

Figure 76: Those self-reporting anxiety or depression

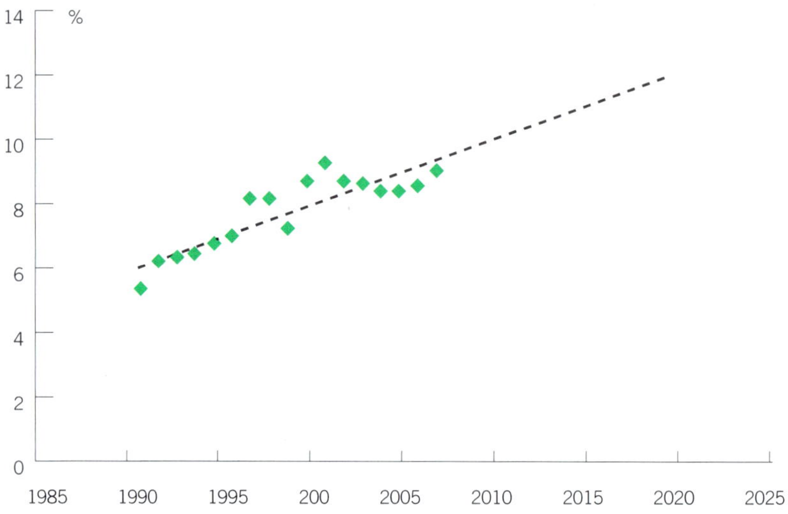

Source: BHPS analysis

Questions taken from the British Household Panel Survey show that on most measures there has been a slight decline in positive responses to statements about people's psychological wellbeing. Those able to respond that they never worry about self-worth or isolation (feel they have someone to rely on) or resilience (are able to face problems) have decreased.

Figure 77: Trends in key psychological need indicators

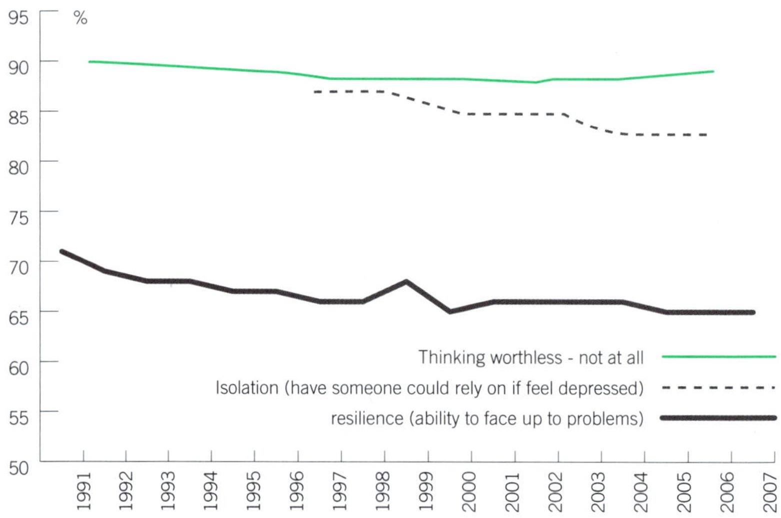

Source: BHPS

Further analysis of this study shows that a combination of these problems (anxiety/depression and the three in the chart above) or higher levels of them occur most often in areas classified as public housing within National Statistics Output Area Classification (OAC) system. These slow and steady trends do not seem to be much affected by the business cycle.

Figure 78: Index of psychological problems by OAC group

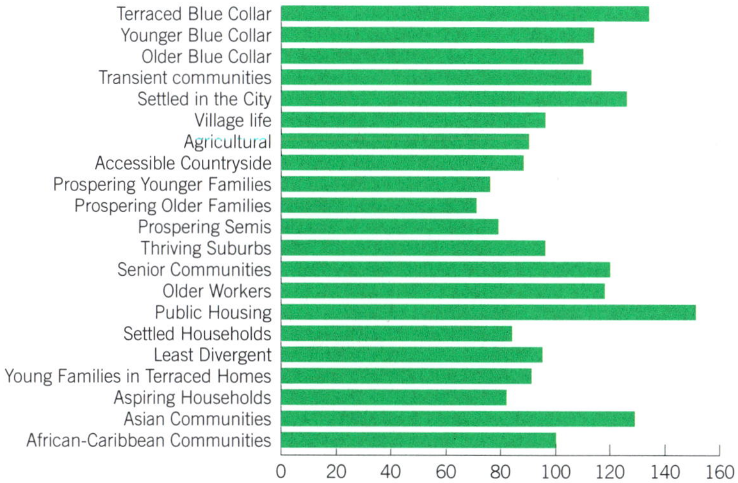

Source: BHPS

The evidence base for what works in meeting psychological needs is much thinner than that for physical needs, partly an effect of massive discrepancies in funding over many years. For example, only 5% of current health research funding is devoted to mental health. A range of approaches can contribute to improving mental health, including full CBT, clinical interventions, informal therapy, social support groups, exercise etc. One hope for the next few years is that there will be a significant improvement in the state of knowledge about what works and for whom. As we saw in the case studies looking at transitions and needs at night, the state is poorly equipped to provide solutions to some of the more complex psychological problems. Professional support often needs to be combined with support from other service providers, and of course from family and friends.

14.8 Damaging consumption

'Damaging consumption' covers any form of consumption that would be considered dangerous or unhealthy, whether because of the intrinsic nature of the substance involved (for example, drugs) or the amount consumed, as with obesity. Alcohol and tobacco consumption clearly fall between these categories, being substances which are to some degree toxic but in practice are problematic mainly due to the high levels of consumption in which individuals indulge. That said, over the past twenty years tobacco has moved from being like alcohol, a substance accepted by society but considered unhealthy in excess, to a position more akin to drugs, with greater stigma attached.

Figure 79: Obesity by gender and income quartile

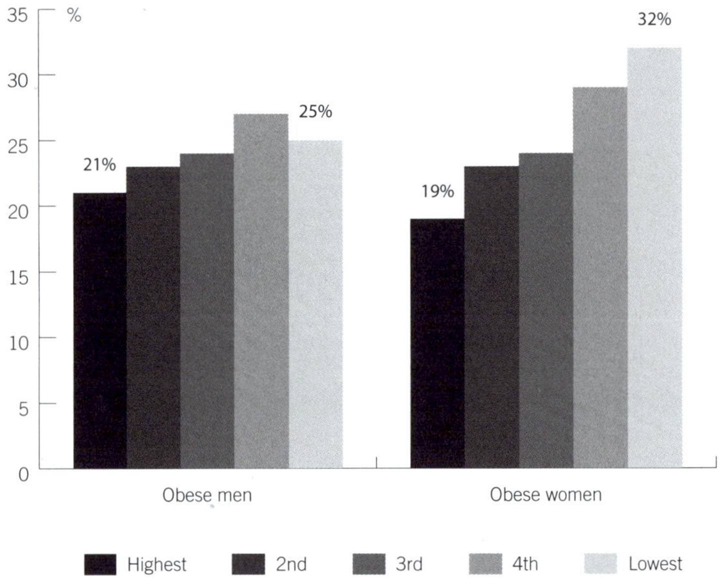

Source: NHS information Centre Health Survey for England 2006

Obesity has been a topic of increasing public debate over the last decade. In 2007 then Health Secretary Alan Johnson declared that obesity in the UK was a "potential crisis on the scale of climate change".[250] Recent statistics have revealed that by 2007 over 60% of adults in the UK were overweight, and almost one-third of children. Half of this group is projected to be obese by 2020. The implications for public health care are clear; an increasing proportion of health service resources may need to be dedicated to treatment of conditions associated with obesity like heart disease and cancer. More draconian responses could become more common – there has already been talk of refusing free treatment to people who will not lose weight – and as public sector spending cuts begin to bite such views may well become more common. While obesity is a problem for all classes, it is more of a problem for lower income women than any other group (see chart).

Figure 80: Proportion of people considered obese (BMI)

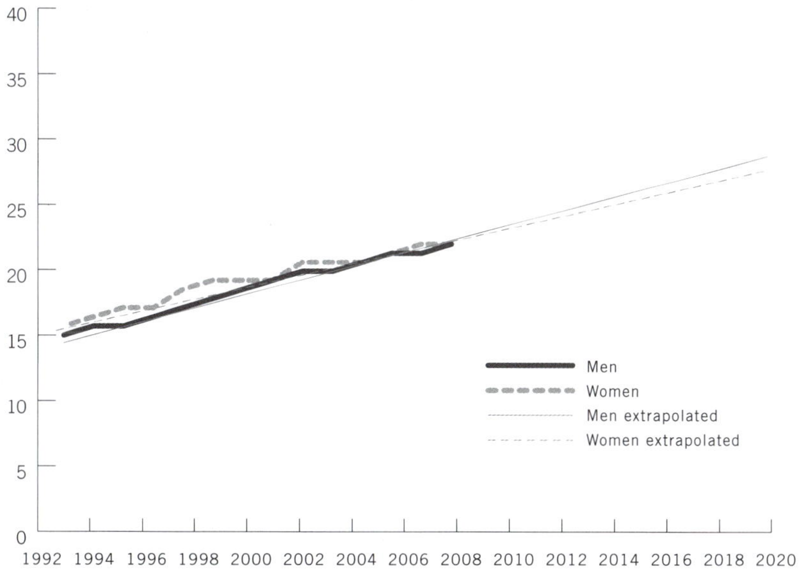

Source: NHS information Centre Health Survey for England 2006

'Vices' such as smoking, and to a lesser extent excessive alcohol use, have come under increasing critical attention, and, as with obesity, the locus of the debate has been the health impact and the costs of treatment, particularly for smoking. Evidence from the Office of National Statistics which indicates that smoking among all classes has remained steady – though more prevalent among those in routine and manual professions – suggests that it is unlikely that more than a small drop in consumption will be seen in the next decade despite an ever more hostile public attitude. Alcohol consumption is the third of the big three forms of dangerous consumption. While the general opinion is that alcohol consumption has rocketed in the UK, fuelled by cheaper supermarket prices and special happy-hour deals, studies indicated that alcohol consumption has remained largely stable over the past decade. Consumption is highest among those in the managerial/professional class, undermining the frequent image of alcohol abuse as a lower class habit. This is a fact that has already begun to be recognised in the press and in health campaigns targeted at middle-class drinkers. This is a group far more likely to be able to afford to fund its own treatment, yet also more adept at securing free provision of services to meet its needs.

For drugs, by contrast, there has been little popular shift in attitudes, though there have been significant movements in consumption. Drug-related deaths do not tally precisely to drug consumption, however they are indicative of wider trends in drug taking. These reached a peak of 3,110 in 1999, then fell back, and have subsequently risen again to 2,928 in 2008.

Figure 81: Drug related deaths (in thousands) in the UK 1997-2007

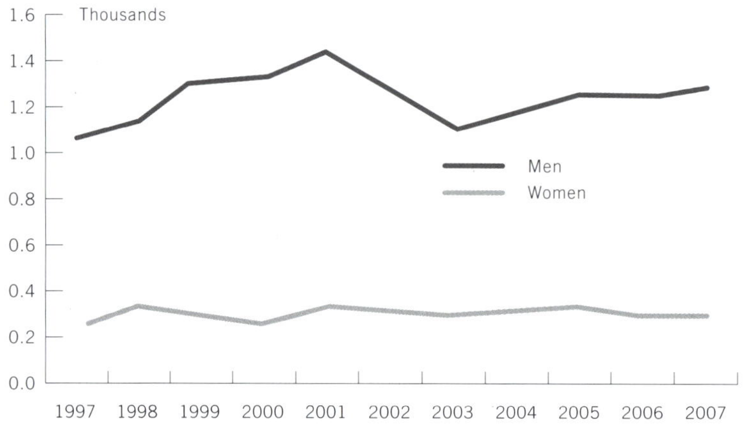

Source: ONS Social Trends 39, 2009

Gambling is another form of damaging consumption which, like drinking alcohol, is generally seen as being harmless in moderation. The Gambling Commission's Gambling Prevalence Survey 2007 found that 68% of the population had participated in some form of gambling in the previous year. Problem gambling, officially defined as gambling to a degree that compromises, disrupts or damages family, personal or recreational pursuits, was estimated as affecting 0.6% of the population in 2007 (1% of men, 0.2% of women); this overall proportion has remained constant since 1999,[251] and equates to around 300,000 people. However, there is considerable evidence that gambling is linked to debt, can be a catalyst for the unravelling of family or work stability and often coincides with other forms of damaging consumption.

14.9 Science and technology: problem or solution?

Science and technology have always had the capability to both improve people's lives and to create new inequalities of access. For example, some expect a dramatic widening of inequalities of life expectancy over the next few years as the wealthy buy tailored treatments based on new medical knowledge.

Technology, or more importantly the lack of it, is already a major issue in social exclusion, whether for the poor children who feel excluded because they don't have a PlayStation or Wii or those unable to access the increasing number of services that are now provided online or those who face extra charges for paper bills (much like the higher cost of various utilities for those who have to pre-pay). With great pressure, for cost reasons, to transfer more public services to online delivery this seems likely to become a pressing issue. Similarly, as social networks continue to spread, lack of access to them becomes relatively more disabling. Conversely, almost universal access to mobile phones has done much to strengthen social ties, as evidenced in many of the case studies where it is seen as a necessity.

Broadband is likely to reach the majority of the population in some form or other but whether people have the training, wherewithal or inclination to use it is another matter. Given the government's commitment to make broadband available to every household by 2012, it is the actual take-up and ability to use it that will be crucial. Broadband (or more broadly connectivity) can be important for employment too. Those using technology to work from home are likely to increase in the future and, of course, it provides new opportunities for those with disabilities.

Those lacking access to the Internet are currently in lower social grades, with lower educational attainment (only 55% of those with no formal qualification have Internet access against over 90% of those educated to degree level or higher, according to a 2008 ONS survey) and most importantly older people (see chart).

Figure 82: Accessing the Internet at home

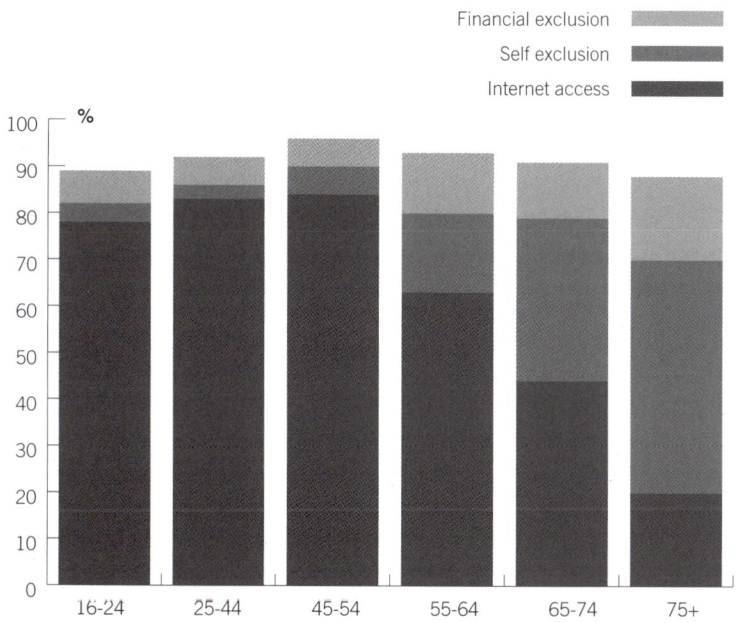

Source: Ofcom 2009

Two factors seem to be excluding older people from using this new technology: the cost (labelled 'financial exclusion' above) and the feeling that there is no need for it ('self exclusion'). One way of attracting older people to the Internet, and helping issues of isolation (see above), is to make them aware of the communication benefits it affords. Many older people are becoming intensive users and specialist social networking sites are starting to emerge such as MyWay Village in the States (www.mywayvillage.com) or Sagazone in Britain (www.sagazone.co.uk). Such virtual networks can provide entertainment and the ability to keep up with family photos and videos. But they can also provide the social networks and support that may be missing as a result of reduced mobility or the dispersal of family and friendship networks.

14.10 Climate change – and rising costs of food and fuel

Climate change is likely to have a range of impacts on unmet need. Air quality is likely to decline in major urban conurbations like London, as temperature aggravates ozone pollution, rising to 2.7 parts per billion (ppb) in the 2020s and up to 4.7ppb in the 2050s. A hotter climate could dramatically increase summer mortality rates; the heat waves of 2003 and 2009 have demonstrated that the emergency services and population as a whole are ill equipped to deal with the effects of very high temperatures. The elderly, the very young and the homeless are particularly vulnerable. Already there is discussion of a buddy system such as that in place in Philadelphia to address the vulnerability of isolated older people, as well as the extension of a range of air-conditioned public buildings with later opening hours to provide those with no other forms of shelter some respite from the summer heat.

Other likely impacts include the prospect of substantial migration into Northern and Western Europe from the East and South, and pressures on land. The UK climate change authority is predicting a possible 11.5 cm rise in sea levels around London by 2020, while the affluent are likely to move away from areas at risk of flooding. The other likely impact on people in the near future could be higher fuel bills and travel costs. Rising costs for food and fuel have already had a big impact in this decade. Under most scenarios the combination of a rising global population and environmental pressures means that these prices will rise further, perhaps by a large margin, with disproportionately big impacts on people with low incomes and on families and people living in rural areas who are dependent on the car. There are likely to be sharper tensions between green priorities and the needs of poorer people, whether in relation to housing (whether to build on the green belt for example), whether to raise the cost of transport, and whether to promote local and organically grown produce which tends to have a price premium. Put another way, supporting cheap and easily accessible alternatives – ranging from Combined Heat and Power (CHP) to local food – may become ever more important.

Longer term, there are likely to be more incidents of heat exhaustion. The elderly, poor and homeless in particular will be vulnerable to increases in summer temperature, particularly those in cities who are susceptible to the 'urban heat island' effect (whereby the built up nature of cities increases ambient temperature by preventing heat from escaping). This will require the development of green and cool roofs which reduce the absorption of heat from the sun, as well as looking into cooling corridors such as those trialled in Japan to reduce the ambient temperature on the streets. But poorer families are likely to be more affected due to their inability to insulate homes properly.

Conclusions

How should we prepare for changing patterns of need? There are some fast moving trends – like the rapid appearance of a new group of refugees from countries with no tradition of migration into the UK or sudden spikes in food and fuel prices. But most of the trends described above move quite slowly.

So in 10-15 years time the UK will remain a relatively unequal society; it is likely to be significantly more diverse (because of the age structure of ethnic minorities); on average older, and potentially more infirm; better educated but with large minorities with poor qualifications and uneven work experience; and with a geography of economic opportunity not greatly different to today.

An optimist would hope that the continuing flood of evidence on the importance of prevention and long-term action to reduce future risks of ill health, prison or unemployment, would have had a major impact on the behaviour of public agencies and others. But it is more likely that this evidence will be acted on in an upswing of public spending rather than in a downswing.

Meanwhile, many of the issues that will be rising up the agenda will be ones involving clusters of behaviour and psychology, social links and blocked opportunities. The focus of concern will be why particular groups and places remain prone to unhealthy lifestyles; why some individuals from all backgrounds are suffering more from stress and anxiety; why some places have become particularly prone to social conflict and mutual resentment; and what can be done to keep people resilient through longer and possibly more turbulent lives.

15 Implications and directions for action

Anyone who spends any time engaged with the everyday issues of unmet needs comes away both depressed and heartened. It's easy to be depressed at the many ways in which people experience unnecessary suffering, whether because of bad luck, the shortcomings of service providers or the vast gulfs of opportunity that characterise modern Britain. But it's also easy to be heartened by the many ways in which people struggle against the odds, and by the remarkable resilience of most communities and most families.

In the previous chapters we have summarised a wide-ranging and complex mass of data and findings. The more you look at individual cases the more you realise that every life is different and unique. Yet there are common patterns, and social science is built on the realisation that what appears to be individual good or bad luck is often the result of much larger social forces.

As we have seen, most people in Britain are living good lives and believe that they live in strong and supportive communities. Most are safer from crime and violence than they were a decade ago, and dramatically safer than their equivalents were a century ago. When they face setbacks most people bounce back.

But Britain is a brittle society, with many fractures and many people left behind. Even during the long economic boom, with unmatched wealth and prosperity, millions were experiencing harm and suffering. The poorest of all grew in number. The numbers not getting qualifications, and the numbers of teenagers without a job, skills or at school, remained high, condemning a great many to a life of poverty and insecurity. Levels of stress and anxiety continued to edge upwards. The places that had always been poor, and the places that suffered most during the rapid deindustrialisation of the 1970s and 1980s, generally remained poor.

Although Britain is a rich country, it still suffers some very old-fashioned types of material want, including poor nutrition and homelessness, and physically run-down buildings and environments. Inequality has grown at both ends of the income spectrum, even though it appears to have diminished in the middle. Needs are both relative and absolute and many are struggling to participate actively in society simply because of lack of money. And for a minority such as asylum seekers, the unemployed, carers and people disabilities money is very tight indeed. For these reasons longstanding arguments about financial entitlements – from levels of state pension to benefits – and redistribution will not go away. How much tax is raised from the relatively prosperous, or from relatively prosperous periods of people's lives, and redistributed to others, or to other periods of our lives, remains a centrally defining feature of any society.

So too are the ways in which opportunities are distributed, whether in terms of jobs, skills, networks or mindsets. A generation of teenagers coming to adulthood in the next few years, against a backdrop of high unemployment, risks a lifetime of insecure employment and low income. Some of the answers lie in the hands of government, including radical reform of the curriculum and opportunities to reengage the thousands of teenagers now doing all they can to escape schooling and college, as well as further attention to the very early years when so many of the patterns of long-term disadvantage are set. As we have shown, life skills are becoming as important as formal skills in shaping life chances, and these are shaped as much by experiences as they are by teaching. But the architectures of opportunity are not just the result of policy choices. Everyone plays a part. Professional parents who secure a privileged internship for their child are contributing, albeit with the best intentions, to inequalities of opportunity, just as they mitigate them if they devote time to mentoring or coaching a child who does not have the access to the skills and cultures that are decisive in finding a job. Every profession, every school with extensive facilities, and every employer, can play their part too in either widening opportunities or keeping them closed.

Britain has done relatively badly in terms of both classic poverty and opportunity compared to other north European countries (though fairly well compared to the USA). Others appear to have navigated the transition from an industrial to a post-industrial age with fewer casualties.

We have also looked at some less familiar views of our needs: our needs for company and companionship and our needs for autonomy and competence. One of the reasons for doing this is the presumption that as material needs come to be largely satisfied, attention will increasingly turn to our needs for things that are less easy to buy: to the intangibles of psychological wellbeing and connectedness. Certainly, this is how the public already thinks about needs, without any presumption that material needs are somehow more real, or more pressing, than non-material ones.

We have also tried to look at some of the dynamics of need. Clearly people with financial assets, or human capital, will on average bounce back more quickly from adversity than others. Living in the right postcode will greatly help you in finding a job if you become unemployed, just as being born into the right family will greatly increase your chances of having the requisite cultural capital or connections to advance your career. But the patterns of resilience are more complex than some of the traditional structural analyses allow. They are influenced by personal qualities, some of which can be cultivated. And they are influenced by how services and supports are organised.

In what follows we draw out some broad conclusions about the directions that follow from our analysis. These are not policy prescriptions – our aim has not been to develop a blueprint or plan. But they are pointers to action and further research, not just by government but by all the institutions that have the capacity to determine whether others suffer harm.

1 Provide preparation, bridges and support for difficult transitions

A first message is that many of the worst clusters of need are the result of difficult transitions. The ways in which we help people make these transitions – from being a teenager to being an adult, or from being in care or prison to independence – are inadequate and miss many of the things that matter most in making them work: good preparation, bridging support from people who understand you, and resources such as housing or money as well as emotional help. Many of these needs are entirely foreseeable, yet the unnecessary misery that results from these failed transitions is striking. If only children in care could rely on someone to help them through to their mid-20s; if only people leaving prison could rely on an initial home and work placement, life for them might be very different. Yet responsibilities tend to be divided up. Public agencies' responsibilities are divided by chronological age, and both public and voluntary organisations tend to divide by function in ways that cut against what people need.

At a time of acute pressure on money, this could be an area for long-term savings as well as one where much greater human wellbeing could be achieved. Failed transitions are invariably very costly, not just for the individual involved but also for the state. Persistent unemployment, levels of recidivism and the costs to the health service of mental illness are all unnecessarily high, and could be substantially cut if services were shaped more along the lines we suggest, with fewer cut-offs and handovers.

2 Isolation – help to connect the disconnected

A second message is that loneliness and a lack of social networks have become a stark feature of a more individualistic society. Millions like living on their own. But again and again we have found that many are suffering because of the absence of people they can turn to for help and support. A growing body of evidence now points to the psychological and physical harm that loneliness can bring. There are many good initiatives trying to address these needs – from befriending schemes to mentors – but they remain very much on the margins of policy and small in scale. Being without a roof over your head or a job to go to brings you entitlements, however meagre. Having no one to talk to does not.

Isolation is not something that government programmes are well suited to solve. Much of the responsibility for addressing it must lie with civil society, with family members and neighbours that keep an eye out and help. But there are also policies that could make a difference – from ensuring funding for low-level supports, street concierges or wardens in sheltered housing, and programmes to support the young elderly in looking out for people ten or twenty years older than them. Mutual support is bound to be part of the answer – using support circles and devices like time banks to connect people with needs to people with something to give.

3 Provide access with 'no wrong door'

A third common theme has been that people often access services that are not the right ones for meeting their underlying need. They may show up at A&E when their real problem is alcohol; they may turn up at a homeless shelter when their underlying problem is a mental illness. People may present the symptoms of a specific issue, but be suffering from a complex combination of multiple unmet material and psychological needs. As a rule, access points need to be less devoted to functions and more to people. We need more institutions, advisers and access points which are holistic, rather than function specific. Equally we still need better ways to route people quickly to the support they need.

These are not easy: they require highly trained staff; better tools to diagnose and assess; and much more sophisticated information systems (as a society we do much better in tracking money and shopping than we do in making sense of human journeys). None of these are new insights, but it is surprising how rare it is to find institutions or front line workers able to deal with people or places in this way.

We have also repeatedly found that the people and families that most need help are the least likely to take it up, sometimes because of chaotic lifestyles but also for reasons of stigma, distrust and disengagement. That is particularly true of 'preventive' services. It is not enough to provide something useful: how it is provided also needs to build trust and confidence.

4 Enhance resilience and psychological fitness

A fourth message is that resilience matters and can be influenced. Everyone is bound to face shocks and setbacks at some point in life. But what makes the difference is how well we cope with these shocks, how well we bounce back. This is in part a matter of social support from family and friends, teachers or GPs, as well as skills and financial assets. But resilience – and psychological fitness in a broader sense – can also be learned, and enhanced. Some areas have introduced it into the school curriculum; some agencies have integrated it with help in finding jobs; and some are beginning to integrate it into healthcare, and in particular the coaching and support for people with long-term conditions, recognising that psychological fitness is as important to life as physical fitness. Resilience can be supported not just for individuals but also for communities (for example, through the availability of assets, leadership and entrepreneurial skills, and social capital).

Not all kinds of resilience are equally useful. Some communities are proving very resilient to economic shocks – particularly the old working class communities that have now experienced several decades of high unemployment. They are good at providing mutual support, and good at absorbing blows. But this kind of passive or survival resilience does not necessarily help people to adapt and prosper; people survive the fall but fail to get up. Passive resilience can stifle innovation and cut people off from opportunities. In these communities what is most needed is a more active or adaptive resilience, that is less comfortable with getting by, more willing to seek out help and build stronger networks outside the community as well as within it.

A final reason for focusing on psychological fitness is its importance for behavioural issues. Inequality is now closely interwoven with issues of behaviour: obesity, smoking, alcohol and gambling. Many factors shape these behaviours, including the environment in which people live, the influence of peers and the availability of damaging consumables. But a common theme is that they are also shaped by people's level of self-efficacy: their abilities to cope with stress and setbacks in ways that are ultimately good for them.

5 Rethink welfare provision through the lens of wellbeing

A fifth message is about welfare. The welfare state grew up to deal with physical and material needs (although it was often justified by its impact on people's dignity as well). It evolved to provide enough food to eat, cures for sickness, homes and jobs. As we have seen, in a society with relative material abundance the critical issues of welfare have become as much about psychology and relationships as about material things. The risks that matter most include mental ill health and relationship breakdown as well as unemployment and poverty in old age. Indeed these psychological and psycho-social risks are more common across classes and regions than the economic ones, and perhaps a stronger basis for mutual support and solidarity. 'It could be you' certainly applies to mental illness, which affects a third of the population at some point in their life, and pretty much every family. Moreover, it intersects closely with other welfare issues, for example in the numbers of unemployed out of work because of mental illness. Currently mental health services remain the poor cousin of services concerned with physical health, despite extensive research showing how much physical health (including recovery from surgery or disease) depends on mental states. Perhaps the time is right to rethink welfare through this new lens, addressing the most important risks that individuals and families cannot deal with on their own.

6 Focus on new and old necessities

Our research has repeatedly confirmed how quickly some things have moved from being luxuries to become necessities. People living in rural areas are not alone in thinking of the car as a necessity. But the mobile phone is much the clearest example of this shift – invaluable and prioritised by everyone from refugees to unemployed teenagers. Given the importance of social contact to mental wellbeing and life opportunities, perhaps this should be reflected in how essential support is provided to people in hardship, and in regulation that already treats some other utilities as necessities. Access to the Internet is also becoming a necessity (not least as public services go more fully online) and for many the mobile will be the main point of access. Other, more traditional, necessities - in particular fuel and food - have meanwhile risen in price and could rise much more, having the most significant impact on the most vulnerable. Many communities are looking at new ways of providing these cheaply and reliably, connecting the imperative of carbon reduction with addressing poverty.

7 Invest in better social accounts

Finally we recommend a better grounding for future action in terms of evidence gathering. The data on need in the UK is complex, patchy and incomplete. What's needed is either a regular national survey or combinations of new survey modules, bespoke ad hoc surveys, the addition of new questions to existing surveys or secondary analysis of existing data sources. Either way, to adequately monitor the state of unmet need and how the most vulnerable are coping with societal change, more comprehensive and integrated longitudinal datasets are required. Specifically we advocate a regular triennial commissioning of research to explore and measure material and psychological need, bringing together the best resources of ONS, academia and conducted independently of government. We have laid the ground with the cognitive testing of a question set on perceptions of need and how it is experienced which shows that developing survey instruments is feasible. Preferably this should be done in conjunction with qualitative research, and would provide important insights to be considered alongside a range of data derived from primary research and secondary data analysis on the objective measurement of unmet need (see Appendix 2).

The UK has a strong track record of statistics and longitudinal studies. But while we still publish regular economic accounts, we do not publish comparable social accounts. And while government shares extensive data on production, consumption and finance, it does little comparable to map wellbeing. Yet there is no reason why regular GDP reports should not be accompanied by regular reports on the psychological fitness and health of the population, which will help to illuminate the many still poorly understood connections between wealth and wellbeing.

Appendix 1: Research methods overview

To investigate changing social needs, we drew on a range of knowledge and experience across four domains/perspectives. We did not just mix a quantitative survey with qualitative interviews as with much mixed method research. We combined different research methods within the two paradigms of quantitative and qualitative research: for example, as well as local ethnographies, we carried out focus groups with service providers and frontline workers and have included methods of public participation and engagement in the research. As well as reviewing current statistical knowledge, we have undertaken new secondary analysis of national survey datasets. By mixing approaches to the research objectives in this way we have generated a rich body of data that will illuminate perceptions of need from the four perspectives.

The table on the next page provides an overview of the different approaches we have taken to research. More detail on the specific methodologies we used throughout this programme is available on our website.

Perspective	Tools and methods
Real life: People who experience and live with need.	• Ethnographic studies in local areas. Each study focused on a different set of research questions, for example around the needs of night workers, NEETS, older people in care, or teenage mothers. • Overview of expert users/individuals research data (evaluations by service users, participatory research). • Public participation and engagement (exact methods to be confirmed).
Front line: People directly meeting need, observing need and involved in the consequences of unmet need.	• Knowledge mining (combinations of surveys, interviews and focus groups) of key individuals/organisations within local studies, including people at the forefront of local services as well as other local experts (taxi drivers, hairdressers etc.).
Service agency: Organisations involved in delivering services to meet need, measuring and assessing need and evaluating the impact of unmet need	• Knowledge mining (combinations of surveys, interviews and focus groups) of key individuals/organisations, including local perspectives on emerging, intensifying and persisting unmet needs. • Overview of local strategies and needs assessments.
Formal: Organisations and individuals claiming expertise through macro-level possession of statistical, academic, policy, strategic and scientific insight into need.	• Knowledge mining (combinations of surveys, interviews and focus groups) of key individuals/organisations, including government, local government, business, philanthropic foundations and civil society organisations • Synthetic overview of current research (across methodologies and specialties) bearing on unmet need. Quantitative analysis of administrative and survey data sets.'Expert' futures work to anticipate emerging, intensifying and persisting unmet needs.

Appendix 2: Exploring perceptions of need and developing survey instruments

1 Background

As we have seen, the circumstances of people's needs and the way that they are experienced and perceived are varied and complex. In order to assess the feasibility of developing survey instruments to measure the unmet material and psychological needs of people, it was considered important to undertake some conceptual work and to test questions with members of the general public so as to be confident that any potential survey tools prove effective and robust. To this end, Young Foundation staff, in association with colleagues from the National Centre for Social Research (NatCen), undertook a feasibility study.

First twelve focus groups were carried out in Scotland, England and Wales. The aim of these focus groups was to explore:

- perceptions of and understanding of what needs are;
- personal experiences of unmet needs, and
- coping mechanisms at times of need.

The intention was to obtain a clear grasp of people's perceptions of need, to understand the language used to articulate needs and how unmet needs are experienced and responded to in day-to-day life. This process was an important first step to take before moving on to develop a series of sample survey questions to ensure that those questions would be appropriate and relevant to people's understanding and experiences of need.

Participants in these focus groups were recruited from the general population according to the following sampling criteria:

- age groups – 18-24, 25-40, 41-60, 60 and over;
- socio-economic status – low and high educational achievement;
- geographical location – urban, suburban, peri-urban and rural.

The sample was monitored to ensure a mix of gender and ethnicity. Ten groups were held in Scotland, England and Wales.

In addition to these focus groups drawn from the general population, two focus groups were conducted with people with recent experience of a major life transition. One was conducted with people who had been made redundant or were unemployed. The other was with older old people (most of whom were over 80) who were experiencing ill-health or disability and loss of independence. This booster sample gave us the opportunity to interrogate the effects of life cycle and life transition, which our other qualitative work had indicated would play a significant role in findings.

Analysis of the data was carried out thematically using Framework, a matrix-based software programme developed by NatCen. This process enabled the key themes and issues discussed in each group to be systematically summarised and then analysed. The findings were then used as a frame of reference to inform the development of the sample survey questions.

The second stage of this iterative research involved testing these questions using cognitive interviews, a process whereby people answered the survey questions and were then asked about their understanding of the questions and the terms used. Undertaking cognitive interviews allows for any problems with the survey questions to be highlighted at the pilot stage. A sample of people was recruited from the general population so as to reflect a mixture of age, gender and geographical location. Twenty cognitive interviews were carried out. These were then analysed and the data ordered using the same thematic matrix-based approach and the key issues emerging from the survey questions were examined.

This appendix sets out the key findings from both the focus groups and the cognitive interviews and makes some observations and recommendations on the feasibility of carrying out a national survey of people's unmet social needs.

2 Findings from focus groups

This section sets out the findings from the focus group discussions, highlighting the ways in which people engaged with the topic, what their views and experiences of needs were including unmet needs and the way they coped with them. General observations and differences according to sample characteristics are also drawn out.

Types of need identified in the focus groups

The focus group discussions began by asking participants very openly and simply what they saw their needs in life as being. It was evident that the notion of needs was one which people readily identified with as a wide range of needs were identified, from food and water; love and fulfilment; to be healthy; to have a job; a roof over your head and so on. However, participants did at times seek clarification as to what was meant by need. We encouraged debate and discussion about what people's understanding was as this was relevant and interesting data for us to collect. In some groups we provided the definition of needs based on Gough and Doyal's work as being items 'without which you would experience harm or suffering' as a way of helping participants to frame the discussions. We also had a series of prompt cards giving suggestions of needs (covering a wide range of different issues from education, love, a job, a home to religion and physical exercise) that we used in some of the groups where participants were finding it more difficult to engage with the subject.

The needs identified by participants can be broadly categorised areas as follows:

Basic survival needs
People talked about having basic, fundamental, primal needs and these were perceived as being universal and essential for life such as food, water and shelter. There was a high degree of consensus amongst participants about this category of needs and the rationale of compatibility with life was fairly incontrovertible. It was seen very much as the building block upon which the other types of needs were founded.

Needs considered essential to live in the UK today
This next category of needs related to items deemed necessary for having a basic standard of living in this country today. People talked about being able to survive without having electricity or education or even healthcare. In this way, although not mutually exclusive this set of needs was set apart from the first category, but there was a broad consensus that there were a range of items needed to have a basic standard of living in the UK today. This covered:

- accommodation;
- the basic utilities, like running water, gas, electricity;
- the universal services provided in this country like education, healthcare and aspects of the welfare state;
- transport, and
- feeling safe where you live.

There was considerable debate about where the threshold for these needs lay, for example, what constitutes a basic level of accommodation, what level of transport should people have access to. The issue of whether items were considered a need, a want or a right were discussed, as detailed below.

Money was another 'need' that generated a lot of debate. Several facets of money were explored across the groups. People recognised that money is a means to an end and that in itself it is just a mechanism for trading goods and services. Societies and cultures where money either does not exist or where the economic system has broken down and currency is replaced by systems of bartering and direct trading were referred to. But there was general agreement that you do need money in order to be able to live in this country today, albeit with a wide range of perceptions as to how much that should be.

There was a close perceived link between having money and having a job - employment was a need which spanned the categories. It was seen on the one hand as being the means with which to provide the money deemed necessary to meet other needs. But on the other hand having a job was also recognised as being an important component of emotional need, with the concomitant benefits of providing self-esteem, security and possibly personal fulfilment.

Physical needs

Health came up recurrently as being a key need. Participants talked about their own health, either having been ill in the past; or having ongoing health problems as well as about the ill health of family members. However, the issue was recognised as being a complex one in so far as experiences of health spans a wide spectrum from good health to very poor health and the whole range in between. The propensity to have a good quality of life despite health problems was recognised, for example, someone in a wheelchair. Expectations of health also varied according to life stage. Not surprisingly, health problems featured to a greater extent amongst the older age groups (41 – 60 and over 60).

Interestingly, sexual needs were only raised on one occasion during all of the focus groups. Given the very private nature of this issue, it is not surprising that people were not forthcoming about it in a group discussion, although it should not be overlooked as an issue that people might feel is an important need.

Emotional needs

This set of needs came across as being of resounding importance across the groups: loving and being loved, having the support and guidance of friends and family. With this love and support came a sense of security, stability and belonging. Although this set of needs was not necessarily articulated as being an underpinning for good mental health, it could be interpreted as such and was certainly described by participants as being of key importance. These needs could be expressed as being as fundamental as the survival needs, with people unable to imagine being able to live without having them met, or they could be more strongly associated with having an enhanced quality of life.

Emotional needs also threaded through other categories of need, with participants talking about the emotional aspects of other types of need, as the following quote illustrates:

> *'A lot of them [needs] are emotional really because even a job, you know that's like your dignity and feeling of self worth.... They're basic needs, but most of them will affect you emotionally somehow.'*
>
> — Male, 25-40

As well as being a category of needs in its own right, emotional needs also performed the function of being a key tenet of people's coping mechanisms, as is discussed in more detail below.

Cultural needs

Included in this category were things like going out and socialising; playing and watching sport; listening to music and taking a vacation. This group of needs was perceived in a differently and was generally recognised as being of a higher order and the furthest away from survival, provoking much debate about whether they should really be classified as needs at all. However, whilst cultural needs did relate more to having an enhanced quality of life, they were sometimes considered to tap into an important aspect of the human condition which should be included in a categorisation of needs.

It was evident that the task of defining was a complex issue and a highly subjective process. Therefore, we have not compiled a definitive list of needs to fit into the above categories. Instead, we have aimed to draw out clarity on the conceptual thresholds between various levels of need. Precisely what those categories consisted of for different individuals could then be explored through a survey.

Different dimensions of need

A number of interesting issues were highlighted as a result of this initial discussion which reflect different dimensions of need as experienced by participants. As already highlighted, there was considerable debate as to what constitutes a 'want' and what constitutes a 'need' and indeed whether some things are a 'right'. The following exchange during a discussion in Scotland illustrates this:

> *Some of them are some are needs and some of them are wants.*
> — Female

> *They can be both. It can vary when you need it and when you want it.*
> — Male

Not surprisingly, participants' perceptions were shaped by a number of factors relating to personal experiences, expectations and their own particular stage of life.

So for example with the younger participants (18-24), the need for social interaction was greater than for the middle age groups but again rose to prominence with the participants of 60 and above, who spoke of their fears of being alone and isolated. Another example was the perception of education as a need which featured prominently as a need in relation to children. There were those participants with very low levels of education who felt that they had led rich and fulfilling lives without being well educated and would not have wanted more. In contrast, some young graduates felt that they were potentially worse off for having degrees: unable to find jobs that matched their expectations and having accumulated high levels of debt.

While the approach taken in these focus groups to assessing needs – asking people what their understanding and experiences of needs is – provides a series of subjective accounts, many of the methods of measuring need cited elsewhere in this report are based on objective measures. For example, dietary needs are based on an analysis of nutrition from the National Diet and Nutrition Survey. These two approaches to exploring need could work in tandem to provide a complementary understanding of the issue of need. Identifying the convergence and divergence between objective and subjective assessments of need would be of great interest and could serve as an illuminating tool highlighting areas of tension, where there are gaps between an outward measurement of needs compared to people's actual perceptions of needs.

The extent, depth and perceived trajectory of particular needs varied. An experience of need could be:

- chronic or acute;
- short-term or long-term and
- more or less likely to be met in the future.

A good illustration of this was some of the experiences participants talked about in relation to health issues. One type of experience was an acute, short-term need for pain relief during childbirth. A contrasting experience was of the need for a range of services from hospital treatment, to social care to Macmillan nurses in the context of a cancer diagnosis with an uncertain prognosis.

Unmet needs

Following the initial discussion of what participants saw their needs in life as being, we asked what they considered their unmet needs to be. This proved to be a more difficult task for several reasons. First when talking about what they saw their needs in life as being, people had already been drawing on their own experiences of times of need, whether that was a period of ill health, unemployment or related to problems with accommodation, all of which are included in the categories of need listed above.

Second as noted above in context of the discussion around education or sexual needs, it could be awkward in a group setting for people to acknowledge that a particular item relating to a personal issue was an unmet need for themselves. Whilst there was certainly a wealth of data about the importance of having friends and family, the flip side is those who did feel alone perhaps felt a group setting was not the appropriate arena to share this. These sorts of issues would be better addressed in one-to-one in-depth interviews.

That said there were a range of examples of unmet need given by participants, which spanned a whole range of different life experiences, from acute agoraphobia to having children with special needs; from going through divorce to trying to avoid getting into debt every month. Some of the issues raised related to the unmet needs of others – in particular, the challenge of caring for elderly relatives.

From the life transition groups there was a strong focus in the group with people who had been made redundant on the importance of employment. Several barriers to finding work were identified and included age discrimination in the labour market and lack of affordable training. The importance of being able to access public transport also came up in this context, particularly with regard to affordability when job seeking and going for interviews. The group with older people who had experienced the onset of ill-health and disability focused firmly on the importance of emotional needs and the importance of having people around, be it friends, family or service providers, to give support and company and prevent a feeling of isolation.

Participants noted that many of the needs which had been identified in the initial discussion were considered everyday things – taken for granted until or unless a barrier to meeting these needs was met. One example was the use of a car which was not considered as a need until it breaks down resulting in the inability to get to work or to ferry children around.

Life Stage

It was very clear from the focus groups that the participants' age and consequently what stage of life they were at had a big impact on their perceived needs. Younger participants (particularly the 18-24 year old age groups) tended to focus more on economic and housing issues, which they saw as being the most pressing set of needs facing them at this point in their lives. The challenge of finding a job came across as a strong theme and was a stark reflection of the current adverse economic climate. Graduates, in particular, described their frustration at having incurred high levels of debt in order to obtain a degree which they had, mistakenly, expected to enhance their career prospects and employability. While having a good job was also discussed by older participants, for younger participants employment was closely linked to a key life stage transition to independence and becoming functional adults in the world.

Accommodation was a key unmet need cited by younger participants in the context of becoming independent and self-sufficient. In particular those younger people who felt they had no option but to live with their parents or rent rooms in "dingy" houses or tiny flats felt that their need for "home" was not being fully met. This was perceived to have had a higher impact in certain contexts, for example where people had been working and considered that they were in effect "lining the pockets of landlords", or where they had begun to think about having children and securing a basis for the future. Great uncertainty as to how this need would be met in the future was expressed.

Broadly speaking, the needs of the younger participants revolved around themselves: starting out in the world and providing a foundation from which they could embark on their adult lives. By contrast, those in the middle age bands (25-40 and 41-60), had a somewhat different perspective. They were much more likely to have dependents, both children and/ or elderly parents. The most pressing needs reported by these participants in fact often related to the pressing needs of their loved ones including both basic needs for living in the UK today e.g. access to transport and education as well as in relation to emotional needs: put crudely, parents were happy if their children were happy.

> *'Children always come first.'*
> —female, 41-60

This issue is a relevant consideration in developing survey instruments and underlines the importance of clarity about whose needs are being considered.

As one would expect, older participants had a wider range of life experiences to draw on in the discussions. In particular, the life experience of having faced challenging problems and "come out the other side" left people with an awareness of how problems can be overcome. In general, older participants also expressed more confidence in managing ongoing problems in their lives.

A shift in perception of the relative importance of different types of needs over the span of the life course was also observed, with older people becoming less focused on material concerns and more aware of emotional issues, in particular the importance of feeling loved. This was particularly evident in the group discussion with older people (mostly 80 years and above) who had been through the life transition of losing independence through ill health and/ or disability. When asked what their needs were, their initial response was to resolutely declare that they had everything they needed. On further probing, it became clear that having basic needs (such as food hygiene etc) met were important but that of far greater importance to them was having company and mental stimulation.

Geographical differences

The discussion groups were held in a range of locations, from cities to rural areas across England, Scotland and Wales. The sample was chosen so as to be able to pick up on any key differences reflecting geographical location. Interestingly, there were no noticeable differences evident in the groups we conducted across the three countries. However, between urban and rural locations the issue of transport needs stood out as being a key difference. Participants in rural locations spoke vividly about the impact of not having access to transport. Having a car was seen as being an absolute necessity. However, this was clearly not achievable for everyone. For young people the lack of access to transport was seen as being a significant restriction to their ability to socialise and they were dependent on their parents to drive them around. Amongst older participants, there was a real concern about becoming very isolated.

Coping mechanisms

The final part of the discussion groups focused on ways in how people had coped at times of need. Participants described a range of strategies that they had employed to cope with difficult situations. The first type of response spanned a spectrum of psychological approaches from the resilient to the destructive including:

- the importance of positive thinking and having hope;
- a determination to overcome obstacles;
- gritting your teeth and just trying to get through every day;
- taking exercise to promote a sense of wellbeing;
- distraction tactics, e.g. having a drink;
- destructive responses including self harm, causing trouble and running away.

As with the other issues discussed in the groups, response was highly subjective and shaped by individual personalities and experiences.

Emotional support was a very strong theme across the sample. Friends and family were seen as providing love, support and encouragement as well as offered practical help during difficult times. Participants in the life transition group who had been made redundant spoke vividly of the importance of having a home and family representing a haven to 'escape' from their problems. It is worth noting the dual nature of emotional needs throughout the discussions, constituting as they do both a need in themselves, in terms of people needing to feel loved and loving, as well as forming an important coping mechanism by way of the emotional support provided by loved ones.

In addition, participants talked about how they had tried to deal with situations of financial hardship using a variety of tactics. Budgeting and attempts to juggle competing priorities were reported, for example, not paying certain bills one month in order to buy children's presents. One young person explained how he had sacrificed his food money in order to be able to take out a girl. Looking for cheap ways of socialising or occupying children were also mentioned. Getting into debt was referred to as a response to the pressing nature of short-term financial difficulties.

Finally there were a range of practical responses where participants talked about the role of formal, external help in addressing unmet needs, for example government service providers and advice or support groups. The means of accessing this kind of support provoked a lot of discussion. Significant problems in identifying and reaching the right service had been experienced by some and was reported to have resulted in enormous stress and frustration. Being able to access information by telephone was discussed, with particular reference to mobile phones – whether these were considered a want or a need or indeed a coping mechanism. The role of the internet also featured and reference was made to the increasing tendency for information to be available online, which is clearly a problem for those, typically older people trying to access the information, who either do not have access to the internet or do not how to use it.

3 Cognitive testing of survey questions

The findings from the focus groups were used to inform the design of a series of sample survey questions around the issue of "unmet need". The aim of the survey question design was to investigate and assess:

- In what ways the public understand 'need' in the UK context
- Which aspects of need people broadly share and which are more contested
- How people with unmet needs respond to them
- How and when people's unmet needs might be met

A list of specific items was drawn up to reflect the spectrum of "needs" that had been identified in the focus groups. The items were presented randomly in order to get respondents' spontaneous, unconsidered reactions to each one. The list of items used is shown in the table on the facing page.

The detailed findings from the cognitive testing component provide valuable data which can ne used to inform the development of survey instruments. The findings reported here are primarily concerned with demonstrating how respondents engaged with the issue of "need" and the extent to which the survey questions were able to elicit individual respondents' "unmet needs".

Perceptions of need

Respondents were asked to look at the list of items and choose one of the following answer options for each one:

- Needed to be able to survive
- Needed for a reasonable quality of life
- Needed for a very good quality of life
- Not a need.

Respondents were then asked to explain how they had understood the different needs and the answer options, and to explain their selections.

The task was generally approached in a conceptual way, but with clear reference to respondents' own circumstances, as well as the circumstances of others close to them or others in their community. It was recognised that something could be a need for others, although not a need for themselves. Deciding what was a 'need' and the level of need was subjective and shaped by people's circumstances (for example, someone who had plenty of support from other people did not need to have written English in order to survive in the UK). To explain why something was felt to be a need, respondents also drew on references to today's world compared to the past, and our own society compared to others.

Carrying out the task and reflecting on it revealed a number of issues around interpreting and understanding needs. The first difficulty was determining whether something was a 'need' or a 'want' – this came up particularly in relation to thinking about a very good quality of life, and whether something which could be seen as making life easier or nicer should be described as a 'need'. Where it was perceived as a 'want' rather than a 'need', respondents felt inclined to classify it as 'not a need'. A second issue was whether an item would be better described as a dependency created over time, but far from essential to life: mobile phones were given as an example here.

Figure 83: Items used for cognitive testing

Item letter	Item description
a	Meeting up with friends for a meal or drink at least once a month
b	Feeling positive about yourself
c	Housing that has heating, a working kitchen and a bathroom and that does not need major repairs
d	The ability to write English to a basic level
e	Access to free healthcare when physically sick or injured
f	A safe area to live in
g	Enough time and money to pursue hobbies such as sport, music, or other interests
h	The ability to get to important places on public transport (e.g. the doctor, shops or a post office)
i	Feeling loved and valued by someone
j	A car, or access to a car
k	Ability to have control over things that affect your life
l	A healthy and varied diet
m	Enough money to buy essential items without getting into high levels of debt
n	An interesting job
o	Feeling part of the local community
p	The ability to handle life's problems well

q	A mobile phone
r	High level qualifications, e.g. a university degree
s	Friends or family to provide support with problems
t	A good state of physical health
u	Enough money to put aside some savings every month
v	Access to free counselling, or other support, when worried, stressed or feeling "down"
w	Knowing how to use a computer
x	Security and stability in your life
y	Ability to take a one week holiday away from home every year
z	Owning your own home

On the whole, the list of needs used for the task appeared to be understood and not cause confusion, particularly the more material and tangible items. However some of the more composite items, such as 'security and stability', 'ability to have control over things', and 'the ability to handle life's problems well' were felt by some to be too broad to categorise easily. Emotional needs, such as 'feeling loved and valued' or 'feeling positive' generated a wide range of responses and reflection, with some respondents feeling they were necessary for survival, while others said they would not classify them as a need, but that they contributed to a good quality of life.

The list was generally felt to be fairly exhaustive, and there were only a few suggestions for additional items (for example, having a job, access to the internet). However, it was felt by some respondents that the list was too random and would have been easier to manage if it had been grouped into categories, for example well-being, community needs.

Respondents often found difficulty in making decisions about which of the four answer options to apply to the items, and clear differences emerged in the interpretation of the categories.

Needed to be able to survive

Respondents used a range of thresholds to understand a need for survival. At one level, it was interpreted as meaning very basic needs, such as food and housing, 'scraping by', but others saw it as a higher quality of life than this, and felt it should encompass aspects such as being happy and healthy, having no debt, and functioning well in society. The term 'survive' also caused some respondents to reflect on whether it should mean a question of life or death.

A reasonable quality of life

Depending on the interpretation people placed on the first category, there was a feeling either that 'survival' was too far from the concept of a 'reasonable' quality of life (and that a middle category was needed), or that it was too near, and they found it hard to distinguish between them. Respondents interpreted 'reasonable' to mean different things: for example, 'getting by', being financially and emotionally stable.

A very good quality of life

There were two main positions here: respondents either felt that the gap between 'reasonable' and 'very good' was hard to distinguish and apply, or they were inclined to assume that 'very good' was some way removed from 'reasonable', meaning a lifestyle involving considerable material wealth. Another view was to link a very good quality of life to emotional fulfilment, such as 'feeling positive', and see these as aspects that are needed for a very good quality of life.

Not a need

This was interpreted in two rather different ways: either that something was not a need because it was more appropriate to describe it as a 'want' (this then caused uncertainty about whether it should be described as 'not a need' or a 'need for a very good quality of life'), or that it was simply not important to life.

In carrying out the task, respondents adopted different kinds of approaches. One approach was to work on the basis that 'reasonable' equated to 'normal', and to position themselves as 'normal', and make their judgements about what needs were required for a reasonable life based on what they did or did not have. Another similar approach was to think of people who may not have the item they were thinking about, and decide whether they felt they managed without it. A different approach was to weigh the different items in terms of how important they were felt to be to the individual, and then allocate them to different levels, i.e. 'needed for survival' if they were felt to be very important.

Identifying unmet needs

The next phase of the cognitive testing exercise was designed to get respondents to consider how the items needed for living in the UK today applied to them personally, and which of these constituted an "unmet need". Two techniques commonly used in cognitive testing were used for this purpose:

- A pack of shuffle cards. The use of a pack of shuffle cards is a valuable tool for getting respondents to sort out things into categories or priorities.
- The Think Aloud process. Respondents are asked to articulate their thought processes whilst they are deciding which pile to allocate a card to.

A shuffle card was made for each of the 26 items show in Figure 83. Respondents were asked to allocate each item to one of the following piles:

Pile 1. I already have this
Pile 2. I don't have this – and I do not want it
Pile 3. I don't have this – but I would like it

Respondents generally found this task easier to do than the first one, perhaps because it less conceptual and more grounded in their own experience of needs and wants. They tended to engage both with the card sort exercise and with the Think Aloud technique.

'Think Aloud' raised issues around the frames of reference people used. Generally people considered each item in terms of their own personal need at present. However, there was some reference to their needs in the future rather than now: for example for public transport or healthcare. In a few cases, the needs of others might be considered when deciding where to put a shuffle card: for example, the issue of local transport might not be a need for someone with a car but a major need for other people in a rural area.

Many of the items generated reflection about what exactly was meant by them and how they should be interpreted. Items that referred to security, stability or control could be viewed in many different ways according to people's own circumstances: some took them to refer to financial needs whilst others related them to emotional needs. It was also clear that assessments of need could vary according to how things were going for a respondent at that particular time: for example a recent event such as redundancy might radically alter perceptions of financial need or the need for stability.

One of the issues raised in the exercise was the fact that some items contained more than one concept and that they could be dealt with differently. For example, the ability to pursue a hobby might be purely dependent on either time or money but not necessarily on both. Similarly, someone could have security but not stability in their life, or vice versa, but these were conceptually different and not automatically allied.

Where respondents did not have an item, it was easy to decide if it was something they did not want or would like to have – piles 2 and 3. Problems occurred, however, where a need was met, but only partially. It was generally felt that the best solution was for option 1 to be split into two parts: one which indicated that the need was fully met and one which indicated that the need was only met in part. There were different aspects of partially met need:

- A need being met sometimes but not always (e.g. ability to have control over things that affect your life)
- Having something but not enough of it (e.g. time for hobbies)

- Having something that does not adequately fulfil the need (e.g. counselling that is of poor quality).

Areas of unmet need differed between respondents. In broad terms, these were focused around: financial security (savings, debt, financial management); lifestyle factors (job, home, time for interests, social contact); and emotional security and wellbeing (feelings about self, ability to deal with life).

Two principal factors appeared to determine what people saw as their area(s) of unmet need: personal circumstances and life stage. It is to be assumed that people's own personal circumstances, including their health (physical and mental), home environment and financial situation, would be a determining factor. However, it was also apparent that people's perceptions of need change over time. For example, needs relating to jobs and social life may be more important at an earlier stage in life whereas needs around health and transport assume a greater importance with age.

Responses to unmet need

Once participants had sorted the cards into the three piles described above they were asked to select one item from pile 3 'I don't have this – but I would like it' as the issue that caused them the most concern or problems in their life. Participants were asked to articulate their thoughts using the Think Aloud technique whilst deciding on their priority issue.

The ease with which participants chose one item varied greatly. While some selected one immediately, others struggled to choose between two or more items. Where participants found it difficult to decide on one item they ranked the different issues depending on the level of control they had over them or whether they could get by without a specific item.

There were a range of factors that influenced what item people chose. Broadly speaking, participants' choices were based on what items caused them concern or problems personally. These experiences varied between problems that people were currently facing, had been a concern for them in the past or could potentially create problems in the future: for example, not having financial security to be able to provide for their children. Items were also selected as a priority if they felt they would help to resolve other issues – so, for example, having more money could help to solve housing costs, living expenses and so on. However, in some cases people's choices were influenced by what caused problems for others around them, for example family members or their local community.

The Think Aloud technique revealed varying interpretations of the question. There were participants who related this to emotional concerns or problems, choosing the item that caused them the most stress or distress. Other participants associated it with a lack of control or something that prevented them from doing what they wanted, while for others it was not just about what caused them concern or problems, but also what impacted on others.

The language used was also raised by participants during the exercise. In a few cases, 'problem' was perceived as unsuitable because people could be concerned about an item but they may still be getting on with life without it causing a problem.

Coping strategies

In addition, participants were also asked how they responded to not having the item they selected in the previous section. They were given a choice of eleven responses and asked for any additional feelings or coping strategies that were not included in the list.

Participants often selected multiple responses and felt the list provided a suitable range of options. Nevertheless several alternative responses were mentioned by participants: working hard, bottling things up, feeling frustrated, and thinking too much about the item.

It was evident that the responses could be interlinked – for example trying not to think about the problem could lead to a feeling of stress and anger. What did emerge, however, was the need to separate out some of the points within a response. For example, people may feel upset but not necessarily angry and vice versa as these can be very different emotions and not automatically linked.

Where people talked about the unmet need, it was most often on an informal basis: usually with friends or family. The list of "informal" people contained some duplication and omissions: for example, someone's partner could also be their boyfriend or girlfriend; it was not clear how to code son/ daughter in law, or mother/ father in law.

In some instances, respondents had talked about the unmet need with others, for example health professionals and support services. Again the list of "formal people" Where respondents reported not speaking to anyone about their unmet need, reasons included: feeling others would not understand, not wanting to worry other people or not wanting others to know their business.

Meeting needs

A question to elicit respondent views about whether or not their principal need would be met at any time in the future was included in the cognitive testing questionnaire. However, due to time constraints, this question was not always included in the interview.
Where respondents were asked whether the need would be met at any time in the

future, people were given the option of saying either “yes” or no”. In some cases, it was possible to give a categorical ‘yes’ answer where it was clear how and why the need would be met, for example where the respondent could achieve this through his or her own efforts or because some specific change was imminent. However, the natural reaction was to say ‘yes’ even if it was not clear how, or even when, this might occur. The perception was based on hope that it would be met and hope was important because otherwise the outlook could be bleak. An outright positive or negative response did not necessarily reflect the respondent’s own response: “possibly” might be nearer to it.

Respondents found it difficult to put a timeframe on when the need might be met. This was especially difficult to predict when the need being met was dependent on factors outside their control. Generally, the last option of ‘in a year’s time or longer’ was selected as a “catch all” response, unless there was some specific event or factor that would provide a speedy resolution. A suggested solution was to provide a different set of less specific timescales, for example: soon, in the foreseeable future, and in the distant future.

4 Key findings

As previously indicated this study has focused on subjective perceptions rather than objective measurements of need. Perceptions of unmet needs may or may not be related to actual experience of need, and if they are the relationship is likely to be a lot more complex than a simple correlation between the two. For example the extent of people’s wellbeing can now be quite comprehensively measured using the Warwick-Edinburgh mental Well-Being Scale.[252] Perceptions of wellbeing are slightly more difficult to capture.

The implication here is that the measurement of actual needs and perceptions of needs might not necessarily need to happen in the same survey, at the same time. To explore perceptions of need a module on an existing general population survey such as the British Social Attitudes Survey or an omnibus survey would provide a shorter (and potentially more cost effective) option than a full exploration of the extent of unmet needs. This study suggests that to be most effective this would be combined with further qualitative exploration in the form of in depth interviews. So there are multiple options for addressing the exploration and measurement of unmet need that are most likely to involve splitting out the collection of data about perceptions and extent.

A regular and full assessment of unmet needs in the UK is likely to need either:

- A bespoke ad hoc survey;
- Existing surveys having new questions added to them; or
- Secondary analysis of existing data sources (if new surveys / questions are not an option).

It is clear that to explore perceptions the list of unmet needs asked about will need to be fairly high level rather than exhaustive to minimise respondent burden. If such a list is at the summary level, then the same list cannot also be used as the basis for fully measuring unmet needs.

The findings from this feasibility study strongly suggests that the use of categories of need may be a key means of exploring perceptions of need through the use of survey instruments. While categorization varies between people, the study provides clear evidence that it is a common feature of the way perceptions of need are conceptualized. As suggested previously a key related issue is whether the study identified common hierarchies of need of the kind once promoted by Maslow. The suggestion of such a hierarchy is not entirely absent in the data collected for this study, as for example the perceived relationship between cultural needs and survival needs referred to above illustrates. However, it is clear that perceptions of any hierarchy vary between respondents and need to be considered in the context of a range of further factors which influence categorization. These factors are also relevant to the potential design of a survey module to explore perceptions of need. They include the following:

- The relationship between perceptions of needs, wants and rights;
- The effect of life stage and context on perceptions of need;
- The presence of emotional responses to material need which are distinct from emotional needs themselves;
- The relationship between personal needs and the needs of others (particularly dependents);
- The presence of facilitators (such as mobile phones, internet access and cars) to meeting needs which may be experienced as absolute or contingent needs in themselves;
- The impact of perceptions of needs in the UK in the past and in other countries on the current perceptions of respondents.

The cognitive interview phase of the study suggests that there is potential for designing a workable survey module in relation to perceptions of need. Overall, respondents were positive about the experience of taking part in the interviews, and felt that the list of needs in particular was comprehensive and identified a good range of different needs. They commented that the process was useful in thinking through what needs they had.

The first task, identifying different levels of needs, was generally considered to have been the most difficult, mainly because respondents had struggled with their interpretation of the four answer options. The key issue here was that while respondents appeared to favour categorisation of needs by type, for example physical or emotional, ascribing needs to levels on a scale proved more problematic. This was, at least in part, because of different interpretations of what might constitute a hierarchy were one to exist.

The cognitive interview stage reinforced the key finding from the first stage that perceptions of need and unmet need are strongly associated with personal context and lifecourse. The second task proved in the first instance to be more straightforward as respondents appeared to find it easier to identify needs as met or unmet. The Think Aloud tool proved particularly effective here eliciting responses which clarified people's interpretation of needs, for example whether they were current or anticipated. However, it emphasised the need for question techniques and routing which enable respondents to identify precisely how types of need were interpreted. This was again particularly the case in relation to composite types of need such as stability of security which could for example, be interpreted as financial or emotional.

In relation to the remaining tasks, two particular issues are worth highlighting here. First when considering how they might respond to needs, it was evident that a series of interlinked responses could arise, each giving rise to another. It would be important for any survey instrument to capture this. Second if asked when they thought needs might be met, respondents not surprisingly had some difficulty selecting an answer.

On balance the study suggests that it would be possible to design survey instruments to explore subjective perceptions of need amongst the general population. It sheds light on a range of question types and approaches that would be feasible if doing so. However, it does illustrate the complexity of the issue, in part because of the highly contingent nature of respondents' understanding and experience. It also underlines the importance of longitudinal research and combining survey instruments with rigorous qualitative data collection.

Appendix 3: Placing yourself on the diagrams of material and psychological prosperity

If you would like to see how you compare with the rest of the UK regarding the indicators of material and psychological need that we have used in this report please follow the procedure below. Note that your results will only be indicative of your general material and psychological wellbeing: a more accurate assessment would require a much longer questionnaire but we wanted to keep this relatively short to encourage participation.

Psychological wellbeing (General health Questionnaire)

Here are some questions about the way you have been feeling. For each question please circle the answer that best describes the way you have felt over the last few weeks.

Have you...

Been able to concentrate on whatever you are doing?	Better than usual **0**	Same as usual **1**	Less so than usual **2**	Much less than usual **3**
Lost much sleep over worry?	Not at all **0**	No more than usual **1**	Rather more than usual **2**	Much more than usual **3**
Felt that you were playing a useful part in things?	More so than usual **0**	Same as usual **1**	Less so than usual **2**	Much less than usual **3**
Felt capable of making decisions about things?	More than usual **0**	Same as usual **1**	Less so than usual **2**	Much less than usual **3**
Felt constantly under strain?	Not at all **0**	No more than usual **1**	Rather more than usual **2**	Much more than usual **3**

Felt that you couldn't overcome your difficulties?	Not at all	No more than usual	Rather more than usual	Much more than usual
	0	**1**	**2**	**3**
Been able to enjoy your normal day-to-day activities?	More so than usual	Same as usual	Less so than usual	Much less than usual
	0	**1**	**2**	**3**
Been able to face up to your problems?	More so than usual	Same as usual	Less so than usual	Much less than usual
	0	**1**	**2**	**3**
Been feeling unhappy and depressed?	Not at all	No more than usual	Rather more than usual	Much more than usual
	0	**1**	**2**	**3**
Been losing self-confidence in yourself?	Not at all	No more than usual	Rather more than usual	Much more than usual
	0	**1**	**2**	**3**
Been thinking of yourself as a worthless person?	Not at all	No more than usual	Rather more than usual	Much more than usual
	0	**1**	**2**	**3**
Been feeling reasonably happy, all things considered?	More so than usual	Same as usual	Less so than usual	Much less than usual
	0	**1**	**2**	**3**

Please ensure that you have answered all the questions.

Now add up each number that you have circled and make a note of the total in the box below. Note the value should be between 0 and 36 or else it is incorrect.

Psychological wellbeing =

We now turn to your material wellbeing.

Material wellbeing (disposable income)

Please note the next steps will roughly calculate your estimated disposable household income as a value that is comparable to other households. This value will not reflect any savings or assets you may have, nor unsecured debt costs such as credit card repayments. Furthermore the figure will not reflect your standard of living as a result of your disposable income expenditure decisions, nor geographic variations in the cost of living. The figure does allow you to see how your disposable income level compares to the rest of the population after some fundamental factors are considered.

You may need a calculator to continue.

Firstly, what is the average monthly 'take-home' earnings (i.e. after tax, national insurance and pension contributions) of each person in your household combined?

Income	**Per month**	
'Take-home' earnings of each person in your household combined	£	**(A)**

Now please list and add up the following monthly household costs.

Costs	**Per month**	
What is the cost of your rent (minus any housing benefit) OR your minimum mortgage repayments?	£	
Council tax?	£	
Ground rent and service charges?	£	
Total	£	**(B)**

Next, please deduct household costs (B) from household income (A)

= £ per month.

Please divide this number by four to give a weekly amount

= £ per week.

One last step...
In the following table[253] please count how many people in your household fit each of the descriptions in column 'A', writing the number in column 'B'.

A	B	C	D
Head of household	1	*0.67	= 0.67
Each other person aged over 14	?	*0.33	?
Each child aged 0-13	?	*0.20	?
		Sum	= ?

Now, please multiply each value in column 'B' by the value on the same row in column 'C' and write the result in column 'D'.

Finally, please add up all the values in column 'D' and divide your weekly household disposable income by that value.

This value is an estimate of your household weekly disposable income after accounting for the number and type of people in your household (i.e. it has been equivalised). Please make a note of the value in the box below:

Equivalised disposable household income estimate (pounds per week) = £

Your results:

Please see the first number you noted regarding your psychological wellbeing. Use this number to place yourself on the scale below (0-36). The right hand side of the scale relates to males, the left to females. You will be able to see how you compare to the UK average.

Distribution of psychological wellbeing (GHQ scores) 2007-08

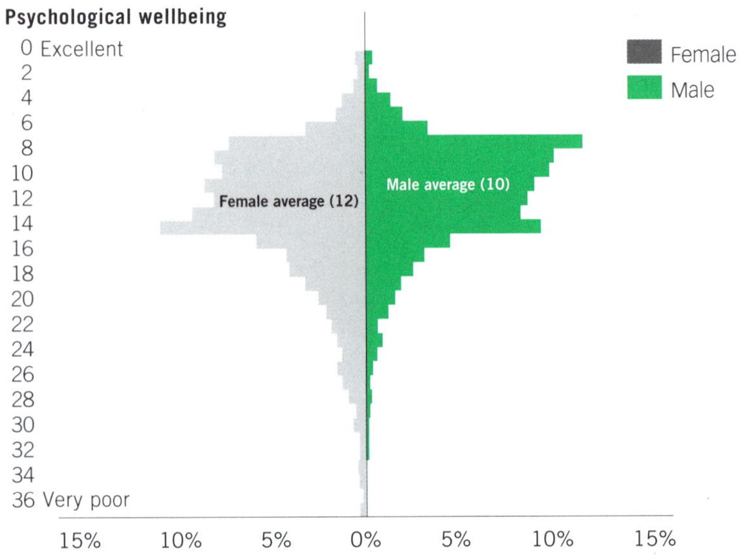

Equivalised disposable household income scale
Now please refer to the second number you noted – your disposable household equivalent income (pounds per week). Use this number to place yourself on the scale below (£0-1000+ per week). You will see that the UK income distribution has been divided into bands of 20% and it should be easy to see which band you fall into. The dotted line provides an indication of how UK income is distributed throughout the population.

Distribution of net household income 2007-08 After Housing Costs

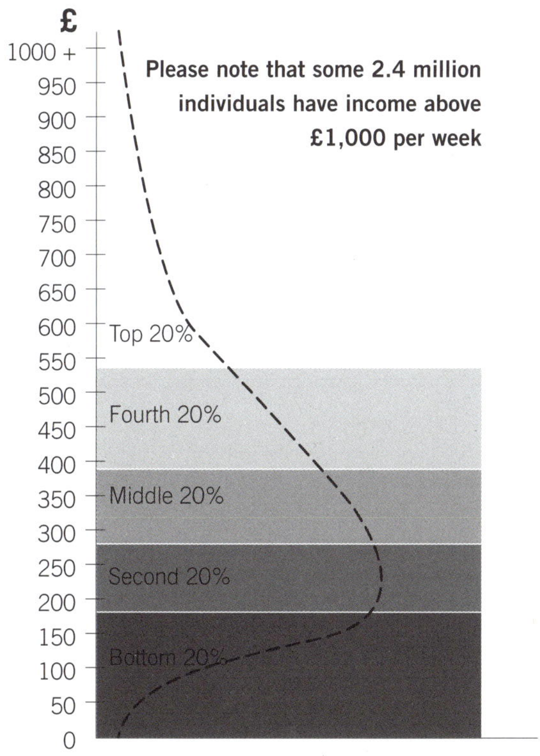

Source: Department for Work and Pensions Households Below Average Income report

References

1. Summarised in Roberts, Y. (2009) *Grit: The skills for success and how they are grown*, London: Young Foundation
2. Townsend, P., and Wedderburn, D. (1965) *The Aged in the Welfare State* London: G Bell. A significant early example of 'needs research', based upon data collected from interviews taken from a large general population sample.
3. Rein, M. (1970) *Social policy: issues of choice and change* New York: Random House, p462
4. Nussbaum, M. and Sen, A. (1993) *The Quality of Life* Oxford: Clarendon Press
5. Doyal, L. and Gough I. (1991) *A Theory of Human Need* Basingstoke: Macmillan Palgrave
6. Hills, J. (2004) *Inequality and the state* Oxford: Oxford University Press
7. Atkinson, A.B. (1999) *The Economic Consequences of Rolling Back the Welfare State* Massachusetts: Massachusetts Institute of Technology Press
8. Wilkinson, R. and Pickett, K. (2009) *The Spirit Level: Why more equal societies almost always do better*, London: Allen Lane; and Wilkinson, R. (2005) *The impact of inequality: How to make sick societies healthier*, London: Routledge
9. Tilly, C. (1998) *Durable Inequality Berkeley and Los Angeles*: University of California Press
10. Maslow, A. (1954) *Motivation and Personality* New York: Harper
11. Watts, B. and Vale, D. (2008) *Mind and Matter: The importance of psychological needs for social policy*, Young Foundation working paper, part of the Mapping Needs programme
12. For just one example, see Wilkinson, R. and Marmot, M. (2003) *Social determinants of health: The solid facts*, Second edition available at http://www.euro.who.int/document/e81384.pdf
13. Caulier-Grice, J., Mulgan, G., Vale, D. (2008) *Discovery, argument and action: how civil society responds to changing needs*. London: Young Foundation
14. Office of National Statistics (2009) *Social Trends No.39* London: Palgrave Macmillan
15. Sims, J. (2008) *The Health Risks of Overweight and Obesity*, available at http://www.weightlossresources.co.uk/body_weight/obesity_health.htm
16. BAPEN Press Release, Issued Tuesday 11 November 2003, available at http://www.bapen.org.uk/res_press_rel9.html
17. Stratton, R.J. and Elia, M. (2006) 'Deprivation linked to malnutrition risk and mortality in hospital' *British Journal of Nutrition* 96, 870–876.
18. Stratton, R.J. (2007) 'Pennington Lecture Malnutrition: another health inequality?' Institute of Human Nutrition, School of Medicine, University of Southampton, *Proceedings of the Nutrition Society*, 66, 522–529
19. Joseph Rowntree Foundation (2000) 'Who is affected by food poverty?' available at http://www.sustainweb.org/page.php?id=235
20. Rayner R., Scarborough P., Williams, C. (2003) 'The origin of Guideline Daily Amounts and the Food Standards Agency's guidance on what counts as 'a lot' and 'a little'' *Public Health Nutrition* 7:4, 549-556
21. Royal College of Physicians of the United Kingdom (2005) *Food Poverty and Health Briefing Statement*, London: Faculty of Public Health
22. Wrigley, N. (2002) '"Food Deserts" in British Cities: Policy Context and Research Priorities' *Urban Studies*, 39:11, 2029–2040
23. Office for National Statistics (2009) *Social Trends No.39*, London: Palgrave Macmillan
24. Grenier, P. (1996) *Still Dying for a Home* London: Crisis

25. Estimated number of rough sleepers in England June 2008, Department for Communities and Local Government

26. Statistics for Wales (2008) *National Rough Sleeping Count*, Wales, 2007 and 2008, Welsh Assembly Government, available at http://wales.gov.uk/docs/statistics/2009/090917roughsleep2007en.pdf

27. The last audit of rough sleepers in Scotland took place in 2003. Laird, A., Mulholl, S., Campbell-Jack, D. (2004) *Rough Sleepers Initiative: Monitoring the Target of Ending the Need to Sleep Rough by 2003*, Scottish Government, George Street Research, available at http://www.scotland.gov.uk/Publications/2004/07/19670/40405

28. St. Mungo's (2009) Facts about homelessness., available at http://www.mungos.org/homelessness/facts/

29. Department for Communities and Local Government (2001) *Preventing tomorrow's rough sleepers: a good practice handbook* available at http://www.communities.gov.uk/documents/housing/pdf/138004.pdf

30. Department for Communities and Local Government (2008) *Rough sleeping 10 years on: From the streets to independent living and opportunity – Discussion paper* available at http://www.communities.gov.uk/documents/housing/pdf/tenyearson.pdf

31. Crisis (2009) *Homelessness Policy Watch: A review of government policies which impact on homelessness by Crisis and NPI 2009*, available at http://www.crisis.org.uk/policywatch/pages/home.html

32. Department of Communities and Local Government (2008) *Statutory Homelessness in England*, Statistical Release, available at http://www.communities.gov.uk/publications/corporate/statistics/homelessnessQ12008

33. Kenway, P., and Palmer, G. (2003) *How many, how much? Single homelessness and the question of numbers and cost* London: Crisis

34. Department of Communities and Local Government (2009) *Statutory Homelessness: April to June quarter 2009, England*London: DCLG

35. Office for National Statistics (2008) *Excess winter deaths remain low in 2007/08*, available at http://www.statistics.gov.uk/pdfdir/deaths1108.pdf

36. General Register Office for Scotland (2008) Increased *Winter Mortality in Scotland, 2007/08*, available at http://www.gro-scotland.gov.uk/statistics/publications-and-data/increased-winter-mortality/increased-winter-mortality-in-scotland-2007-08.html

37. Office for National Statistics (2008) *Excess winter deaths remain low in 2007/08*, available at http://www.statistics.gov.uk/pdfdir/deaths1108.pdf

38. Office for National Statistics (2008) *Excess winter deaths remain low in 2007/08*, available at http://www.statistics.gov.uk/pdfdir/deaths1108.pdf

39. Age Concern (2009) *Excess Winter Deaths*, available at http://www.ageconcern.org.uk/AgeConcern/ftf_winter_deaths.asp#

40. Palmer, G., MacInnes, T., and Kenway, P. (2008) *Cold and Poor: An Analysis of The Link between Fuel Poverty and Low Income* London: New Policy Institute

41. Scottish Government (2009) *Review of Fuel Poverty in Scotland*, available at http://www.scotland.gov.uk/Topics/Built-Environment/Housing/access/FP/fuelpovertyreview

42. Department of Environment, *Food and Rural Affairs* (2008) The UK Fuel Poverty Strategy: 6th annual progress report, London: DEFRA

43. Ofgem (2009) *Protecting energy consumer interests now and in the future Annual report 2008-09*, available at http://www.official-documents.gov.uk/document/hc0809/hc08/0824/0824.pdf

44. Palmer, G., MacInnes, T., and Kenway, P. (2008) Cold and Poor: *An Analysis of The Link between Fuel Poverty and Low Income* London: New Policy Institute

45. NPI UK Poverty website, available at http://www.npi.org.uk/

46. NPI UK Poverty Site, available at http://www.poverty.org.uk/r75/index.shtml

47. Department of Work and Pensions (2009) *Households Below Average Income: An analysis of the income distribution 1994/95 – 2007/08*, London: DWP

48. Gregg, P. Harkness, S. Machin, S. (1999) *Child poverty and its consequences*, York: Joseph Rowntree Foundation

49. Department of Work and Pensions (2009) *Households Below Average Income: An analysis of the income distribution 1994/95 – 2007/08*, London: DWP

50. Department of Work and Pensions (2009) *Households Below Average Income: An analysis of the income distribution 1994/95 – 2007/08*, London: DWP

51. Eurostat data (website), available at http://epp.eurostat.ec.europa.eu/portal/page/portal/eurostat/home/

52. Department for Works and Pensions (2006) *Households below average income 1994/5 - 2004/5*. London DWP

53. Office for National Statistics (2009) *Social Trends No.39*, London: Palgrave Macmillan

54. ReallyWorried (2009) *UK Worry Index* 2008, available at http://www.reallyworried.com/WorryIndex.aspx

55. Office for National Statistics (2009) *Labour market statistics August 2009*, Statistical Bulletin, Newport: ONS

56. The Scottish Government (2005) *Employability Framework for Scotland: Report of the NEET Workstream*, available at http://www.scotland.gov.uk/Publications/2005/08/30111605/16069#f

57. Rennison, J., Maguire, S., Middleton, S. And Ashworth, K. (2005) *Young People not in Education, Employment or Training: Evidence from the education maintenance allowance pilots database*, Research Report 628, Department for Education and Skills

58. Sen, A. (1999) *Development as freedom* New York: Anchor books, p. 74-5

59. Department for Education and Skills (2003)'The Skills for Life survey: A national needs and impact survey of literacy, numeracy and ICT skills', *Research Brief RB490*, Norwich: DfES

60. Heckman, J. (2006) *Investing in Disadvantaged Young Children is an Economically Efficient Policy*, presented at the Forum on Building the Economic Case for Investments in Preschool, Jan 10 2006, New York

61. Hart, B. and Risley, T. (1995) *Meaningful Differences in Everyday Parenting and Intellectual Development in Young American Children*. Baltimore: Brookes

62. Crick, R.D. Broadfoot, P. Claxton, G. (2004) 'Developing an effective lifelong learning inventory: the ELLI project,' *Assessment in Education*, 11:3, 247-72

63. Flynn, J. (2007) *What is Intelligence?: Beyond the Flynn Effect* Cambridge: Cambridge University Press

64. Blanden, J. Gregg, P. Macmillan, L. (2006) 'Explaining Inter-generational income persistence: non-cognitive skills ability and education', *Working Paper No 06/146*, The Centre for Market and Public Organisation, Bristol: University of Bristol

65. See for example. 'Statistics 1: How common is mental distress?' MIND, available at http://www.mind.org.uk/Information/Factsheets/Statistics/Statistics+1.htm#Prevalence_of_mental_health_problems_in_Great_Britain

66. Statistics on mental health, Mental Health Foundation, available at http://www.mentalhealth.org.uk/information/mental-health-overview/statistics/

67. Office for National Statistics (2009) *Social Trends No.39* London: Palgrave Macmillan

68. Office for National Statistics (2009) *Social Trends No.39* London: Palgrave Macmillan

69. London School of Economics. Centre for Economic Performance. Mental Health policy Group (2006) *The Depression Report: A New Deal for Depression and Anxiety Disorders*. London: LSE Research, available at http://eprints.lse.ac.uk/archive/00000818

70. The NHS Information Centre (2009) *Mental Health Bulletin: Second report on experimental statistics from Mental Health Minimum Dataset (MHMDS) annual returns, 2003-2008*, Leeds: The NHS Information Centre

71. The NHS Information Centre (2009) *Mental Health Bulletin: Second report on experimental statistics from Mental Health Minimum Dataset (MHMDS) annual returns*, 2003-2008, Leeds: The NHS Information Centre

72. The NHS Information Centre (2007) *Adult psychiatric morbidity in England, 2007, Results of a household survey*, Leeds: The NHS Information Centre

73. Christopher, J.C. (1999) 'Situating Psychological Well-Being: Exploring the Cultural Roots of Its Theory and Research', *Journal of Counseling & Development*, 77, 141-152

74. Willitts, M., Benzeval, M., Stansfeld, S. (2004) 'Partnership history and mental health over time,' *Journal of Epidemiology and Community Health*, 58, 53-58

75. Vale, D. Watts, B. Franklin, J. (2009) *Receding Tide: Understanding unmet needs in a harsher economic climate*, London: Young Foundation

76. See for example Deci, E., and Ryan, R. (Eds.) (2002) *Handbook of self-determination research*, New York: University of Rochester Press and Doyal, L. and Gough, I. (1991) A theory of human need, Basingstoke: Palgrave Macmillan

77. For a fuller account of debates are definition and measurement see Emler, N. (2001) *Self-esteem: The Costs and Causes of Low Self-worth*, York: Joseph Rowntree Foundation

78. Emler, N. (2001) *Self-esteem: The Costs and Causes of Low Self-worth*, York: Joseph Rowntree Foundation

79. Walker, A., Flatley, J., Kershaw, C., Moon, D. (Eds) (2009) 'Crime in England and Wales 2008/09 Volume 1, Findings from the British Crime Survey and police recorded crime', 11/09, London: Home Office

80. Kershaw, C. Nicholas, S. Walker, A. (Eds) (2008) 'Crime in England and Wales 2007/08: Findings from the British Crime Survey and police recorded crime', 07/08, London: Home Office

81. Povey, D. (Ed.) Coleman, K. Kaiza, P. Roe, S. (2009) 'Homicides, Firearm Offences and Intimate Violence 2007/08 (Supplementary Volume 2 to Crime in England and Wales 2007/08)', 02/09, London: Home Office

82. Northern Ireland Office (2008) 'Experience of Domestic Violence: Findings from the 2007/2008 Northern Ireland Crime Survey', *Research and Statistical Bulletin 16/2008*, Belfast: Northern Ireland Office

83. Hamlyn, B. Brown, M. (2007) 'Partner abuse in Scotland: Findings from the 2006 Scottish Crime & Victimisation Survey', *07/2007*, Edinburgh. Scottish Government Social Research

84. Eastertin, R.A. (1974) 'Does economic growth improve the human lot? Some empirical evidence' in David, P.A. and Melvin, W.R. (Eds) *Nations and Households in Economic Growth*, Palo Alto: Stamford University Press

85. Taylor, S. Jenkins, S. Sacker, A. (2009) 'Financial capability and wellbeing: Evidence from the BHPS' *FSA Occasional Paper Series, 34*, Essex: Institute for Social and Economic Research University of Essex

86. Office for National Statistics (2009) *Social Trends No.39* London: Palgrave Macmillan

87. Office for National Statistics (2009) *Social Trends No.39* London: Palgrave Macmillan
88. Department of Work and Pensions (2009) *Households Below Average Income: An analysis of the income distribution 1994/95 – 2007/08*, London: DWP
89. Office for National Statistics (2007) *Key Population and Vital Statistics 2007 Series VS No 34, PPI No 30*, Newport: ONS
90. Office for National Statistics (2009) *Labour market statistics August 2009*, Newport: ONS
91. Greater London Authority (2009) *Economic impact on the London and UK economy of an earned regularisation of irregular migrants to the UK*, London: GLA
92. Migrants' Rights Network (2009) *Irregular Migrants: the urgent need for a new approach*, London: MRN
93. Gibney, M.J. (2000) *Outside the Protection of the Law: The Situation of Irregular Migrants in Europe, a synthesis report commissioned by the Jesuit Refugee Service–Europe*, Oxford: Refugee Studies Centre University of Oxford
94. All-Party Parliamentary Group for Children who Run Away or Go Missing (2007) *Safeguarding children and young people who runaway or go missing from home or care,* available at http://www.missingpeople.org.uk/uploads/files/safeguarding_children_and_young_people_who_runaway_or_go_missing_from_home_or_care.pdf
95. All-Party Parliamentary Group for Children who Run Away or Go Missing (2007) *Safeguarding children and young people who runaway or go missing from home or care*, available at http://www.missingpeople.org.uk/uploads/files/safeguarding_children_and_young_people_who_runaway_or_go_missing_from_home_or_care.pdf
96. Safe on the Streets Research Team (1999) *Still running: Children on the streets in the UK*, London: Children's Society
97. Home Office (2004) *Paying the Price: A Home Office Consultation paper on Prostitution*, London: Home Office
98. Hester, M. & Westmarland, N. (2004) *Tackling Street Prostitution: Towards an Holistic Approach*, Home Office: London
99. Cusick, L., Martin, A., May, T. (2003) 'Vulnerability and involvement in drug use and sex work', HORS 268, London: Home Office
100. May, T. Edmunds, M. Hough, M. Harvey, C. (1999) *Street Business: Links Between Sex and Drug Markets*, London: Home Office
101. Barnard, M. Hart, G. Church, S. (2002) *Client Violence Against Prostitute Women Working From Street and Off-Street Locations: A Three City Comparison*, Available at: http://www1.rhbnc.ac.uk/sociopolitical-science/vrp/Findings/rfbarnard.PDF
102. Church, S. Henderson, M. Barnard, M. Hart, G. (2001) 'Violence by clients towards female prostitutes in different work settings: questionnaire survey,' BMJ, 322, 524-525
103. Singleton, N. Murray, R. Tinsley, L. (Eds) (2006) 'Measuring different aspects of problem drug use: methodological developments', *Home Office Online Report 16/06*, available at http://www.homeoffice.gov.uk/rds/pdfs06/rdsolr1606.pdf
104. Hay, G. Gannon, M. McKeganey, N. Hutchinson, S. Goldberg, D. (2005) *Estimating the National and Local Prevalence of Problem Drug Misuse in Scotland, Executive Report*, Glasgow: Centre for Drug Misuse Research, University of Glasgow Scottish Centre for Infection and Environmental Health
105. European Monitoring Centre for Drugs and Drug Addiction (2007) 'Table PDU-1, Prevalence of problem drug use at national level: summary table, 2001-2005, rate per 1000 aged 15-64', Statistical bulletin 2007, EMCDDA, available at http://www.emcdda.europa.eu/stats07/

pdutab01a

106. European Monitoring Centre for Drugs and Drug addiction Prevalence of problem drug use at national level: summary table, 2001-2005, rate per 1000 aged 15-64
107. Lloyd, C. (1998) 'Risk Factors for Problem Drug Use: Identifying vulnerable groups', *Drugs: education, prevention and policy*, 5:3, 217-232
108. Office for National Statistics (2008) General Household Survey 2006, table 3.3 (GB), ONS, online edition, available at http://www.statistics.gov.uk/StatBase/Product.asp?vlnk=5756
109. GfK/NOP (2006) Spotlight 2006 survey, London: Help the Aged
110. ICM Research (unpublished), *Christmas Day survey* 2007, London: Help the Aged
111. Age Concern and Help the Aged (2009) *One Voice: Shaping our ageing society*, London: Age Concern and Help the Aged
112. Victor, C. Scambler, S. Bond, J. Bowling, A. (2003) *Loneliness, Social Isolation and Living Alone in Later Life*, Swindon: Economic and Social Research Council
113. Ipsos MORI (2000) *Poverty And Poor Health Create Isolation In Older People*, London: Ipsos MORI on behalf of Help the Aged and British Gas
114. Department for Transport (2001) *Older people: Their transport needs and requirements*, London: DfT
115. Cattan, M. (2002) *Supporting older people to overcome social isolation and loneliness*, Leeds: Leeds Metropolitan University on behalf of the British Gas Help the Aged Partnership Isolation Campaign
116. Department for Transport (2001) *Older people: Their transport needs and requirements*, London: DfT
117. Ofcom Consumer Panel (2006) *Position paper on why connecting older people is important* [online]available at http://www.communicationsconsumerpanel.org.uk/smartweb/older-people-and-communications/older-people-and-communications
118. Stewart, D. (2008) 'The problems and needs of newly sentenced prisoners: results from a national survey' Ministry of Justice Research Series 16/08 (all definitions detailed in this report)
119. Hansard (2009) House of Commons written answers, 12 January 2009, available at http://www.publications.parliament.uk/pa/cm200809/cmhansrd/cm090112/text/90112w0117.htm
120. National Association of Probation Officers (2008) *Veterans in Prison report August 2008*, British Armed Forces Federation, available at http://www.baff.org.uk/personnel-issues-12
121. Webster, R. Hedderman, C. Turnbull, P.J. May, T. (2001) 'Building bridges to employment for prisoners', HORS 226, London: Home Office
122. Hartfree, Y. Dearden, C. Pound, E. (2008) 'High Hopes: Supporting ex-prisoners in their lives after prison',*Research Report No 509*, London: DWP
123. Stewart, D. (2008) 'The problems and needs of newly sentenced prisoners: results from a national survey', *Research Series 16/08*, London: Ministry of Justice
124. Rother, M. (1955) 'The natural history of mental disorders in old age.' *Journal of Mental Science*. 101, 281-301.
125. Evans, M. (1994) 'Dementia', *Psychiatry in General Practice*, available at http://priory.com/dem.htm
126. Department of Health (2009) Living well with dementia: A National Dementia Strategy, London: Department of Health
127. Joseph Roundtree Foundation Poverty website (2009) available at http://www.jrf.org.uk/work/poverty
128. Berridge, D. Brodie, I. Pitts, J. Porteous, D. Tarling, R. (2001) 'The independent effects of

permanent exclusion from school on the offending careers of young people', *RDS Occasional paper 71*, London: Home Office

129. Department for Children, Schools and Families (2008) *Back on Track A strategy for modernising alternative provision for young people*, London: TSO
130. Department for Children, Schools and Families (2008) *Improving the Educational Attainment of Children in care (Looked after Children)*, London: DCSF
131. Meltzer, H. Gatward, R. Corbin, T. Goodman, R. Ford, T. (2003) *The Mental Health of Young People Looked After by Local Authorities in Wales*, London: TSO
132. Ford, T. Vostanis, P. Meltzer, H. Goodman, R. (2007) 'Psychiatric disorder among British children looked after by local authorities: comparison with children living in private households,' The British Journal of Psychiatry, 190:4, 319-325
133. House of Commons (2009) *Children, Schools and Families Committee – Third Report: Looked-after Children*, London: House of Commons
134. Traveller Law Research Unit (2001) *Factsheet: Travelling People in the United Kingdom*, Traveller Law Research Unit, Cardiff Law School, University of Cardiff, available at http://www.law.cf.ac.uk/tlru/Factsheet.pdf
135. Ofsted (1996) *The Education of Travelling Children: A survey of educational provision for Travelling children*, available at http://www.ofsted.gov.uk/Ofsted-home/Publications-and-research/Browse-all-by/Education/Inclusion/Traveller-children/The-education-of-Travelling-children.
136. Department for Education and Skills (2003) *Aiming High: Raising The Achievement of Gypsy Traveller Pupils – A Guide to Good Practice*, Nottingham: DfES
137. Parry, G. Van Cleemput, P. Peters, J. Moore, J. Walters, S. Thomas, K. Cooper, C. (2007) 'Health status of Gypsies and Travellers in England,' *Journal of Epidemiology and Community Health*, 61, 198-204
138. Friends, Families and Travellers website (2009) *Gypsy & Traveller Mental Health Event*, Clair Hall, Haywards Heath, June 25th 2009, available at http://www.gypsy-traveller.org/mental-health-and-wellbeing
139. Department for Communities and Local Government (2004) *Gypsies and Travellers: Facts and Figures*, London: DCLG
140. Friends, Families and Travellers website (2009) *Working with Gypsies & Travellers – A brief note for Mental Health Practitioners*, available at http://www.gypsy-traveller.org/mental-health-and-wellbeing
141. Institute of Psychiatry Neurodevelopmental Disorders webpage (2009) King's College London, available at http://www.iop.kcl.ac.uk/departments/?locator=1039
142. A The NHS Information Centre (2007) *Adult psychiatric morbidity in England, 2007*, Results of a household survey, Leeds: The NHS Information Centre
143. Finkel, M.F. (1997) 'The diagnosis and treatment of the adult attention deficit hyperactivity disorders,' *Neurologist*, 3, 31-44
144. The NHS Information Centre (2007) *Adult psychiatric morbidity in England, 2007*, Results of a household survey, Leeds: The NHS Information Centre
145. Department of Health (2009) *A Better Future: A consultation on a future strategy for adults with autistic spectrum conditions*, London: Department of Health
146. National Audit Office (2007) *Improving services and support for people with dementia: report by the comptroller and auditor general* London: The Stationary Office
147. Quilgars, D., Johnsen, S. and Pleace, N. (2008) Youth Homelessness in the UK, York: Joseph

Rowntree Foundation

148. The Prince's Trust (2004) Reaching the hardest to reach, available at http://www.princestrust.org.uk/Main%20Site%20v2/downloads/Reaching.pdf
149. Department of Work and Pensions (2009) *Households Below Average Income: An analysis of the income distribution 1994/95 – 2007/08*, London: DWP
150. Get Set London 2012 – a world city webpage (2009) available athttp://getset.london2012.com/en/the-games/about-london-2012/london-2012-a-world-city
151. Prime Minister's Strategy Unit (2004) London Project Report. Cabinet Office: London
152. Price Waterhouse Coopers (2008) Young London Matters
153. Greater London Authority (2008) Planning for a Better London. GLA: London
154. Greater London Authority (2007) The State of London's Children. GLA: London
155. Bell, M., Ford, I. and McDougall, D. (2008) *London Asylum Seekers Consortium A warm welcome, public services and managing migration in London: Scoping Research and Introductory report.* London: Michael Bell Associates
156. Greater London Authority (2007) The State of London's Children. London: GLA
157. Data Management and Analysis Group (2008) Pay Check. London: GLA
158. Almost half of all children living in Inner London come from relatively poor households (48% inner 37% outer AHC). http://www.london.gov.uk/gla/publications/factsandfigures/dmag-update-10-2008.pdf.
159. Data Management and Analysis Group (2008) Pay Check. London: GLA
160. Child Poverty Action Group (2008) *Child Poverty – the stats: analysis of the latest poverty statistics*, London: Child Poverty Action Group
161. London Child Poverty Commission (2007) *Monitoring Child Poverty in London.* London: GLA
162. Greater London Authority (2009) Ending Rough Sleeping – the London Delivery Board. London: GLA
163. Homeless Link (2008) *Homelessness and Rough Sleeping – Some Key Facts*, available at http://www.homeless.org.uk/policyandinfo/facts/rskeystats1
164. Greater London Authority (2009) *Ending Rough Sleeping – the London Delivery Board.* London: GLA
165. Homeless Link (no date), *Homelessness and Rough Sleeping – Some Key Facts*, available at www.homeless.org.uk/inyourarea/london/keyfacts
166. Greater London Authority (2008) *Living Well in London – The Mayor's Draft Health Inequalities Strategy for London.* London: GLA
167. Piggott, G. (Ed) (2008) 'Chapter 8: Housing', *Focus on London 2008*, London: GLA
168. Greater London Authority (2008) *Living Well In London – The Mayor's Draft Health Inequalities Strategy for London.* London: GLA
169. Greater London Authority (2004) *The Case for London.* London: GLA
170. Data Management and Analysis Group Update (2008) *Employment rates by ethnic group*, London: GLA
171. Vaid, L. (2006) 'Family and Children's Study 2004', *DMAG Briefing 2006/21*, London: GLA
172. Piggott, G. (2004) 'Londoners' qualifications: Analysis of 2001 Census data', DMAG Briefing 2004/6, London: GLA
173. Green, A. and Owen, D. (2006) *The Geography of Poor Skills and Access to Work.* York: Joseph Rowntree Foundation
174. Green, A. and Owen, D. (2006) *The Geography of Poor Skills and Access to Work.* York: Joseph Rowntree Foundation

175. Department for children, schools and families (2009) available at, http://www.dcsf.gov.uk/1419/index.cfm?go=site.home&sid=42&pid=343&lid=337&ctype=Text&ptype=Single
176. London Child Poverty Commission (2008) *Capital Gains- London Child Poverty Commission Final Report*, London: London Councils
177. Vaid, L. (2006) 'Family and Children's Study 2004', *DMAG Briefing 2006/21*, London: GLA
178. Piggott, G. (Ed) (2008) 'Chapter 12: Education', *Focus on London 2008*, London: GLA
179. Piggott, G. (Ed) (2008) 'Chapter 12: Education', *Focus on London 2008*, London: GLA
180. London Health Commission (2007) *Looking Back – Looking Forward: 2006/07 Review of Trends, Progress and Opportunities*, London: London Health Commission
181. Greater London Authority Economics (2009) *London Economic Development Snapshot*. London: GLA
182. Greater London Authority (2007) *The State of London's Children*, London: GLA.
183. Greater London Authority (2008) *Living Well in London – The Mayor's Draft Health Inequalities Strategy for London*. London: GLA
184. Greater London Authority (2008) *Living Well in London – The Mayor's Draft Health Inequalities Strategy for London*. London: GLA
185. Greater London Authority (2008) *The State of London's Children*. London: GLA
186. London Development Agency (2006) *The Mayor of London* – Food Strategy. London: LDA
187. Prime Minister's Strategy Unit (2004) *London Project Report*. Cabinet Office: London
188. Greater London Authority (2008) *Living Well in London – The Mayor's Draft Health Inequalities Strategy for London*. London: GLA
189. Greater London Authority (2008) *Living Well in London – The Mayor's Draft Health Inequalities Strategy for London*. London: GLA
190. Greater London Authority (2008) *Living Well in London – The Mayor's Draft Health Inequalities Strategy for London*. London: GLA
191. Greater London Authority (2008) *Living Well in London – The Mayor's Draft Health Inequalities Strategy for London*. London: GLA
192. Greater London Authority (2003) *Availability of Mental Health Services – A Report for the Mayor of London*. London: GLA
193. Greater London Authority (2003) *Availability of Mental Health Services – A Report for the Mayor of London*. London: GLA
194. Greater London Authority (2008) *Time for Action: Equipping Young People for the Future and Preventing Violence – the Mayor's proposals and call to partners*, London: GLA
195. Greater London Authority (2008) Time for Action: Equipping Young People for the Future and Preventing Violence – the Mayor's proposals and call to partners, London: GLA
196. Greater London Alcohol and Drug Alliance (2007) *London: the highs and lows – A report from the Greater London Alcohol and Drug Alliance*. London: GLA
197. Greater London Alcohol and Drug Alliance (2007) *London: the highs and lows – A report from the Greater London Alcohol and Drug Alliance*. London: GLA
198. Joseph Rowntree Foundation and the New Policy Institute (2005) *Monitoring poverty and social exclusion in Wales 2005*. York: Joseph Rowntree Foundation
199. Welsh Assembly Government (2008) *Economic Inactivity in Wales 2007 – Statistical Bulletin 61/2008*, Cardiff: Welsh Assembly Government
200. Allen, J., Nicholas, S., Salisbury, H. and Wood, M. (2003) 'Nature of burglary, vehicle and violent crime' in C. Flood-Page and J. Taylor (eds). *Crime in England and Wales 2001/2002:*

Supplementary Volume. Home Office Statistical Bulletin 01/03. London: Home Office.

201. Kreitzman, L. (1999) *The 24 Hour Society London*: Profile Books
202. Horwitz, I.B. (2004) 'The impact of shift work on the risk and severity of injuries for hospital employees: an analysis using Oregon workers' compensation data.' *Occupational Medicine* 54:8, 556-563
203. Engleman, H.E. and Douglas, N.J. (2005) 'Sleep, driving and the workplace' *Clinical Medicine* 5:2, 133-117
204. Pati, A., Chandrawanshi, A. & Reinberg, A. (2001) 'Shift work: Consequences and management' *Current Science* 81:1, 32-52
205. Pati, A., Chandrawanshi, A. & Reinberg, A. (2001) 'Shift work: Consequences and management' *Current Science* 81:1 32-52
206. Rouch, I. (2005) 'Shiftwork experience, age and cognitive performance' *Ergonomics* 48: 10, 1282-1293
207. Megdala, S. (2005) 'Night work and breast cancer risk: A systematic review and meta-analysis' *European Journal of Cancer*, 41:13, 2023-2032
208. Kubo, T. (2006) 'Prospective cohort study of the risk of prostate cancer among rotating-shift workers: Findings from the Japan Collaborative Cohort Study' *American Journal of Epidemiology*, 164, 549-555
209. Lahti, T. (2008)'Night-time work predisposes to non-Hodgkin lymphoma' *International Journal of Cancer*, 123, 2148–2151
210. Knutsson, A. (1989) 'Shift work and coronary heart disease' *Scandinavian Journal of Social Medicine*. Supplementum, 44, 1-36.
211. Pati, A. Chandrawanshi, A. Reinberg, A. (2001) 'Shift work: Consequences and management' *Current Science* 81:1, 32-52
212. Pompeii, L. (2005) 'Physical exertion at work and the risk of preterm delivery and small-for-gestational-age birth' *Obstetrics & Gynaecology*, 106, 1279-1288
213. Scheer, F (2009) 'Adverse metabolic and cardiovascular consequences of circadian misalignment' *Proceedings of the National Academy of Sciences* 106: 9
214. Day Care Trust (2007) *Listening to lone parents about childcare* London: DCFS
215. Mason, C (No Date) *Healthy Nights* Report for the Home Office Policing and Reducing Crime Unit. London: Home Office
216. Padfield, B (2009) 'Preparing for the new asbestos?' *The Guardian* 16 June 2009
217. District Data from The Poverty Site available at www.poverty.org.uk/maps/district%20data.xls
218. DCSF (2007) NEETs data, available at www.dcsf.gov.uk/14-19/documents/NEET2007.xls
219. Oxford Consultants for Social Inclusion (2005) *Bedfordshire and Luton Economic Development Partnership: Needs Analysis for Investing in Communities Business Plan* Oxford: OCSI
220. NEET Data from The Poverty Site, available at District Data from The Poverty Site available at www.poverty.org.uk/maps/district%20data.xls
221. Save the Children (2007) *The Poverty Premium: How poor households pay more for essential goods and services*, available at http://www.savethechildren.org.uk/en/54_2523.htm
222. This definition draws on the work of Walker, B. Holling, CS. Carpenter, S. Kinzig, A. (2004) 'Resilience, adaptability and transformability in social-ecological systems', *Ecology and Society*, 9:2
223. Ramon, S. (2007) 'Inequality In Mental Health: The Relevance of Current Research and Understanding To Potentially Effective Social Work Responses,' *Radical Psychology*, 6:1
224. Connor, K.M. and Davidson, J.R.T. (2003) 'Development of a new resilience scale: The Connor-

Davidson Resilience Scale,' *Depression and Anxiety*, 18, 76–82
225. Skuse, D. Reilly, S. Wolke, D. (1994) 'Psycho-social adversity and growth during infancy', *European Journal of Clinical Nutrition*, 48:1, 113-30
226. Masten, A. Best, K. Garmezy, N. (1990) 'Resilience and development: Contributions from the study of children who overcome adversity', *Development and Psychopathology*, 2, 425–444.
227. Masten, A.S. Hubbard, J.J. Gest, S.D. Tellegen, A. Garmezy, N. Ramirez, M. (1999) 'Competence in the context of adversity: Pathways to resilience and maladaptation from childhood to late adolescence' *Development and Psychopathology*, 11, 143–169
228. Gralinski-Bakker, J., Hauser, S., Stott, C., Billings, R. & Allen, J. (2004) 'Markers of Resilience and Risk: Adult Lives in a Vulnerable Population' *Research in Human Development* 1(4):291-326
229. Mancini, A. & Bonanno, G. (2006) 'Resilience in the face of potential trauma: Clinical practices and illustrations' *Journal of Clinical Psychology* 62 (8): 971 - 985
230. Ballas, B. Dorling, D. (2007) 'Measuring the impact of major life events upon happiness', *International Journal of Epidemiology*, 36, 1244
231. Williams, A.W., Ware Jr, J.E. and Donald, C.A. (1981) 'A model of mental health, life events, and social supports applicable to general populations', *Journal of Health and Social Behaviour*, 22:4, 324-325
232. Waugh, C., Fredrickson, B. and Taylor, S. (2008) 'Adapting to life's slings and arrows: Individual differences in resilience when recovering from an anticipated threat' *Journal of Research in Personality* 42(4): 1031–1046
233. Hillegers, M.H.J. Burger, H. Wals, M. Reichart, C.G. Verhulst, F.C. Nolen, W.A. Ormel, J. (2004) 'Impact of stressful life events, familial loading and their interaction on the onset of mood disorders'. *British Journal of Psychiatry*, 185, 97
234. Rutter, M. (1985) 'Resilience in the face of adversity. Protective factors and resistance to psychiatric disorder', *British Journal of Psychiatry*, 147, 598–611.
235. Baldwin, A.L. Baldwin, C. Cole, R. (1990) 'Stress-resistant families and stress-resistant children'. In Rolf, J.E. Masten, A.S. Cicchetti, D. Neuchterlein, K.H. Weintraub, S. (Eds.) *Risk and protective factors in the development of psychopathology* New York: Cambridge University Press.
236. Waysman, M. Schwarzwald, J. Solomon, Z. (2001) 'Hardiness: an examination of its relationship with positive and negative longterm changes following trauma'. *Journal of Traumatic Stress*, 14, 531–548
237. Cutrona, C.E. and Cole, V. (2000) 'Optimizing support in the natural network' in Cohen, S. (Ed.) Underwood, L.G. Gottlieb, B.H. *Social Support Measurement and Intervention: A Guide for Health and Social Scientists*, Oxford: Oxford University Press
238. Kidd, S. and Shahar, G. (2008) 'Resilience in Homeless Youth: The Key Role of Self-Esteem', *American Journal of Orthopsychiatry*, 78:2, 163–172
239. Rickwood, D. and Braithwaite, V. (1994) 'Social-psychological factors affecting help-seeking for emotional problems', *Social Science and Medicine*, 39:4, 563–72..
240. Aalto-Setala, T., Marttunen, M., Tuulio-Henriksson, T., Poikolainen, K. and Lonnqvist, J. (2002) 'Psychiatric treatment seeking and psycho-social impairment among young adults with depression', *Journal of Affective Disorders*, 70, 35–47
241. Andrews, G., Issakidis, C. and Carter, G. (2001) 'Shortfall in mental health service utilisation', *British Journal of Psychiatry*, 179, 417–25.
242. This chapter draws in part on work done by Michael Wilmott and the Trajectory Partnership for

this project.

243. Godfrey, C. Hutton, S. Bradshaw, J. Coles, B. Craig, G. & Johnson, J. (2002) 'Estimating the Cost of Being "Not in Education, Employment or Training" at Age 16-18', *Research Report RR346*, London: DfES

244. Available at http://www.dcsf.gov.uk/rsgateway/DB/STR/d000751/NEETQuarterlyBriefQ12009.pdf

245. Office for National Statistics (2009) *Population Trends no 136, Summer 2009*, Basingstoke: Palgrave Macmillan

246. Office for National Statistics (2009) *Population Trends no 136, Summer 2009*, Basingstoke: Palgrave Macmillan

247. British Social Attitudes surveys, 1986 and 1995.Some findings from the surveys are in McGlone, F. Park, A. and Roberts, C. (1996) 'Relative values: kinship and friendship' in Jowell, R. Curtice, J. Park, A. Brook, L. and Thomson, K. *British Social Attitudes: the 13th report*, London: Social and Community Planning Research; and in McGlone, F. Park, A. and Smith, K. (1998) *Families and Kinship*, London: Family Policies Study Centre

248. Dench, G. Gavron, K. Young, M. (2006) *The New East End: Kinship, Race and Conflict*, London: Profile Books

249. As reported by the BBC in October 2007. http://news.bbc.co.uk/1/hi/health/7043639.stm

250. Wardle, H. Sproston, K. Orford, J. Erens, B. Griffiths, M. Constantine, R. & Pigott, S. (2007) *British Gambling Prevalence Survey 2007*, London: National Centre for Social Research

251. NHS Health Scotland (2006) *Warwick-Edinburgh Mental Well-Being Scale (WEMWBS)*, available at http://www.healthscotland.com/documents/1467.aspx

252. Organisation for Economic Cooperation and Development (OECD) equivalence scale cited in Department of Work and Pensions (2009) Households Below Average Income: An analysis of the income distribution 1994/95 – 2007/08, London: DWP